The shining splendor of our Zebra Lovegram logo on the cover of this book reflects the glittering excellence of the story inside. Look for the Zebra Lovegram whenever you buy a historical romance. It's a trademark that guarantees the very best in quality and reading entertainment.

UNDER PASSION'S SPELL

"Charity, I've wanted to hold you like this since the first minute I set eyes on you. To touch you . . . to feel you against me . . ." Rane whispered hoarsely.

His kiss was fierce, consuming, and when it ended it left her dazed and swaying. When she managed to open her eyes, he had removed his elegant coat and spread it on the ground nearby. He lowered her to it and sank to the ground beside her, pressing her back against the softness of the cradling grasses.

"I want to love you, angel," he murmured against the bare skin of her throat. "But a gentleman never goes anywhere uninvited."

"Touch me."

It was the purest invitation he'd ever received . . .

Midnight Magic is fabulous and funny, lighthearted and loving. Betina Krahn is magic.
> —Kathe Robin
> ROMANTIC TIMES

". . . a warm, endearing love story filled with humor and sensuality. Krahn's unique ability to interweave a tale with hilarious characterization is magic in and of itself. Superb!"
> —Mildred Burkett
> AFFAIRE DE COEUR

MIDNIGHT MAGIC

BETINA M. KRAHN

ZEBRA BOOKS
KENSINGTON PUBLISHING CORP.

ZEBRA BOOKS

are published by

Kensington Publishing Corp.
475 Park Avenue South
New York, NY 10016

First printing: July, 1990

Printed in the United States of America

For the milestone people in my writing career:

Bonnie Bloom,
who gave me my first romance

Shari Hinzman,
who was a signpost when I needed direction

Pesha Finkelstein,
who bought my first book

Mary Knibbe,
a dear reader, who gave me hope

and, most importantly,

Sharon Maynard Stone,
whose insight and encouragement
have nourished me all my life.

Foreword

Gypsies know things nobody else knows . . . all sorts of things. They know about the power of Fridays and sevens and wishing on the new moon. They know about the supernatural "sight" of black horses and about the strange effects the color red has on people. They know that "if a man dies bald, he turns into a fish" and that old shoes are much luckier than new ones. Long experience has taught them that to kill a spider is to invite poverty and illness. They know about the luck that nature stores in metals and bottles up in wood . . . and how to release it with a touch or a knock.

Through centuries of roving life, they've collected the deep secrets of life and luck from the far corners of the earth. And under winking stars, around their smoky campfires, with hushed voices and widened eyes, they pass those precious secrets on to their children. Hand signs and respect for the moon and reading fortunes in a human palm . . . lucky charms and animal lore and the many practices for repelling bad fortune and attracting good. . . . There is a very great deal to pass along, indeed. It takes many years of smoky campfires and close attention for a gypsy to learn all the things a good gypsy should know.

And in the end, there is still one lesson that every good gypsy must learn for himself. *Luck,* that most treasured of commodities in gypsy life, has limits. People can beg their luck or borrow their luck, or press their luck, or stretch their luck, but in the end it will only reach so far, and no further. There is only one thing in life which has no limits, every good gypsy must learn. The only thing without limits is *love.*

Chapter One

Rain. It was the very last thing she needed. It was already the worst day of Charity Standing's life, and now it was taking yet another drastic turn. *It's true, what they say,* she sniffed miserably. *No matter how bad things seem . . . they can always get worse.*

Fresh tears welled in her honey-brown eyes as she looked up at the wind-driven drops beginning to pound against the glass of the arched stone window well nearby. She slipped a black-gloved hand beneath her silk veil to dab at her eyes and sat a bit straighter against the hard pew, trying to compensate for the awful sinking feeling inside her.

Her gaze drifted around the little stone church, searching for solace in the familiar gray stone walls, the simple, carved stone arches, and the massive oak timbers that supported the roof. Her titled ancestors had helped to build this sturdy chapel centuries ago, and in its day it had served the countryside for miles around. Now, the damp, earthy chill of the thick stone walls and worn oaken pews carried the forlorn mustiness of age and disuse. Forgotten, she realized; it smelled forgotten. The thought sent another pair of tears squeezing from beneath her wet lashes. There was no comfort for her here . . . perhaps not anywhere.

The funeral service had just ended; echoes of the benediction still hung on the thick, moist air. Suddenly the expectant hush in the little stone church became a low, drumming

9

roar of rain. It sent a rustle of disquiet through the other mourners, who had shunned the front seating to wedge themselves into the pews at the back of the chapel. A rainstorm at a burial boded ill, west-country folk believed. They looked at each other uneasily and turned back to watch black-veiled Charity Standing, some with sympathy, some with bald curiosity.

The rites for Squire Upton Standing had been modest and sincere, befitting both his station and his character. Most of the folk attending had been the squire's neighbors all his life. Some were low-level gentry with small holdings of land in the area, some were tenant farmers who inhabited the modest cottages that dotted the squire's land, and some were tradesmen from the nearby town, with whom he'd done business in bygone days. To a body, they had known and respected Squire Standing. But to be truthful, their attendance at these rites had more to do with the chance to peruse the squire's beautiful daughter and his eccentric mother-in-law, Lady Margaret Villiers, firsthand. Over the last ten years, the goodly squire had withdrawn his family further and further from public notice and roused speculation on his reasons for doing so.

The graying, black-clad rector cleared his throat nervously, one eye on the downpour, and stepped back into the pulpit. "We shall continue in . . . silent prayer and reflection."

A palpable wave of relief went through the group at the back; the reverend had just saved them all a good drenching. But the reprieve had only added to Charity's misery, delaying the inevitable, prolonging the agony. In a short while they would put her beloved father into the cold Devonshire ground, cover him over and tamp him down to wait for eternity.

She strangled a sob in her handkerchief and felt her grandmother's hand searching for hers on the pew between them. She raised her head and through the dark haze of her veil glimpsed Lady Margaret's weathered, unveiled face, now tight with shared misery. Then she turned to the sight of

10

the simple oaken box that held her father's mortal shell. A fresh wave of sorrow crested in her and broke, releasing yet more tears. When she could lift her head, her eyes drifted across the aisle to the pew box on the other side and her spirits sank to a new low.

There, in the only other family box in the small chapel, sat Sullivan Pinnow, *Baron* Pinnow of the nearby town of Mortehoe. Tall, lean, and smartly dressed, he was the very picture of angular, tautly bred nobility. Charity could feel his lidded gaze, with its ever-so-sincere sorrow, reaching for her, somehow touching her, as if . . . anticipating something. Yes, Charity groaned dismally, things could always get worse.

It was nearly half an hour before the rain stopped and the congregation in the little church roused again, rustling with expectation. The rector beckoned the pallbearers forward and the plainly clad fellows stumbled past Charity and her grandmother, keeping to the far side of the aisle and making nods of respect as they passed. Charity lifted her chin and tried valiantly to smile her heartfelt gratitude at two of them, Gar Davis and Percy Hall. The inseparable Gar and Percy were long-time hunting companions of her father's and, despite their modest station in life, were considered dear friends of the family. They smiled back through eyes that were bloodshot from a long night of toasting their dear old friend, the squire.

The coffin was borne out by six bearers, three laboring on each side. The rector followed, pausing to open the wooden gate to the Standing family box for Charity and her grandmother.

"I shall escort them, Reverend," Sullivan Pinnow announced, stepping out of the other box, smoothing his closely tailored waistcoat and adjusting the small, tasteful ruffles at his wrists. The good rector nodded and hurried out behind the coffin, leaving Charity and Lady Margaret in the baron's ever-so-sincere hands.

A clearing wind had risen through the Devonshire coastland, breaking up the trailing end of the storm and blowing it further inland. The sun now streamed through the tattered gray clouds, caressing the gently rolling fields with long hazy fingers of light. The combination of wetness and light gave everything a rich, jewel-like radiance of lush, mature emerald, icy sapphire green, deep golden topaz. The lush vitality of the countryside, its vibrant color and resurgent sense of life, was a stunning contrast to the somberness of the rites being enacted across it. Today the last male of the Standing line, a lineage which could be traced back to the Norman conquest, was being buried. And all knew that as he was laid to rest, the family's dwindling expectations were being laid to rest with him.

The funeral procession left the inland vale and wound its way through a meandering woods and across the fields on a rutted lane that muddied shoes and boots and wetted skirts. Their destination was a gentle slope near the rambling stone manor house, Standwell, that nestled beside the craggy Devonshire coast.

Behind Charity Standing, Lady Margaret Villiers, and the lanky baron, the other mourners hung back several paces and whispered amongst themselves, watching shapely young Charity and her aging grandmother. Both of the women were dressed in black, high-waisted gowns of good bombazine, newly stitched, and both had eschewed proper bonnets. Charity had chosen to wear a black crown-like circlet on which her veil could be draped but Lady Margaret had spurned even a veil, preferring a simple mantilla that left her face bare.

The blustery wind tugged capriciously at Charity's veil, giving the mourners glimpses of the glorious honey-blonde hair that trailed in a bright river down her back all the way to her gently swaying bottom. Those tempting little flashes of gold and subtle undulations only piqued their curiosity about her, and turned more than one male mind amongst the mourners to less than reverent contemplations.

Walking beside her, with her slender hand on his sleeve, Baron Pinnow had the best view of all. He could scarcely mind his own footing for watching her exquisite shape and demure, unconsciously sensual movement. But Charity's heart and mind were so clouded with grief that she scarcely felt their bold scrutiny or the baron's too-familiar hands on her arm and elbow . . . with their sly fingers that occasionally brushed the side of her breast. Nor did she hear her grandmother's mutterings nor the rector's incantations of the Twenty-third Psalm.

The pace quickened and a noticeable wave of relief went through the entire procession as they left the lane and approached the gravesite. But when the bearers reached the foot of the grave opening and peered in, they began to murmur, hastily shedding the coffin from their shoulders onto the muddy clay beside the hole. Charity watched their reaction with pained surprise and shoved free of Baron Pinnow's possessive grasp to hurry graveside.

The bottom of the grave was filled with at least a foot of muddy water from the recent storm, and Charity stiffened visibly at the sight. When Lady Margaret saw it, she tucked her chin and crossed herself in triplicate. And when the other mourners crept close enough to see what had caused their reactions, they quickly withdrew to the far side of the grave, in agitated huddles. Normally, water in a grave would be no great cause for distress . . . but the good squire had died of drowning. It seemed downright eerie, they whispered amongst themselves, that he was bound for a *second* watery grave.

"Let's get on wi' it," the stocky, ever-practical Percy Hall declared, tugging up his breeches as though they contained his fortitude. His pragmatic tone cut through the tension and at his firm example, the other pallbearers jerked stiff nods and set to work. The sooner they were done, the better. They uncoiled the ropes that two of them carried on their shoulders and slid them beneath the coffin, head and foot. Then they heaved, hauling the box up and over the hole as the rector, at the head of the grave, read the words of comfort from his service book. The straining bearers glanced at the clergyman, visually entreating him to make it a short one. But the rector was determined to maintain the dignity of the

13

occasion and pronounced the words of committal in his roundest and most stentorian tones.

"It is written that: 'Man that is born of woman is of few days and full of trouble . . .' "

Suddenly there was a raspy, creaking sound—a grating scrape—and the rope slipped off the head of the coffin. The squire's box slid and fell, splashing muddy water everywhere as it came to lodge, head-first, at an angle, in the muck at the bottom of the grave.

The murmur of shock grew to a ripe clamor as the mourners gaped and the dazed pallbearers stumbled back a step, staring at their empty, mud-slicked ropes and the upended casket. They turned incredulous looks on one another and it looked for the moment as though the squire was going to have to await eternity with his heels above his head!

"Please!" The rector raised his trembling hands for silence. "No more of this . . . untoward commotion! Let us observe some decorum . . . some proper reverence for the man and the occasion!" He sounded a little strangled by the end.

Charity bit back a sob and turned to seek her grandmother's arms only to find herself captive in Sullivan Pinnow's, instead. How could this be happening, she moaned. And how could they just stand there, gawking? "Oh *please*. . . ." She pushed back in the baron's embrace to raise a tortured plea to his ever-so-sincere face. "Please don't let him go to eternal rest . . ." she choked, "on his *eeear*. . . ." She buried her face in her hands and sagged against him to weep in earnest.

"Oh, for god's sake!" the baron growled, absorbing every inch of her sweet form pressed against him. He waved a command at wiry, thin-faced Gar Davis. "Have you no sense a'tall? Right and settle the thing properly . . . and be quick about it!"

Gar paled and swallowed hard as he looked between the imperious baron and his old friend's coffin. Every eye in the crowd settled on him, including Percy Hall's. Percy nodded gravely at him, adding weight to the order. Gar edged forward toward the brink of the watery grave. His chin was

14

tucked and his beagle-brown eyes were huge with trepidation. He braced and squatted on the muddy bank, sticking one boot out to give the coffin a nudge. But it was too far to reach and he teetered breathlessly on the edge for a moment, then recovered.

"Go on. . . ," the baron commanded. And though there was no further sound, his lips might have been framing a "dammit."

Gar got down on his knobby knees, as close to the muddy edge as he dared, and leaned over, reaching, stretching. His fingers brushed the foot of the oak coffin lightly and withdrew as he flailed for balance. The others gasped as he narrowly regained the safety of the edge and they "ooohed" and "ahhhed" as the foot of the coffin shifted downward. But the squire was still heels-over-head, and Gar drew a ragged, miserable sigh and cast pleading looks at both the baron and Percy Hall. Their combined, prodding glares offered no hope of reprieve.

Again he leaned, hugging the edge, then leaning further, straining. Suddenly he was suspended over the opening . . . then teetering and scrambling for a hold on the eroded edge.

"Aaahhh!!!" He flailed and flapped and fell full into the grave with a screeching wail of surprise. There was a great, sloshing thump as the coffin dropped fully into the grave and a split second of tomb-like silence before pandemonium broke loose all around.

The baron eagerly embraced the anguished Charity, pulling her hard against his taut body, as though protecting her from the sight. The rector stuttered like a wide-eyed schoolboy and the bearers and mourners gasped and recoiled, huddling together and exclaiming horror. The diminutive Gar Davis scrambled to rise on the buoyant coffin and clawed at the slippery edge of the grave. His face was deathly white and his soulful eyes were filled with raw terror.

"Help me, Perc—" He strained mightily to haul himself above the slippery, muddy edge that was just more than chest high on him. "I-I can't get out!"

"O'course ye can." The usually pragmatic Percy Hall stiff-

15

ened back and grayed at the sight of Gar beckoning, pleading with him from the grave itself.

"Please Perc—" Gar was panicky now, grappling to pull himself up and over the slippery edge and failing. "H-help m-me! Ye gotta help me, Perc—"

"Ye gods, man," the baron barked hoarsely, "give the wretch a hand up!"

There was a long, breathless pause before Percy edged forward, scowling, locked wrists with the hapless Gar, and pulled. No sooner had Gar's muddy feet cleared the edge, than he was clambering up on them, clinging to Percy as they scuttled away from that ominous hole. He looked around at his neighbors and acquaintances, reading their comment on his fate in the pity and fear their faces contained. His eyes flew back to the grave he'd inhabited briefly and the full impact of his fall dawned on him. He turned and grabbed Percy's coatfront with frantic hands.

"Perc—I-I fell in!" Gar's eyes arced wide and his face drained of color. "A feller what falls in a grave dug fer somebody else . . . it means . . . he'll be next to go. That's what it means . . . don't it?" When Percy didn't answer, Gar tried to shake some response from him by his crumpled lapels. "Don't it?!"

But Percy's blocky jaw clamped against reply and he turned his face away, looking devastated indeed. Gar stiffened and released him, turning to the others to refute his statement. "Don't it?" But they backed a step and shook their heads and would not meet his eyes either. In desperation, he turned to Lady Margaret, whose dark scowl and tragic expression sent his panic into full flight.

"I'm gonna die." Gar staggered back so that he bumped into Percy. He turned in a flash and grabbed his friend's coat again. "I'm gonna die, Perc! I fell in . . . and now I'm gonna die, too!"

"No. . . ," Charity moaned and covered her face with her hands to blot out the sight. How could this be happening . . . here, of all places, and now, of all times? Grief boiled up in her, fiery and uncontainable. Suddenly it was too much—

16

the water, the rope slipping, Gar Davis's fall . . . Trouble upon trouble! Every eye in the crowd suddenly seemed riveted on *her;* she sensed the sly, suspicious looks, the bold, speculative looks. And then the oppressive weight of those stares, added to the panic in Gar Davis's face, was more than her burdened heart could bear. She groaned from the anguished depths of her being.

"No . . . no . . . nooooo!"

Wrenching free of the startled baron's hold, she wheeled and started to run across the grassy field, away from their stares, away from the grave and the empty manor house, away from the treacherous sea and all the other reminders of her terrible loss. Tear-blinded and sobbing, she tripped and stumbled over her damp skirts. Frantically, she snatched up handfuls of her black bombazine and soft muslin and began to run harder.

"Miss Charity!" The baron recovered sharply, calling after her, "Stop! Where are you going?!" But she kept running across the field, her black veil billowing on the wind, and her long, honey-blonde hair streaming behind. When it became clear that she wasn't going to stop, he sputtered and bolted after her.

The baron's speed was hampered by his gentlemanly attempts at grace . . . and by a pair of fashionably snug knee-breeches, a viciously starched collar and a tightly wrapped stock. Stiff-backed and chin up, his rangy legs churning, he looked remarkably like an enormous ruffed grouse in full courting display. His gaze was riveted on her raised skirts and shapely, bared ankles, such that he completely forgot to mind his own feet. Just as he began to close the distance between them, one of his feet hit a patch of muck, sinking and sticking fast. The bottom half of him jarred to a halt, while the top half hurtled past, careening headlong. When he tried to catch himself, his other leg hit a second patch of slippery mud, jerked, twisted, and shot from beneath him, sending him sprawling on his side and back in the muddy field.

Pain seared up his right leg, up his spine, then burst in his

17

brain like fireworks. "ARGHH!! Oww! Oh God!" He shoved up, clutching his knee and his screaming ankle and rocking in pure agony. At the far edge of the field, his quarry was disappearing over a rise, oblivious to his pursuit and his pain.

Charity ran, unseeing, toward the meandering woods in the valley. Her heart was pounding and her lungs were aching; she was scarcely able to expel one breath before she was forced to gulp another. She swiped her veil from her wet face and blinked furiously to dislodge the tears that blurred her path. Behind her lay a trail of pure disaster, a string of small calamities that had ruined her last, solemn farewell to her father and turned his burial into a spectacle. Before her lay a murky future in which the only certainty seemed to be penury. And within her lay a bleak, chasm-like void caused by her father's untimely death.

She ran without intent or direction, across the sunlit fields and pastures, trying to escape . . . and mercifully unaware of the turbulent wake she created in the deep, silent waters of fate as she passed.

Not far away, a black, high-wheeled phaeton with crimson markings flew down the London Road at a blistering pace, drawn by two flashy, high-stepping blacks with manes flying and nostrils flaring. The sight would have turned heads in any part of the realm, even in fashionably blasé London. But in the provincial Devon countryside, where carriages of any sort drew considerable notice, it caused quite a sensation as it passed. Hands stilled, heads turned, and low whistles and murmurs expressed universal admiration for both the vehicle and its driver.

At the reins was a gentleman dressed in gray from the top of his high-crowned, narrow-brimmed hat, to the soles of his expensive leather pumps with their silver buckles. The dove gray of his garments was exquisitely neutral, cannily chosen to blunt the impact of the gentleman's dramatic coloring. Raven dark hair curled slightly at his temples and lapped with fashionable carelessness over his impeccable standing collar and midnight blue stock. Taut bronzed skin was stretched over cleanly sculpted bones and a square, patrician jaw. Only the gentleman's eyes matched his raiment; they were the same light gray, though there was certainly nothing dovish about them just now. Indeed, they glowed with hawk-like intensity.

Rane Austen, Viscount Oxley, tore his eyes from the road to glance at the rumpled copy of the *Times* on the cordovan leather seat beside him. His light eyes narrowed and the muscles in his jaw worked visibly as he ground his teeth together.

"Married!" he muttered furiously as he searched for that devastating, bold-faced heading one more time. The wording wouldn't have changed, he knew; it was futile to look. But he read it again anyway. *Sutterfield-Harrowford Betrothal.* It was still Miss Gloria Sutterfield and she was still going to marry the Viscount Harrowford . . . scrawny, ineffectual Archie Lattimer, who had only recently become Viscount Harrowford.

"Fine! Let the little tight-arse marry that juiceless toadwart! She'll get exactly what she deserves . . . a limp stick in a cold bed and a lifetime of wondering what it would have been like with a *man!*" His powerful hands clenched on the reins, unconsciously telegraphing his anger down the lines to his high-spirited blacks. They slipped a bit more of their restraint and raced a bit wilder.

It wasn't losing the highly decorative and impeccably pedigreed Miss Sutterfield herself, that galled him so. After all, one typically refined, standardly accomplished young deb was basically the same as another. But this wasn't the first time he had lost the young deb he had so assiduously courted to another man . . . nor even the second! It was the third, b'dammit! *The third bloody wretched time* he had lost out to some idle, worthless rag-rack with an "untainted" title, a "respectable" family and a "proper" living. And it was the second year in a row that he'd been publicly humiliated before London's almighty ton!

His uncommonly broad shoulders swelled inside his silk-lined coat and his full, sensual mouth compressed into a grim line. In his mind's eye he could see the head-wagging and the ill-suppressed smirks he would have to endure when he got back to London. The ton had made their opinion of him abundantly clear in the last six years, and for a moment he despaired that his title and money might never be enough to overcome their prejudice against him.

He knew his appearance branded him an outsider in their eyes; they made no secret of it. His hair was unthinkably black, however silky and stylishly cropped, and his skin was permanently tanned from the harsh tropic sun of Barbados, where he had lived and grown to manhood. Together, they gave him a dark, exotic look that belied his solid English ancestry, his proper English birth and the fact that he'd spent his earliest years in Sussex.

But to be fair, Rane Austen's coloring was only part of the reason that the ton had never accepted him. He was outlandishly tall, to their way of thinking, his shoulders were vulgarly broad — like a common laborer's — and his movements were altogether too physical. His light eyes and his speech both were too bold and he gamed and drove and even danced with unseemly intensity. In short, he seemed far too much like his disreputable, fast-living father and grandfather, neither of whom had quite been ton material, either.

A sharp jolt from a storm-washed hole in the road brought his mind back to the business at hand. The high-wheeled phaeton swayed and lurched and he reined the blacks a bit, scowling at the way they resisted him at first. The road was far worse than he remembered and the morning's downpour hadn't improved it any. He was beginning to regret bringing his new rig and his hot-blooded blacks out onto these rough, provincial roads.

His discerning gaze scoured the still glistening countryside from habit, cataloguing its character, its assets, and potential for profit. He saw lush, greening fields, healthy stands of woods that nestled in hollows and huddled cozily on hilltops, neat cottages, and full-running brooks. It was a blessedly pastoral and picturesque country. The thought came reflexively that "picturesque" was a term in vogue in London. An instant later, he was angry with himself for thinking it.

It seemed everything he did of late was governed by what "they" thought, those nameless, faceless arbiters of fashion and sensibility that controlled the lives of England's most privileged class. His dark, feathery brows lowered and his eyes took on the luster of mirror-polished steel as he banished those thoughts. He had other concerns on this hasty journey into the west country. He turned his mind briefly to the inn where he would lodge and wondered whether his man, Stephenson, had found it from the directions he had given. And he thought about how he would go about contacting the party he had come to Devon to confront.

After a few moments, his grip on the reins slackened again as his mind's eye returned to the elegant London scene, where he seemed always to be on the outside, looking in. He began to mentally sort through the remains of this year's crop of eligible young debs, cataloguing their marital assets and their accessibility. There were still several weeks left in the waning season and if he wrapped this business up quickly, he could probably still make it back in time for a few dances and parties . . . if he could wangle some invitations.

Inescapably, his thoughts turned to his last encounter with Miss Gloria Sutterfield, at the Mountjoys' ball. Through the two dances that propriety allowed them, she'd batted those big, blue eyes at him, and fluttering her fan afterward, she had gazed up at him as though he were the only man in the world. The very next day he had sent a messenger to her father, asking for an appointment. His messenger returned with word that Sir Horace Sutterfield was absent from his home for a few days. After "a few days" had passed, he was still away. Now, a mere two weeks later, she was publicly declared the acquisition of that mealworm Lattimer. Why the hell couldn't he get what every milksop wretch and bacon-faced sod in the west end of London had . . . a *wife?*

With his mind on his London troubles and his hands slack

21

on the reins, Rane Austen sped down that rutted road, growing less and less attentive to his driving and to the surrounding countryside. When a small, dark speck appeared, moving over a hillside, far ahead and to his right, he didn't notice it at all. It grew larger as it streaked along on a path perpendicular to his own on a course that was bound to intercept his. Soon it took on a human shape and after a time became recognizable as a female form, clad in black, with skirts billowing and silky veil flying above a wind-whipped banner of long, blonde hair.

The road worsened abruptly, bouncing the elegant, long-spoked wheels of the phaeton like spinning jackstraws and jarring Rane Austen back to the present. He reacted instinctively, reining the blacks and fighting to turn them toward the less rutted berm of the road. The sudden tightening of control and the muddy, treacherous footing tested the limits of the horses' training and discipline, but as they found the more solid footing, they began to calm.

Then something darted out of the row of trees, ahead and to the right of the carriage, startling both Austen and his high-strung blacks.

His first half-formed perception was that it was a cat—a big, black cat. It took another split-second for him to realize that it was a human blazing across his path.

That instant his reflexes took over, and he worked the reins as hard as he could. He was caught at the left edge of the road, blocked ahead by the startled human form, and blocked on the right by a quagmire of water-filled holes, rocks, and ruts. In a mere heartbeat, the choice was made and he strained at the reins to force his blacks into that treacherous course, just as the woman—he had managed to somehow collect that impression—continued her flight toward the safety of the far side.

But something dark had lifted on a gust of wind; like a specter, it came straight at the blacks' heads. They laid their ears back and their eyes rolled as they broke stride, leaping and balking. The silken specter brushed and clung to their faces just as they hit the slippery muck in the middle of the road. One reared and then the other, and they lurched and scrambled in the sucking mud, breaking into a panicky flight that utterly defied Austen's considerable skill at the reins. When their hooves struck firmer ground, they began to run pell-mell, dragging the swaying, bouncing phaeton behind them like an unwieldy toy.

Austen had lost his grip on the reins as he was tossed about, and clutched at the footboard to keep from being tipped out of the carriage. Before he could recover, he was thrown back in the seat by the forward lurch of the vehicle. He fought the backward thrust and threw himself against the footboard to retrieve the reins, only to see them slip over the front boards. His arm shot out in time to snatch one line, but one line out of four was useless when both animals were so out of control. He shouted at them as they hurtled down the road, but they were already past both horse and human sense. He was reduced to hanging on to the trouncing vehicle as best he could and shouting hoarse commands.

Just then, one of the slender, elegant wheels hit a huge rock, bounced, and came down sideways between two other rocks, snapping several crimson spokes. The carriage tossed violently as the wheel splintered and came off, leaving the carriage dragging and bouncing wildly behind the panic-stricken horses. As they rounded a great curve in the road, Rane Austen was flung from the carriage, head-first into a grassy thicket near a stand of trees.

The carriage kept going, thrashing wildly behind the frightened horses, until it crashed into the stout trunk of a tree at the edge of road and smashed like a child's tin trinket. Splintered debris went flying as the break-hitch released and the horses charged on, dragging parts of the mangled harness with them as they left the road to escape across nearby fields.

Rane Austen's hard head had managed to find the only rock in that entire thicket as he landed on the rain-softened ground. He lay sprawled on his stomach, unconscious, oblivious to the ruin of his expensive phaeton and mercifully unaware of the force that had just disrupted both his journey and his life. Black-clad Charity Standing had just crossed his path and he'd been caught briefly in the unseen turbulence that seemed always to surround her passage through the world around her.

Chapter Two

Charity stumbled to a halt and sank to her knees in an old hayfield not far from the London Road. Her lungs were burning, her blood pounded thunderously in her head, and her eyes felt like they were full of dry sand. She couldn't go another step, not another inch. Her pain and anger had finally burned themselves out, and the last of her energy had been consumed with them.

She collapsed onto the ground, feeling charred and numbed to all but the barest impact of her perceptions. It was some time before she could right her senses enough to feel the dampness of the ground beneath her and the warmth of the afternoon sun on her black dress and bare face. And it was longer still before her screaming body quieted and the memory of her father's disastrous burial settled harshly on her heart again.

What should have been a tribute to her father's memory had degenerated into a series of mishaps that had unnerved everyone present. She should be used to such things by now, to the accidents and mischances that always occurred around her, but, miraculously, seemed never to involve her personally. Her father had always declared it was her unthinkably *good* luck that kept rampant calamity at bay, and over the years she'd accepted his cajoling explanation.

But if she was personally immune to disaster, those about her seemed doubly susceptible. And their pains and misfortunes grieved her tender heart so, she felt compelled to try to help anyone who was troubled or destitute or suffering. From her earliest years, she had adopted every hurt or lost animal she encountered, brought home vagrants for a bit of

25

food or shelter, and watched anxiously over Standwell's sickbeds.

But her compassionate heart and Standwell's resources could only bear so much misfortune and her father had gradually withdrawn from society, and drawn a veil of seclusion about her. The less she saw of the troubles around her, the better, he had decided. And it was only in the last year, as she approached and passed her eighteenth birthday, that she realized what he had done and just how isolated their lives had become. The Standings had never been greatly social, but it had now been years since they had paid or received calls, attended town celebrations, or seen anyone but tradesmen or tenants, and her father's friends Percy Hall and Gar Davis.

She lay in the yellowed remnant of last season's grasses that mingled with the new green of the summer's promised growth, feeling caught between past and future herself. Glimpses of her life with her father bloomed in her mind and faded gently into the sepia tones of memory. The day he taught her to sit a horse . . . the way he would steal into her room at night, thinking her asleep, and watch her with that sad, angelic smile of his . . . the frazzled look he wore when she brought home yet another half-drowned puppy, or gave away her petticoat to a tenant's child who didn't even have a skirt to wear it under.

Mingled with those memories came dim foreshadowings of the future that no one at Standwell ever talked about or permitted her to ask questions about. On her own, bright young Charity had projected the present through clouds of "if's" and "when's" and had carried present things to logical conclusions. The household had become progressively thinner in the last few years—fewer servants, fewer purchases, plainer food—and it would get thinner still. Someday the aging Lady Margaret would lie on the slope beside Upton Standing and her beloved mother, Chanson, and Charity would feel even more alone than she felt now. What would she do then?

She pushed up slowly to find herself sitting in a grassy

field, not a house, a barn, or another soul in sight. A closer look told her it was one of Mr. George Burford's far-flung holdings, more than six miles from her home, Standwell. She had no clear recollection of the mad flight that had brought her here. A brief glimpse of an onrushing carriage and lathered black horses, huge and powerful, came to her. She shuddered in the warm sun, thinking she'd only imagined it.

"Well, you're whole, Charity Standing. That's something, anyway," she whispered. It was as hopeful as she could be just now. "And you've got a precious long walk home."

The mention of her home darkened her winsome face and she stilled, trying desperately to hold onto that blessed numbness a bit longer. Wasn't there anyplace else she could go? Anyplace, as long as it didn't smell of vinegar and juniper smoke . . . and death. A moment later, she recalled her grandmother's lined face as it had been in the church. Gran'mere would probably be frantic with worry, perhaps even be searching the countryside for her this very minute. She had to go home.

She struggled to her knees then to her feet, concentrating on the painful movement to keep her painful thoughts at bay. Her legs and arms seemed each to weigh a ton, in spite of the odd, empty feeling in the rest of her. She brushed her rumpled, dusty bombazine, flicking haystraws and dead leaves from her skirt. Her veil was gone and her fingers relayed that her thick hair was a mass of tangles. Her cheeks were hot, and probably red from the sun and the salt of her tears.

Keeping to the grassy edge of the road and the shade of the trees that lined it, she'd gone more than half a mile when she rounded a large curve and stopped dead. A part of a wheel rim with several broken spokes lay in the middle of the rutted road. Her eyes followed an alarming trail of wheel wreckage down the road to a carriage that was wrapped partway around a large tree trunk, like so much wastefully crumpled paper. The sight jarred some of the protective numbness from her faculties and she began to walk faster, then to run, toward the demolished carriage. A carriage wreck always meant injuries, often dire ones.

Her eyes caught on a figure sprawled in the grass near the roadside and without the slightest hesitation, she ran to help. It was a man—a gentleman, from the looks of his clothing and what was left of his carriage. He lay face down with his arms and legs sprawled at graceless angles, probably just as he'd fallen. She knelt beside him and set tremulous hands to his back to give him a shake.

"Sir? Sir, are you badly hurt? Can you move?" Her anxiety mounted as she roused no response. "Can you hear me?" She began to feel a bit light-headed and her heart began to thud erratically. Something in the sight of him, lying limp and unconscious, dredged up the freshly traumatic memories of her father.

"Oh please," she whispered hoarsely, "please don't be dead. You can't be dead, too." How did one tell? She steeled her nerve and put her ear to his broad back to listen for his heart, then had to press harder . . . and harder. The muffled thudding sent a warm tide of relief through her.

She straightened, her cheek glowing where it had lain against his coat. Scanning his long frame for visible signs of injury and finding none, she bit her lip, trying to decide what to do. There still could be broken bones or other internal injuries. Her grandmother had never allowed propriety to stand in the way of helping someone who was hurt, and in so doing had set Charity an example. Humanity took precedence over propriety. She shifted on her knees to run her hands gingerly over his arms and legs, checking for broken bones, as she had so often seen her grandmother do.

Beneath her hands, his limbs were hard and warm—reassuringly warm, disturbingly hard. She'd never really touched a man's body before and the thought occurred to her that she'd never imagined one would be so firm.

Everything seemed to be in place and she risked rolling him over carefully, onto his back. She stopped, arched halfway over him, staring. There was a nasty blue swelling near his right temple, but it was the rest of his face that held her attention. It was stunning. His features seemed a sort of living bronze framed on bold cheekbones, a high, clear forehead, and a square jaw and chin. His nose was straight and given to a slight arch, his brows were graceful, feathery wings above crescents of long black lashes. She found herself staring at his lips, fascinated by the contrast of their broad, gentle curves and their distinctly chiseled borders. And soft . . . They looked as soft as the rest of him seemed hard.

She tore her eyes away and they flowed down his once impeccable collar, his blue stock and elegant gray coat with silver buttons. He seemed to be dressed in the height of fashion but, somehow, to her inexperienced eye, the clothes seemed of little consequence compared with the man himself.

"Sir?" She leaned near his face and a lock of her hair slid over her shoulder and came to rest on his chin, as if caressing it. She risked patting the smooth bronze of his cheek with her hand. "Please wake up. I—I can't just leave you here. . . ."

His eyelids fluttered in response to her call. She sighed relief and lifted his head to encourage him to waken. But he was much heavier than she'd supposed and she had to put both arms around his neck to hold his head up. He stiffened suddenly in her arms and his head raised of its own power, coming up nose-first, straight into the bared skin of her breasts.

"Ohhh!" She recoiled, arching back while trying not to drop him. "Sir! A-are you badly hurt? Can you move? Can you stand?"

He groaned and blinked and flopped his arms ineffectually, as if trying them out to see if they still worked. Then, finding them in his command, he braced on them and tried to push up, bumping into her and falling back abruptly, with a breathless "uffff."

Charity, startled, just managed to keep his head from smacking the ground again. "You've had a terrible accident, sir, and you've cracked your head. I don't know if anything else is broken." He obviously could hear her, for he had responded. "Open your eyes. Can you see?"

Rane Austen obeyed slowly. The centers of his eyes were huge and dark, giving them a glassy, unseeing look and making everything seem glazed with light and indistinct to him. When he finally focused, his beleaguered mind registered a woman's face, a blushed, beautiful oval of a face, long blonde hair dangling free around him, falling on him, and pale, half-bare breasts just an inch or two away. He was lying on his back and caught against her in an embrace, and in his irrational state he made what sense of it he could. Blonde and beautiful . . . in part deshabille . . . He did what came most naturally, obeying the urgency that had ridden his mind in his last rational thoughts. He proposed.

"M-marr-r-r-y — mmmm — "

Dismay filled him; his tongue wasn't working properly! But he had to ask her! How could he make her know? He felt her pulling away and struggled mightily to follow her up into a sitting position. The sudden movement sent searing pain through his head and shoulders and he grimaced and grabbed his head between his hands, curling bodily. But the urgency of his need forced him to uncurl and sit straighter. Where was she? He peeled his eyes open and found her sitting on her knees beside him, so very blonde and lovely.

He blinked repeatedly, as though he were having difficulty seeing her, and Charity realized that he wasn't quite lucid yet.

"Perhaps you'd best stay here, sir." She drew back, unsettled by how big he seemed, now that he was upright and staring at her with those dark, glazed eyes. "You probably shouldn't try to walk. I'll fetch you some help."

"N-nooo." There was genuine pain in his deep, tattered voice. His big hands snaked out to grab her arm and a fistful of her skirts, holding her back as she tried to rise. "Don't go. I-I — " He squinted against the brightness and tried to pull her closer. "M-marr-y m-mee."

"Really sir, you must let me up! I have to get you some help." She was busy fending off his hands and was unable to make sense of his mumblings at first.

"N-no, please." He became desperate, watching her shrink

from him, and he abandoned his grip on her skirts to reach for her other arm and pull her resisting form closer. He sucked a deep, steadying breath and swallowed hard, concentrating. This time it came out right.

"M-marry me. P-please. *Marry me.*"

Charity stared, owl-eyed with shock. "What?"

"M-marry me . . ."

"Ohhh, sir . . ." Her face flushed and her heart gave a queer lurch. He was out of his head, raving, she realized, to say such a thing to a perfect stranger! But the bronzed intensity of his handsome face and the power evident in his big frame jolted her anxiety onto a whole new level. If his head were cracked that badly, there was no telling what he might do. She wrested her arms from his grip and skittered back on her bottom, staring at him. "I have to go—"

"N-no!" he rasped, reaching for her again, frantic she would get away. When she made it to her feet, he began to scramble, desperate to get to his feet as well. "M-marry you . . . I have to. . . ."

Charity watched him wobble and flop and struggle to rise. "Are you quite sure you should be. . . ?" She agonized a moment, deciding, then lurched to his aid, putting her arm about his waist to lift and steady him as he stood. He made it onto his feet, and an instant later, he turned and had both arms locked about her, engulfing her like a great, unwieldy bear. He gazed dazedly down into her face and his head began to bend toward her.

His mouth came boldly down on hers, a bit off center, but very emphatic. Her first reeling thought was that his lips really *were* soft and her second was that it was fascinating— frightening!—feeling his lips so warm on hers and feeling so engulfed physically. She could scarcely breathe as his mouth swayed and moved over hers.

It took a moment for her to realize that more than his mouth was moving. His whole body was suddenly tilting. His warm lips slid off the edge of hers and careened down her jaw line as he went over, staggering this way, then that, pulling her along while he struggled to stay afoot. His face paled dangerously as his blood drained from his head and his glazed eyes crossed and uncrossed themselves at random.

"Sir, you can't possibly—" She pushed and struggled frantically to keep them both upright as he began to lean, then to fall on her as the strength ebbed from his legs. "Oh, don't fall! I can't *caaaatch*—" She felt her own balance going and tried to push him back onto his own feet to keep him from falling on her. But her maneuver worked too well. He keeled over and kept going backward, with his hands locked around her so that he carried her with him as he stumbled and fell.

He hit the ground, with a great, muffled thud. Charity found herself sprawled atop him, jarred breathless. She shook her head and gasped for air, then recovered enough of her wits to realize that she was lying atop a strange man's body, with his arms clamped around her in a death grip. She twisted and wriggled over him, finally breaking his hold, and scrambled off his inert form and onto her own bottom.

"I'm sorry." She skittered back and began straightening her clothes frantically. "I said you shouldn't try to get up. Are you all right?" She paused and made herself touch him again, to give his shoulder a shake. There was no response and she raised onto her knees beside him, searching the paleness of his face beneath his tanned skin with growing alarm. His big, hard hand seemed icy when she touched it and his cheek now felt cool and clammy.

Icy waves of memory again invaded her perceptions, distorting them. His head seemed to be lying at an odd angle and his color worsened rapidly, as if. . . .

"What have I done?" The accumulated shocks and stresses of the day bore down upon her, besieging her still-rattled wits. She pressed the back of one hand to her mouth and her eyes flew wide. "Merciful Heaven—have I killed you? Oh, please, *please* don't die!"

Fresh panic set her heart racing and squeezed her throat so that she couldn't swallow. She leaned down to press an ear to his chest and could hear nothing but the frantic coursing of her own blood in her head. She sprang up, truly frightened, and touched his forehead. It was colder still. Her thought processes were being invaded by icy tendrils of fear. It couldn't be. He was so young and so strong and so . . . cold.

Cold. Like her father had been cold.

Cold like the sea. Cold like the grave, a watery grave.

She skittered back on her knees and scrambled up, shaking, trying not to think it. He was likely dying. *Or already dead!*

"No! Noooo!"

For the second time that day, she snatched up her skirts and began to run, spurred by anguish and pursued by loss.

Standwell was a rambling gray stone manor house built around a modest stone keep that had stood watch over the Devon coastland for more than four hundred years. In all that time, held and inhabited by the descendants of the original Earl of Standier, it had proven a worthy guardian of its venue. But cannons and long guns had eventually made such fortresses obsolete and, like an old soldier whose glories were now only memories, Standwell had settled stoically into the lush countryside, surrendering gallantly to the onslaught of time.

Now there were gaps in the stone walls and numerous slates missing from the roof. The house was filled with doors that wouldn't quite close and windows that wouldn't quite open, with chairs that didn't quite sit straight and dishes that didn't quite match. The rugs were now more warp than woof and the floors had such eccentric and specific creaks that they could be used to track a person's progress through the house with amazing accuracy.

From the battlements of the stone tower of the old keep, Lady Margaret Villiers kept a watch not unlike those of centuries before, scouring the countryside.

"Damnable trees," she declared, peering from one of the shoulder-high stone crenels, searching what she could see of the nearby fields and the road leading to the front doors of Standwell. "Upton should have listened to me and had the

33

wretched things cleared out years ago. They ruin the damned view. Make a body feel hemmed in, feel half planted herself! Hell's backwater, what am I tellin' you for?" She clamped her jaw tight and shot a dark look at the huge mastiff-wolfhound cross that sat staring at her from the top of the wooden stairs. Turning back to squint off into the distance, she examined first one speck, then another on the horizon. Dismissing them with a shake of her head, she scowled, "Where in blazes is she?"

She drew her black shawl tighter around her and abandoned one chiseled embrasure in the stone wall to take up another, from which she could see further inland. She scowled and rubbed her sun-browned chin with a weathered hand. She had cast off her new black mantilla in favor of her customary blue silk stole, which she wore wound about her head, turban fashion. And she'd exchanged that awful black bombazine that the dressmaker insisted was the latest in mourning fashion, for a worn, yellow on blue, print cotton bedgown. Over that loose gown, she'd pulled a bold crimson and green paisley print smock that was part overdress and part apron with pockets. Two enormous golden hoops had appeared in her ears and a clutch of odd-shaped amulets, made of bones, pebbles, metals, and paws, were again visible around her neck. Only the black shawl remained as outward evidence of her mourning for her son-in-law.

"If only I could see like I used to," she muttered. The huge, much-scarred dog made a yawning whine-moan that sounded startlingly like a laugh and the old woman stiffened, glaring at the animal irritably. "Well, you're no prize yourself!" She glared pointedly at the creature's missing ear and patchy gray coat, and at his lip that, missing on one side, gave him the look of a perpetual snarl. "If you were worth the air you breathe, you'd be out looking for her with Gar and Percy, instead of sitting there on that huge rump of yours, lookin' ugly as a head on a boil."

The dog pulled its enormous head back, as if offended. Lady Margaret harumphed unrepentantly and trundled on to yet another observation post. There was a weight of genuine worry in her deep sigh as she scanned the grassy fields that sloped gently toward the seaside cliffs.

"Still nothing. She was in such a state."

She fidgeted indecisively for a moment, fingering a crescent moon-shaped amulet that hung around her neck, then picked up her skirts and sailed for the stairs. She moved with notable vigor and ease for a woman of uncertain, but certainly numerous, years. The massive dog was hard put to keep up and to squeeze through the wooden door at the bottom of the rickety steps before she slammed it shut and dropped the aged bar into place. Her step was quick and sure as she hurried across the creaky flooring of the round room at the top of the tower and down a broad set of stone steps built into the thick stone walls. She passed through a series of narrow stone archways and emerged into a plastered hallway that marked the boundary between the house proper and the round stone fortress it had been built around. Pausing, she looked down the east hallway toward her granddaughter's bedchamber and tried to decide whether to check Charity's room again.

The sound of voices drifting into the hallway from the nearby center stairs caught her ear. In her haste to reach the stairs and the entry hall below, she trod on the dog's foot, then baldly ignored his deep growl of warning.

Sturdy, square-featured Percy Hall and the shorter, slighter Gar Davis stood on the worn slate floor of the modest entry hall, shifting from foot to foot. They were panting hard from their long run, and their boots were caked with drying mud. At the sight of Lady Margaret, they dragged their knitted caps from their heads and jostled past old Melwin the butler to make their report.

"Nary a trace," raspy voiced Percy Hall said.

"Not a thing? Not even a glimpse?" Lady Margaret's lined forehead puckered above her piercing brown eyes and her sunken mouth pursed into a firm line.

"We looked everplace, asked everbody we seen," Gar added. "We even went back an' tracked 'er across them fields where she run, after we got the squire," his voice dropped nervously, "planted proper." He shot an uneasy look at Percy, then again faced Lady Margaret's penetrating glare.

"She has to be somewhere close by," Lady Margaret whispered, fingering her moonstone amulet with the seven silver stars around it. "I can feel it in my bones." Gar and Percy glanced at each other and nodded warily. They'd had years of experience with Lady Margaret's bones and knew that they were seldom wrong.

Suddenly the dog whined and bolted down the stairs, jostling Lady Margaret violently. It raced pell-mell through the hall and lunged at the heavy front doors, raking them from top to bottom with its massive paws. Everyone in the hall braced for what they knew came next. "Woof!" It was thunderous. "*Woof!*" Deafening. "*Woof, Woof!*" The picture hanging in the entry hall nearly danced off its nail, the walls sang with the vibrations, and the slate tiles underfoot hummed.

"For God's sake!" Lady Margaret shouted, clamping her hands over her ears. "Let the bloody brute out!!"

Percy peeled his hands from his ears and lurched to obey. As soon as the heavy, paneled door swung open a few inches, the dog squeezed through and bounded out, barking, leaving a startled vacuum in the hall behind him. It took a minute for Percy to recover and he closed the door on the unholy racket the dog was making.

"Mangy beast," Lady Margaret muttered mutinously, heading for the main parlor. She waved Gar and Percy along with her through a wide, arched doorway over which seven upturned horseshoes had been nailed.

What was now called Standwell's "parlor" was actually the old great hall, a huge chamber with vaulted ceilings, a massive marble mantel and heavily screened hearth, and a long expanse of tall windows facing south. The leaded windows collected the heat in a most pleasant way in winter and a most unpleasant way in summer, and the sun which shone through them had long since faded the furnishings to a dusty gray-pink and a sickly celery green. Heavy, old, mutton-legged Jacobean furnishings were the standard throughout the house, but in this room, they had been augmented by later acquisitions in the now antique Queen Anne style. Even with its splendor faded, it was still the most elegant place Gar and Percy had ever seen, and they instinctively began to tiptoe as they followed Lady Margaret into what had once been the sanctum of belted earls of the realm.

"She's taking it so hard. Did you check the chapel?" She turned on them with a scowl and waved them toward chairs. "Sit down before you fall down. Or the church in town?" She trailed to a halt, cocking her head, listening. Gar and Percy were caught mid-sit by her sudden attention to the sound and, with a wary glance at each other, straightened. The dog's thunderous barks could still be heard through the front-facing windows, and their nature had just changed significantly.

"Rolf!" They burst like quiet bombs in the sudden tension of the parlor. "*Rrrrolf, rolf, rolf. ROLF, ROLF!*" It was the kind of manic bark that signaled a scent caught or a quarry cornered. It could only mean one thing.

"Miz Charity . . ."

No sooner had Gar breathed her name than all three were in motion, heading for the door, with Lady Margaret elbowing the others back. They swung open the creaking front doors and charged out into the weedy entry court, scouring the yard and nearby road for the source of that canine call.

In the middle of the road, some hundred yards away, Charity was on her knees, clinging to the side of the huge, battered-looking dog as he stood over her, barking for help. They ran to help her up, but she was utterly exhausted, too weak to stand, and breathing in gulps. She transferred her grip to Gar's sleeve and to her Grandmother's skirts as she tried frantically to say something between gasps.

"D-dead . . . he may . . . be . . . d-dead. . . ." Her eyes stared wildly, unseeingly at them as she struggled to make herself understood.

Gar bit his lip, his eyes misting up, Percy had to look away, and Lady Margaret crossed herself and felt for her amulet made of three white rabbit's feet. Charity's grief was just too large for her to bear, they realized, shaking their heads at the extreme to which it had driven her. Her gown was soiled and wrinkled, her long blonde hair hung in tangles, and, though her eyes were dry now, the tracks of old tears were still visible in the dirt on her face.

"Don't just stand there gawking. Carry her inside!" Lady Margaret ordered. Gar and Percy hesitated until the old woman's eyes narrowed with a look that was peculiarly compelling. They then hurriedly made a chair of their arms and, at Lady Margaret's gruff directions, lifted and carried Charity toward the front doors that were wreathed in dried mountain ash and overhung with no less than seven upturned horsehoes.

"B-but, if he's not d-dead . . ." Charity wailed half coherently, clutching at her grandmother's sleeve. "H-help him . . ."

Lady Margaret patted Charity's hand, nodding darkly and shushing her. Shoulders rounded and body knotted up like a cannon ball, the old lady burst through the front doors, barreled through the entry hall and bustled up the long flight of steps to the upstairs hall. She led them down the east hall to Charity's room, threw back the door with a bang, and instructed them to place her granddaughter on her great postered bed. But no sooner had Charity touched the counterpane, than she was struggling to sit up, clutching at Percy's sleeve and at her grandmother's hand frantically.

"No . . . he may be dead . . . maybe not. Please, we have to help . . . I have to help . . ."

"He's dead, child." Lady Margaret squeezed between Percy and Gar to lean over Charity, gently pushing her shoulders back down each time she tried to rise. The old woman's face was stony with double anguish, her own and Charity's. "You must accept it. He's dead now, and in the angels' hands. He's beyond our help. Merciful sakes!" She began brushing and fussing distractedly. "Look at you, fretting and grieving yourself into such a state!"

"No!" Charity tossed her head wildly on the bolsters. Her mind was fogged by exhaustion and one grief mingled so with another that even she could not separate them. It was little wonder that her grandmother and Gar and Percy failed to understand that she wasn't rambling about her father's accident and death. "Th' accident! He was hurt . . . maybe dead."

"He *is* dead." Her grandmother smoothed her hair and tried to restrain her twisting shoulders.

"But I saw 'im!"

"Shhhh. You've had a terrible time of it, child, but you're safe now." She turned aside to Percy with wide, horrified eyes. "She's purely daft with grief. Stay with her whilst I mix her up a double draught of my healing comfort!"

The old woman left the room at a run, and Gar and Percy patted Charity's hands uncomfortably, shushing and soothing her grief as best they could. Above her head, they exchanged worried glances as she rambled about accidents and dying, and pleaded incoherently for their help.

They knew all about Miss Charity's problem, about the accidents and mishaps that happened around her with unnerving regularity. They'd known since she was a wee thing, having been on the receiving end of her peculiar "luck" numerous times themselves. Their sweet little Charity had both the face and the disposition of an angel. The rest of her feminine charms were equally as heavenly and they were convinced: *the angels must want it all back!* To their minds, nothing short of so fantastic an explanation could account for the strange things that always seemed to happen around her.

A few minutes later Lady Margaret returned with a cup of her potent concoction of secret herbs and sleeping powders. They helped her sit and made her drink and finally were forced to promise that they'd go look for "him" on the road "somewhere." With that assurance, she calmed, and Lady Margaret, with a grave nod that absolved them of their promise, dismissed Gar and Percy to "see to it." When they left, Lady Margaret settled on the edge of the bed beside her, and Charity seemed to ease enough for tears to fill her half-focused eyes.

"W-why, Gran'mere?" she asked, stammering in her ex-

39

haustion. "Why do such bad things always happen? Troubles, always troubles. People have such troubles everywhere."

"Shush, child, you musn't talk so." Lady Margaret looked about nervously and released one of Charity's hands to once again finger the rabbits' feet hanging from her neck. "It's bad luck to speak of your luck."

"B-but I never have troubles." Charity was beyond all admonitions as the effect of the potion began to take hold, calming her and making her eyes grow heavier. "I tried to help. I always try to help. Papa always said I was lucky. B-but I always see such troubles. Oh, Gran'mere, I think I killed him!"

"Rumnoggins! You haven't killed anybody!" Lady Margaret cast a worried look about her, then delved into her pocket for a pinch of salt to toss over her shoulder.

"B-but, he was so han'some . . . an' so cold. And he's dead, too. Oh, Gran'mere, why did he have to die?"

"We all have to die, child . . . sooner or later." The old lady bit her lip and banished the mist forming in her faded eyes.

"Why don' things work out better?" She didn't seem to hear her grandmother. "Am I jus' *too* lucky?"

Her grief-darkened eyes drifted shut a final time and Lady Margaret sagged with relief. Too lucky? Lady Margaret groaned privately; hardly that. She stood, laid Charity's hand gently on her waist, and gave her cheek a pat. Then she pulled the girl's shoes from her feet, so as not to spoil the bedclothes further, and shook her head at the state of her stockings and skirts. Then her eyes traveled to her granddaughter's lovely face and for the thousandth time she felt a deep, wrenching pain on her behalf.

All Charity's life, they had done their best to shield her from what Upton Standing had tactfully called "her problem." They had accident-proofed the house as much as was humanly possible, had withdrawn from what society their dwindling fortunes would have otherwise allowed them, and had persistently explained away the accidents and small troubles that their precautions could not prevent. But as Lady Margaret stood by the bed, watching her granddaughter's troubled sleep, she felt that protective network of isolation and arrangement unraveling all around them. With Upton gone and no money in the coffers, and with Charity now a young woman who was bound to attract attention wherever she went, circumstances could come to a head quickly. If only Upton hadn't gone and got himself killed.

Lady Margaret sighed and wet a cloth to gently wipe her granddaughter's sun-reddened face. She pushed back a few tangles of thick blonde hair, thinking how much like her mother Charity was, so shapely, fair, and fetching, and so very tender-hearted. She would sleep now; sleep was the very thing she needed. The old woman took the crescent moon amulet from her own neck and slipped it over Charity's head, smoothing the girl's hair across the pillow once again before settling in a nearby chair to keep watch.

Strikingly lovely, with a compassionate and generous nature that befitted her name, Charity Standing was simply the most desirable young woman in Devonshire, perhaps in the whole south of England. But her irresistible little person was like fate's baited trap. A wave of calamity seemed to follow her wherever she went, sometimes causing small accidents and embarrassments, and other times generating grand catastrophes and wholesale disasters. Over the years, the faithful Gar Davis and Percy Hall had conjured their own explanation for the misfortunes that trailed her; thieving from the angels, they reasoned, was a serious and irredeemable offense. But Charity's grandmother had quite another explanation. Her granddaughter was simply and undeniably a moon-crossed *jinx*.

Chapter Three

Rane Austen awakened at the side of the road, face up in the grass, feeling as though he'd been put through a washer-woman's mangle. He moved, only to groan as pain shot up his spine and burst through his shoulders and arms. He opened his eyes to meaningless patches of white and blue that were shifting so that they made him dizzy. It took a few blinks and some effort for him to realize that he was looking up at the sky. And for a brief, unsettling moment he had the powerful impression that there was a woman quite near him.

The pull of that strong and seductive intuition made him push up too quickly, and he clasped his head between his hands, fighting down the explosion of pain this caused. The aura of "woman" was dispelled as quickly as it had come and he growled irritably, then, after a moment, pushed up onto his knees. With dogged persistence, he focused his eyes on the tall grasses around him, the overhanging trees above, and, finally, on the nearby road, trying to make sense of them.

His head swam, and his ribs hurt too much to breathe. There wasn't a spot on his body that wasn't complaining. But all those pains were minor beside the one that coursed through him as he staggered to his feet and caught sight of his precious, crimson-wheeled phaeton crumpled around a tree trunk like a discarded rag. He reeled. His eyes disengaged and drifted in separate directions so that he saw everything in identical pairs.

"Dammit!" he muttered . . . then roared, *"B'dammit!"* The volume was itself a punishment for his profanity and he grabbed his head and staggered, first one way, then the other. He crashed into a nearby tree with his shoulder, tight-

42

ening all over at the explosion of pain from the impact.

"Not my phaeton. Anything but my phaeton and my—"
He straightened, scanning the wreckage and then the area
for sign of his fancy-blooded blacks. They were nowhere to
be seen, and he didn't know whether to be relieved or not.
They'd obviously escaped the crash and run for their lives.
But run where?

He closed his eyes and made himself recall what had happened. He'd been nearing the town of Mortehoe, driving
. . . wretched roads . . . something had spooked his blacks.
The rest was a merciful blur, but his mind was clearing
enough to wonder the extent of his injuries. He felt his aching head and discovered two nasty lumps, one in front, one
behind. He gritted his teeth and tested the contusions with
his fingers; neither was bleeding, at least not anymore. He'd
somehow managed to bash his head two directions at once.

"Probably some sort of damned record," he snarled as vehemently as his aching head would allow. But then, Rane
"Bulldog" Austen, was not known for doing things by half
measures.

Early in life, raised in the crucible of his father's bitter
exile and the topic heat, Rane Austen had learned harsh
lessons in survival and in making something out of nothing.
Thus upon returning to England, a nineteen-year-old viscount, and learning he had nothing again, he had been determined to make something out of it, or die trying. Since a
good name and good will keep neither meat on one's bones
nor a roof over one's head, he had at first concentrated all his
efforts on the acquisition of capital and goods. The niceties
of society and sensibility, he reasoned, would have to wait.
And with characteristic Austen singlemindedness, he had
not always been so choosy about just how his money was
made.

Now, nearly eight years later, he had earned enough
wealth to be solidly established in the world of commerce.
He had earned enough to dress and drive in the height of
fashion and to own a grand house on one of London's desirable west side "squares." He had also earned the nickname

"Bulldog," for the tenacity with which he pursued and achieved his goals. The one thing he had *not* earned, was entry and acceptance into the elite society to which his birth and education should have entitled him. And increasingly, acceptance by London society was the thing he craved in his deepest soul.

The criterion by which he judged his acceptance was fixed, in his mind. He would know he was accepted into their midst only when they took him into the family literally, by giving him one of their elegant, purebred daughters in marriage.

A wife. He wanted a lady wife. And he'd sworn to himself that he would have one by summer . . . or die trying.

His head, his ribs, and shoulders were severely bruised, his long, muscular fingers told him. But everything still seemed to be in place and at least marginally functional. He pushed off from the tree trunk with his shoulder and staggered toward the wreckage. His small trunk was still in the wrecked stowage, he realized distractedly. Studying the remains of his prized carriage, he winced at the realization that the financial deal he'd come to Mortehoe to arrange would barely cover the loss he'd just incurred.

The sun was lowering as he dragged a hot breath and began the painful walk down the London road, toward the little town of Mortehoe. With each jarring step, his pain and agitation grew, so that by the time his man, Stephenson, appeared, bent low and riding hard for him, Austen was in a foul state indeed.

"M'lord!" The burly, platter-faced fellow reined up sharply and pounced to the ground before Austen. His eyes widened at the sight of the wound and the dried trickle of blood which marred his employer's face and elegant gray coat. "Are ye all right?"

"Excellent. I'll die in the bloody pink of health."

"Yer blacks made it into town wi'out ye. Somebody caught 'em and bro't word to the inn. When I saw 'em, I knowed somethin' was up."

"Damned astute of you—" Austen weaved. His bare head

was griddle-hot and his eyes were parting company again. "Then you did manage to find the place. . . ."

"Here, m'lord," Stephenson caught him as he swayed and propelled him toward the horse. "Climb aboard. I'll walk ye back."

Austen managed to do as his servant-cum-bodyguard had suggested, though not without some help. Soon they were turned back toward the town, Austen's large frame slumped rather disgracedly in the saddle while Stephenson led the horse.

"M'lord?"

"What now?" he moaned.

"They ain't got any fresh fruit. Ain't never even heard of bananas."

"Damn."

By the time they reached the inn, both the horse and the servant were at a run and the master had sunk again into oblivion.

Three full days and two unsavory visits from the local quack-salver later, Rane Austen was back on his feet, albeit with his head still aching and his pride still raw. The wreck had cost him time as well as money. He had done nothing for the first two days but take the local physic's foul-smelling nostrums and sleep. The third day, he had awakened as hungry and impatient as a bear. He had no time to waste in this backwater province. The end of the London season was approaching, and he had to get back to London and mount yet another campaign for matrimony.

Stephenson, at his direction, had managed to get a message to the party they had come to Devon to see. And Austen had spent most of a very uncomfortable night in a cold, dripping woods, waiting for the wretch to show himself and growing increasingly incensed at the rogue's insolence. The next day, they'd sent another message, this one accompanied by dire warnings of what would occur if the fellow refused to show himself. They were to meet that very night, at an abandoned stable located near a small stone church in the nearby valley. If the wretch failed to appear, Austen reasoned grimly, then at least the wait would be warm and dry this time.

Just past ten o'clock that evening, Austen donned a black coat and boots and slipped down the inn's rickety back steps. Stephenson had their hired horses saddled, and they led them away from the inn before mounting and riding off into the countryside. But they hadn't gone far before Austen's hired saddle mount pulled up lame, forcing him to dismount.

"What the hell is it now?" He growled softly, lifting the horse's leg to check the cannon and hoof for signs of heat or swelling. "In this light there isn't any way of telling how bad it is." His jaw clamped tight and pain radiated up through his head, a lingering effect of his recent accident. After all the time he'd waited and the threats he'd made . . .

"Dammit to ditchwater! I'll not put this off another night. Give me your mount and walk this one back."

"B-but—"

"None of your damnable pissing and moaning! I'm finishing this bloody business tonight. I have to get back to London."

Stephenson knew his employer too well to take offense at his strong language or his testy mood. When Austen was irritable he often reverted to what Stephenson had dubbed his "Barbados French."

"He could bring his gang, or have 'em lay in wait. Ye could be walkin' straight into a trap." Stephenson scowled at the sardonic grin which spread over his employer's chiseled face. He exhaled disgustedly and handed over the reins. A bit of danger was never a deterrent to Rane Austen.

Austen swung up into the saddle and looked down into Stephenson's shadowed face with a roguish, half-pained smile. "If I don't like the lay of things, I won't show myself," he assured him. "And if I'm not back by breakfast, you can earn those fancy new boots of yours by looking for me."

* * *

46

The small stone chapel in the vale was bright, even in the dim light of the new moon, and it was not difficult to locate the ramshackle stable nearby. Austen watched it for some time from the shelter of the edge of a nearby woods, until he was satisfied that no one was there. The field around was clearly visible from his vantage point and he watched with growing tension for signs of movement. It was nearly an hour, probably close to midnight before the two dark specks appeared, bobbing and weaving, approaching the stable.

Two of them, unmounted; Austen felt a wave of physical relief at the sight. Then, out of habit, he continued to watch the area, scanning the nearby church and trees for signs of others. When he was satisfied that they were alone, he led his horse forward into the moonlight to join them, his hand on the pistol lodged inside his coat.

As he approached, they caught sight of him, coming across the field, and drew together, coming to a halt beside the entrance to the old stable. He confronted them with a low, irritable snarl.

"I said to come alone."

"There's been . . . compli-ca-shuns," the taller, stouter one answered, with a kind of artificial depth to his voice that hinted he was forcing it. And the shorter, slighter fellow, standing one step behind the speaker, nodded vigorously, echoing, "Compli-ca-shuns."

"Indeed." Austen appraised the pair. Afoot, seemingly unarmed, they weren't quite what he had expected. He'd never actually seen the fellow he'd done business with for the last two years, but from the few written messages they'd exchanged, he'd somehow gathered that the smuggler was a gentleman. He cast a careful look about them before motioning toward the door of the stable, then ducking inside himself.

The weathered door creaked shut behind them and Austen moved instinctively, feeling for the low roof beams and keeping his back to the wall as his eyes adjusted. "There's a lantern on a barrel in the middle," he declared in low, com-

47

manding tones. "Light it."

There was a muffled bang, like a boot hitting wood, and the sound of startled breath. Shortly, light bloomed from the tallow lantern and Austen squinted against the brightness, searching the two plainly clad fellows before him. One had a broad, square-featured face, the other a lean, peckish countenance with a frown-knot in his brow that looked to be almost permanent. Neither had the look of a hard-driving businessman or a leader of a band of smugglers. And they were staring at him as though they were beholding Satan himself.

"My shipment." Austen laid his demand on the table. "Where is it?" The square-faced fellow swallowed, stuck his thumbs in his belt, and shifted feet.

"We said there wus compli-ca-shuns. A wreck. It were a bad night an' the boat wrecked on th' first run, haulin' it ashore." His voice sounded choked near the end and he stopped. In the ensuing silence the other fellow took it up with a hushed quiver in his voice.

"One o' our fellers . . . got kilt."

Austen was struck momentarily speechless by the long-faced looks and the air of desolation that had descended on the pair of them. They had made their announcement as though they expected *sympathy*. He recovered quickly and felt himself tightening all over. They had just managed to surprise him and he didn't like surprises, not in this sort of business. It was a second unpleasant surprise when he opened his mouth and said, "My condolences."

He drew an irritable breath and planted his fists at his waist so that his broad shoulders spread wider and jutted forward threateningly. "Look, you scrubs, I paid a quarter faith on a shipment of brandy and I have buyers waiting all over London for the stuff. My buyers expect me to deliver and I expect you to deliver — *brandy*, not excuses!"

The two looked at each other and the square-faced one looked back at Austen and scowled. "Well, we ain't doin' it no more. We ain't bringin' no more shipments ashore. We be gettin' out of the smugglin' bizness." He paused, then ex-

48

plained with hushed seriousness, "It's dang'rous."

Austen nearly swallowed his tongue.

"Of course it's dang—" He stopped dead. Were they trying to gull him? "Look you, I've paid hard money and I'll have the goods due me or you'll learn first hand just how dangerous *I* can be!" Austen began to tighten muscle by muscle, bracing. "If you're getting out of the damnable business, you can bloody well do it *after* you haul one last shipment ashore, do you hear?!"

"B-but we cain't!" The skinny one paled, his eyes wide. "Our con-tact's gone. We don't know—" But an elbow in his side stopped him.

"What he means is, the king's cutters be heatin' things up an' our suppliers is . . . not sure they can get more." Then came yet another of those utterly guileless pronouncements: "There's a war on wi' France, ye know."

"B'dammit!" Austen fairly choked on his own juices. "Of course there's a bloody war on! Why do you think French brandy is at such a premium?!"

Out of sheer frustration, and desperate to inject some proper menace into the situation, he pulled the sleek little pistol out of his coat and leveled it at the pair. The sight of their widened eyes and blanching faces was momentarily gratifying. But when they turned toward each other and huddled a bit closer together, as though seeking refuge, Austen suffered a pang of conscience for having reacted so drastically. But what was done, was done. He had to convince them it was dangerous to cross him, or he'd never get his brandy.

"I said I intend to have that shipment of brandy. I'll have it before I leave Mortehoe, or I'll find you and go through you and your gang like a bucket of hot lead!"

"B-but—we ain't got it. Honest!" The skinny fellow looked ready to faint.

"I don't believe you," Austen growled savagely, even while suffering the infuriating suspicion that they were probably telling him the truth. What was it about these two?

"See here, sir—" The square faced fellow faced him with a

pitiful, pleading look. "We already spent most o' yer money. But we'll give the rest back and we'll be willin' to work it off, we swear."

"Work it—? Oh, you'll work it off, all right!" Austen was now quivering with humiliating fury that was as much aimed at himself as at them. The landmarks of menace and danger that usually charted the way in such a meeting had been stripped away in these few exchanges and, for once, Bulldog Austen was at a loss for how to proceed. He stalked forward, his wide shoulders inflating even further, filling, then crowding the small stable.

"You'll get word to your contact and arrange another shipment, straight away or," he was becoming desperate, "I swear, I'll find you. And when I do I'll hang you up by the heels until your blood fills your head and runs out your ears!" He saw their eyes widen and, like the gruesome little boy he felt like just then, he pursued his ghoulish tack enthusiastically.

"Then I'll personally sew your fingers together. And then, I'll have my men play noughts and crosses on your bare bellies with their knives." Their jaws drooped in satisfyingly horror.

"Y-you dasn't h-hurt us, sir!" The square-faced fellow managed a pale bit of bravado. "W-we have a *protect-or*, a powerful one!"

"Right!" the thin one squeaked, clutching his comrade's arm. "An' he's *powerful bad luck*, he is!"

"Bloody Hell!" Austen roared, startling them back another step. His jaw squared pugnaciously and his light eyes took on a silvery glow in the dim light. "I don't believe in luck— there's no such thing! A man either makes it or he doesn't. And you'd better make it, or I'll—"

There was quick flash of movement and the barrel that held the lantern crashed onto its side. The stable was suddenly engulfed in blackness and there was a sound of scuffling. Austen lunged forward to grab the fellows and bashed his head straight into a low hanging beam.

"Ugghhh—OWWWW!" He recoiled, gasping, and

50

dropped his pistol. While he was bent over, seeing stars in the blackness, he caught the silvery flash of a slice of moonlight as the door creaked open, then banged shut again with a muffled smack. They'd escaped him!

"Dammit to bloody deep ditchwater," he cursed feebly, holding his pounding head together with his hands. Now he had razor-sharp flashes of new pain to compound the old. Several concentrated breaths later he was able to straighten fully. And when he did, a nasty trill of pain-spawned anger went through him.

What was the matter with him, letting them get away like that? He needed their blasted brandy. And what the hell kind of smugglers were they anyway? He'd done business with smugglers all over England and he hadn't met one yet who honestly called him "sir." And he couldn't imagine any of that rough, dangerous brotherhood offering to work off a debt, like a wretched *tenant farmer!*

He felt the growing knot on his forehead and winced. He'd been had, in spades. Pained heat flooded his head and spilled over into his coiled shoulders. Those two weren't smugglers, he'd stake his name on it. But if they weren't the smugglers he'd dealt with before, then just who in hell were they?

"Perc—" Gar Davis panted, clutching at his partner as they reached the shelter of the trees. Percy Hall slowed and they halted, staring back at the stable and the horse still standing beside it in the dim moonlight. "Perc, what're we gonna do? We cain't get no more brandy! We don't even know where that stuff come from!" His thin face was pinched more than usual and the knot in his brow drew tighter as a sense of doom settled on him.

"Perc—he's gonna kill us!" When Percy didn't respond right away, Gar's anxious gaze drifted back toward the stable again and he recalled aloud, "O'course, I'm gonna die anyway. . . ."

"You're not gonna die," Percy snapped, scowling, thinking desperately.

"Oh, yes I am. I fell in th' grave, an' a feller what falls in a

51

grave dug for another man, he's gonna die next." Gar looked sickly indeed as his hands came up to feel his stomach forlornly. "I jus' never tho't it would be by fellers playin' noughts an' crosses on my belly." Percy grabbed his shoulders and glared at him.

"Nobody's gonna carve up your belly, numbskull, nor mine. Not if I have anythin' to say about it."

"Well, what can we do, Perc? He's got a gang . . . an' guns." He shuddered, fingering his stomach again. "An' knives . . ."

"Well, we gotta scare him off somehow, make him think we got a gang, too. An' guns." He turned to watch the stable and was gratified to see the fancy cove's horse still just standing there. "He'll have to go back to town through Rowden Woods, an' my cottage ain't far away." A spark of ingenuity showed in Percy's blocky face as he lurched into motion, pulling Gar along. "Come on!"

A quarter of an hour later, Percy and Gar were running as fast as they dared through the brambled Rowden Woods, bound for a spot near the road that wound through them. When the road came in sight, Percy finally lumbered to a stop, panting savagely and clinging to a nearby tree with one arm. His other arm held an old flintlock rifle. Then Gar caught up, carrying an old soldier's kit containing lead and powder, and heaving so that he could scarcely stand up.

"Over there . . . should be . . . 'bout right," Percy called, panting and waving Gar toward some bushes that would provide both cover and a decent view of the moonlit road. They were soon on their knees behind the scrubby growth and fumbling to load the old firearm.

"What if he already come this way?" Gar swallowed hard and whispered half-hopefully, "Mebee we already missed 'im."

"We ain't missed him. He'll be along," Percy declared, tamping the wadding down tight and loading in the lead ball.

"B-but Perc—I ain't never shot nobody before. Have you?" Gar was turning a ghastly shade of green in the dim light.

"We're not gonna *shoot him.*" Percy huffed disgustedly. "We're gonna shoot *at* him! But he's gonna *think* we're tryin' to kill 'im, and he'll take the rest of his money back an' go." At Percy's assurance Gar tried to be a bit more enthusiastic about the plan. It was the only one they had at the moment, and it would have to work. Percy put the gun to his shoulder and sighted down the long barrel toward the road.

"Likely he'll be riding fast," Gar observed wanly. "You ain't never even hit a rabbit with that thing."

"The idear's to *not* hit him, remember?" Percy snapped irritably, sighting again. Then he suddenly crumpled up and grabbed himself, gasping as pain speared through his stomach. "Owww! Oh, sweet Jesus."

"What is it Perc?!"

"M'stomach . . . that danged ul-cer-ation o' mine! You'll have to do it. I cain't!"

He thrust the gun into Gar's hands with a moan, and before Gar could protest, there came the first muffled, then increasingly loud thud of hooves headed their way.

"Mebee it's not him."

"It's him! Ye got to, Gar!" Perc clutched his stomach as though in real pain and pushed the gun up toward Gar's shoulder. "Now! Ye got to do it now!"

Gar was ashen, trembling, as he raised the old rifle to his shoulder and looked down the cold steel barrel toward the figure looming out of the woods onto the moon-brightened road. "Now, Gar, now!" Percy's urgings were suddenly clanging in Gar's head, and fear was squeezing his throat and knotting his innards. His heart thrashed violently against his ribs, making it hard for him to hold the old flintlock steady. And from down the barrel of that gun, a powerful, thundering specter materialized, a dark, unearthly vision. On it came . . . and on . . . and then it was upon him.

"Now, Gar!" Percy shout-whispered, and as the rider drew even with them, Gar jolted with the realization that the horseman was already passing them by, and swung around in a panic. When Percy yelled *"NOW!"* into his ear, it startled him so that his finger clenched. The gun flashed and fired.

The rider jerked in his seat and the horse broke stride and reared a half-second later, dumping him in the middle of the road. The animal laid its ears back and began to run, harum-scarum, leaving its rider sprawled in the half-hardened mud. Soon there was just the moonlit road, a human in a heap, and profound silence.

Gar and Percy watched from their hiding place, shocked, waiting. When the fancy gent didn't rouse or rise, they looked at each other and swallowed hard. A few alarming minutes later, when the fellow was still just lying there, Percy crept from the bushes to see what had happened. Gar went all clammy-palmed and light-headed as he stood up and he dropped the gun as though it burned him.

Percy gave the bloke a prod with his boot and then squatted down to turn him over. When he pulled his hand away it was wet, and even in the spare moonlight they could make out the color. *Red.*

"Ye shot him," Percy choked.

"B-but . . ." Gar came running up. "I didn't mean to! It jus' went off. Oh, Perc, is he dead?"

"Cain't tell." Percy sprang up, staring at his wet hand in abject horror. "Looks like ye got 'im low." Then he looked at Gar with frustration mounting. "Ye were supposed to *miss* 'im!"

"I ain't never hit nothin' before, Perc, I swear!"

"Well, ye picked a fine time to come up a crack shot." Percy winced, shaking his bloody hand and going to wipe it on the grass at the side of the road.

"It's Miz Charity's luck, that's what it is." Gar stared at his victim, reading his grim future in the sprawl of the fellow's big body. "I fell in the grave an' now I've went and kilt a feller." He began to quake as he put the two together. "He's dead, and now I'm gonna die . . . by hangin'."

"Shut up, Gar. You're not gonna die," Percy growled, feeling his own panic rising. "I gotta think."

But before Percy could come up with another of his plans,

the sound of hoofbeats reached them in the gloom, faint, but growing louder.

"Somebody's comin'! Whadda we do, Perc?" Gar shook his hands with anxiety. Percy looked at Gar's ashen face, looked down at their erstwhile customer, and grabbed Gar's arm as he bolted for the bushes.

"We run like hell!"

Baron Sullivan Pinnow, one foot swathed in bandages and sticking stiffly past his stirrup, came riding along that moonlit road with his small contingent of king's men. They were homeward bound after a fruitless evening of tracking and chasing poachers in Sir Hugh Luddington's woods. That is, Pinnow's men had tracked and chased poachers; Pinnow himself had spent a rather profitable evening in Sir Hugh's comfortable parlor, his sore foot propped on a pillow collecting sympathy while he collected winnings at the card table and savored the good knight's excellent port.

Penniless peerdom had disadvantages, but in Pinnow's experience, they didn't totally outweigh the numerous advantages of merely being a peer — any kind of a peer — when it came to the choicer things in society. Even a penniless titleholder, as long as he kept up appearances and maintained a cultured, gentlemanly demeanor, could be expected to be entertained in the finest of homes, with the finest wines, wit, and women.

Since coming to Mortehoe to accept his demeaning scrap of a preferment, Magistrate of the District of Mortehoe, he'd made good use of that principle and of his otherwise worthless title. He'd worked hard to cultivate the local gentry and, in general, had them believing that his rigid hand on the reins of justice had singlehandedly snatched the district back from the jaws of anarchy. Meanwhile, he'd acquired a suitable house in town, seized by himself for non-payment of tax, of course, and had begun to feather his nest with a few extras trimmed from the financial edges of his administration. Added to this, his modest winnings from pleasant evenings like the one just past were enough to keep him looking like a well-fixed nobleman while he cast about for an opportunity that would actually make him into one.

"Somethin' on the road, yer lordship!" The sergeant pulled Pinnow from his wine-induced reverie as he slowed the patrol and pointed ahead. When, cautiously, they had ventured forth, the "something" proved to be a shape of a man. Pinnow ordered the sergeant to investigate and waited, watching from horseback, while the fellow examined the body and spoke with his men.

"He's bleedin' bad, yer lordship," the sergeant reported as he knelt by the body. The baron liked hearing "your lordship," despite the fact that he was not technically entitled to such address. "Likely shot, somehows, but still alive. Dressed like a gent'lmun, too."

A bleeding gentleman in his path was the last thing Sullivan Pinnow wanted just now, when his mind was set on his warm, comfortable bed in town. But wait . . . A gentleman could be grateful. "Any papers or . . . money?"

"No papers, yer lordship, but a fair bit o' coin an' foldin' flash." The sergeant rose and held up a substantial stack of bank notes and a small pouch of coin.

"Indeed." Pinnow came fully awake now, his eyes widening as he beckoned the sergeant closer and snatched up the money. "I shall take charge of that, sergeant . . . the safe-keeping of evidence, of course." The amount of the injured fellow's purse made Pinnow appraise his inert form with fresh interest.

"What'll we do wi' him, yer lordship? He needs tendin' bad."

"A gentleman of means deserves proper care. He should have the nearest bed, which would be at Standwell, of course." Pinnow's eyes narrowed as he envisioned a tableau which would please him immensely. "What a pity to have to rouse Miss Charity Standing from her soft bed at this hour of the night . . . and Lady Margaret too, of course." The lascivious curl of his lips belied his seemingly gentlemanly lament. He turned his horse toward Standwell and barked orders over his shoulder.

"Make a litter of your coats and rifles. And be quick about it!"

Chapter Four

A ferocious pounding at the aged front doors slowly roused the house and the servants' hall of Standwell. By the time old Melwin, the butler, and Bernadette, his wife, finally answered the summons, Lady Margaret was barrelling downstairs in her nightcap, her eyes wild and her wrapper flapping.

"Wait! Don't you dare set a finger to that door!" she called to the old butler in a loud, frantic whisper as she raced toward the door. "At this hour of the night, it's mischief tryin' to get in, you can be sure." The pounding on the heavy door intensified as if in response to her worry. She drew up between the old retainers and the doors, to keep the former from doing something irresponsible . . . like opening them. "It's a new moon," she reminded them, "and it just crossed over into Friday." She watched old Melwin's scowl of confusion and interpreted for him with an outraged huff. "Bad luck, the Friday of a new moon." Why didn't Melwin ever remember these things? "Where's my salt?"

Melwin muttered and scratched his white head, turning away to fetch the little bag of salt that Lady Margaret kept stowed inside the drawer of the hall table, for just such happenings. A good gypsy was always prepared to ward off bad luck and to attract the good. And in that regard, Lady Margaret Villiers was a better gypsy than most of the sons of Romany who plied the roads of England in traveling bands. The more the years piled upon her, the more gypsy-like she became, and the more extensive and exotic the precautions she took with Standwell's luck — on her granddaughter's behalf.

Lady Margaret, youngest daughter of the Duke of Clarendon, had been abducted by a band of gypsies when a child. She had traveled and lived with them for three years before being returned, safe and whole, to her parents at the tender age of twelve years. Gossip concerning her adventure with the gypsies—and its unfortunate liberating effect on her—had kept her from making a proper marriage. It seemed no one wanted a shoe-shunning, outspoken daughter-in-law who knew more about reading moonsigns and cooking chickens than she knew about reading clothing trends and arranging seven-course menus. But being ineligible in London's fastidious "marriage mart" had allowed her an unprecedented amount of say in her own future, and she had eventually married Henri Villiers, son of the French Comte de Villiers, for love.

Twenty years ago, when Henri died, she had come to live with her daughter, Chanson, and her son-in-law, Upton Standing. And when her beloved daughter died of a fever, leaving a deep, painful hole in the world where her vibrant presence had been, Lady Margaret had risen to the challenge of patching up their lives. In the process, she had resurrected her gypsy heritage to cope with her grief . . . and with her little granddaughter's growing "problem."

From the very night of Charity's birth, Lady Margaret had known she was destined to be different, special in some way. The new moon had been strange that night, shimmering, casting unusually bright light edged with prismatic rainbows. But it was only after her daughter's untimely death that Charity's unusual propensity for precipitating disaster began to reveal itself. From that time on, Lady Margaret had spared no effort to search out and employ the surest methods of insuring good luck.

"Salt over the doorstep," Lady Margaret spoke in the singsong voice of memory as she sprinkled a tiny line of salt across the stone threshold, "and salt on the sill. Guard against wickedness and mischief, they will . . ."

"Last week, salt was fer witches," Old Melwin muttered under his breath as he moved to unbolt the doors and swing one of them open.

Outside in the spare moonlight stood Baron Pinnow, leaning on a stout cane, flanked by a brace of uniformed king's men. Old Melwin fell back, swinging the door wider as he went. "B-baron!"

"Go tell your mistress—" he stepped inside with an imperial air, then spotted Lady Margaret. "My Lady Margaret! I do apologize for this gross intrusion—and at such a hideous hour . . ." His sudden ooze of charm had a suffocating quality about it. "But justice keeps a poor clock, Ma'am, and I must be abroad whenever duty calls. I am come to beg your aid for a gravely injured gentleman we discovered on the road. He's been shot and is in peril of his life. I fear that if he is not tended soon—"

"Mischief," Lady Margaret muttered, casting a scalding glance at Melwin before elbowing her way through the startled baron and his men and out into the entry court. "Where is he?"

She stared down at the long, limp frame of the gentleman lying on the ground, and felt a tremor through her very reliable bones. She turned and cast a quick glance at the grinning crescent of the new moon. She didn't like the looks of this at all. Taking a deep breath, she turned back and growled at the soldiers, "Don't just stand there like stumps. Bring him inside—and be careful about it!"

Charity sat bolt upright in her big, postered bed. Her heart was thudding and her eyes were wide with confusion that melted slowly at the reassuring sights of her darkened room. Then suddenly, from just inside her closed door, came the clicking and a scraping of something against the floor. She heard hoarse panting and an unearthly groan. . . .

She sighed, relieved.

"What is it Wolfie?" she called, peering through the gloom to where the great wolfhound paced, moaning, in front of the door. "What is it, boy? Do you want out?" Another moan ended in a half whine. Then she heard it, too. Voices, in the hall, in the dead of night. Her heart beat harder. "What's happening?"

She threw back the counterpane and slid from the bed, neglecting her slippers, and just remembering to snag the dressing gown that lay across the end of the bed. Hurrying to the door, she listened to the voices growing louder . . . men's voices, their deep, vibrating tones penetrating the walls around her. She opened the door and the dog bounded out, growling with hair-raising ferocity.

Charity was only a few steps behind him, pulling her dressing gown onto her shoulder, when she stopped dead. Hurtling down the west hallway, was a heaving knot of red-clad soldiers, in front of which her grandmother's familiar white nightcap and muslin wrapper bobbed. Trailing behind, swaying on a cane, was the dismayingly familiar figure of Baron Sullivan Pinnow.

The massive dog charged the knot of soldiers, knocking the cane from under the baron in the process and sending the redcoats flying and bouncing off the walls like nine-pins. Briefly, his thunderous barks and snarls produced raw pandemonium, as the soldiers snarled and scrambled to keep the beast at bay, while Lady Margaret held her ears and yelled at the beast and Baron Pinnow shouted orders nobody could hear.

"Wolfram, stop that! Wolfram!" Charity's voice pierced the chaos as she ran toward the west hallway, her robe billowing. The dog responded instantly, quieting to mere growls, then went to investigate the injured gentleman's body, which lay where the soldiers had dropped it. All were astonished to see the massive beast recoil slightly, stiffen, then keel over on its side in what appeared to be a dead faint. Lady Margaret was the first to recover her senses.

"Thank the Lord. You," she motioned brusquely to the soldiers and to the open doorway nearby. "Get the blighter in there and onto the bed before he bleeds to death on the hall runner." She spotted Charity running toward them. "Hurry, girl! The baron's found a man on the road, shot and bleeding badly. I'll need your help." She darted into the room after the soldiers and Charity followed, slowing and stooping to check the dog with a caressing hand. Once assured that Wolfram was sleeping peacefully, Charity slipped quickly past the baron and into the little-used guest chamber.

"Wh-whaat happened to it?" The rattled baron finally peeled himself from the wall, staring at the dog in raw disbelief.

"Blood." Old Melwin answered as he headed downstairs to heat water and fetch Lady Margaret's salves and herbals. "He cain't stand the smell of it."

Charity hurried into the dimly lit chamber and made her way through the soldiers to the foot of the bed. "Did you say someone was shot?"

"It appears so," Lady Margaret declared tersely, inspecting the man's blood-soaked garments for the source of the blood. "We'll need more light. There's blood all over."

Charity hastily lit more candles in the candlestand and brought it beside the bed. Her eyes fell on a large male body, sprawled face down, filling more than half of the bed . . . and both her breath and her heart stopped.

The man's broad shoulders were encased in black, not gray, but his hair was dark and gently curled, and from what she could see, the curve of his cheek was the same. His long, muscular frame was stunningly familiar, and when she reached out with tentative fingers to touch his booted leg, it was hard and reassuringly real. She stood, spellbound, reliving it, seeing him face down in the grasses again, as she'd seen him in her troubled sleep these last three nights. It was the same man . . . it had to be! And she *hadn't* been dreaming—or driven to distraction by grief!

For the last three days, since she awakened from her grandmother's "healing comfort," she'd been plagued by powerful, recurring impressions of the man everyone told her she'd just imagined. Grief-sick, they had explained. Yet the half-remembered incident had lingered hauntingly in her mind. She had lain in the quiet darkness of her draped bed each night, recalling the surprising hardness of his limbs beneath her hands, the fascinating bronzed strength of his features, the feel of his lips on hers. How could she ever have conjured something as unexpected as all that in her mind? Then an ineffable sadness had filled her, a sense of loss somehow greater than if he'd been real.

"Gran'mere, it's him! It's the man in the accident." She hurried around her grandmother to the head of the bed and leaned over him, holding the light closer. She examined his drained features and compared them with her re-emerging memories. Then she brushed his hair from his left temple with a trembling hand and pointed to the faded-to-green swelling that confirmed her story. "There it is . . . the same bruise, only healed a bit! And—heaven—he's struck his head again; look at this!"

Lady Margaret started and looked at her, then at the man on the bed, scowling. "He's the one you saw on the road, hurt? But they've just brought him from the road . . . hurt." The old lady's eyes widened as connections were made in her mind. Then this was the *second* time the fellow had been hurt on the road? And the second time fate had cast him into Charity's hands?! Lady Margaret's bones were suddenly rattling with premonition. She ran to the window and threw it open, leaning over the stone sill to locate the moon and search its sly silver arc for some hint of what was transpiring around her.

Charity watched her grandmother fly to the window to read the moon and she felt a rush of unprecedented annoyance at the old lady's behavior. This was no time for moonwatching! "Gran'mere, he's hurt. We've got to help him!"

Lady Margaret wheeled around, stared wide-eyed at Charity, then at the man sprawled on the bed, then rushed from the room, leaving her granddaughter sputtering.

"Gran'mere?! B-b-but . . ."

Charity looked down at the large, dark-haired stranger who had haunted her recent nights and felt a troubling surge of feeling that seemed to be only part compassion. The ache of compassion, she knew quite well, for others' pain and suffering had always touched her deeply. But the sight of the powerful and handsome man who had haunted her dreams, lying hurt and helpless at her fingertips, produced a very different sort of ache in her. This ache was so large, it permeated her bones and flesh and sinew as well as her tender heart.

As she stared at his strong, handsome features, a blast of dry heat blew the fog of recent grief from her senses. Suddenly she recalled it all: the fascinating feel of his lips moving over hers . . . the breath-stealing sensations of being surrounded by his hard body and his masculine heat. . . . He'd *kissed* her! What else could it be called when lips met and held like that? And he'd asked her to *marry* him, even if it was after a vicious knock on the head. He'd proposed to her and now he was here, under her roof. . . .

A confusing wave of feeling crested in her, finding expression in a flush of chagrin at her shocking thoughts and a compensating determination to help him. Her beloved father had been ripped from her life without warning, and she sensed that fate was somehow evening the score. A life taken from her, a life restored to her hand. She was being given a second chance to help this tall, dark stranger, and she wouldn't be found wanting this time!

"Hold this steady!" She turned and thrust the candlestand into the nearest soldier's hands. Then she ordered another soldier to gently remove the stranger's boots as she began peeling his coat to reveal his blood-soaked back and the ominous hole in the seat of his breeches. The soldier holding the light let a low whistle.

"He be *butt-shot.*"

"Good Lord!" Sullivan Pinnow declared from across the bed and hobbled around hurriedly to have a look for himself. "Miss Charity, you cannot possibly tend so . . . *personal* a wound. It simply isn't decent."

"It isn't *decent* to let a man die because it's not 'proper' to tend his wound." She straightened and looked up into the baron's sharp, disapproving features. The purity of the compassion in her lovely features was a stunning rebuke to the baron's sanctimonious concern for propriety. "If it will ease your mind, Baron, you may stay and help me to be sure there are no 'improprieties.' "

Melwin arrived just then with the herbals, bandages, and water, and she turned immediately back to her patient. She asked the baron to cut the fellow's bloody shirt and breeches from him, but halfway through the process, the baron went green around the gills and staggered back a pace or two. Old Melwin was pressed into service and soon the gentleman was disrobed and modestly draped in a sheet; all but his wound . . . and the firm, tight buttock around it.

By the time Charity, having steeled herself, began to remove the lead ball, Lady Margaret returned, elbowing her way through the curious soldiers to reach the bed. She was turbaned once again and wore every amulet she owned, some hanging down her front, some down her back.

They worked together to clean and close the wound. It was a surprisingly neat injury, for all its bleeding, and the surrounding flesh was firm and healthy. The bleeding slowed quickly once the source of irritation was removed. The stitching-up and the poulticing and bandaging went well.

"He's young and strong, and he can make up the blood he lost. He'll be right as rain in a few weeks," the old lady predicted, setting hands to the small of her back and arching over them with a grimace.

"One must certainly hope so," the baron declared, craning his neck to have a look at the stranger, who was looking handsomer and more naked under that sheet by the moment. "Your generosity is to be commended, Lady Margaret. To relieve you of further obligation, I shall leave one of my men to tend him."

"That won't be necessary, Baron, thank you," Charity declared firmly. "I shall tend him myself."

"B-but . . . surely not. Lady Margaret, I must protest . . ."

"Protest? Pish!" Lady Margaret replied, eyeing her granddaughter's determined glow. She'd never seen such a look on Charity's face before. She turned her gaze to the injured stranger on the bed and remembered the moon. It wouldn't do the least bit of good to try to separate them, anyway. "My granddaughter is an upstanding and decent young woman, sir. And we have male servants to see to the fellow in 'personal' ways."

"Oh, well, of course. I only meant to say . . ." Pinnow forced a gentlemanly smile, wishing vehemently that he'd had the foresight to get shot in the buttocks, instead of just cracking his ankle. Then *he* might have been carried to Charity Standing's doorstep and it might be *his* bum that desirable little Charity Standing would be cosseting for the next fortnight. The very thought of it was enough to set his loins warming, and it was that heat that glowed in his smile as it turned on Charity's tousled, golden hair and slid down the unconscious provocation of her open robe.

"Rest assured, I shan't abandon you with this burden. I shall call frequently so that I may question him as soon as possible. This heinous crime must not go unpunished."

The baron lavished a wet kiss on Charity's hand, then took his leave, weaving out of the chamber on his cane. Recalling his hot eyes, Charity looked down and snatched her dressing robe together, tucking her arms about her protectively. "I don't like that man very much. And for the life of me, I can't say why."

Lady Margaret beheld Charity's troubled innocence and

sighed. As long as Charity didn't know *why* she disliked Sullivan Pinnow so much, there wasn't much need to worry; the irksome baron hadn't yet acted on the desires in his eyes. She nodded agreement and hurried to the doorway to sprinkle a trail of salt across it anyway. By the time she had finished sprinkling a trail of salt across the window ledge to keep evil and mischief from entering the room, Charity was bending over the stranger's head, washing the accessible side of his face with a cool cloth.

Fascination glowed in her eyes as she stroked his hard cheek, ran her cloth over his ear, and brushed his dark hair back with her fingers. Her cheeks were flushed and she was biting her lower lip the way she had when a child desirous of a sweet-treat, but afraid to ask. Lady Margaret scowled at the extent of Charity's interest, then shook off her grandmotherly misgivings to make a protective gypsy hand sign over the stranger. Propriety was the last thing she had to worry about. With Charity around, they'd have their hands full just keeping the fellow alive!

For three days and most of three nights, Charity tended the injured gentleman, refusing to be dislodged from her post. She was "an upstanding and decent young woman," she would say, using Lady Margaret's own words against her when the old lady objected to her constant presence and her intimate duties with him. And, after all, he was unconscious. Thinking that things couldn't go too far wrong, Lady Margaret had let her stay by the fellow that Melwin and his wife, Bernadette, were beginning to refer to as "Miss Charity's stranger."

But something did go wrong; the fellow began to contract a fever. Lady Margaret went into one of her tizzies, fashioning protective amulets and hanging them from the bed canopy above him. When these didn't seem to help, she ripped three of the amulets from her own neck and placed them around his, muttering gypsy "somethings."

Whether it was the amulets, or the herbal poultices and nostrums, or Charity's persistent cold baths, the fever finally subsided and left him resting easily under Charity's tender touch.

Somewhere in those long, quiet hours, Charity began to think of him as "her stranger," too. Over and over she recalled their encounter by the side of the road and his shocking proposal of marriage, which became a little less shocking, though more puzzling, with each remembrance.

Marriage. She'd never even thought about it, and obviously no one else had, either, for the subject had never been mentioned. She certainly thought about it now. Marriage. It had a grand and intriguing sound to it which set her imagination in flight. Images rose inside her: a stately house and fine linen and gleaming silver and crystal . . . servants that called the mistress of all that solidity and substance, "madam," or even, "my lady." She conjured in her mind fine vellum imprinted with invitations to balls and parties . . . beautiful dresses with silk slippers and long elegant gloves . . . and a man's arm while walking, a man's face, and eyes, and shoulders. . . . Marriage meant a *man* in a woman's life.

Her eyes drifted tellingly back to her patient. His dark hair was thick and soft with just a hint of curl lapping down over his neck and caressing his hard cheekbones. He had a broad generous mouth that was rimmed with firm borders that seemed to be straining to keep the lush velvet of his lips in bounds. At the corners of his mouth, there were tiny lines that spoke of laughter and matched the crinkles that were starting at the corners of his eyes. She imagined those long, black lashes fluttering open, imagined a soft smile crinkling those crinkles, imagined the broad sweep of those lips drawing back in a smile to reveal healthy white teeth beneath.

Her fingers came up to feather gently over her lips and she sighed, feeling a strange tightness in her chest. A man in *her* life. . . ?

She was moon-spinning again, she realized, trying to shake off the strange clinging warmth that settled over her shoulders. What was it about him that made her do that, imagine things? She straightened and wetted her cloth to bathe him, trying to make her strokes less caressing. But soon they were drifting down his neck to the broad planes of his bronzed back, where they slowed again, skating with wistful leisure over those ridges, mounds and valleys. Her stranger's arms were thick and mounded at the tops, and tapered to corded forearms and then to muscular, long-fingered hands that made the breath catch in her throat. His was so different from her own body. . . . She had never guessed a man could be so different. But then, she'd seen very few bodies, just her father's, without his weskit, and an occasional farmer in the field.

But her stranger wasn't just "a man," she realized. He was the man that had kissed her and asked her to marry him — even if it had been while he was out of his head and drunk with pain. Whether she wanted it to or not, that knowledge somehow changed things. It made him special.

Now, in a quiet moment beside his bed, she fashioned for him a character and a life out of the cloth of her imagination. He was even-tempered, soft-spoken, and as noble as his straight, beautifully carved nose. He was wealthy and generous, and he often put those broad shoulders to work for those less fortunate than himself. He was witty, well-educated, and impeccably well-mannered. He had businesses in London and estates, large ones, which he ran with Solomon-like hand. He was, of course, unmarried. And in search of a wife . . .

Austen rose through the dark, protective layers of sleep as if pulled, summoned by something he neither trusted nor wanted to obey. The inky mists that swirled around him gradually paled to shades of gray and finally dispersed. Someone was speaking . . . around him, above him, or inside him? He had no sense of place or separateness. Was someone calling him?

His eyes opened up on a landscape of rumpled white linen, then closed involuntarily. But the glimpse was enough to orient him to his own sensations. Without fully conscious thought, he knew he was abed and lying on his front. A moment later, something cool and moist slid down the left side of his face and down his neck. When it reached his shoulders and kept going down his spine, he shivered. Then the cool, caressing sensation traced a leisurely path down his arm and seemed to ruffle gently through his fingers.

In his half-wakened state he managed to think it was heavenly. Then he heard the voices again, a woman's voice. A woman? Bed? It was sufficient motivation for him to try opening his eyes again. When he had, they focused on a lock of long, blonde hair that had fallen in front of his face. He managed to follow it up to the face that was bending over him.

It was a vision of a face, with perfect marble skin and unusual golden-brown eyes framed in a rim of glowing blonde hair which contrasted with a broader border of black. Blonde on black. Light on dark. His eyes closed involuntarily, trapping that vision in his reeling mind. It shimmered through the feverish heat inside him, ethereal and beautiful and comforting—and so oddly familiar. It had to be an angel, his fevered mind reasoned. A warm presence surrounded him and he smelled faintly of attar of roses tinged with lavender. A lush, earthy angel he'd seen before, somewhere. . . . Suddenly he was struggling toward full consciousness, pushing up on his arms. Where? Where was she?!

Pain charged up his spine and burst in his head, sending him crashing back to the bed, gasping and groaning. Hands lifted his head and put a cup to his lips. Then bitter liquid filled his mouth and he simply had to swallow it in order to breathe. He took a second swallow and a third. . . . Hands lowered him and something cool again stroked his hot face. And before he could rouse himself, he was once more engulfed in dark, merciful mist.

The next time Rane Austen awakened, it was to discomfort and a regrettably clear conscious state. He gritted his teeth and opened his eyes, finding himself lying in a bed, a general ache in his lower half and a rather more specific burning pain in his left buttock. His mouth felt like a moldy oat sack, and his head was throbbing as he lifted it and squinted, trying to make out what was beyond the half-pulled drapes of the bed. His vision was none too clear, and he blinked and blinked again, forcing his perception past the dull pounding in his head.

Nothing he could see was familiar to him at all. The door visible through the bed drapes on the far side was arched and paneled, the bedposts dark, ropy pillars. The bed drapes, washed gray in the dim light, gave the impression of age and disuse, though he couldn't have said why just then. Despite the pain in his lower half, he pushed up onto his elbows, determined to investigate both his own condition and his whereabouts.

Resting on his elbows, he rubbed his face and squeezed his eyes shut until he could master the explosion of pain the movement caused. Taking a deep breath, he unsteadily pushed back onto his right side. He arched and stretched his shoulders and neck, realizing that he was stiff all over, as though he'd lain in the same position for days. He could scarcely move his head. He pushed up shakily, locating the prime source of his discomfort. He reached back with a stiff, clumsy hand and felt his left buttock. Bandages. Lord, his arse hurt!

And as he turned and craned his stiff neck to look, something above him brushed his head. He started back, squinted, and blinked, trying to locate it visually.

His unsteady eyes widened at the clutch of dark and spiney shapes which dangled above him, dancing, jiggling, wriggling.

71

Oh, God—*spiders!*

"Uggghhhh!" He recoiled in horror, not realizing that he was perched on the edge of the bed. He rolled right off and smacked the floor, flat on his already battered buttock.

"AAAGGGHHHHHH!!!"

Chapter Five

Charity heard the thud and subsequent wail as she reached the top of the main stairs with the tray of broth which was to be breakfast for her patient. She started, shed the tray on the hall table across from the stairs, and flew down the west hallway to his room. Her stranger was sprawled on the floor on his back, groaning, gasping, and using far more explicit language than Charity had ever expected to hear from his handsome lips.

"Hell's burning balls! Aagghhhggod, it hurts!" He was stiff as a board, clenching his fists, his eyes squeezed shut and his bare toes curled. Pain radiated in sizzling flashes down the nerves of his legs and speared through the muscles of his belly, stopping his breath.

She jolted to a halt, then backed up a step, startled by the dusky anger in his face and the powerful heat emanating from his half-bare body as he flexed and writhed.

"Damnation!" His roar became a soul-deep groan. "My whole arse is split open — I can feel it." His face contorted as another wave of pain crashed over him. "Ohhh-ohh-ohh-god!"

He'd fallen from the bed and landed right on his wound! Charity rushed to him and knelt on the floor by him. The poor man was in agony! "Please, don't thrash and don't move until I see how much damage is done," she ordered, setting hands to his waist and hip to roll him over. But the live resistance of the flesh beneath her hands shocked her and she jerked them back with widened eyes. "You shouldn't have tried to get out of bed . . . y-you're much too weak."

But even as she said it, she realized how absurd it was. Weak? Him? Her eyes widened further at the sight of his big, writhing form. Coping with a limp, silent gentleman was one thing; dealing with a live, raging, half-naked man was quite another.

"My bloody achin' arse. I'm ruined!" he gritted through his teeth. Then human presence registered in his beleaguered mind and his eyes sprang open, searching for it wildly as she drew back to go for help. He grabbed whatever he could reach and pulled. "Spiders," he rasped, as though it would explain everything. "There are damned spiders everywhere!"

He had grabbed her dress; specifically, her rounded scoop neckline and the gathered chemise beneath. When he crunched the black bombazine and ruffled lawn in his fist and pulled, she resisted but her dress surrendered, popping numerous stitches as it slid off her shoulder. She gasped and sputtered, staring down her pale, bared shoulder at his pain-bronzed face and silvery eyes. Between his pulling and her straining lay the threat that at any moment her bodice would tear.

"Sir, please — you're not yourself," she groaned, tugging, too afraid to attempt more directly to pry his hands from her dress. She suddenly recalled his strange behavior upon awakening before, and realized she hadn't the foggiest notion of what he was truly. Perhaps raging irrationality and brute force were his usual mode of behavior!

A heartbeat later she found herself grabbed by the shoulders and being pulled down onto his chest.

"Ohhhh!" Her nose was suddenly within a half-inch of his. She could feel his panting breaths against her lips. Suddenly those silvery, pain-glazed eyes overcame some inner obstacle to focus on her. He froze, his fingers tightening on the soft, bare skin of her shoulder as if, shocked by her presence, he was testing her reality. She froze, trapped against him, her heart skipping beats and her face and breast filling with becoming heat.

In that startling, breathless moment occurred to her the absurd thought that his eyes weren't dark after all; they were light gray, striking and beautiful, framed in a fringe of jet lashes. In the next moment she realized that, beneath her hands, which were trapped between them, his heart was pounding . . . just like hers.

Through pain-charged senses, he absorbed the sweet-taffy warmth of her eyes and the silky coolness of her bare shoulder under his fingers. His eyes grew to take in more and slid to the luxurious curve of her Cupid's bow lips, then to the soft mounds that were spilling from her gown onto his chest. Shock pounded through him in physical waves.

"Merciful Lord!" Lady Margaret's exclamation snapped the slender thread of discovery between them.

Charity came hurtling back to her senses to find herself lying on top of her injured stranger for the *second time*, a mere breath away from a second kiss! Panicking, she pushed hard and won release, skittering back to sit on the floor beside him. Her grandmother and old Melwin were standing a few feet away, staring at her with expressions that trod the thin line between horror and fascination. Her eyes followed theirs to her own bared shoulder and nearly-naked breasts. She washed crimson as she hauled her bodice up to cover them.

"I-I heard him fall from the bed and ran to see . . ." she tried to explain.

Lady Margaret's scowl deepened. She'd never have guessed things could possibly go so far between them with the fellow lying senseless as a toadstool! But then, with Charity all sorts of calamities were possible.

Charity shoved to her feet above his groaning form and the sudden movement made her sway. "We've got to get him back into bed; I fear he's reopened his wound."

Lady Margaret and Melwin hurried forward to seize his arms and legs and lift him. "Come on, lad. We'll have you back in your bed in—"

"No! NOOOOOOOO!!" he roared, coming to life. When Charity had left his body, she had left his limited sphere of consciousness, and pain and confusion had surged in to take her place. He had no idea where he was or what was happening to him, but he did know he wasn't going back into a damned nest of spiders. Lord, how he hated spiders! "NO!" He stiffened, then flailed so that they almost dropped him. They had to set him down again and stared at each other in confusion.

"Dammit, there's spiders—they're everywhere!"

"Don't be absurd. There aren't any spiders in there," Lady Margaret declared, adding under her breath, "Not any big ones, anyway."

"What the hell do you call *thossse?!!*" Wild-eyed and pain-drunk, he punched a furious finger up at the bed canopy. His bellow carried surprising force for a man recently just two steps from death's door.

"Spiders?" Charity stepped quickly around him to push back the bed drapes. There were her grandmother's homemade talismans and health charms, dangling, jiggling over the bed. She bit her lip to keep back an involuntary smile of surprise. "We call them health charms. My grandmother made them to help you get well." The smile bloomed fully on her face.

When she had reentered his vision, she had plunged straight into the middle of his consciousness again, crowding everything else out, suspending even his bodily discomfort. There she stood, blonde in black, beautiful—and hauntingly familiar. Then her lush presence was gone again; he was abandoned in his pain and, somehow, angrier for it.

"Imagine a bracer like you, being worried over a little spider or two!" Lady Margaret chided. "Get hold of him."

The three of them overwhelmed his weakened resistance, lifting him back onto the bed and rolling him onto his stomach. Charity and Melwin held him still while Lady Margaret lifted the long shirt they'd dressed him in and inspected the damage. "He's opened it up, partway," she announced irritably, crossing herself and giving Charity a wary glance as she set to work.

"Where the hell am I?" he gritted out through his teeth when he had conquered the pain enough to drag a breath again. His broad shoulders twitched and he wrapped his arms around the feather bolster with lethal force.

"You're at Standwell, our home," Charity answered against a strange squeezing in her throat. The flexed and bulging muscles of his arms, visible through the snug sleeves of the shirt he wore, held her eyes transfixed. And the feel of his warm, hard shoulders beneath her hands made her stomach feel very empty and odd indeed. "And you're in safe h-hands."

"Owwww!" He flinched at something Lady Margaret had done to him and ground his teeth together. "Like bloody hell I am! Let me up—"

"No! You must hold still!" Charity struggled to push his shoulders back down, in desperation adding the weight of her own body over his back to hold him down. "You have to let my grandmother fix you—where you were shot."

Lady Margaret stared, open-mouthed, at her granddaughter's brazen bodily contact with the fellow. Mer-

77

ciful Lord! From now on she would have to watch them every blessed second!

Charity felt her stranger's resistance slacken beneath her and interpreted it as the triumph of reason. "I'm sorry about the pain." Her voice softened to a pain-numbing caress as she leaned a bit closer to his face. Her breath ruffled the hair at his neck. "But my grandmother knows what she's doing; she's better than any physician. You were shot in your . . . your . . ."

"Arse," he supplied, evidence that he was at least somewhat rational. "Shot in the bloody arse."

"Yes." She blushed furiously and began to retreat from her intimate contact with his back, pushing up. "And Baron Pinnow, our district magistrate, found you on the road and brought you here. Can you tell us your name?"

He pried his clenched jaws open to hiss, "Austen. Rane Austen." He was beginning to remember more. Images of his wrecked phaeton flashed through his mind. His head began to pound furiously as remembered pain joined and magnified his present discomfort. Suddenly he recalled it all: his reason for coming to Devon, the night, the road. . . .

"Damnation!" he thundered, remembering his hapless confrontation with the smugglers. "The bastards shot me!" In a blink he was up, twisting his torso, struggling to leave the bed. Charity was hauled down on the side of the bed to meet his molten glare. "What the hell am I—where the hell is . . ." He ground to a halt, staring at her. This time she registered fully in his mind as well as in his senses.

"You." He recognized her somehow. The feverish glimpses he had had, the brief respites from pain that had accompanied his perceptions of her were now recalled in his mind. A blonde in black. That face—like an angel's—with such earthy, opulent lips and such extravagantly warm eyes. She was staring at him as if

78

he'd taken complete leave of his senses. "Who the hell are you?"

"I . . . I'm Charity Standing." She swallowed hard, feeling his hostility softening as he pulled her tighter against him and examined her with those compelling gray eyes. She felt him touching her hair, her cheeks, her lips, with his gaze. Her voice grew hushed, confessing. "I've been caring for you since you were brought to our home."

"You've been . . ."

"Caring . . . for you." She could scarcely swallow. Their noses were almost touching. His lips were parted and she could feel his breath grazing her chin. "Caring . . . for your . . . your . . ."

"Arse," he supplied. His wits, like his senses, were otherwise occupied.

She nodded, equally thoughtless.

For another fragile moment, everything else in existence faded from awareness. There was only the two of them, their bodies molded warmly together. Both hearts were beating erratically; both faces were heating slowly.

He was so: overwhelmingly male.

She was so: delectably female.

His eyes lidded; her lashes lowered. His tongue made a circuit of his upper lip. Her lips parted and began to redden. She was remembering. He was anticipating.

"Where have I seen you before?" His voice dropped to a potent whisper, meant for her ears alone. His eyes poured over her, searching her startling beauty, and his hand boldly followed, feathering along the silky curve of her cheek. She felt cool and fragile, like fine porcelain.

Charity felt the warmth of his touch spreading through her, opening inner doors of sensation and awareness. The strength and gentleness of his hand on her face were breathtaking.

"I tried to help you . . . after your carriage wreck." She blushed, lowering her lashes. Would he remember? Her gaze drifted to his mouth and her lips parted in unconscious invitation.

"Carriage wreck?" He was totally absorbed in the way her white skin flushed tantalizingly under his sunbrowned hand. Then his hand slid down the side of her head and curled about the silky nape of her neck. His arm muscles contracted of their own will, pulling her closer as his eyes fastened on her lips. . . .

"Blarm me," Lady Margaret choked. If she didn't do something, it was going to happen right here before her eyes! She cleared her throat loudly and declared, "Not a particularly convenient place to get blasted, a *buttock.* You lost a lot of blood and blame near took a ragin' fever on top of it. Now you've reopened yourself with a fall. Not a very lucky sort, are you, lad?"

She'd managed to penetrate their little haven, all right. Both stiffened visibly and reddened with acute embarrassment. The reminder set off an explosion of humiliation in Rane Austen and he jerked back, releasing Charity abruptly. She sprang up, stunned and breathless from the encounter.

"Damnation! I wasn't exactly given a choice on where they leaded me!" He craned his stiff neck and shoulders about to find an old woman in a gaudy print smock and a blue turban glaring at him, her arms crossed over her waist. Her accusing look both baffled and rankled him. "Nor do I recall being given choice on where I was carried."

He heard Charity's surprised intake of breath at his rude retort and halted, feeling her eyes on him and fighting the overwhelming urge to stare at her again. His lovely blonde vision had taken care of him, he realized; she'd cared for his blasted . . . Oh, God. It was just too humiliating.

"Where the hell is 'Standwell'—and where is Stephenson?"

"Stephenson?" The old lady came forward with a scowl and he noted several bizarre looking objects hanging about her neck.

"Yes, Stephenson. He's my—" he stopped short of saying *bodyguard,* "valet." He took a ragged breath and tried to take himself better in hand. The flaming pain in his head and his arse was bad enough; now his bloody pride was on fire as well. He strained for more gentlemanly language, but he could do little about the underlying surliness in his tone.

"See here, if you'll be so good as to send a message to the Trayside Inn in Mortehoe, straightaway . . . I trust I am somewhere near Mortehoe?! My man Stephenson will make arrangements to unburden you of my care."

Rane followed them out with his eyes, then slumped against the bed and squeezed his eyes shut. In the midst of his discomfort, a tantalizing oasis of tranquility lingered. A face framed in honey-colored hair. Her face. He groaned. Was he mad with fever? Drugged witless? What in heaven's name was happening to him?

Lady Margaret bustled down the center stairs, leaving Charity standing in the hallway, staring at the guest room door, scowling and chewing her lip.

Whoever, whatever her Mister Austen was, he certainly wasn't the gentleman she had expected. Asleep he'd seemed handsome and gentlemanly and full of admirable qualities. Awake, he was powerful and intimidating, and his temper and language were shocking. It embarrassed her to realize that the disparity was mostly the result of her own moonspinning, and worse, that her imaginings had been fired by a proposal of marriage and a kiss from a man who was clearly irrational!

81

She sighed, remembering the storm of pain and emotion she'd glimpsed while looking into those dove gray eyes of his. He hadn't seemed particularly rational just now, either, cursing and flailing, pulling her on top of him bodily, staring at her—and touching her. Then Charity thought of her own behavior: she had touched his body, pressed herself against him, stared brazenly into his eyes . . . wishing he'd remember.

Her conduct had been abysmal. But even more troubling was the wild jumble of strange new feelings these potent touches and looks had produced in her. In the tangled knot of emotion and sensation inside her, she managed to recognize threads of compassion, pleasure and anticipation and curiosity . . . and even a bit of girlish fear. She'd never felt so many different things at one time. She'd never felt some of these things before in her life!

She shivered and wrapped her arms around her waist, dragging her thoughts back to the unexpected nature of her Mr. Austen. A moment later, she flushed from head to toe. Whatever else Mister Austen was, she realized with a sinking in her chest, he certainly wasn't *hers*.

As it happened, it wasn't necessary to send a message to the Trayside Inn at all. Within the hour, Baron Pinnow was on the doorstep of Standwell Hall with an air of importance greater than was customary and a stocky, flat-faced fellow in tow. He was shown to the sunlit "parlor" and after his usual effusion of apology, introduced the burly fellow to Lady Margaret as Stephenson, the very man Rane Austen had demanded they contact.

Lady Margaret scowled and led them out of the parlor and up the stairs to see her patient. "He wakened fully this morning, foul of temper, and with tongue enough for two sets of teeth."

"Not *his lordship's* usual manner, I'm sure." Pinnow arched a meaning-filled look at Lady Margaret. "Mr. Stephenson here informed me that *his lordship* was involved in a carriage mishap a few days back . . . a head injury, I believe."

Lady Margaret came to a dead stop on the stairs, causing both the magistrate and the manservant to fall back to avoid banging into her.

"His *lordship?* Old rusty guts is a lord of some kind?"

"The Viscount Oxley." Pinnow preened, congratulating himself on his own good sense in recognizing an opportunity when he saw it. A well-rigged *viscount* was certainly the sort of person one wanted to assist when one could. "His lordship has been under great personal strain of late, and I'm sure he will be eternally grateful once he recovers his customary verve and vigor." In fact, Pinnow was positively counting on it.

Lady Margaret's eyes narrowed and she "humphed" and barreled up the stairs and down the west hallway. As they entered the chamber, "his lordship" was rearing up on braced arms among the tousled sheets, clawing at something about his neck.

"I'm bloody well strangling! What the hell *is* this rubbish?!" He managed to loosen the itchy yarns, the vine, and the leather thong about his neck, and then pulled a handful of strange artifacts around from his back and still more from underneath the shirt he wore.

"M'lord!" Stephenson hurried around the thick-pillared bed to the far side, where Rane lay on his stomach, grappling to stay upright and glaring at the objects under his nose. "Are you alright, m'lord?"

"What the hell is this stuff?" Austen choked, curling his noble nose at the smell emanating from one shriv-

83

eled, meaty-looking mass. "It's not bad enough I'm butt-shot and half bled to death! Now they're trying to suffocate me?!" He looked up to witness Stephenson's eyes widening on him in confusion. "Don't just stand there; help me get this rubbish off!" Then as Stephenson lurched to obey, he demanded, "Where the hell have you been?"

"Don't you dare touch those amulets!"

Stephenson froze and Rane turned his entire upper body in one stiff, agonizing movement to find the gaudily garbed old woman who had tended him earlier standing near the foot of the bed. Beside her was a tall, pallorous gentleman dressed in a fashionable swept-back coat, buff knee breeches, and what appeared to be *one* riding boot. He was leaning heavily to one side on a stout cane and staring fixedly at Rane's damaged posterior. Rane gritted his teeth in anticipation of yet another round of humiliation.

"Those are healing powers, and as long as you're in this house, you'll wear them proper!" She bustled forward and smacked Stephenson's hands away, inserting herself between the manservant and his master to force the charms and amulets back down on Rane's neck.

"Healing powers? You mean, like those hunks of soup bone and shriveled bits of dead god-knows-what up there?!" he demanded, punching a finger back over his shoulder toward the charms hanging from the bed canopy. Lady Margaret tucked her chin, insulted mightily.

"They are not hunks of . . ." She stiffened and snatched up what appeared to be a bone fragment on a length of red yarn, from around his neck. "This is not *soup* bone. It's from the broken bone of a cow's leg that miraculously healed. And this," she held up a flatly shaped piece, "is part of a wolf's shoulder blade. And this," she held up a small, whitish rock wrapped in a leather thong, "is from the gizzard of a rooster that lived to be *seven years old!*"

"Gizzar—?!" Austen shuddered and tried to pull the leather string over his head, but she wrestled it back down. He began tugging feverishly at a bit of dried vine about his neck, trying not to look at the blackened, shriveled thing hanging from it.

"Absolutely not!" Lady Margaret came nose to nose with him. "That's a chain of pusley . . . taken in the full of the moon and kept over the winter in a jar of garlic."

"And what the hell's this on it?" he snarled, holding up the grisly withered thing on the end by two disdainful fingers, "a bat snout?!"

"It's a lizard tail!" the old woman declared furiously. "After the lizard lost it, he grew another one, and you're wearing it so it'll help *you* grow a new one!" The blaze in Lady Margaret's eyes said she'd been vindicated. The horror in Austen's eyes said she'd gone stark raving mad.

Austen gaped at the old woman and sputtered, speechless. He was wearing a lizard's tail to help *him* grow a new tail?! Please God, let him only be delirious with pain and not really experiencing all this! He was simply too stunned to resist when the old woman brushed his hands away and resettled the putrid things on his neck again. In the process, she pulled another amulet around from his back, one that had been caught on the shirt he was wearing.

Paws. His eyes unlocked and each went spiraling off in its own direction. He was wearing an iron circle with a dead something's shriveled paws in it! He didn't ask, didn't ever want to know.

"P-please, your lordship," the baron jolted forward, anxious to appease his injured nobleman. "Lady Margaret Villiers," he gestured to the old lady, "is a renowned herbalist and something of a physic in these

85

parts. Her methods may be somewhat . . . unorthodox . . . but they are vastly effective, nonetheless."

The baron's rational-sounding intervention jarred Rane back to his senses. "And just who . . . are you," he bit back "the hell" just in time and managed to add, "sir?"

"Baron Pinnow, Magistrate of the District of Mortehoe, at your service, my lord." Pinnow nodded with impeccable intonation and deference. "It was I who found you on the road that night and brought you here. I knew you would receive the finest of care here."

"My undying gratitude," Rane gritted out nastily as sharp pains began shooting up his neck and curling around his scalp. The muscles in his shoulders began catching fire. He'd never felt more miserable in his life, or felt less in control.

The baron was visibly startled by Austen's ungracious attitude and began rethinking both his generosity toward the viscount and his hope of gain. He drew himself up to his full height. "Actually, I've come to ask you questions concerning the shooting, your lordship, if it wouldn't put you to too much trouble. Have you any idea who shot you?"

"None," Rane said through his teeth. The throbbing in his rear and the irritation in his tone were both growing worse by the minute. The tendrils of fire in his shoulders were now migrating down his arms.

"Then perhaps you can tell me something of what happened . . . what you saw . . . heard. . . ?"

"I have no earthly idea what happened. I was shot — apparently on a road somewhere, since that is where you found me. Obviously, I was riding back to the inn —" He stopped himself just in time and managed a convincing grimace of pain to cloak his near misstep. He couldn't possibly reveal that he'd been out strongarming smugglers.

86

"He was comin' back from appraisin' a bit o' local muslin." Stephenson stepped forward and winked insinuatingly at the baron. A look of comprehension dawned in the baron's worldly face. "His lordship's in commerce, y'know. Got a tradin' company in London . . . an' he come to check on . . . the local goods."

"Muslin. I do understand, being familiar with such *commerce* myself. Go on, your lordship."

"There's nothing to go on about," Austen said tersely. "I recall nothing of the incident. It was probably just riff-raff, thieves of some sort." The drop in his tone declared the subject closed and the inquisitor dismissed.

"Thieves . . . Perhaps, since there were no papers or funds on your person when we found you." The baron stiffened and his eyes and long features sharpened with covert indignation. "No doubt you will recall more later."

The baron's questions had jarred Rane Austen's thinking past his bodily discomfort to other, more important considerations. If there was anything he didn't need just now, it was a toadying local magistrate asking questions and poking around in his affairs. He had to get out of here before . . . a panicky sense of urgency gripped him. He had to get back to London — today, now. He had business to attend and customers to pacify. Then the most horrifying thought of all struck. While he was lying here with a hole in his arse, the rest of the social season was slipping away! He turned on Stephenson, his eyes silvering with pain.

"Hire a carriage immediately. I'm going back to London today . . . now!"

"What?" Stephenson stared at him as though he'd lost his senses.

"Rumnoggins!" Lady Margaret sputtered. "I've only just retightened your stitches from where you fell out

87

of bed this morning. You're not going anywhere."

"Oh, yes I am! I'm going back to London this very afternoon." Rane felt the baron's and Stephenson's startled gazes upon him and turned to the old lady, eyes burning with humiliation. "I am much in your debt already, madam, and I shall *not* impose upon you further. The carriage, Stephenson," his voice rose to teeter on the edge of irruption, "as soon as is humanly possible!"

"Horsefeathers! You'll open yourself up!" "Are ye sure, m'lord?" "My lord *viscount*, please reconsider —"

Everyone began talking at once, trying to persuade him or to persuade each other to persuade him, while he insisted on having a carriage and traveling back to London forthwith, even if it meant bleeding to death in the process.

Charity had slipped into the room, unnoticed, and stood by the drapes at the far side of the bed watching Rane Austen. What kind of man was he? In the last minute she'd witnessed his powerful aura of command, and glimpsed his determined and sometimes high-handed nature. He was a very direct and forceful man. And he was obviously in pain. His knuckles whitened as they gripped the sheet and, in unconscious response, her hands curled into tight balls at her sides. She watched his broad shoulders tremble with strain and her back stiffened against the ache. When his eyes and jaw tightened grimly, she experienced a fleeting sensation of pain and winced.

She bit her lip and edged around the bed, where she was ignored by everyone except Rane Austen. The minute she came in view, she walked straight into the middle of his aching sight, into the heart of his pain-spawned anger, and into the center of his reeling thoughts. And this time he absorbed every bit of her.

She was dressed starkly, in a black, high-waisted dress that was utterly devoid of ornament and all the

88

more noteworthy for it. Her thick blonde hair was dressed in soft curls by her face and drawn up into a casual, feminine swirl on the crown of her head. The simplicity of her gown and coiffure were stunning counterpoints to the lush perfection of her skin, the vibrant colors of her lips and eyes, and the exquisite, classical contours of her features. As she came a step closer, her softly draped dress caressed a very womanly set of curves, drawing his eyes downward and causing his breath to rattle in his throat.

"Are you hurting, Mr. Austen?" Her words came softly and were all but obscured by the others' strident voices.

Rane Austen stared at his earth-bound angel with the sweet caramel eyes and soft satin lips, who seemed to know exactly what was happening inside him. Hell yes, he was hurting. All over. Everywhere. But his jaw clenched tighter and his neck stiffened of its own accord, making him incapable of a word or a nod of agreement.

She turned abruptly to the trove of bottles and jars on the table near the window. The brash combination of vulnerability and pride she read in the stubborn set of his jaw undercut her indignation at his surly behavior. He was hurting and he didn't want to admit it. A small, aching hollow began to open in the middle of her. *She just had to help him.*

Sullivan Pinnow started about, following the viscount's intense gaze to her. He quickly followed her to the table. "Miss Charity, we must prevail upon his lordship, the *viscount* to consider how it will blight us all if something untoward happens to him."

"His *lordship?*" The baron's emphatic use of the term finally registered with her. Her head came up and her hands paused in the midst of measuring medicinal powders into a glass of water. Her handsome, irascible Mr. Austen was a titled man, a *viscount?* Something in her shrank and slid with disappointment at that news, and it took a moment to recognize just what it was in her that had been dealt such a blow. Hope.

She frowned. A nobleman. She should have guessed. She lifted her chin and carried the cloudy mixture back to his bedside. He had slumped down onto one shoulder, glaring, and she found herself watching his facial muscles working whitely beneath his sun-browned skin. A strange liquid surge occurred in her middle, and her voice softened in spite of her.

"This will help the discomfort . . . your lordship."

His lidded eyes opened and a small trill of panic went through him as she took possession of his senses again. It was the heat and sickness, surely, that caused this bizarre, feverish reaction every time he set eyes on her. When he finally relented and reached for the medicine, his hand curled over hers around the glass, trapping it, bringing it closer. Bringing her closer. Relief poured through him at the substantial feel of her hand beneath his. Until now, he'd harbored an unacknowledged anxiety that she was a product of his pain-induced delirium.

"What's in it?" he whispered hoarsely. "Bat fingers and spiders' knees?" He watched her golden brown eyes darken briefly, then brighten as she determined to ignore his sarcastic remark.

"Willowbark . . ." She bent closer, urging the glass to his lips. Warmth was spreading up her arm from where his hand covered hers. "And tansy . . ." His hand tightened further around hers on the glass and she swallowed hard. "And secrets."

"What secrets? Yours?"

She swayed a bit closer, unable to answer. Then, because she couldn't seem to resist the urge, she dropped her eyes to his. And because he couldn't resist, he caught her gaze and pulled her slowly toward him until she was bent close and their faces, almost

90

touching.

She softened visibly; he tightened tellingly.

His eyes were turbulent gray, like storm clouds that swirled, cloaking dangerous lightning. Her eyes were serene honey-brown, like the rich, patient earth herself, sheltering deep mysteries.

Powerful, she marveled.

So very powerful, he recognized.

A long, scintillant moment later, Rane recoiled abruptly from that unnerving insight to find the others staring at him, slackjawed. When he pulled away, Charity felt the severance of the deepening connection between them all through her, like a physical pain. She abandoned the glass to his hands, blushing violently, and Rane buried his nose in it, downing the stuff out of sheer embarrassment. Neither had the faintest notion of how long that potent visual exchange had lasted. But both the baron and Charity's grandmother had timed it as well past the limits of decency, and now all in the chamber were reassessing the viscount's determination to leave Standwell.

"Of course, we must certainly respect your lordship's desire to recuperate at your own pace . . . and under your own auspices," the baron declared testily. His eyes narrowed irritably on the flush of Charity's cheeks and the awakening of sensual interest in her lash veiled eyes.

"I'll go straightaway and mix up some of my healing comfort for you to take along." Lady Margaret barreled toward the door, then halted and turned back to stare darkly at Charity and her moon-hexed nobleman. "You'd better come with me." She snagged her granddaughter by the arm.

Charity flushed hotly, delaying long enough for a last tumultuous look at her erstwhile patient. She wouldn't have a chance to help him at all; he was going to *leave!*

The baron curtly excused himself to wait below and that left only Stephenson in the chamber with Rane. He stared at his handsome employer with a wry, insinuating grin. He'd never known Austen to pass up an opportunity like the one that little wench had just offered him in front of God and everybody. "I suppose ye'll not be needin' that carriage now. . . ."

Rane struggled to rise above the humiliating heat in his body and turned a ferocious glare on Stephenson. "Then you damn well suppose wrong. The sooner I'm out of this crazy place, the better!"

Chapter Six

Less than an hour later, there came a fierce pounding on Standwell's weathered doors, and when Melwin answered he found the baron, pink-faced and heaving, hanging onto the dried wreath of ash limbs around the doorframe.

"Get your mistress," he panted hoarsely into old Melwin's face. "That Stephenson fellow . . . broken his damned leg!" Melwin startled and raced off to fetch his mistress.

Lady Margaret came flying and stopped dead when she saw the jinxed nobleman's equally jinxed servant. She clucked distress, pulled a bone amulet from the pocket of her smock, and hurried to drape it about the injured fellow's neck.

Charity was not far behind and stopped short, seeing the burly servant's face twisted in pain and feeling a strange sinking feeling in the middle of her. Troubles. It was happening again. First her stranger . . . now his servant. . . . She watched her grandmother fiddling with her amulets and glancing nervously up at the sky, where a hawk was tracing lazy circles far above, and she wondered for the thousandth time, what things the old lady seemed to know and never told.

They trundled the viscount's man up the stairs and settled him in a dusty guest room just down the hallway from his employer's. Charity and Lady Margaret quickly set about filling him with herbed brandy and setting the rather painful break, while Baron Pinnow rattled on about how the fellow's mount had stepped in a hole and rolled over onto his leg. They had been only a few minutes away from Standwell and he had selflessly hauled the poor blighter up onto his own horse and brought him back to Lady Margaret for tending.

"My deepest apologies, dear ladies," the baron hovered irritably at the edges of the faded bed drapes, "to have inflicted the inconvenience of *two* unhappy invalids upon your good graces."

Lady Margaret was finishing the wrappings about the splint on Stephenson's leg and she looked up and scowled. Charity discerned the implications of the baron's apology in the same moment and looked up, right into her grandmother's piercing eyes. She straightened, and her thoughts mirrored the baron's words as he said, "With his man unable to take him or even tend him, I'm afraid there is no question of his lordship removing to London now." Pinnow tightened disagreeably at his conclusion, recalling Miss Charity's fascination with the handsome viscount. "He shall have to depend upon your abundant mercies."

Charity excused herself, and by the time she quitted the door, her eyes were glowing again and her lip was caught between her teeth. She paused in the hallway, staring at her injured nobleman's door, and suddenly the smile she had been fighting overwhelmed her. Her eyes warmed and her face glowed with an expression that would have been immediately recognizable to any woman seeing it . . . and a profound mystery to any man.

Gray-eyed Rane Austen was going to have to *stay*.

With a thudding sense of alarm, Baron Pinnow had watched Charity's voluptuous little person sway from the chamber. He dragged a smothering layer of propriety over the kindled sparks of his desire and turned to Lady Margaret. "Lady Margaret, you simply cannot permit Miss Charity to tend to his lordship too . . . personally."

"Ummm." Lady Margaret was thinking the same thing,

though for altogether different reasons. "I'll send for Gar and Percy, straightaway."

A short while later, Charity and her grandmother carried Rane Austen the bad news of his manservant's mishap. As expected, the viscount took it rather hard.

"Broke his damned . . ." He went rigid and pushed up out of the sheet he'd clamped about his neck the minute they came into the room. He looked for all the world like a surly turtle coming out of his shell. "I don't believe it! Damn Satan's bones," he swore without thinking, and when he realized what he'd done, he did it again, out of raw embarrassment. "B'dammit! I—I won't stand for it!"

"Looks like you won't be able to *stand* for anything, for some time yet," Lady Margaret harumphed irritably, sending her eyes to his bandaged buttocks. "It looks like both of you will be staying on with us for a while."

"The hell it does! I can't stay here—not another bloody night!" He raised on both arms, turning, and glimpsed Charity standing near the foot of the bed. *Her* again. Please . . . *no*. He began to coil with unholy expectation.

"Why can't you?" Charity came forward with a thoughtful frown. She was thinking of her lordship's London life. Was there something . . . *someone* . . . in London he needed to hurry back to? The question sent a cool draft through the warm spot in the middle of her.

Why? Rane tightened all over, like a block of ruddy granite. Lying there, prisoner to her gentle scrutiny, he had never felt so powerless or so absurd in his life. *Why* indeed? Because he was hurting and embarrassed by it. Because he was behaving utterly unlike himself, like a boor and an ingrate and a colossal jackass—and he didn't seem to be able to stop it. Most of all because he didn't understand what happened to him every time she came in sight, what was happening to him this very minute.

She was standing there, close enough to touch, with

those extraordinary eyes of hers and that precious ivory oval of a face and that warm, satiny skin. His fingers were remembering exactly what it felt like to touch her and his lips were *anticipating* what it would feel like to touch her . . . all of her. Every ache and discomfort in his body was somehow fading, banished, suspended by her mere presence. The sight of her was as powerful as any medicament known to mankind. And he knew exactly what came next. Once the pain was gone, the seductive lure of her womanly aura would take hold, a rousing awareness of her desirable mouth and softly curved body. . . .

"I—I h-have to get back to L-London," he stammered, horrified by the way he'd let his gaze follow his thoughts. It rested hotly on the full curve of her breasts. His face caught fire and his head turned with a jerk. He was desperate to come up with reasons, any reasons, that didn't involve *escaping her.* "I-I have a trading concern to run. And I have appointments—important negotiations, and . . . and there are still several weeks left in the season and I have to—" He clamped his jaw shut in horror.

"Have to what?" She swayed a bit closer, searching him with those devastating caramel eyes and invading him with that warm, seductive presence.

Rane's jaw tightened and his sculptured features bronzed. "I—I have to return to London to find . . ." To find a wife! He veered from that potentially humiliating course just in time. "I simply cannot remain here—not another night!"

"If I may be so blunt, your lordship . . ." Her gaze settled warmly on his tight face and coiled shoulders. "I don't think you have much choice."

She was absolutely right, of course. He knew it in the marrow of his bones. This was the crowning calamity of the worst two weeks of his life. He'd lost an expensive shipment of brandy, lost a long cultivated acquisition in the bride market, lost his expensive phaeton, been bashed senseless — *twice,* and been shot in the rear by two of the most cunning simpletons it had ever been his misfortune to encounter. And now he was trapped in an isolated country house with a crazy old woman who hung bizarre animal parts all over him . . . and with a voluptuous blonde angel who uprooted his soul and took hold of his senses everytime he saw her. Surliness was his only defense against total brainless humiliation! And he had only to meet her devastating eyes for a brief moment to put that in peril!

Charity watched him burrow sullenly back into the sheet as he grudgingly surrendered to his fate. The strangest wave of warmth swept her from head to toe. She had the distinct impression that Rane Austen, Viscount Oxley, wasn't accustomed to surrendering . . . not to anyone or anything. More likely, he was used to conquering, to having his way with servants and employees and perhaps everyone and everything else that crossed his path. It was probably very difficult for him to lie there hurting, isolated, and powerless; the insight surprised her. It was little wonder he was so angry and irritable just now.

Melwin appeared at the door, just at that moment, with the news that "that Stephenson feller" was "moanin' and thrashin' somethin' fierce." Lady Margaret scowled at his lordship and then at her granddaughter, debating whether they could be trusted together in the same room. Then she hurried out to see to their other patient.

"How bad is he?" Rane growled, refusing to look at her. Twice already he'd made a complete jackass of himself, staring at her. He wasn't about to make that mistake again. There was something about the wench . . .

"It's a simple break. He's hurting now, but he'll be fine." She suddenly had an overpowering urge to reassure him, to let him know she truly wanted to help him. If only he would look at her again . . .

The pull of her irresistible presence and the push of

his own stubborn desire combined to make the urge to see her, to experience her again, overpowering. In a mild panic, he buried his chin in the pillow and squeezed his eyes shut. Perhaps she'd be insulted enough to leave.

She sighed very quietly. She knew he was dismissing her, and something in her rebelled at the idea. She was determined to help him—whether he wanted her help or not.

"Is there anyone we should send a message to in London? Your business partners, perhaps?"

"I have no business partners," he said through clamped jaws and a formidable, unseeing scowl. Her image rose on the lids of his closed eyes, all pale satiny skin and lush curves that made his skin heat, soft hair that begged to be released and touched.

"Then perhaps we could write to your family. . . ."

"No family," he growled, trying desperately to find some solid ground on which to take a stand against her. His complete lack of gentlemanly connections had always been an acute embarrassment to him; he never spoke of it to anyone, ever. What in hell was he doing, letting her pry into his personal affairs like this? Why was he even answering her?

"A message to your . . . wife?" Would he ask strange women to marry him if he already had a wife?

Wife. He always flinched privately when the word was said in his hearing. But something in the soft caress she gave the word as she said it, took the everpresent sting from it this time. Wife. It came from her lips a warm, full syllable that had room in it for all sorts of tantalizing possibilities. He suddenly had to look, to see if she really did have that soft, irresistible glow in her face, in her eyes. He turned to her and her gaze, warm and searching upon him, sent a painfully sweet surge of confusion through him. How had he known she'd look like this?

"No wife," he rasped.

"Oh." She let out the breath she'd been holding and felt

a ripple of pleasure through her, despite the formidable scowl that was trained on her. She watched the powerful tension of his shoulders and facial muscles and sensed a great deal of feeling beneath his gruff denials. No family, no partners, and no wife . . . It tugged unexpectedly at something inside her.

"Then perhaps your betrothed would like to know. . . " She held her breath.

"I'm not betrothed," he answered with confused heat. The idea of her being curious about him was dangerously pleasurable.

"Oh." She chewed her lip to forbid it to curl at the ends. She'd come this far, inventorying his life. She might as well go a step further. "Is there *anyone* we should notify?"

"Meddlesome, aren't you?" he growled without real heat. "My butler, Eversby. By all means write him . . . he's mad about letters."

"I don't mean to be meddlesome," she said, reddening. "I just want to help you." She came a step closer, wishing she could reach out to stroke his soft hair and trail her fingertips over his hard cheek. "I know you're hurting now, but with rest and nourishment and proper care, you'll be up and walking in a few days. And in a few weeks, you'll be good as new."

He drew back sharply, feeling exposed and off-balance and deathly afraid of the way he was losing himself in the seductive honey-pools of her eyes again. In sheer panic, he retreated into his quarrelsome temper again. "Weeks? A few *weeks?!*"

"Well, two at least . . . three or four before you can sit a horse. Surely you can bear with us for two or three weeks." Her voice and eyes lightened with teasing reason. "We shall certainly have to bear with you."

He stiffened visibly as her good-natured taunt struck home. "Look here—*you* don't have to lie here with your ar—" he changed directions abruptly, "with these

99

wretched things draped all over you!" He snatched up several of the amulets hanging around his neck and glowered at her. It struck him that she wasn't wearing a single amulet across that splendidly unadorned bosom of hers. The old lady wore a ton of them and even the blessed butler wore them. "You . . . you don't have to wear them?"

"No, I don't have to wear lucky pieces." A small, charming smile bloomed on her features, deflecting his glare. "I'm too lucky as it is."

"*Too* lucky?" he felt himself melting, surrendering again and he panicked, jerking his face away. "That's absurd," he snorted gruffly. "Whoever heard of anybody claiming too much luck? Anyway, there isn't any such thing as *luck.*"

"Oh, but there is." Her eyes sparkled as she sensed he was fighting to maintain his peckish attitude. It was her first real clue that there was a different man beneath all that sulk and snarl, and she was suddenly burning with curiosity about him. "My father even agreed there was. It's just that he and Gran'mere differed strongly on whether a person could do anything to influence or change it. Gran'mere believes all kinds of things can change your luck and Papa . . . always let her try, as long as she didn't tamper with his food or make him wear anything too . . . unusual."

"Your father?" The mention of him surprised Rane and he looked up, coming partway out of his sheet-shell again. "He sounds like a refreshingly rational sort. Where is he? I wish to speak with him . . . right away."

He wanted to speak with her father? Charity stiffened and backed a step. She was completely unprepared for the sense of loss that suddenly descended on her. She wished she could speak with her father, too. And she wished she could bury her face in his shirtfront and feel his warm, callused hand around hers again. The sparkle fled her eyes and her throat tightened so that she couldn't respond. For a moment she just stared, unseeing, feeling lost.

Gradually the pull of his gaze brought her back to the present. She took a deep breath and forced her voice past the knot in her throat. "I'm afraid that won't be possible. My father died . . . almost a fortnight ago."

Silence grew between them and as it lengthened, Rane was drawn from the cocoon of his own misery. The strength of her response unnerved him. She was paling, her vibrant eyes had darkened, were oddly vulnerable, even hurting. The unguarded pain he glimpsed in her suddenly vibrated strings of understanding all through him. Of course . . . the black dress. She was in deep mourning. Her father had died a mere fortnight ago. An instant later, his face was aflame. Demanding to see her dead father—he ought to be chained up!

"Miss . . . Miss . . ."

"Standing," she supplied quietly, thinking he'd forgotten her name. "Charity Standing."

Charity. He hadn't forgotten. But it was only now, as he started to say it, that its full impact registered in him. Lord. What else would she be called? With her pain-numbing presence, gentle voice, and comforting eyes, she was charity personified. His tongue was suddenly too thick to work properly.

"We'll send to the inn for your things this afternoon." She took a deep breath and squared her shoulders, once again her determined and helpful self. "It might help to have your own razor to shave with and your own things to wear."

She had no way of knowing that his dark, startled look was mild shock that she would think of such things. A proper young London deb would scarcely even know what comprised a gentleman's toilette, much less speak of it. But Charity Standing knew about such things, and was apparently insightful enough to understand that a man's personal items could provide some comfort in strange surroundings. Charity Standing was clearly no ordinary girl. The realization sent another wave of confused heat through him. He grappled for something, anything, to say.

"It would feel good to get out of this wretched shirt." He flexed his powerful shoulders and arms in irritable demonstration. "It's miles too small."

"Yes," Charity managed a wan little smile of agreement, "I'm afraid it is. You're much larger than Papa was."

Rane watched her go, feeling as though he'd been gut-punched. The door and his eyes closed in the same moment. What a perfect bonehead! Here he was, wearing her dead father's shirt and braying about it like a bloody stupid jackass! He dropped his face into the pillow.

"Damn."

Charity paused in the hallway, halfway to the stairs. A thoughtful look came over her. His lordship didn't have a family and didn't have a wife . . . or a fiancée. He didn't seem to belong to anyone at all! Her eyes lighted at the thought.

But the next instant, she recalled the strange feeling she had had when looking in his eyes just now, a feeling that she'd somehow struck a very sensitive nerve by asking about his personal life. Why didn't he belong to anybody? Why didn't he have a wife or at least a betrothed? She frowned. It was plain to anybody with two good eyes that more than just his body was hurting. There was something else . . . deep inside. A broken heart? The idea of him filled with unrequited love and longing produced a sinking sensation in her stomach.

She squared her shoulders and lifted her chin. It was her duty, she believed, to try to counter the troubles and comfort the pain she saw all around her. Her thoughtful look gave way to a brimming smile. Rane Austen's posterior wasn't the only thing that was going to improve . . . his temper would, too. Whatever his problem was, she was going to help him with it!

Two lame guests residing on Standwell's upper floor meant a good bit of additional work to be done in a household unused to the disturbance of guests. There were special meals to fix and ferry up the stairs, and dirty dishes to cart back down to the kitchen. There had to be extra water for cleaning and bathing; it had to be heated and then also hauled upstairs. Additional linens and laundry were needed . . . upstairs and back down again . . . and necessaries to empty, and candles to light . . .

The servant staff consisted only of old Melwin, his wife, Bernadette, and two of their grandsons, who worked primarily in the garden and stable. The routine cooking, cleaning, and tending were all the aging pair of retainers could handle, and their young grandsons were already fully occupied with the spring chores of tilling and planting the kitchen garden, and tending the stable and poultry and small livestock. Thus it fell to Charity and Lady Margaret to don dust caps and aprons and tidy up the dusty guest room where Stephenson lay in a "healing comfort" sleep.

As they rolled up the rugs to be carried out for a beating and dismantled the bed hanging to be trundled out for a good airing, Lady Margaret watched the blooming color in her granddaughter's cheeks and knew it had precious little to do with the exertion of cleaning. She scowled, and seized the moment to have a serious word with her much-too-sheltered and much-too-desirable granddaughter.

"I've sent word for Gar and Percy to come to take over his lordship's care."

Charity paused in the middle of unhooking the last of the faded velvets that hung from the rods about the bed canopy. "Gar and Percy? But why bother them? I'm perfectly capable." Lady Margaret stood on the other side of the bed, her arms full of dusty bed hangings, wearing her narrowest, you-know-better-than-that look.

"It's not proper, a young lady tending a man's . . . a man's . . ."

"Arse?" Charity supplied.

"Wound! Tending a gentleman's *wound!*" Lady Margaret flushed at having been caught mincing words. She had always prided herself on ignoring the mindless niceties expected of ladies, and now found herself in the awkward position of resorting to them. "See there! He's got you talkin' like a swaggering tar already." She fussed with the bed drapes in her hands as she tried to think how to phrase her thoughts. Finally, she just shoved the things into a pile on the bed near Stephenson's feet and came out with it.

"It's simply not proper for a young girl to have such personal dealings with a man."

"But, Gran'mere," Charity blushed a bit guiltily, clasping the dusty old velvets against her. "I'm not having 'personal dealings' with his lordship. I'm only tending him, helping him."

That's what you think, Lady Margaret thought. She said, "That's not what he'll think. Men, especially noblemen, think differently about these things than women do. Where he comes from, in high society, a decent woman would never *want* to help a man . . . it wouldn't even cross her mind. In their world it's for men to help each other, or to help themselves. So to his way of thinking, when a woman comes close and touches him, she's already declared she doesn't care about things like decency and morality, much less about higher things like compassion and kindness. To a man like his lordship, a touch is a pure invitation to 'night work.' " She stopped and stiffened. But she could see from the way Charity's eyes were widening that it was too late to recall her words.

" 'Night work'?" Charity reddened, having the strangest

104

feeling that she knew exactly what her grandmother meant.

Lady Margaret swallowed hard and fidgeted under her granddaughter's expectant stare. She'd been meaning to have this talk with Charity for the last five years, since Charity came to womanhood. But like everything else with consequences for the future, she'd put it off, hoping against hope that somehow it wouldn't be necessary. "See here, girl. There are things that happen between men and women. . . ."

"You mean . . . like what happens in the dark, between husbands and wives . . . in the blessed marriage bed? That sort of 'night work'?"

Lady Margaret's jaw dropped. "W-well, y-yes. How do you know about. . . ?"

"Papa told me about it, a long time ago." Charity winced at her grandmother's look of dismay. "All about the woman's fertile field and the man's seed and the plowing that had to be done. I'm afraid I asked why we couldn't get a baby brother, since we had a fair cabbage patch . . . and he said it wasn't quite as simple as looking under a cabbage leaf. Then he told me how babies are really made."

"He told you? Everything?!" Lady Margaret choked. She didn't know whether to feel scandalized or relieved. She tottered around the end of the bed in shock and pulled Charity to the dusty windowseat, bidding her sit. Then she eased her knowledgeable bones down onto the seat, too.

"I think so. About the cock on the hen's back, and the stallion on the mare, and husband on the wife's—"

"Yes, well!" Lady Margaret broke in, reddening uncomfortably. "You do seem to have the gist of it." She looked away trying to collect her wits and recall just how this conversation had begun, and where she had intended it to go. Then Charity helpfully put it all back on track.

"I can't imagine that his lordship would think I'd invite

him to such 'night work' with me," she whispered, feeling strangely empty in her middle at the thought. "I'm not his wife."

Lady Margaret turned to stare at her. Apparently in emphasizing the procreative aspects of the process, Upton had left out some rather major details. Like desire. And pleasure. And their volatile potential for misuse. Lady Margaret stared at her granddaughter's lovely, guileless face and understood completely why Upton had left them out. But she also understood that Charity couldn't go on in ignorance of those things any longer . . . especially now that she was beginning to experience them.

"I'm afraid it doesn't have much to do with being married . . . or even with making babies," she said quietly. "It has to do with pleasure and with one's need for another . . . in that way. Men take much pleasure in mating . . . and somehow, the sight of a beautiful woman makes them crave that pleasure. And I'm afraid it doesn't much matter whether they're properly married or whether they scarcely even know the woman . . . or whether they make a baby or ruin a woman's name in the process. They just want the excitement, the pleasure."

Charity sat listening to her Gran'mere's explanation, feeling both enlightened and confused. The viscount certainly didn't seem to take much pleasure in his brief contacts with her. On the other hand, "pleasure" was the perfect word to describe what she felt whenever she looked at his handsome face and manly frame. And excitement was exactly the name for what caused her heart to race and her face to warm when he looked deep into her eyes and wrapped his big hand over hers or brushed his fingers over her cheek.

"And women," Charity murmured, searching her Gran'mere's wise face for reassurance. "Do women take pleasure in men, too?"

Lady Margaret's gaze drifted back through the long, dusty halls of her memory, to a time when she had experienced such things. And in the strong grip of those memories, she answered too candidly. "Yes, they do. With the right man, 'night work' becomes *night magic*. It's a magic that makes your bones soften and your flesh melt and your blood burn in your veins. It carries you into distant worlds of colored dreams and untold delights. Sometimes it makes you think you'll explode, you're stuffed so full of pleasure, and other times it makes you feel so quiet and so peaceful . . . like you're hardly being at all." She sighed, rousing from her very personal reflections to continue.

"Gypsy men know about night magic. They carry it in their hands. And they weave it for their women in the dark . . . with soft touches and caresses." Joy and sadness mingled memorably in her lined face. "Your Gran'pere had the night magic in his hands . . ."

"But, Gran'pere wasn't a gypsy. He was a Frenchman." Charity watched her grandmother's longing remembrance and glimpsed the greater scope of the old woman's life: the spirited woman, the loving wife, the mother that had all come before this last phase of life, grandmother.

"Yes, well, apparently some Frenchmen have it too. I guess some of them have it in their hands . . . and some don't. But if a man has it, he can touch a woman and know just what she's feeling and how to make her deepest—" A startled look came across the old woman's face as she realized where her lecture of warning had led. *Night magic?!* Ye gods! Horrified, she turned on Charity and straightened, becoming *Gran'mere* again with a vengeance.

"I've sent for Gar and Percy, and when they come, they'll care for his lordship and you'll have no need to be in his room a'tall. Until then, you'll see that the door is left open at all times and you'll keep away from his . . ." She was going to say "hands," but the dazed look of discovery on Charity's face warned that she'd already said too much. Instead of educating Charity on the dangers

107

of men and passions, she feared she'd only succeeded in opening up a whole new realm of intriguing possibilities for her.

Indeed she had. For Charity was sitting, clutching the dusty bed drapes, remembering the odd warmth of Rane Austen's muscular hands when he touched her, wondering . . .

"Gran'mere, do you think his lordship has any gypsy in him?"

"Not a drop!" Lady Margaret twitched at the trend of her granddaughter's thoughts. "Not a drop of gypsy in him anywhere!" She shoved to her feet and snatched the bed curtain from Charity's lap, heading then for the others on the bed, then for the door. Charity rose, oblivious to her grandmother's irritation.

"But he's so dark. Wouldn't you think—"

"Old rusty guts is more likely part panther." The old woman turned back to make a protective sign on the air. "And the only thing they make at night is trouble!"

Alone in the sun-drenched chamber, Rane Austen had the rest of the morning to stare at the yellowed walls and faded bed hangings, thinking about his trading company offices and his buyers, who would soon be howling with disappointment, and the matrimonial opportunities he would be forfeiting while his wound healed. The potential for loss in his absence was enormous, for much of his trade depended upon his own personal force as a trader and negotiator. It was dismal and depressing thought-fodder, indeed, but he was desperate to keep from thinking about the strange household where he lodged and the people who had taken him in.

He didn't want to think about *her* especially, didn't want to conjure up her thick, blonde hair and her warm, caramel eyes, or her fair skin. Lord, she had such magnificent skin, so pale and translucent . . . like fine Florentine marble, only warmer . . . much warmer.

After all his years in the tropics and with his own skin so brown, he found nothing more erotic than the contrast of a woman's pale, bare skin against his own. It was an excruciatingly small step from trying *not* to conjure so specific an image — light on dark, pale skin on tanned — to doing exactly that. And in a breath he was imagining the sight of her creamy shoulders covered with a sensual curtain of blonde hair, the sight of his own tanned hands releasing her snowy breasts from the stern, unadorned black of her dress. Dark on light, his sun-bronzed fingers cupping those pale globes . . .

Desire thickened his blood and congealed in his loins, and it took a moment for him to recognize it among the dull aches in the rest of his lower half. The abrupt completion of his arousal genuinely horrified him, for he honestly hadn't intended to summon desire at all! It was on him fully before he had realized what was happening. . . .

The door opened just at that moment and Rane burrowed furiously under the sheets, flushing hot with humiliation. He was only slightly relieved to see it was the aging butler.

Old Melwin dragged a straight chair from the far wall to the door and climbed up on it. He plucked a huge iron horseshoe from his forearm, extracted a hammer and spikes from his sagging coat pockets, and before Rane's disbelieving eyes, he pounded two spikes through the horseshoe and into the wall. When he finished, he pulled another horseshoe from his arm to fasten it the same way. Rane's surly shout stopped him.

"What in hell is all this foolishness?" he demanded. Old Melwin turned gingerly on the chair bottom to frown at him.

"It's iron . . . fer luck. M'lady swears by 'em." The old servant waved his hammer offhandedly and turned back to his task. "Got 'em everwhere." When he finished pounding the last nail, Rane tore his hands from his ears and forced his eyes open. The old fellow was replacing the chair against the wall when Rane craned his stiff neck to see.

"What? Only three?" Rane snarled as the butler passed. The old fellow paused briefly.

"Odd numbers is the lucky ones," he explained, puzzled that Rane wouldn't know something as basic as that. "Three's good. Five's odd, but it's real easy to turn the wrong way on ye. An' seven's next up. Real lucky. Did ye want seven, instead?"

"God, no!" Rane blurted out, "three is just fine . . . three is excellent! God knows, I'm not a greedy man."

Old Melwin knew sarcasm when he heard it. He "humphed" and shuffled out, leaving Rane roundly irritated with his crazy old hostess. Who the hell asked her to fiddle with his luck in the first place?! There wasn't any such thing as *luck!* He glared at the bizarre collection of things hanging around his neck and sorted through them with a wary finger to find the one that stunk like something dead and rotted. It was shaped like a leathery, withered ball and seemed to be stuffed with dried plant-like material. He slipped the yarn it was on over his neck and head and, lacking any more permanent means of disposal, gave it a satisfyingly vicious heave under the bed.

An instant later, he caught himself mid-oath, and was suddenly as irritated with his own surly, unpredictable behavior as he was with his dotty old hostess. Where the hell were his gentlemanly standards? For years he'd struggled to curb the intensity and toughness his hard early life had built in him. Was his hard won polish really so thin that a small mishap or two could turn him into a snarling, uncouth brute?

Every time he opened his mouth, he made a royal ass of himself, as when he'd demanded to speak with Miss Charity's dead father, then complained about having to

110

wear his blessed shirts. He'd been too humiliated, afterward, to even frame an apology, though certainly she had deserved one.

Unbidden, her image came to his mind, wearing the same sweetly melancholy expression she'd worn when speaking of her father. A strange hollow opened deep in the middle of his chest and he sent a hand to rub the spot over it, scowling. He looked down at the linen shirt stretched snugly over his arms and chest and thought about this Upton Standing. What kind of man could father such a girl? A curvy blonde angel who ignored his crude language and answered his surliness with genuine consideration, whose mere presence could make him forget that someone had blown a hole in his arse.

And what kind of man would it take to . . . His eyes widened at the unholy bend of his thoughts. He didn't want to ravish her! Didn't want to touch her or hold her or talk with her, didn't want anything to do with her at all! He just wanted to survive long enough to get out of this crazy place and get back to London, back to his comfortable house and his offices and his companies, and back to an uncomplicated bit of pleasure.

His mind raced. His mistress, Fanny; he hadn't seen her in four, five — no, *six* weeks! That prolonged period of abstinence, coupled with the physical pain and mental duress of his injuries, was probably enough to explain his bizarre reaction to the girl. A wave of bone-melting relief went through him. This Charity Standing was an extraordinarily fetching young thing, and a disturbingly powerful combination of guilelessness and sensuality. It was probably understandable, in his weakened, deprived state, that he'd been roused by the close personal contact he'd had with her. To think of it in such logical terms had a calming effect on him.

He took a deep, settling breath and vowed that when he got back to London, he'd pay Fanny a long visit to work this wretched steam out of his blood. Until then, he'd have to find a way to keep the very disturbing Miss Standing, with her tantalizing marble skin and her seductive charitable impulses, at bay!

Chapter Seven

Old Melwin found the viscount in a foul mood indeed when he carried up his evening tray of tea and broth. The April sun had streamed in through the south window all afternoon, heating the closed room drastically. Since he was in no condition to leave his bed and had no means of calling for assistance, Austen had suffered in silence, unable to sleep and growing damp and itchy against the sheets.

The old butler scowled at the stuffy condition of the room as he deposited the draped tray on the table by the bed. "Beggin' yer pardon, but do ye think it seems a mite warm in here, yer lordship?"

"Warm? Lord, no. Not for a bloody oven!" Rane snapped. "I thought the entire idea was to roast me to a turn and have me for supper!"

Melwin's chin drew back sharply and his eyes narrowed on the sweaty nobleman. He shuffled over to the window to throw it open wide. Cool air flowed into the room around him and he carried a draft of it back to the bed with him as he returned to the tray.

Rane wiped his damp, tousled hair back from his face and, propping himself up on his elbows, watched the old fellow pour tea and lift the cover on a steaming bowl of beefy-smelling soup. He was starving! With an intent scowl, the old butler picked up a broad spoon, filled it with soup, and ferried it toward Rane's mouth, his other hand cupped under it to catch any drips.

"What in bloody hell do you think you're doing?" Rane pulled back, staring at Melwin.

"Feedin' yer lordship. Mistress's orders. Ye'll have to open up, sir." Melwin was concentrating fiercely on the spoon in his gnarled hands and so missed Rane's incredulous expression.

"Like hell you will!" Rane coiled back further and clamped his mouth shut in defiance.

"M'lady's busy wi' yer feller down the hall an' Miz Charity . . . she's . . . busy helpin'. So it's me stuck wi—Open up, m'lord." Melwin's bent posture was giving him a crook in his lower back. And when he had a crook in his back, Melwin was not a man to trifle with. "Wi' all respect, m'lord, open yer yap!"

"No!" Rane's tightly pursed lips scarcely moved. "I'll feed myself, dammit."

Aging brown eyes met steely gray gaze over the spoonful of broth, and for a long moment, neither blinked or budged. Then Melwin's face drew up like a withered prune. He straightened his aching spine and glowered at his uncooperative charge. "As ye say yer lordship. Feed yerself."

"Splendid. Excellent. I shall be more than happy to do for myself. If you will just place the tray here." Rane smacked the feather pillows at his head with an authoritative hand.

The tray was plopped on the pillows in front of Rane and the old butler lurched out, muttering to himself. When the door closed, Rane took a deep breath of satisfaction, having finally won a contest of wills in this crazy place—even if it had been with only the crusty old butler.

It was clear beef soup, piping hot, a whole beautiful dish of it. He removed the lid on the tea pot and inhaled the vapors. A whole, generous pot of steaming tea. His mouth watered violently and he snatched up the spoon and shoveled some into his mouth, then had to swallow the blistering stuff fast and suck in air to cool his half-burnt tongue. Dammit! His entire throat was now aflame and there was nothing on the tray to cool it with. Even in the best of houses, food got cold and tea got tepid on its way from the kitchens. Why did the one thing they got right in this place have to be keeping food *hot?!*

A moment later, drawn by the warmth radiating from the open window, a bird flew into the room, lost its way out again, and promptly panicked. Rane heard the flapping and scraping about the ceiling and whipped his head around, craning his neck and searching for the source of it.

A small, gray and brown sparrow was flapping and bumping against the ceiling and swooping from corner to corner, only to bump and scramble again. It was a pathetic sight, and one that touched sympathetic nerves in Rane, who was feeling quite trapped himself just now. He wrestled up onto his left elbow, watching the creature and ignoring the slow slide and slosh of the hot liquids on his tray.

"There's the window," he waved his arm toward the opening. "Over there," he waved, dodging the bird as it flew under the bed canopy, flapping until it had blundered its way out of the bed only to soar for the corner of the ceiling again. "Over there, bird-wit!" he called, waving, and wincing as the poor thing again bashed into the wall. "There's the window."

He didn't realize his rolling weight was tilting the bed and that the tray was sliding, headed straight for him. When he caught the motion from the corner of his eye and reacted, it was already too late. The edge of the tray hit his chest, the hot consommé spilled, and the teapot toppled, roiling straight at him. The hot soup and scalding tea hit his chest in a burning wave and poured down his front.

"YYEEEOOOOWW!!"

Charity heard his howl from across the hall, where she was sitting with the still sedated Stephenson and working on her mending. She was on her feet in a flash and running for his room.

She found him pushed up in the bed amidst a sea of upset dishes, hot soup, and soaked linen. He was clawing at the steaming front of his shirt, which was plastered to his chest and belly.

"Oh — ohhhmygod — I'm scalded!"

"Heaven!" She was around the bed in a wink. What had happened was all too clear. She quickly shoved the jumble of dishes back onto the puddled tray and set it off onto the floor nearby. When she turned back, he was pulling the wet fabric out from his skin, fanning it. Her purest helping instincts took over.

"It was that bird . . . A blasted bird flew in," he tried to explain.

She reached for the shirt, raising and lifting it away from his skin, and he found himself shifting instinctively to allow the long tail of the shirt to slide up and over his body.

"It got trapped and was swooping and banging into things."

"Here — take your arms out," she ordered. He did as he was bade, one arm after the other, understanding that she was pulling the garment from him so it wouldn't hold heat against the burn.

"Then it got trapped in the bloody bed and I turned and tried to wave it toward the window," he paused briefly as she pulled the shirt over his head, then dropped it onto the floor by the bed. She hurried across the room to the washstand and a bit of toweling with cool water as he continued, "The damned thing kept bashing into the ceiling, and then I saw the tray start to slide and tried to stop it — the damnable tea was boiling hot — What the hell was it doing boiling hot?!!"

"I believe that's the way tea is made, your lordship, by boiling . . ." She hurried back with the cold cloth and pressed it against his reddened chest. He raised further up on his arms to allow her access and she settled her bottom on the edge of the bed to have both hands free. Her slender hands molded the cloth to his muscular chest. His eyes closed as the cool cloth drew the blistering heat from his skin.

"God, that feels good."

Those suggestive words were no sooner out of his mouth than he froze. Her hands stilled on his chest and a heartbeat later, his eyes opened, straight into hers. There they sat, inches apart, touching, staring into each others' faces.

The reality of their unthinkable position was slowly dawning on both of them. He had just allowed her to strip his only garment from his shoulders and now he was lying stark naked before her, with only a sheet draped precariously over his bottom half, offering his bare chest and belly to her. She had just stripped the last of his clothes from his back and was sitting on a bed, inches away from his bare, bronzed body, rubbing his hot, naked chest with her cool hands to soothe him.

Her hands stilled, fingers splayed over his thudding heart. She couldn't move. He was so warm and hard and powerful, so different from anyone she'd ever known. Night after night, she'd lain in her bed, letting her imagination wander over his broad back and wondering . . . about his front. It was every bit as marvelous. Ridges of muscles crossed his shoulders, ending in sleek caps of muscle which extended over the tops of his arms. His chest bore taut mounds of smooth, bronzed muscle, flat nipples that were shockingly similar to hers, and a light furring of black hair that trickled down to his waist . . . and kept going. Of their own will, her fingers abandoned the cloth to move again over that broad, fascinating expanse, exploring as

117

much as comforting.

His big hand came up to feather hard fingers over her heat-polished cheek. She was so cool and soft and smooth. As her touch drifted further over his burning body, his hand ranged wider over her as well, caressing her silky lips, her slender throat, her pale, inviting shoulders. His touches drifted down her perfect marble skin to the tops of the maddening mounds curving above the rim of her bodice. He let his fingertips linger over the erotic crevice between them.

He feared that at any minute she would pull away from the overpowering intimacy of his eyes and his touch.

But she stayed, touching him still.

And he stayed, wanting that touch, needing it somehow.

"It just proves the rule," she murmured, wandering lost in the silvery lights of his eyes.

"What rule?" he asked, immersed totally in the sweet liquid warmth of her.

"Birds in houses are bad luck." She swallowed hard. He was touching her with his *hand*. Was her skin catching fire? A delicious, icy-hot shiver ran up her spine. Was he bending closer?

"I don't believe in luck."

"What do you believe in?" Her gaze slid to his expressive lips to watch them answer. Her whole body was warming, growing pliant under his hand.

"Hard work. Hard money. Hard bargaining. And—" He had almost said, "hard loving." But hard-driving passion wasn't what he wanted just now. He was being consumed by an urge for something altogether different, something new, something . . . tender. He wanted to savor both her and the swirling heat she'd generated in his body with her curious fingers. "And soft skin," he declared too candidly. His thumb came up to trace the outline of her jaw. "I believe in soft skin."

118

Charity couldn't swallow, couldn't breathe. He was talking about her skin; she could see it in his eyes, and could feel it in the womanly depths of her body. He liked the softness of her skin . . . the way she liked the hardness of him . . .

"Merciful Lord!" came a strangled voice from the open doorway. Lady Margaret swayed, ashen-faced, her hands clutching her throat and bosom. Charity and her moon-hexed viscount were nose-to-nose on the bed, him naked as the Almighty made him, and her with her hands all over the Almighty's creation!

In a blink, Charity started back, ripping her hands from his chest, and Rane jerked away and sank to the bed, hauling the sheet up over him. She shoved to her feet, beet-red and stammering, and he flushed fiery crimson and barked out an explanation. The bird in the room . . . the hot tray . . . she had just been trying to help . . .

Lady Margaret stood listening to their jumbled story, trying to decide what to do. It was plain as a parson's daughter that they were telling the truth. And it was plainer still that her little talk with Charity had probably done more harm than good. She harumphed and snorted indignation and ordered Charity to wait downstairs for her.

Charity bit her lip and nodded, feeling utterly humiliated and avoiding Rane's eyes. He didn't notice; he was too busy avoiding her gaze and trying to frame some defense of his vile, ungentlemanly exposure of himself to the delectable young girl he'd sworn to avoid only a short while before. So much for logical defenses, manly determination, and self-control!

When Charity was gone, the old woman turned on him. But instead of the scathing denunciation he expected, she just stared at him with unnerving intensity, searching him with snapping brown eyes.

"Take a lesson, your lordship. You're the unluckiest

119

lump of human flesh I've ever seen. And if you expect to live to use that arse of yours again, you'll keep a healthy distance from my granddaughter." She paused and her voice lowered. "I'll not have your blood on her head." With that cryptic threat, the old woman turned and left, banging the door soundly behind her.

Below in the kitchen, Lady Margaret ordered Melwin to ferry up the trunk that had just arrived from the inn and clothe the fellow decently, and to carry his lordship yet another tray. Bernadette resurrected her consommé and brewed another pot of tea. When old Melwin had returned to carry the food upstairs and Bernadette had gone to see to clean linens for his lordship's bed, Lady Margaret settled a troubled look on Charity.

"I'm sorry, Gran'mere." Charity interpreted the look as a censure of her behavior. "It was the truth . . . he did burn himself and I only tried to help." Even as she said it, she knew there was more, much more. But did one have to confess to things like excitement and pleasure and fascination?

"You've been raised decently, Charity Ann Standing. And I'll not have you forgetting your morals and manners and flaunting yourself. He's a titled man, used to London standards and proper ladies. I've told you what he'll think. Now you've gone and seen him naked—"

"Not completely, Gran'mere," she protested, red-faced.

"Well that's a mercy," the old lady muttered, reddening a bit herself. "Look, child." She took Charity's hands in hers. "No good will come of touching him, or watching him, or thinking about him. He's the blamed unluckiest man I've ever seen. And he's double unlucky for you."

Unlucky. Gran'mere was right, Charity realized. His lordship did show an alarming propensity for disaster. His cracked head, his gunshot wound, his fall from the bed . . . And now he'd gone and scalded himself!

A moment later her face warmed in the sunniest, happiest smile Lady Margaret had seen from her in years. The old lady's heart sank when Charity gave her a kiss on the cheek and said stubbornly, "Then I'll just have to share some of my luck with him!"

Well into the night, when the coals in the great stone hearth had been banked and most of the candles in the house damped, there came a scratching at the weathered kitchen door of Standwell. When Bernadette roused to answer it, two dark forms slipped hurriedly inside the door and shushed her gasp of surprise.

"Go for m'lady, Bernadette," Percy Hall begged. "And hurry."

Lady Margaret appeared shortly, garbed in her bed-cap and muslin wrapper, to find the two huddled near the kitchen door, looking disheveled and dispirited. She held her candlestick aloft and squinted to get a better look. Their clothes were rumpled and their chins sported several days' growth of beard.

"Where in hell's backwater have you two been?" she demanded. "I've been lookin' all over for you. I've got a sick nobleman upstairs I need help with."

"We been hidin' out," Percy rasped.

"On the moors," Gar added dolefully.

"Merciful Lord, you're chilled to the bone! Sit down before you fall down." She waved them to the table and benches along the wall. "Bernadette, warm them some wine." Soon she was demanding, and getting, the story of where they'd been and why.

"We shot a feller," Gar announced dismally. "Didn't mean to . . ." He saw Lady Margaret's jaw loosen and her eyes widen and he hurried to add, "I tried to miss 'im, I swear! It were some fancy London cove—"

"Come to collect that last shipment of brandy what the squire sold 'im," Percy took it up. "We told him

121

there weren't no more brandy an' he pulled a pistol an' got right nasty, so we figured to give 'im a good scare." He looked at Gar and both nodded in earnest.

"You shot a London fellow?" Lady Margaret grabbed their arms across the table and demanded, "Where?"

"In Rowden Woods, where we knowed he'd come thru—"

"No! I mean, where did you *hit* him?"

Percy pulled in his chin and glanced irritably at Gar. "Gar hit 'im low somewheres. That's all we know. We heard horses comin' and we scrammed, quick."

They watched Lady Margaret pale, push up from the table, and begin to pace, wringing her hands. "It's come to this. I knew it. I told Upton it was pure fool-ishness, smuggling in brandy. He wouldn't listen, wouldn't hear a word." They looked at each other and frowned. She stopped a moment later and turned on them. "He's here."

"Who's here?" Percy scowled, confused.

"Your fancy London cove. He's here, in this house. Baron Pinnow found him on the road and carried him here. I've been looking for you all day to come and tend his lordship." She stopped stock still, staring into space, her eyes searching something only she could see.

"Lord, we cain't tend 'im. We *shot* im! It's Miz Charity's luck is what it is," Gar whispered miserably. "I went and fell in th' grave and then I went an' shot a feller." He stared at Percy with fresh horror. "A noble-man, Perc! I shot a *lordship!* I'm doomed fer sure!"

For once, Lady Margaret was inclined to agree with Gar's gloomy predictions. The entire situation smacked of her granddaughter's calamitous influence. And expe-rience had shown that once such events were set in motion, there was nothing to do but ride them out, countering Charity's "luck" wherever possible.

Her eyes rolled toward the ceiling and the second floor chamber where the Viscount Oxley lay, an unwitting victim of Charity's jinx. There was little doubt in her mind that he was well on the way to becoming a victim of her charms, as well.

Later, as the moon was rising, Gar and Percy slipped from the house and into the shadows once more. Lady Margaret watched the growing crescent of the moon, reading in it the waxing passions of a pair of moon-crossed lovers. She feared it could only end in heart-break. She drew a deep, unhappy breath and enlisted what help she could to keep them apart. She stuck her head out the kitchen door and called softly, "Wolfram? You wretched piece of flea-bait, where in blazes are you?!"

The upstairs hallway was lit by a single candle held high in Lady Margaret's hand as she moved down the west hallway toward the viscount's room. The only sound was the old lady's hoarse whisper as she spoke to the massive wolfhound stalking by her side.

"Get it right, you hear?" she demanded, glaring at the dog.

He glared back, pulling in his hall-runner of a tongue and looking rather miffed at her disparaging tone.

"Get in there, *under* his bed, and *stay*. And if Charity comes, or if he tries to leave the room, you bark like a fiend. Is that clear?" He made a huffing sound that in a human would have been pure indignation.

"All right, then, go," Lady Margaret's voice lowered to a bare whisper as she opened the door and pointed at the bottom of the bed. "Go on. Under the bed." She pointed irritably and, after a moment's hesitation, the huge beast slunk into the darkened room and began to claw and stuff himself under the bed. The door closed softly and quiet again descended.

Wolfram lay in the blackness, smelling Rane Austen's

foreign scent and listening, and feeling cramped. In his canine mind came fond visions of the soft bit of old rug by the door in Miss Charity's room. *No. Under. Stay.* He took a deep, resigned breath and stopped halfway through. *Food?* His head came up and banged against the bottom of the bed. *Food! Where?* He pushed his big wet nose against the sagging bed above him and sniffed. No, it was not quite in that direction.

Wolfram followed his nose to a shriveled, meatysmelling ball lying on the floor under the bed. It was a smell he'd know anywhere. Chicken liver! Being a devout carnivore, he picked it up and chewed it off its inedible string. At the very end, just before he swallowed it, he got a wild burst of the bitter herbs and garlic that had apparently been stuffed inside it. He shuddered, but swallowed it anyway.

Having unsuspectingly snacked on one of Lady Margaret's most potent amulets, Wolfram licked his onesided lip and laid his great head down on his paws for a short nap. It wasn't long before Lady Margaret's herbs made themselves felt. The great dog rolled onto his side in his sleep to better accommodate the irritation in his stomach. And as the discomfort grew, it invaded his canine dreams and he reacted to it in both worlds, waking and sleeping.

Rane wakened with a start in the inky blackness of his bed. His heart was racing, and his mind was scrambling to keep up with it. Something had wakened him, some noise, something . . . There it came again. A groan, an unearthly, disembodied sound that seemed to be coming from the confines of his bed itself. He stiffened all over, muscle by muscle, tendon by tendon, developing rigor mortis from night-spawned anxiety.

For a brief moment, in the quiet, he listened to the familiar pounding of his own heart and told himself he had imagined it. But then came a low, hair-raising snarl and another of those grisly, death-like groans. He wasn't imagining that! He felt a bump against the bottom of his bed and pushed up on his arms, eyes wide, blood pumping furiously. Panting rasped the air around him, a dark, grating sound, a hungry, desirous, fiendish sort of sound. In his ears it grew louder as it continued. The bed jolted again and he twisted around, looking over his shoulder. The amulets hanging from the canopy moving in the dim light. Jiggling, wriggling, like spiders . . .

Suddenly the air was alive with the memory of Caribbean night sounds and with the dark dangers of his tropical boyhood. Panting and scratchings . . . things wriggling in the dark . . . Suddenly the amulets about his neck seemed to be weighing him down, tightening, strangling. He had to get up, get out of there!

His heart pounding in his head and his wits beguiled by recent dreams and strange perceptions, he slid to the edge of the bed and stuck his legs over the edge. Ignoring the painful pulling sensation in his rear, he stiffly lowered himself over the edge of the bed so that his feet hit the floor. Then he pushed up with his arms and managed to stand and straighten. Blood rushed from his head and he swayed and clutched at the bed drapes to stay upright.

The groaning and panting became an earnest growling and clawing and scraping. One instant it seemed far away and the next, it seemed to be coming from all around him, closing in on him!

He staggered back dizzily and stepped smack in the middle of the dishes on the spilled tray Charity had placed on the floor earlier. The delicate china splintered under his weight and he howled, jerking his foot up and lurching wildly as he grabbed at it. His half-healed buttock felt like it was ripping apart as he hopped and blundered about, bent over and unable to straighten. Blood surged back into his head and he gasped and reeled, bashing headfirst into the stout bedpost.

As he fell, he managed to twist so that he landed on his front, but then something pounced on his back. It was the bloody fiend, come to get him, and suddenly there were great, banging roars, like claps of doomsday thunder.

"Rrolf! *Rrrolff! RRROOLF!!!*" Wolfram had risen to his duty, despite his attack of indigestion, and now had his man pinned safely to the floor. He stood on Rane's shock-frozen shoulders, barking ferociously, daring him to move so much as a finger.

Charity came running in her bare feet, her nightdress billowing and her unbound hair flying like a pale banner behind her. Wolfram's barks were so frantic, she hadn't bothered with a candle or a robe. She burst through the door and into the viscount's moonlit room to find the massive dog standing on his lordship's back and barking to rouse the devil himself.

"Wolfram!" she bolted forward and grabbed the great beast by the neck, struggling to pull him away from his prisoner. "Wolfie — stop it! Wolfram! What in heaven's name are you doing in here?! How did you get into the house?" He quieted and she wrestled him to the door and finally succeeded in pushing him out into the hall. "If you've hurt his lordship, I'll never forgive you! Now *stay!*"

Wolfram whine-growled and thumped down onto the floor in a sulk, watching as she hurried back to Rane's sprawled form on the floor. He was raising his head, shaking it, and trying to make sense of his surroundings. His head hurt like the devil, pains were stabbing up his left leg from his foot, and he was having mad illusions of Charity Standing again. She seemed to be there, beside him, glowing palely in the moonlight, and asking him if he was alright.

"Oh, god," he moaned. "I think I'm dead."

"No, you're not." She knelt beside him, her cool fingers stroked the side of his face anxiously. "I'm so sorry about Wolfie. He didn't mean any harm, really. Wait—don't move! I'll light a candle."

She came back to him in a golden halo of light and set the candlestand on the floor nearby. "Can you tell where you're hurt? It's not your *hands*, is it?"

"No," he flexed them, finding them operational, and she let out a breath of pure relief.

"Then is it your . . . your . . ."

"Arse?" he finished for her again. He sent a hand back to explore that territory through his voluminous shirt and it came back unbloodied. "I think that survived. It's my foot." He sucked in an anguished breath. "I must have stepped on something."

"I'll have a look." She started for his feet, but he grabbed a handful of her night dress.

"No!" He was suddenly burning with fresh humiliation. In the light everything had become sane again. In the doorway he could see the beast that had attacked him. It was a dog. A massive beast of a dog that looked like a compilation of numerous nasty nightmares, but still, just a dog. And demure little Charity Standing had hauled it off him single-handedly, and had even apologized to him for it!

"No! Really, perhaps if you could just help me to the bed . . ." He suddenly realized that he held her by her thin night garment and that she didn't seem to be wearing anything beneath it. Good Lord—it was happening again! He was in an unthinkably compromising position with her, and the thudding in his head and the spearing pains in his foot were subsiding, dissolving in the warmth of her presence, as they always did. He released her abruptly. "If you'll please just fetch someone else . . . anyone else."

"Let me look at your foot first." She settled the candles on the floor and lifted his foot into her lap. Of their own will his toes seemed to snuggle against the soft heat of her belly and thinly-clad thighs. She felt that suggestive motion all through her. "You've a nasty cut here." She raised dark, topaz-clear eyes to him. "I'm afraid it may need stitching." As she pressed the cut with one hand, the other drifted in a reassuring caress over his square toes, up his high arch, and around his ankle.

Suddenly the pain in his body was entirely gone and his senses were opening wide to her. He couldn't seem to stop it.

Mesmerized, she let her fingers drift higher onto his muscular calf, exploring the gentle raspiness of the hair on his leg. Bit by bit, she was coming to know all of him — thanks to his penchant for disaster. She spoke her unthinkable thoughts aloud.

"You're so brown, and so hard. You're so wonderfully hard all over."

He was turned half onto his side and he watched her eyes traveling shyly up his bare leg, up his shirt-clad thigh and hip, and up his chest. Other women had commented on the shade of his skin, and every one of them, even his mistress, had considered it a flaw, something to be excused. But Charity spoke of it with a sense of wonder, making it seem interesting, desirable. He tightened, realizing that it was a mark of her innocence that she considered it so.

As she sat there, in the candlelight, her honey-golden hair swirling around her and her nightdress slipping off one shoulder, holding his hurt foot in her lap, she seemed the most genuine and appealing creature God ever put on earth. Out of nowhere came a towering urge to collect that precious innocence against him, to hold it and protect it . . . against even the rising call of his own desire.

"Charity, you shouldn't touch me like this." He couldn't help the rasp of desire in his voice or the way his eyes were beginning to shimmer with sensual heat. But he could end the delicious torture her fingers were inflicting. He had to. He summoned the scraps of his tattered gallantry and tried to drag his injured foot from her lap. She wouldn't let it go.

"How did you get so . . . hard all over?" she asked, too intent on the delicious excitement curling through her to realize just how shocking her secret curiosity sounded, or how erotic. She lifted her jewel-clear eyes and the only way Rane could handle the rush of fire through his veins was to rechannel the heat into the irritation that could protect them both.

"I worked," he tightened visibly and struggled to produce a forbidding scowl and a sardonic tone. "I worked like a common laborer, shirtless, on my father's sugar plantation on Barbados. That's where I grew up. Barbados. In the hot sun, among the savages . . ."

He said it challengingly, as if to shock her. And beneath his resurgence of ill temper, Charity glimpsed a flicker of pain that had nothing to do with his fall or his foot. His boyhood, his tanned skin, the hard work that had made his body hard . . . he spoke as if . . . It washed over her in a warm wave of understanding. He was ashamed of them. And he obviously expected her to be shocked by them. For a moment she watched his hot eyes narrow and his chin rise defensively. She saw clearly that his rash temper and caustic tongue were his prime defenses against the scorn he expected, and against his own shame.

"I've heard Barbados is . . . very beautiful in the mountains." Her stubborn, accepting smile melted gaping holes in his irritation. "And I suppose that's where you learned to believe in 'hard work.' "

Rane stared at her, feeling the moorings of his lifelong defenses being eroded from beneath him by the relentless tide of her acceptance. "How the hell do you know Barbados has mountains?!"

"I've read about it." Her voice dropped to a husky caress. "It sounds wonderful."

129

"It's a hellhole." He tugged at his foot again, and found it still trapped against her. "Like living in pure steam. The wretched sun always blazing, burning everything in sight. Nothing except cane will grow there—"

"That's not true," she argued gently, pulling his shimmering eyes into hers. "You grew there. You grew to be strong and hard . . . and handsome. . . ."

He pushed up onto his arms, staring at her, feeling her admiration storm through his chilled heart and blow through his vulnerable body. Handsome. It flashed through him like a lightning bolt. Lord, she really liked his oversized body and his sun-browned skin.

"Merciful Heaven!"

They started and looked up to find Lady Margaret standing in the doorway, staring at them in full horror. Charity blushed furiously and Rane sputtered and shifted to try to cover a bit more of himself with his long shirt tail. How much had she seen? Heard?

Enough. The old woman had witnessed the charged visual flow between the pair. She had seen the viscount gallantly refuse to take advantage of Charity's innocence, and had seen Charity's patient refusal to be put off by either his inelegant background or his irritable bluster. She wished with all her heart it hadn't happened.

"This is unthinkable!" She charged in. "How dare you, your lordship?! Charity, I ordered you specifically—"

"Yes, Gran'mere, I know!" She jumped to her feet and faced the old woman squarely. "But Wolfie got into the house somehow and was about to eat his lordship alive. I couldn't let that happen, could I? And then he cut his foot when he got out of bed, and I was just seeing to it. It's a bad cut. . . ."

While she was explaining, standing before the candles

which were still on the floor behind her, her body was outlined in tantalizingly explicit silhouette against her thin muslin gown. Full breasts, a gently curved waist, and a deliciously rounded bottom atop sleekly tapered legs . . . The beleaguered bounds of Rane's passions dissolved somewhere with the borders of that voluptuous outline . . . dark on light. His loins caught fire and he couldn't have pulled his eyes away to save his life. To make matters worse, Lady Margaret was also witnessing the sight . . . and his instinctively lusty reaction to it. She pulled Charity out of the way and glared at him.

"You're going straight back into bed, your lordship! And first thing tomorrow morning, I'll send for one of the baron's men to come and tend to you. The sooner you're healed and out of this house, the better!"

In a flash, the old woman had him by the arm and was tugging. As they struggled up, Charity flew to Rane's other arm and draped it over her shoulders to help. Lady Margaret stopped dead, glaring fiercely at Charity across Rane's crumpled form.

"Let go!" she demanded.

For the first time in her life, Charity looked her grandmother in the eye and said quietly, "No."

They put him to bed and tended his cut foot in tense, volatile silence. When the door closed behind them, Lady Margaret turned to her granddaughter with a hot spark in her eye and on her tongue. Charity met that look with an equally fiery one. For a long time they stared at each other, both realizing the extent of the changes occurring between them and around them.

"You don't need to send for the baron's man, Gran'mere. I'll take care of his lordship."

Her grandmother scowled and glared, but in the end, remained silent. Charity took one lighted taper from the candlestand to see her to her room, handing the rest to her grandmother. She was halfway down the hall, and well out of hearing, before the old lady whispered, "Oh, but child . . . Who will take care of you?"

Chapter Eight

The next morning old Melwin brought the viscount a breakfast of thin porridge, milk, and plain tea. After another stubborn confrontation, he allowed the viscount to feed himself . . . or to not feed himself. His lordship didn't seem to think much of Lady Margaret's choice of menu.

By the time Charity appeared with a large kettle of hot water for his bath, Rane was starving and itchy and in no mood to see anybody, much less her, with her unnerving presence and determined helpfulness. He'd just spent a very confusing and very miserable night, wrestling his physical passions to a standstill and scourging himself mentally for letting things get so shockingly physical and personal between them. Never mind that she didn't seem to mind; she was an innocent. But he certainly knew better. He was in no mood to be reminded of her unthinkable impact on him, or to feel that deep, insatiable stirring inside him that seemed to involve more than just his blood and sinews. Again, surliness became his refuge.

"I'll bathe myself!" he declared irritably. "Just put the damned basin here on the bed between these pillows, and I'll do for myself!"

She did as he had so ungallantly asked, then stood there, her eyes warm and unannoyed. Would he like Melwin to come back up to help him shave? His refusal was a bit less gracious than her offer. Would he like more goose-grease salve for his burn? He glowered and declared it didn't hurt anymore, which wasn't entirely true. She offered to check the bandage on his foot and

133

he gripped the sheets tighter under his chin as though daring her to touch him. She stood looking at him for a long moment, making him feel vulnerable and ashamed of both his urges and his foul humor. Why did she have to be so blasted even-tempered and helpful, so desirable?

"Is there anything else I can get you?" she asked as she carried his shaving things to the bed.

"Some decent food," he announced testily. "A fat beefsteak or boiled fowl with oyster sauce, or a reasonable ragoût of veal."

"Oh, I'm afraid not. Today is strictly sops; Gran'mere is quite adamant about it. Your stomach has to have time to adjust."

"My stomach won't survive long enough to adjust unless I get some decent food! Salmon, trout, or sole, or a fricand of veal with a rais'd giblet pie . . ." She shook her head.

"Then a vegetable pudding and some larded sweetbreads!" More head shaking, and a bit lip that seemed to be forbidding a smile.

"At least a cottage pie and buttered peas and macaroni," his mouth was now watering violently, "or an open tart syllabub or berry cobbler—or just some damned jam on bread!" Still nothing.

He was mildly shocked to realize that his curvy blonde angel seemed to have the same unholy stubborn streak as her dotty old grandmother. In desperation, he resorted to demanding what he really wanted . . . since he wasn't likely to get it anyway.

"Alright then, fruit! Bananas—I have to have bananas!"

"I've never seen bananas," she observed calmly, fighting the twitching at the corners of her mouth and losing. "Do you think they would qualify as sops?" He made a growling sound, low in his throat, that was the essence of frustration.

In the hallway she paused, scowling, her helpful urges

134

burning with frustration. His surliness was especially troubling after what had passed between them in his room last night: she knew he didn't always act so difficult. Then her insight of last night came back to her; he acted this way to defend himself. But why would he think he had to defend himself against her? She was trying to help him, to share her luck with him. She blushed. Well, there was perhaps a little more involved.

On her way downstairs, she happened upon Wolfram sprawled across the top of the stairs, still pouting from last night's scolding. She stooped to pet him and make up with him, and in the process had a wonderful idea. "Come with me, Wolfie."

She retraced her steps down the hall to the viscount's room and pressed her finger against her lip as she faced the great beast. "Shhhhh. I want you to go in and lie by the foot of his bed, and if he needs help of any kind, you come straight for me. Understand?"

Wolfram stuck out his chest and his lone ear came to attention. He took on a very serious and trustworthy look. He'd do anything for Miss Charity.

She opened the door and pressed her finger to her lips in a "shhh" and he skulked quietly inside and across the chamber to lie at the foot of the bed. Boredom soon set in and the dog began sniffing the air and sorting out the scents around him.

Porridge. The one his humans called "lordship" had had porridge to eat. He sniffed again. *And milk.* He licked his one sided lip and briefly considered nosing about to see if they'd left any dishes setting about. But experience had shown that Melwin seldom left anything lying about. Then came the faint smells of the freshly used "necessary," from under the bed. That wasn't terribly interesting. He yawned silently. He'd smelled a few chamberpots in his time, and if you'd smelled one, you'd smelled them all. There was a trace of a noxious odor that might have been from a bloody bandage . . . *Phew!*

Then suddenly all other smells were obliterated by great rolling billows of some woody, sweet smell that was utterly tantalizing. And it was coming from the fellow himself. He had to find the source of that delicious smell!

Rane was braced gingerly on his elbows beside the basin of warm water that was propped between pillows. In one hand was the remains of his shaving mirror, which had been broken in the carriage crash, and in the other was his unstropped razor. His face was lathered generously with sandalwood-scented soap, and he was endeavoring to scrape the dark growth from his face while keeping a wary eye on the basin of water. Then he lifted his head and shifted the mirror to view his right side better as he drew the razor along his jawline.

A huge, shaggy monstrosity of an animal head stared back at him from the mirror. Great burning eyes and bared fangs were propped on the bed behind him, a mere chomp away from his own damaged rear, and staring hungrily at him! Rane startled and jerked, scraping and cutting his chin nastily.

"Owwww! Dammit!" He drew back from the hurt and lurched onto his far side to escape, bringing his elbow and his weight down on the side of the basin, flipping it up and emptying it all over him. Rane found himself bleeding from the chin, soaked to the skin, lying on a soggy mattress, and eye to eye with the deranged, mangy-looking wolf-beast that had attacked him in the night.

"B'dammit!"

Wolfram took off at a dead run.

The aged mattress was thoroughly soaked and for all purposes, ruined. Lacking any other chamber that was fully furnished and generally habitable, they had to move the unlucky viscount across the east hallway and

136

into the room that had been Upton Standing's . . . directly across the hall from Charity's room. Melwin brought his trunk and helped him change into a dry shirt again, then left to fetch Lady Margaret, who would see to the cut on his face.

In the brief solitude, Rane found himself lying in a stately, aged bed in a large bedchamber with papered walls and a ceiling decorated with once-elegant plaster reliefs of grapes and leaves. The bed and the chamber's two long windows were draped with faded crimson brocades, and the furnishings and rugs bespoke the bygone grace of the Queen Anne period. The chamber was a ghost of its former elegance, and somehow it seemed perfectly fitting that he should be there; he felt like a ghost of his former self, too.

Soap was drying on his face in streaks, his black hair was in wild disarray, there were strain-smudges under his eyes. His buttock and cut foot and frequently banged head were all throbbing, his face burned where he'd scraped and cut it, and his chest was still tender from yesterday's scalding. What next?!

He pushed up onto his elbows, rubbing his chest through the shirt and the clutch of amulets beneath it. He was itching—it probably meant his burn was healing. But when itching intensified, he pulled out the open neck of the shirt and swept the amulets aside to have a look. There were raised, rashy patches across his reddened skin.

A rash. He was getting a bloody rash!!

Just then Lady Margaret and Charity appeared to see to the cut on his face. His dark scowl and humped posture warned them of renewed resistance.

"Don't you come near me, either of you!" he ordered, holding up a hand to halt them. "And no more of your bloody wretched 'cures.' One of your damnable 'healing powers' has given me a rash!"

"Where?" Lady Margaret started and hurried forward,

137

reaching for the neck of his shirt. "Let me see." He huddled back furiously, but after a visual tug-of-war, he surrendered and allowed her access to his itchy, burn-tender chest. She scrutinized the rash and began to shake her head.

"It's the ferret feet," she sighed. "Some folks just can't tolerate them . . . get a rash all over. We'll have to switch to rabbit — they're not as powerful, but —"

"The hell we will!" Rane snatched the neck of his shirt together and vibrated with indignation. "We'll not switch to anything! In fact," he began clawing and tugging at the amulets about his neck, pulling them off in bunches, "I'm getting rid of the lot of them! No more, do you hear?! There isn't any damned thing such as *luck*. I'll get better as a rational man or —"

"Or not at all!" Lady Margaret warned, coming nose to nose with the jinxed nobleman. "If you take them off, you may not get well at all!"

"Then at least I'll *die* a rational man!" he shouted, pulling the last talisman over his head and shoving it into her outraged hands.

Lady Margaret staggered back, gasping and clasping the rejected charms to her breast. Apparently the viscount hadn't learned much from his recent brushes with disaster. He was really in for it now! She straightened and made an impassioned gypsy sign in the air, glaring at him.

"I bet you were born on a *Friday!*" Lady Margaret snapped. "You're the blamed unluckiest man I've ever seen!"

Rane's eyes followed her narrowly as she bustled out, then closed in an attempt at self-control. Ferret feet. He'd been wearing a *dead ferret's feet!*

A soft rustling and the quiet fall of steps about the room began to register in his mind. It was Charity Standing. He somehow knew the sound of her movement, and he could feel her presence in the peculiar warming of his skin that always occurred when she came near. He groaned silently. He didn't want to have to see her, to confront her perfection, not in his present chaotic state. When he finally opened his eyes, he found her standing by the bed with her slender hands folded patiently before her. Beside her, on the night table, was a basin of water and toweling and shaving articles.

"What are you doing here?"

"I'm going to tend to your cut, then help you bathe and shave," she declared with quiet determination. And when he drew breath to protest, she did that for him, too. "I know; you're perfectly capable, under normal circumstances. But, I think you'll agree, these aren't normal circumstances. And I'm not sure you can be trusted with liquids again just now." A slow, irresistible smile crept into her lovely features.

Rane felt that strange bit of calm, that unnerving respite from discomfort and frustration, blooming in him again. And this time, looking at her warm, sparkling eyes and softly exquisite features, he found himself wanting it, craving it. He wanted to have her near, wanted to look at her and talk with her.

Charity watched his coiled muscles and tight jaw begin to relax and sighed quietly. She'd been afraid he was going to snap and snarl again. She stooped to investigate the cut on his face and found it already closing. She applied a bit of grainy salve from a jar in the pocket of the long apron she wore. "That wasn't so bad, was it?"

She turned to the basin and wet a washing cloth in the warm water. He drew back with a frown of confusion, feeling his face tingling where her cool fingers had touched it.

"I have it figured out." She picked up the soap and rubbed it over the cloth, then offered the soapy combination to him. "I'll soap and rinse the cloth; you'll do the bathing while I turn my back to give you privacy."

She put the cloth in his wary hands and did exactly that.

Rane lay stunned, looking at the cloth in his hands and then at the delicate determination of her back. He swallowed hard. Her utterly sensible solution made a shambles of his gentlemanly prejudice concerning the dearth of wits in well-born young ladies. He took a deep breath and began to wash himself.

Charity could hear the soft shushing of cloth over skin and smiled to herself. "I'm sorry about your soap."

"My soap?" he paused, then sniffed the cloth, finding it smelled of plain, homemade soap instead of his sandalwood.

"I'm afraid Wolfie ate it." She chewed back a laugh, but her shoulders twitched and betrayed it. "It was the sandalwood scent in it. He has a weakness for sweet-smelling things. If it's any consolation, he's not feeling very good just now."

One corner of Rane's generous mouth quirked up as he imagined the great, ferocious beast brought low by a cake of scented soap. It was the closest he'd come to a smile in two weeks.

"That is the ugliest damned dog I have ever seen in my life."

"He is, isn't he?" Charity's soft laugh escaped. "And worthless as worm's fingers—at least, according to Gran'mere. But he has a very good heart. I pulled him from a drowning sack in the river when he was a puppy and brought him home and tended him. My father always said it would have been kinder to let him drown." Rane's muffled snort indicated he agreed with her father . . . again.

"I'm afraid he's not a very lucky dog. He's always getting hurt somehow. His missing lip on one side—he lost that in a fight with a badger. Then he got his foot stepped on by a rogue horse . . . Took off two of his toes. His ear . . . We're not sure if he got it caught in

140

something or had it bitten off. And every so often he comes home with another hank of hair missing or another slash or scrape, and I have to patch him up, again."

Rane felt a brief, unnerving sense of empathy for the great beast. They seemed to have a common knack for personal calamity, he and old Wolfram.

When he finished soaping as much as he dared, he nudged her elbow and she turned just enough to rinse the cloth in the basin beside her and hand it back to him. The process was repeated twice, and then she handed him the towel, removed her father's razor from its case, and began to strop it with quick, expert flips of her wrist. He watched, surprised, wondering where on earth she learned to sharpen a razor.

Surprise turned to dismay when she turned to lather his face and he realized what she intended. He jerked back. "Oh, no."

"Oh, yes," she said determinedly. Then she eased back. "You needn't worry I'll cut you. I'm experienced at shaving." She stopped short of revealing that part of her experience had been with him . . . as he lay unconscious.

"You—you are?" His frown was diluted by surprise . . . and by the tantalizing contrast of her somber black dress and white marble skin. She was leaning closer with the soapy shaving brush.

"My father broke his arm twice and I had to shave him. I'm really very competent."

"See here, I don't doubt your . . ." He realized he was retreating into a corner with no reasonable way out. And when reason failed, he drew the sheet up under his chin and resorted to propriety. "Miss Charity, I cannot allow you to do this."

"Melwin shakes, Gran'mere is positively dangerous with any sort of blade, and Bernadette, our cook, would faint dead away at the thought of touching a strange man. That leaves just me." She began to swirl the brush

141

over the fascinating plane of his cheek and he grabbed her wrist, looking up into her glowing face.

"But it's not . . . not very . . ."

"Ladylike of me?"

Rane flushed violently in spite of himself and released her hand abruptly. To his agonized delight, she didn't move away.

"Gran'mere has been giving me extended lectures on 'ladyhood' ever since you came. I find it more than a little hypocritical of her, since she's always inveighed against the emptiness of manners just for the sake of manners. And now it seems you're worried about my 'ladyhood' as well." She sighed quietly and a golden glint appeared in her warm, caramel eyes.

"Well, it's easily dealt with," she said in a teasingly sensible tone. "Once you're well and gone, if I should happen to be in London and we should happen to meet on the street, I'll look the other way and you may do the same." A quick, unexpected quiver of pain went through her heart at the thought, causing her to catch her breath. The conviction drained from her voice as she went on. "I'll pretend I've never shaved you or bathed you or tended your . . . person. And you can pretend you've never seen me before, that I'm just another face in the street." She swallowed hard. "All perfectly proper."

He saw the dark flicker in her eyes as she said this and watched the way her lashes lowered briefly. Something in his chest tightened, telling him he could never, from this moment on, pretend he didn't know Charity Standing. For in that moment he knew her utterly. He knew her gentle determination, her compassion for others—even for surly, ungrateful strangers. He knew her gift of healing presence, and her irresistible good sense, put the world and its stilted ways in a very human and very bearable perspective.

"Now." She lifted her chin and dragged her spirits up

142

with it. "Hold very still." She began to ply the shaving brush again, and he allowed it. Soon she was urging him onto his side and settling on the edge of the bed beside him. She tilted his chin up with one finger and deftly plied the razor up his throat and then around his one bristled jaw and over his hard plane of a cheek. When she came to his generous mouth, she paused. "You'll have to stiffen your upper lip . . ." She stretched her upper lip down and pursed her mouth to demonstrate. "Like this."

He complied too well with her request and looked like a prune-mouthed old schoolmaster. The sunny shower of her laughter filled the room and trickled in warm, seductive rivulets through Rane Austen's opened core. He'd never heard a woman laugh like she did, so spontaneously, so contagiously. He was suddenly laughing too, quietly, sheepishly. It had been a long time since he had laughed with anything but a vengeful or sardonic tone.

"I'm sorry," she chewed her lip, trying to sober and hoping she hadn't offended him. He was redfaced, but he seemed to be chuckling. "That wasn't very ladylike of me. I'll try to be better . . . I really will."

She was achingly aware of those beautiful gray eyes settling on her, searching her. She took a nervous breath and color bloomed brighter in her cheeks. Trills of expectation raced up her spine, over her shoulders, and down her creamy breast. Her lips heated unaccountably and her eyes sought his hands, wondering, remembering the feel of them on the skin of her breast.

"I don't think that would be possible," he said quietly. "I don't think you could be any better . . . not even if you tried."

Her lashes lowered in confusion. What did he mean? That she was hopelessly unladylike and unmannerly? Her heart skipped. What else? Humiliation broke over her, washing her from head to toe. She probably should have listened to Gran'mere and kept a proper distance from him.

He lifted her chin and when she looked up he was leaning closer, his bold, beautiful lips parting. Warm and impelling, his hand moved to the nape of her neck, sending shivers back down her spine as he rose on the bed and pulled her closer. An instant later, the sensual suspense she'd lived with since that first day, by the side of the road, was ended. His lips pressed into hers gently, testingly. They were so soft and yet so firm against hers, moist, resilient velvet that slowly turned to sleek, commanding satin as they opened to cover hers fully. His mouth canted across hers and his lips flexed gently in massaging, caressing motions that sent surges of warmth through her cheeks and plunging down her throat into her breasts.

Her head tilted under his and her eyes closed. Her shoulders softened as the wonder of his kiss swirled through her. It was as though the boundaries of her body were melting where his mouth touched hers. She drank in every shade and nuance of position and pressure and texture, thirstily savoring every drop of sensation. Then with vague surprise, she realized the tip of his tongue was tracing her lips, stroking and caressing her. It felt shockingly hot and liquid and sent streams of shivery new pleasure flowing along her nerves and pooling in the sensitive womanly parts of her. Her body was coming to life in a way she'd never imagined.

It was Rane Austen, her handsome stranger, her powerful enigma, her surly, hurting nobleman, who was making this stunning pleasure for her with his mouth. Instinctively she knew that this was only the beginning of what could occur between a man and a woman, between herself and this man. If he could make her feel such deep, physical delight with his mouth, then perhaps he had the powerful *night magic* in his hands.

144

Just at that moment, Lady Margaret was bustling down the east hall with the still queasy Wolfram in tow. "You stick to him like a mustard pilaster," she ordered in a hushed voice, slowing as they neared the door. "And if he starts to touch her, you get yourself between them, even if it means climbing into bed with him! You understand?"

Wolfram's head was lowered, his great shoulders were rounded, and his patchy looking tail was tucked. When he looked up at Lady Margaret, there was a pathetic droop to his eyes that showed a ring of white beneath the great brown orbs. His groaning whine said he understood. *Miz Charity . . . the "lordship" . . . no fight, no bite.*

She straightened and waved the dog toward the room and departed. He whined and lumbered forward, padding through the doorway to find: *the "lordship" chewing Miss Charity!* He streaked frantically across the master bedchamber to protect his mistress.

One minute Charity's bones were melting from the pure splendor of Rane's deepening kiss, and the next she was gasping and struggling against a great, snarling ball of dusty fur and hot breath that had a sandalwood scent. "Wolfram! Stop it! What's gotten into you?!"

She scrambled free and shed the razor from her hands in order to haul the beast from the edge of the bed and give him a sound swat on the nose. "Wolfram, how dare you?" She turned to Rane with love-stung lips and cheeks burning with embarrassment. Having little experience with such things, she attributed the bronzing of his face and the molten silver glow of his eyes to angered heat.

"I'm so sorry," she breathed miserably. For the first time ever, she wished she'd left Wolfram in that drowning sack, too.

Rane couldn't say a word, but his shock had little to

145

do with the dog's unnerving attack. The impact of their growing intimacy and of his impulsive behavior crowded out more mundane considerations . . . like the possibility of being torn apart by a very big and very jealous dog. Looking into her glowing eyes, he could still feel the yielding sweetness of her mouth against his, and he let the delicious tendrils of pleasure he felt curl through him at will. He'd never felt such wholesale stirrings in so many unrelated parts of him before. His lips were burning, his blood was flowing like a thick, molten river, his skin ached, his chest felt tight, his fingers tingled, his loins throbbed . . . It was madness, a delicious, enthralling madness!

When Charity finished scolding Wolfram, Rane roused to consciousness enough to recoil a bit when she led the beast to the edge of the bed. But despite the glare on Wolfram's battered face, he lifted one massive paw and flopped it sulkily onto the edge of the bed.

"He's trying to say he's sorry," Charity interpreted. "And he won't do it again," she narrowed one eye meaningfully at the dog, *"ever."* Wolfram tucked his chin in a flaming pout and made a huffing noise. "And he wants to shake hands and be friends."

Rane watched his right hand extending to take the animal's paw as though they'd just met in his gentleman's club in London. A moment later, he drew back in raw disbelief. Shaking paws?! He must be losing every scrap of sanity he possessed!

Lady Margaret came puffing through the door, out of breath from her run back up the stairs. From the snarling and shouting she'd heard, she fully expected to find a bloody disaster in the master chamber! Instead, there was his lordship, soapy-faced, and Wolfram, shaking hands, and Charity looking on with a great streak of soap drying on her face, right beside her kiss-swollen lips.

Lady Margaret groaned audibly. There'd been a disaster, alright. His lordship had finally gone and kissed her jinxed granddaughter. It was what he got for removing his protective amulets. Lord knew what calamities were in store for the poor wretch now!

Something terrible had happened in that kiss; Rane felt it in the aching depths of him. After Charity's grandmother had spirited her off, he lay there, reliving it, to discover that even its memory had the power to rouse him to full, throbbing desire for her. In the midst of him, freshly carved in his proud, stony core, he felt a new emptiness, as though she'd somehow taken a piece of him with her. He felt hungrier somehow, having tasted her. And having shared her vital, enchanting presence so memorably, he now felt all the more alone. That hollow, vulnerable feeling sent him into a cold, suffocating panic.

He slid from the bed on his stomach and lowered his feet onto the floor. He had to get out of here . . . today . . . now! With considerable effort, he managed to stand and to steady himself against the bedpost until he had achieved some equilibrium. He located his trunk on the floor nearby and headed for it with stiff, dragging steps. Somehow he managed to pry it open with his foot and to snag his gray trousers with his toes. He grimaced as he bent to grasp the garment with his hand.

The very next second Wolfram's massive jaws appeared, sinking his teeth deep into the trousers. "Hey!" Rane staggered frantically, just keeping his balance. *"Let go!"* He pulled fiercely on the trousers, glaring at the huge mongrel.

Wolfram's dark eyes glinted. He'd tussled with far more vicious sorts than a wounded "lordship." And with a wily, twisting lunge, he succeeded in ripping the trousers from Rane's hands.

Rane watched helplessly as the beast disappeared out

the door with his last pair of breeches and his last chance of escape.

"B'dammit!"

He hobbled and dragged himself back to the bed and fell on it, face down. A moment later, Charity Standing's face rose in the middle of him and the turmoil in his mind and body began to quiet, just as it did in her physical presence. As he quieted, he began to understand. He wouldn't be able to escape her, even if he did manage to get to Mortehoe . . . or London. The minute he'd touched her lips, a bit of her had somehow taken up residence inside him. Even as he realized it, he felt her moving through that new empty spot in the middle of him, paradoxically both enlarging it and filling it at the same time.

He lay a long time, examining the odd little glow of her presence inside him. In his greed, he'd claimed a little piece of Charity Standing. What in heaven was he going to do with a piece of an angel?

That evening, Charity appeared in Rane's twilight-rosy room with books in her hands and a very determined look on her face. She'd spent the afternoon banishing the strange physical longing his kiss had evoked in her and summoning the courage to face him again. He already thought she was a hopeless hoyden; he'd said as much. So what was to be lost by pursuing her own course of helping him? Except, of course, that she didn't want him to think her a flaming tart or a mannerless lout. Increasingly she wanted him to think of her as a person of decency and worth and substance. No, she made herself face it, what she really wanted was for him to think of her as a *lady*. And it was obviously too late for that. It was what she got for letting her helping urges get all mixed up with . . . other urges.

Under Wolfram's watchful eye, she announced that

148

she'd brought him some books to help him pass the time, and offered to read to him, if he would like. He declined in surprisingly gentlemanly fashion and she set the books on the night table along with a lighted candlestand and turned to go, feeling small indeed.

"Miss Charity," he called after her. She turned so quickly that it embarrassed her.

"Yes, your lordship?"

"Thank you."

She stood near the door, feeling his eyes on her and remembering the feel of his lips on hers. Was he remembering too? Was that why his voice had that rough velvet texture to it? She smiled the most dazzling, radiant smile of her life.

"You're most welcome."

Chapter Nine

The sun was beaming brilliantly the next morning when Melwin appeared in Rane's borrowed room with a huge, heaping tray of food: poached eggs, sausages, porridge with real cream, buttery scones, and tea with sugar. Rane demolished it, down to the last sip and crumb, then collapsed against the pillows to luxuriate in his overstuffed condition. But he was not to enjoy it for long. Melwin soon brought word that Wolfram had made strings of his expensive gray trousers, and then produced a scarcely recognizable ball of chewed textile in evidence. While Rane was still grumbling, Lady Margaret appeared, her arms laden with all manner of bizarre animal, mineral, and vegetable matter, to "proof" his room against "bad luck."

Rane watched her from a braced posture on the bed, and suggested tartly that she apply her dubious protective arts to that Wolfram creature, since he seemed to be the main cause of disaster around the place. Lady Margaret harumphed and ignored him pointedly until it was time to check the poultice and dressing on his wound. By the time she was finished with her poking and prodding, his rear parts were burning and throbbing again and he would have sworn she'd purposefully done something to cause it.

Charity appeared in his room late that morning, and found him sunk into a testy mood once again. She opened the windows to let the fresh air in and came to stand by the bed, apologizing for not having come earlier to see if he needed anything. She stopped short of saying she'd been helping with the weekly wash; no respectable household operated without a laundress, even a hired one. And no lady ever set her hands to such work.

"But I've brought you something to keep you company." Her eyes sparkled as she reached inside the deep pockets of the long apron she wore and drew out two small bundles of fur. She held them up, one in each hand, turning them about for Rane to admire. They were kittens, very young ones. One was a dusky, tabby color, the other a spotted gray and white. Their eyes were newly opened.

"Their mother, apparently, abandoned them, and I've been feeding them." She turned and found him scowling up at her from beneath a tight, disapproving brow. "I thought perhaps—"

"I don't like cats." He drew back slightly, dragging his eyes away from the disturbing glow of pleasure in her face. The discomfort in his posterior parts was subsiding, right on schedule. "I can abide dogs if I must, but I *detest* cats."

Charity cradled the mewing kittens against her bosom, puzzled by the way he rejected her surprise out-of-hand. She frowned as she studied his mood and his response. Last night his flinty shell had seemed to be yielding, but this morning, he was clearly his old barnacled self again.

"Spiders, cats . . . Is there anything else you dislike?" The soft rebuke in her tone made him look at her. There were gray mists swirling in the depths of his eyes, cloaking that inner distress she sometimes glimpsed in him. Was there something about *her* he disliked?

"Boredom. I hate being idle," he said, feeling the warm searching of her eyes and sliding inescapably into the same rough-velvet tone he'd used last night. "I'm not used to it. I'm used to . . . used to . . ."

"Hard work?" she supplied, realizing a heartbeat later

151

that she'd probably blundered by recalling what he'd re-vealed in an unthinkably intimate moment. "I meant— you're probably very busy in London with your trading company and your . . . London society . . . invitations and parties . . . elegant operas and glittering balls. . . ." Her cheeks reddened. *And silk-gowned ladies with milk-white hands,* she continued dismally inside her own head. The kittens, mewing and squirming and sinking their needle-like claws into her bodice, suddenly seemed a naïve and girlish idea to her. Whatever possessed her to think a wealthy, worldly nobleman could possibly enjoy the com-pany of something as simple and provincial as kittens . . . or a poor country miss with chapped hands?

But in the same instant, Rane was recognizing the fullness of the gesture that was meant to comfort and cheer him, to take his mind from his hurts and troubles. She'd wanted to give him something warm and live. . . . The idea stirred him massively. Both his loins and his eyes heated as he watched the little beasts' free access to her lush breasts. For the first time in his life, he found himself envying cats!

"It's true." Rising fully onto a braced arm, he came nearly eye to eye with her. His voice came, deep and challenging at first. "I am used to hard work, more used to it that I am to London's *elegant society.* I'm not one of the idle rich. I have to work for my money, every far-thing! I spend most of my time at my offices or on the docks negotiating for cargoes." He caught her eyes in his and she reddened slowly, from her breasts up.

Was that why there was no "wife" or "betrothed" in his life, she wondered. Did he spend too much time and energy on his business affairs? Or did he spend so much time on his business *because* there was no woman in his life?

She was suddenly very aware of how close she was to him, how a lock of his black hair hung roguishly over his forehead, and how full and soft his lips looked.

Every inch of her exposed skin was aching for the feel of his eyes upon it. And there her awareness stopped, for she was drawn into the lightning-charged depths of his turbulent gaze. She forgot about the kittens squirming against her and about keeping a proper lady's distance and about her grandmother's disapproval. She was caught up in powerful currents of feeling and fascination, and when he reached for her hand, she was overwhelmed by a churning whitewater of sensation. She couldn't resist.

"What are you used to, Charity Standing?" His tone softened memorably. "How do you spend your time?" He carried her hand into his broadening gaze and took in her pared nails and the soap-reddened cast of her skin. Several impressions he'd garnered about the household came together in his mind: the faded furnishings, the simple fare, her telling enumeration of the household when she shaved him. Standwell was a household far gone in decline. He answered for her with fresh insight.

"Hard work?"

She was speechless, absorbed in the shifting silver streams in his eyes and in the subtle, sensual hardening of his features. She wanted to touch him, to feel his lips against hers. . . . What was he saying about work? The word rumbled about inside her, rattling her wits back to duty. He was holding her hand, reading in it the raw evidence of her unladylike activities.

"The house is too much for Melwin and Bernadette now." She managed to dilute her confession. "So Gran'mere and I . . . help."

"And when you're not *helping?*" he pressed, dragging her closer. "Who waits to fill your other hours . . . and your future? Callers? A sweetheart? An intended husband, perhaps?"

"No, there's . . . no one," she admitted, lowering her eyes.

"That's hard to believe. The men of Devon must be a

backward lot."

Her utter lack of expectations was suddenly embarrassing. A betrothed? A future? No one had ever spoken of such things with regard to her. She had always assumed it was because they lacked money, but Rane Austen was implying she might have a betrothed, despite her obvious lack of funds.

"I have no time. There are so many things to do."

"I'll bet there are," he murmured, pulling her closer. Miss Charity Standing didn't seem to belong to anyone, he realized. The idea brought a very male smile to his roguish face. "We seem to have that in common, hard work. It makes one wonder what else we might share."

"Neither of us is—" She caught herself just in time.

"Is what?" he coaxed, releasing her hand to lift her chin.

"Married," she said impulsively, wishing instantly she could recall it.

"No, we're not." He smiled wryly. For the first time in his adult life, his unmarried state actually pleased him.

She swallowed hard, finding herself sitting on the edge of the bed, facing him, her heart thudding and her lips feeling hot and conspicuous. He didn't seem outraged that she'd raised so personal and suggestive a topic. When his hand moved to her shoulder, she tried desperately not to look at it, not to wonder what pleasurable mysteries it contained. His eyes glowed dangerously and his lips were parted in sensual invitation . . . so close to hers.

"I don't want kittens for companionship." His deep, seductive tones vibrated all through her warmed, receptive body as he leaned toward her.

"What do you want?" she whispered helplessly.

"You."

His lips unleashed a hot, liquid wave of pleasure in her as they covered hers. It poured through her like honey, coating, clinging to every part of her, lingering

154

warmly, priming her for more. And more came, in trickles and streams and full rivers of sensation as his mouth moved on hers. She knew what to expect this time and she softened, absorbing those free-flowing pleasures into the womanly core of her. She scarcely felt herself shifting, yielding him position, lowering. But somehow she was lying on her back and he was over her, lowering . . . until the mewing cries of the half-squashed kittens between them stopped him.

The pressure of his mouth on hers eased. He arched his chest away and spoke into her lips, "Another good reason to dislike cats." He gently dislodged first one wriggling ball of fur wedged between them, placing it somewhere on the bed behind him, and then the other.

She waited, scarcely breathing. Then his chest came down over hers, both crushing and caressing her, and his arms sank around her like a big, hard cradle. She was engulfed, overwhelmed by the feel of his body on hers. Her lips parted in surprise and his tongue traced the opening between them with maddening leisure. She opened to his subtle coaxing, stunned by the fluid intimacy of their open mouths and the tentative brushes of the tips of their tongues.

Of their own will, her hands came up to touch him, gliding lightly over the soft linen of his shirt, then seeking the hard, familiar muscles beneath. Gradually they circled him in a gentle embrace that drew tighter and pressed him harder against her tingling breasts. He slid his mouth onto her cheek and dragged it down her jaw line to the side of her neck. Her breath stopped. His kisses became gentle nibbles that fired white-hot bolts of pleasure along her nerves. Her skin caught fire and her breasts ached and burned against him, craving something more. As if responding to her most secret desire, his hand withdrew from her shoulder to trace the curve of her side, then slid possessively over one breast.

She moaned from deep in her throat, an expression of

pure pleasure, a wordless entreaty for more. His fingers closed over the cool skin exposed above her rounded bodice, caressing and exploring the pale satin that had obsessed him since he first saw her. The rim of her bodice yielded, and he groaned as his hand slid beneath it, over that full, resilient mound. He tightened sinuously, as though waves rippled through his fingers.

Powerful new feelings took control of her movements and responses. She arched against him, quivering, realizing that these delicious icy-hot shivers and hungry-feeling aches were wrought by his *hands*. He touched her and she ached and burned; he caressed her, and her body vibrated with response. Were these part of the *night magic*, these breathtaking sensations and startling new cravings for closeness, for joining with him?

Her arms tightened about him and she urged his mouth back to hers, meeting it with an irresistible demand. He obliged her fierce new hunger, kissing her deeply, exploring the liquid depths of her eagerness, demanding and claiming yet another bit of her.

Suddenly, he froze against her and his mouth stilled on hers. He stiffened with a small jolt, his back arching. Then he twitched again, arching into her and raising his head sharply, his jaw tight. Through passion-dulled senses she managed to open her eyes and focus on him.

"Claws," he whispered raggedly, twitching again as one of the kittens continued climbing his shoulders, sinking needle-like talons through his shirt.

It took a moment for her to surface from submersion in pleasure. Then what was happening registered in her mind. She lifted her head to glimpse one of the kittens clinging to his back. Poised, staring at that tenacious ball of fur, she felt a wave of frustration rushing through her. She slid from beneath him to sit up and remove the creature from his shirt to her lap. Then she turned slightly as he pushed up on the bed beside her. Her dark-centered eyes met his and lowered in helpless longing to his kiss-swollen lips.

Their faces were close. Their shoulders were touching. Her entire body was filled with awareness of his long, muscular frame, now warm with expectation and taut with desire. She lifted her eyes to his again, seeking, and realized that their moment of stunning intimacy was past. She slipped from the bed, holding the kitten in hands that trembled. He reached for her arm as she moved away, but halted short of touching her, then withdrew. His hand curled with embarrassment, making a fist as it lay on the bed.

"At least it wasn't your raging bull of a dog," he whispered hoarsely.

"It's a good thing Wolfie isn't here. He . . . hates cats, too," she murmured softly.

Rane stared at her crimson face, her bee-stung lips and love-flushed breasts. He was in chaos inside, roused beyond bearing, frustrated beyond words . . . and suddenly grateful beyond measure for the little beast's untimely intrusion. His massively lusty urges toward her were totally out of his control, ungentlemanly in the extreme. And for some dread reason he couldn't muster any real outrage at his behavior.

Charity stood there, looking at him with the remnants of desire glowing in her eyes and in her delectable skin, searching him for clues to what had happened between them. He had kissed her and touched her in ways she hadn't known to desire, and she'd encouraged it, entreated it, with her brazen conduct. What must he think of her brash, unladylike behavior? She bit her lip and waited for his response.

"Hates cats, does he? I guess I can't hold that against him." His voice came thick and low, filled with lingering feeling he made no attempt to hide. "But his manners could definitely use work. As could mine. We both seem to overstep our bounds with appalling regularity." He caught her gaze in his. "Especially where you are con-

157

cerned."

Relief poured through her. His gray eyes were unguarded windows on the pleasure she'd brought him. He didn't regret kissing her, they seemed to say, except in the most gentlemanly sense. Blushing furiously and hoping her pleasure in that discovery wasn't too obvious, she turned to leave. But Rane's voice called her back.

"Your other animal, Miss Standing." He was holding a stiff, howling kitten out to her and she came back to the bed to collect it. Just before he placed it in her arms he paused, holding it in midair as he sought her eyes.

"Will you come this evening? I'll mend my manners. . . ."

Her eyes sparkled and a warm smile spread from her face to his.

"I'll come."

Just at twilight that evening, she appeared in the doorway to his room with an armful of books, an unlit candlestand . . . and Lady Margaret and Wolfram in tow. Rane managed to hide his disappointment beneath a layer of gentlemanly acceptance as the old lady bustled about arranging chairs and lighting so her granddaughter could read to them. Then as Charity read from a mix of her favorite books of poetry, classical works, and travelogues, he forgot all about Lady Margaret, who lolled in her chair and sank into a genteel snore, and Wolfram, who sprawled on the rug between them on his back and snored prodigiously.

He concentrated wholly on the expression in Charity's face and frame as she read. She became learned and sage while reading passages that expounded, was whimsical in light verse and impassioned in dramatic soliloquies. She had voices for each character in a fable and had shades of tone to equal the hues on an artist's pallette when describing a sunset or temple in a far-flung land. She was a treasure, an unexpected treat for both eyes and ears. And when she ended the last passage and put the book aside, he studied her with unabashed fascination.

"Poetry, geography, natural philosophy . . . you've studied all that?"

She blushed, finding her gaze caught in his. "Papa . . . liked to read . . . and to travel. We couldn't afford to go see the world, so he brought the world to us . . . in books. He used to call us 'arm-chair adventurers.' " Her smile dimmed briefly as she weathered another sudden wave of memories of her father. "He has—he *had* a marvelous library." She straightened, her eyes dark and luminous. "You're welcome to use it when you're up and about again. But I suppose you'll find the travelogues rather dull going. You've probably traveled quite a bit, yourself."

"Some." He watched her shrugging off the sadness that he knew was connected with her father. Some of the melancholy she had shed found its way inside him. It baffled him that her moods could have such an effect on his own. "Mostly the West Indies and the Americas. And a few years ago, I made the obligatory grand tour of the continent."

"Would you tell me about it? Where you've been, what you've seen?" she came to the edge of her chair, her countenance coming alive again. "The Cathedral of Nôtre Dame, and the canals of Venice, and the ruined temples of old Greece? Have you seen them?" When he nodded, she melted visibly. "Tell me, please?"

He obliged, sketchily at first, then in greater detail as her questions probed his recall. He was stunned by the contrast between her sense of wonder in even borrowed experience and his own lack of enthusiasm for the travels he'd gone to great lengths to undertake. In retrospect, he saw that he'd taken little pleasure in the journeys and experiences that were meant to add a burnish

159

of refinement to his Barbados-formed hard edges. But then, enjoyment hadn't been the purpose of spending all that time and money. Every cathedral and statue and performance had been simply one more rung on the ladder of social acceptance.

It was only now, reliving his own experience through Charity Standing's eyes, that he realized how much more there had been, and how blind he'd been to it. Charity Standing would never come away from Venice complaining of the dampness, or leave Paris recalling only the dirt and beggars in the street and the brothels. Suddenly he realized there was another whole world to be seen . . . through her eyes.

By the time Charity had roused her grandmother and ushered her out, Rane was besieged by disturbing new hungers that had little to do with his body's volatile cravings. What would it be like to see that other world with her, he wanted to know. What would it be like to experience her joy and excitement, and even her sorrow, with her? Lord, he was already feeling some of them . . . Why didn't that thought seem to alarm him anymore?

Charity read to Rane again the following evening and listened eagerly to his increasingly vivid descriptions, of his continental travels, of London's noteworthy sights and the ton's elegant habits, the tearooms, the morning calls, the plays, the concerts in Vauxhall, the soirées. Determined to chaperone them more closely, Lady Margaret tried to stay awake longer this time, but was soon nodding in her chair.

Charity turned to him, seizing her chance. "And Barbados. Tell me about Barbados next."

The genial look froze on his face and after a moment he took a very controlled breath. "There is precious little to tell. It's a rock in the middle of the ocean . . . and it's hellaciously hot. Did I tell you about the Cathedral of Cologne—"

"Does it really have beaches that look like white sugar?" She persisted, levelling a persuasive look at him.

He paused a moment, searching the feminine challenge in that look. She was going to continue until she made him tell her what she wanted to know, he realized. And just what was it she really wanted to know?

"Yes."

"Is the water as blue as a robin's egg? And do the hillsides look like green velvet in the distance?"

"The water is blue, the hills are green," he admitted tightly, royally annoyed by the half smile she wore and the irresistible glow in her eyes. "Perhaps you'd rather hear about Madrid and the bull fights. . . ."

"And the flowers? Hibernius . . . and cannas? Of course they must have pineapples . . . and your bananas?" She came toward the edge of her chair, her face alight with purpose. She was determined to make him tell her about it. She needed to know about him, wanted desperately to know what lay beneath that wall of hostility he raised at will. She knew Barbados was some part of it.

He watched her with a guarded look, deciding whether or not to answer. The warmth of her eyes made him want to believe it was not mere curiosity that made her insist.

"*Hibiscus*," he declared. "Scarlet-red hibiscus. And a few pineapples and too damn few bananas. Most of those come by boat from Venezuela." The smile of delight that bloomed on her face made it almost worth dredging up uncomfortable old memories.

"Tell me about the lagoons, and about the moon rising, please."

He did tell her, reluctantly at first. But as he talked, his voice warmed from tropic currents of memory and he began to speak of the mountain flowers and palm

161

trees and the way the water shimmered like diamonds beneath the full moon. Soon somehow he was telling her about the Anglican minister and his good wife, who gave him lessons with their children, about the cane fields and how the sugar was pressed and how the cane had tasted when he chewed it as a boy. About the flower blossoms as big as dinner plates, the bugs to match, about lizards and colorful birds and flying fish. . . .

She sometimes closed her eyes while listening, to let his words paint pictures in her mind. When he paused, watching her, she opened her eyes and saw the thoughtful troubling in his brow.

"You loved it, didn't you," she whispered. "It's in your voice as you speak."

His jaw clenched, his eyes narrowed. He was unnerved and somewhat irritated at the way she used his fondness for her to pry into his most private feelings. But try as he might, he could find no real anger in him. She was right, so painfully right.

"I . . . did like some of it." It was happening again; he was seeing things with her wonder, recalling experiences he'd locked away and things he had taken for granted or disparaged.

"Then why do you call it a 'hellhole'?" She saw his surprise, and she blushed at her language, but not at her curiosity. This was too important to her. His face tightened and fully five different emotions crossed his features before he forced himself to ease. He chose his words carefully.

"It was not always pleasant for me, growing up there." He paused, as if weighing each syllable. "And it is not *fashionable* to be from Barbados, any more than it is fashionable to have skin darkened by the sun."

She stared at him, understanding more, but not quite all. Fashionable? She would never have guessed that hardheaded Rane Austen would let the opinion of others cause him undue concern. But the guarded heat in his

162

eyes as he searched her reaction for signs of disapproval said he was perfectly serious. Not fashionable. It baffled her that anyone would think less of him for having such an unusual and exciting background, or for having such deliciously sun-browned skin. How could anyone look at his long, muscular frame and his striking eyes and think him anything but marvelous?!

The question slammed straight into her other curiosity about him, sparking insight. He wasn't considered "fashionable." Was that why he didn't have a wife or a betrothed? The certainty of it swept her, stunning her momentarily. Why else?

She lifted her eyes to his formidable countenance and glimpsed a vulnerable young boy with sun-burned cheeks peering out at her from inside those shimmering gray eyes. That little boy worked so hard, and seemed so lonely . . .

She rose, eyes glowing golden, and came to the side of the bed.

"I like the sound of your Barbados, whether it is fashionable or not." Her voice was low and tender as she picked up his hand and ran her fingers over it lovingly. Impulsively, she brought his fingers up one at a time, kissing their tips. "Do you know," she quieted to a whisper that beckoned him closer. "When you touch me, I can feel the hot Barbados sun in your hands."

He contracted visibly, trying to contain the explosion of shocked heat her words set off in the core of his body. She shivered, watching flames being struck in the backs of his eyes.

"And I taste the nectar of island flowers in your kiss."

"Charity," he groaned.

Her fingers touched his lips, silencing them, as she flicked a cautionary glance at her sleeping grandmother. When she sank onto the side of the bed, he groaned silently, turning a wince of apology toward the old lady. But a moment later, his conflict dissolved in the glowing

163

invitation in Charity's eyes. He lowered her to the bed with him, trapping her beneath his chest, and paused to absorb the delicate beauty that beckoned him to such earthly delight.

She felt his arms tighten around her and familiar pleasures began to swirl through her again. She opened to his kiss, parrying the gentle thrusts of his tongue and luxuriating in the wet heat of his mouth on hers. He nibbled her lips and toyed silkily with her tongue, devouring her by slow, seductive increments. Soon his warm hands were tracing her shape through her dress, setting her skin on fire. She whispered a sigh of pleasure and arched, rubbing the side of her breast against the inside of his arm, entreating his touch. His fingers slid beneath her stern bodice, coiling around the soft mounds of her breasts, closing deliciously on the ragged velvet peaks at their tips. Each brush of his fingers sent a spasm of fiery pleasure echoing through her body to lodge in the tender center of her womanflesh.

His kisses lowered to her jaw, to the base of her throat, then to the aching peaks of her breasts. He pushed back her bodice and chemise and rubbed his hot, bronzed face over a burning nipple. Her eyes opened and focused through the steam in her head, just as his lips opened and his tongue began to swirl that rosy velvet in hypnotic circles. A moan ripped free in her throat and she just caught it with her teeth.

Her whole body was hot, her muscles melting, blood steaming. She felt him lavishing the same adorations on her other breast and shuddered as he added one more, a gentle suckling that vibrated strings of sensation all through her. She pulled his head back to hers and responded in the only way she knew, with a deep, voluptuous kiss. He moaned softly and his hand left her breast to tighten at her waist then to slide possessively down her hip and across her belly. Her breath stopped as it came to rest hotly on the sensitive mound at the top of her legs.

She waited, heart pounding, senses open and hungry. Heat from his hand radiated through her clothes into her most sensitive flesh. Only heat. No movement. Just Barbados heat . . . from Rane Austen's big hand.

Her perception focused totally on that sensation, savoring it, exploring it, claiming it. Stillness and heat. Tropic steam.

Aching and hot, burning with suspense, she moved against that torrid weight, a small, shifting movement, seeking. His fingers shifted, pressed, then stroked slowly. She quivered, anticipating more . . .

Lady Margaret made a snuffling noise that seemed as loud as a gunshot in the stillness of the chamber, and shifted abruptly in her chair. They froze, listening, staring helplessly into each other's eyes.

Charity sprang up, her heart pounding, slid from the bed, smoothing her bodice and hair, composing herself frantically. She took one step toward her chair when Lady Margaret started awake and her head jerked up.

"Time to retire, Gran'mere." Charity hurried to take the old lady's arm and urge her to her feet, taking advantage of her confusion upon wakening. The old lady paused to glance at Rane, and nod him farewell, then allowed Charity to usher her to the door.

"I forgot to douse the candles. Go ahead, Gran'mere, I'll be right along." Charity turned back to collect the candlestand as the old lady shuffled out. She paused and lifted her eyes to Rane. He was reclining on one elbow, watching her with a very controlled look. His face was dusky with embarrassment, but his eyes shone with unslaked hunger.

"Thank you for telling me about Barbados."

"Thank you for reminding me about Barbados, Charity."

She smiled and doused all but one candle, carrying it out the door with her. She checked on Gran'mere and then paused in her doorway, staring at Rane's door.

He needed someone . . . a wife. And she needed someone . . . a husband. Her winsome smile broadened to a determined grin. He wasn't fashionable and neither was she. He had too little luck and she had too much. They were a perfect match.

Now all she had to do was convince him of it.

Chapter Ten

The next day, Rane's eighth in their household, Lady Margaret checked his wound. She found it knitting surprisingly fast, given the minor catastrophes it had suffered and the dismal state of its bearer's luck. The viscount was fit enough to be on his feet for brief periods, she announced, though she refused to take responsibility for his safety if he left the protection of his heavily "charmed" room. The prime obstacle to his freedom then became his lack of breeches. Charity saw to that, producing a pair of her father's breeches, let out to accommodate his larger frame.

When Melwin finished dressing his lordship, Charity reappeared in his room with a cane her father had used whenever he cracked an ankle. She halted at the sight of him and her eyes widened as he came forward to take the cane. He was so big, so intimidating, so *different* standing up! She was speechless for a moment.

Above her, Rane was discovering the same change in perception. From so far above, with his perceptions finally righted and put into usual perspective, she seemed quite demure, feminine and fragile. It knocked him back on his emotional heels. The things he'd been thinking and desiring suddenly seemed base and loutish, throwbacks to his old Barbados self. It embarrassed him to think that he'd inflicted himself on her bodily, trapping her beneath him on his bed on more than one occasion. And it perfectly appalled him that he'd spent half his nights dreaming about doing this again . . . and more.

Charity recovered enough to suggest he might like to visit Stephenson, down the hall. He nodded dumbly and she led the way, stealing shy glances at his tight expression and trying to force her thudding heart to calm. She hoped it was the discomfort in his hip and leg that caused his forbidding frown, and not anything she'd done.

They found Stephenson in a snarl of tangled bed-linen and odoriferous amulets, hungry as a bear and irritable as a caged boar. He and Lady Margaret had just gone a round over "sops" and he was still muttering and growling about it. Not even the sight of his half-mended employer could improve his temper, or his language, which had slid irretrievably into "Barbados French."

Rane saw himself in Stephenson's impotent fume-and-fury and reddened, wondering if he'd been this ridiculous, too. He watched Charity's determined offers of help and Stephenson's prickly refusals and knew that this was exactly what he'd been like, foul language and all. By the time they left the room, Rane's hip was aching and his gentlemanly pride and his conscience were both burning.

All he could think about was how crude and un-gentlemanly he'd been toward her, on every count. He'd snarled and demanded and cursed and pouted. He'd been coarse and insulting and even ungrateful. He'd exposed himself to her innocent eyes and touched her at every opportunity, he'd kissed her, dragged her beneath him, pawed her as though she were some ignorant little tavern scull. And last night he'd invaded her clothes and damn near . . . and in front of her sleeping grandmother! She had every right to loathe him.

"He's not usually like this." His voice was a constricted rasp as he paused in the hallway. Then he raised his head and found himself staring into sweet-taffy eyes that were looking shyly up at him.

168

"I know. He's hurting, both in his body and his pride," she whispered, wishing she could do something about the darkness in his eyes and chisled features, wishing she could touch him.

Rane realized she spoke about both of them and suffered yet another sting of conscience. "It's good of you to take care of him . . . in spite of his attitude."

Charity smiled, sensing he spoke not just for Stephenson. Was that what was troubling him? His surly, uncouth behavior? She answered him in kind. "People do and say things when they're hurting that they wouldn't say and do otherwise. Gran'mere taught me long ago to separate the pain from the person."

Rane stood there, thinking that she really was an angel of sorts, a warm, earthly bit of undeserved acceptance. She'd seen nothing but his baser side and yet, she'd somehow discerned that there was more to him than the disagreeable sum of his anger and coarseness and pain. In that moment, he resolved to reclaim the gentlemanly part of him he'd abandoned in the throes of disaster. From now on, he'd treat her with the respect — and restraint — she deserved.

She escorted him back to his room and he paused in the doorway, blocking her from entering with him.

"I must thank you, Miss Standing, for your care of Stephenson and me."

"It has its compensations, your lordship." She forced a puzzled little smile. "I'm coming to interpret what Mister Stephenson calls 'Barbados French,' rather well."

He looked quite pained suddenly, bade her good morning, and closed his door.

Charity stood in the hallway, feeling a staggering wave of loss and longing for the intimacy she'd shared with him at his bedside. It was regret she'd seen in his eyes just now. Was he embarrassed by his ungentlemanly behavior . . . or was he appalled by her unladylike conduct? Was he seeing her through his "London eyes" now? Remembering the differences in their status and expectations? She had abandoned every bit of decorum and propriety she'd been taught in her eagerness to be with him and to help him. Was he regretting spending those deep kisses and intimate touches on a meddlesome country miss with no fortune, no expectations . . . and no manners?

Her stubborn heart bent under that load of doubt and guilt, but it flatly refused to break. She hadn't been very ladylike, she reasoned, but then, he hadn't exactly been the perfect gentleman. He'd wanted her kisses as much as she wanted his. He'd been as eager to hold her and touch her as she had been to be held and touched. Could a simple thing like getting out of bed affect a man's desires so much?

After a moment, her honey golden eyes glowed with new determination. He'd wanted her lying down . . . she'd just have to make him want her standing up as well.

Over the next three days, Rane became a model patient and a paragon of gentlemanly demeanor. It was a real challenge to Charity's determination. The sole lapses in his new persona came as he increased the range and duration of his movements about the upper floor of Standwell only to encounter Wolfram repeatedly. Something about Rane's use of the cane, or his halting gait, absolutely fascinated Wolfram, who made an exasperating game of stalking Rane from behind and darting unexpectedly through the gap between him and the cane, knocking it from under him. The maneuver naturally threw Rane off balance and sent him flailing. He bruised an elbow one time, went sprawling on the hall runner and wrenched a shoulder another, and scraped his hand on a doorlatch still another time. When Charity came running to see what had hap-

170

pened, Rane always evaded her helping touch and Wolfram was invariably parked against a far wall or curled up in a corner, with an infuriating, droopy-eyed look of innocence that made mincemeat of Rane's hot complaints against him. She put it down to an unlucky combination of Rane's boredom and his unfortunate history with Wolfie, and seized the chance to persuade Lady Margaret to allow Rane to come downstairs for meals with them. Once there, she intended to remember her manners . . . and to see that he forgot all about his.

She supervised Rane's progress down the stairs that afternoon and he limped from room to room on the first floor, observing the peculiar arrangement of household items and furnishings at Standwell.

Almost everything at Standwell seemed to be placed a little out of reach. Pictures were hung abnormally high on the walls and the candle sconces could only be reached by yard-long taper lighters. All the knicknacks and small objects in the house were lodged on shelves set above shoulder-height and surrounded by sturdy railings. The hearths were enclosed by armored grates and fences of iron bars that bore heavy latches. In the dining room, a great glass-fronted china cabinet had been refitted with narrow wooden slats over the doors. In the library, books were crammed into the uppermost shelves and instead of the customary ladder, there was an odd contraption like an exceptionally long pair of fire tongs that was used to retrieve books. And it took him a while to realize that the legs of chairs and tables in the house had all been shortened.

He scratched his head, puzzling over the bizarre arrangements, and finally mentioned it to Charity. She smiled a bit ruefully and divulged that things were arranged that way to reduce household accidents and mishaps . . . which had been something of a problem in earlier days. He scowled and rambled off to study the number and location of horseshoes over doorways and to try to identify the dried plant materials that were tacked and stuffed and draped into and around nearly every available opening.

Mountain ash, Charity finally informed him . . . and selected instances of moonwart and pusley, depending on the application, and of course, strings of acorns. Very good luck, acorns. And he mustn't move the old shoes her grandmother had placed strategically on windowsills, mantles, and hearths. And the grainy little trails on the window sills were salt, to keep mischief out of the house. . . .

"What the hell kind of 'mischief' requires all this?" he demanded, gesturing at the burdened doorways.

"The kind in Gran'mere's worries and fears," she ventured with reassuring sensibility. "Papa always said that if her charms and notions made her feel better, there was no harm in it."

She could tell he didn't like what he was hearing and offered to show him the old keep, to take his mind off her grandmothers' superstitions and direct it into more productive channels. He found himself sinking into the melted caramel of her eyes and agreeing, before he could catch himself. He tightened inside with both dread and expectation, and followed. She set a pace that accommodated his stiff movement, leading him slowly up to the second floor. Opening a set of arched doors into what appeared to be a massive, round stone chamber, she lit a candle and stood a moment, staring up at him in the flickering golden light.

"Beware the footing, your lordship," she said softly, suddenly very aware of his broad shoulders and bronzed warmth in the dimness. "The stone steps are worn and uneven."

He nodded wordlessly, having been caught staring at

172

the maddening little cleft in the flesh that showed above the rim of her bodice. When she began to ascend the circular steps built into the sides of the tower, his eyes fell to the gentle rocking of her curvy bottom, now just at eye level, and his hands began to tingle with temptation.

It had been three very long days since he'd last kissed her and his renaissance of restraint had done nothing to lessen the need she built in him with her admiring looks and unconsciously sensual movements. Every night as he fell face-down across his bed, he recalled every line and movement of her body and the feel of her mouth under his, yielding, responding. And he lay in a swollen agony, waiting for the fire in his blood to burn itself out.

Now watching her mount the stairs before him, he felt his control unraveling. The heat was rising in him again, filling his belly and licking up his spine. That rhythmic motion, that divine, swaying pendulum of femininity. . . .

With his thoughts narrowing, he managed to mind his feet, but not to notice the narrowing passage and shrinking headroom through the stone arches. A small veer to the left and—*THWAAACK!!*—his hard forehead smacked resoundingly into the stone arch and he recoiled, grabbing his head and staggering.

Charity wheeled, wide-eyed, just in time to see Rane stumbling backward toward the sheer drop at the edge of the steps. She jolted, just as he began to lose balance, and dropped the candle to grab his coat with both hands and pull with all her might. He lurched back onto the step, crashing into her and knocking her against the far wall with a thud. For a long moment, both hearts pounded frantically with fright. Their senses vibrated and filled with each other. Then in the darkness, the unspent heat of reaction erupted, releasing suppressed desires.

Rane's mouth found hers in the dimness and his arms circled her, pinning her between the cold stone of the wall and his burning body. Her arms coiled around his lean waist as she arched, seeking and returning the pressure of his body on hers. His kiss was the same hard-soft wonder, the same liquid lightning that always exploded her senses and left her without boundaries or limits. Guided by feminine intuitions, she clung to his hard body, opening to him, giving him her mouth, yielding him the treasures of her full response. It was some minutes before he could raise his head.

"I swore I wouldn't do this again," he said against her lips.

"People swear ridiculous things all the time," she murmured breathlessly. "I don't think the Almighty pays much attention to such things. He knows what's possible with humans and what's not."

"Are you saying it's not humanly possible for me to behave in a gentlemanly manner toward you?" His lips drifted down her neck to fasten on the sweet skin of her shoulder.

"I'm saying . . . it's not necessary."

He groaned and his hands moved feverishly over her back and sides, caressing and adoring the curves that had become the new template of his desires, the standard to which his passions were now molded. Through her clothes, he confirmed the smallness of her waist, the supple elegance of the curve of her spine, the silky strength of her shoulders. She was the perfection of desire, the encompassing sensual pleasure, so soft in his arms and so tantalizingly insistent against his rousing hardness. His legs began to tremble, his loins tightened, and his powerful arms flexed. He clasped her buttocks and lifted her tightly against his swollen desire, thrusting in hot, sinuous rounds against her woman's heat.

Air-starved and reeling from the flood of sensations,

she went taut in his arms as he grazed her tingling womanflesh with a hard, undulant movement. All existence was suspended in the clear, low trill of pleasure that spread along her nerves and resonated in the innermost recesses of her flesh. As she waited, breathless, it came again, a quivering spasm of excitation that focused in one burning point at the center of her woman's heat, then radiated up through her to collect in the burning tips of her breasts. She contracted around that stunning sensation, holding it, savoring it until it came again . . . and again.

She moaned softly, giving herself up to the aching need in her, seeking a closer joining, a fulfillment she didn't fully understand. Her thighs parted at the gentle nudging of his and she gasped as he pressed full against her, rubbing, thrusting in imitation of the completion both now sought. She wriggled in his hands and against his arms, arching, catlike, into him, purring, imploring. . . .

"Woof!" It came from the distant edge of reality to invade their constricted consciousness. They tightened, holding each other closer to seal it out. "Woof, woof! . . . *Woof!* . . . *WOOF— WOOF— WOOOOF!!"*

The muffled thud of wood smacking stone echoed up through the darkness, fanning through the veil of their senses. The scraping sound of movement over stone rushed at them, joined by the ominous rasp of panting. But immersed in hot sensation, locked in both embrace and discovery, they were helpless against the threat.

"WOOF!" Wolfram lunged at them out of the black well of the tower, knocking them into the wall and effectively jostling them apart. They stumbled and scrambled in the darkness, trying to hold onto each other while fending him off. The thunderous echoes of his barks in the stone tower were deadly disorienting, and the dim outlines of walls and steps and dog gyrated crazily around them.

"B'dammit, dog!" Rane swung forcefully at Wolfram, connecting with something furry, but the animal's reckless leaps and barks continued. Then Charity scraped her wits together and yelled at Wolfram while trying to constrain Rane's anger. She was feeling none too charitable toward the dog herself, at the moment, but she had a dread-filled appreciation of just how far below them the floor of the lower chamber was.

"Wolfie stop it! Get off! Who let you up here?!"

"Miss Charity?" A voice and a dim gold shaft of light speared upward from the tower floor, far below. A single candle . . . and Baron Pinnow's voice. "Good Lord, are you alright? What's happened?"

The sound of his ever-so-sincere voice caused Wolfie to break off his purposefully noxious intrusion and he raced up the steps, out of reach. Charity could feel Rane's silent fury in the darkness beside her and clamped her hand over her throat to send her heart back into her chest so she could answer.

"I'm afraid Wolfie surprised us . . . I dropped the candle . . ."

"Stay where you are!" he called valiantly, "I'll be right there." And shortly, the golden circle of light approached and broadened to reveal Sullivan Pinnow's long face and rigid shoulders. "How fortunate that I came when I did!" He paused, glimpsing her reddened face and swollen lips, and felt a massive rush of irritation. "Fortunate *indeed*."

"If you would please lead the way, Baron," Rane waved him ahead, and the threesome trailed in thick silence up the remaining steps. Charity frantically smoothed her bodice and sent trembling hands up to right any disturbance of her hair. Her knees felt like jelly and her whole body throbbed with unspent passions. But no amount of embarrassment or frustration could dim her joy in the knowledge that she'd broken through Rane's gentlemanly wall.

176

Behind her, Rane was making critical adjustments to his borrowed breeches and his chaotic thoughts, while gritting his teeth. Angry as he was at the dog, he did realize that without the brute's intervention, he'd probably have been caught making love to her against a blessed wall! So much for days of gentlemanly restraint, he thought grimly. All he'd done was bottle his desire for her, only to unleash it all in one greedy, humiliating lunge.

Wolfram met them in the tower room below the battlements, rearing and wagging his tail, looking pleased with himself for having rescued his mistress from the lordship's gnawing. He easily dodged Rane's foot and waited until all three had climbed out onto the tower's walk before following.

Charity shaded her eyes and turned away, using the brilliant sunlight as an excuse to compose herself before facing the baron or Rane. She led them around the battlements, pointing out aspects of the view and collecting compliments that had nothing to do with what was really on their minds.

"Lovely as it is, I've come on an official matter." The baron finally maneuvered between her and the viscount to capture her hand and lean insinuatingly close.

"I've told you, Baron—"

"Not *your* business, your lordship," Pinnow tossed over the shoulder he'd turned in Rane's direction. He poured a smile over Charity that was suffocating at such close range. "It concerns some acquaintances of yours . . . and your late father's. Gar Davis and Percy Hall. They haven't been seen in Mortehoe in quite some time and certain creditors have grown concerned as to their whereabouts. I came to see if you had any knowledge of them."

"Gar and Percy, missing?" Charity searching her memory and finding that her last encounter with them was hazy, bound up with indistinct recall of her father's

177

burial and its chaotic aftermath. "Why, no, now that you mention it. I haven't seen them in a week or two . . . since Papa's funeral. Surely nothing untoward has happened to them." Her eyes widened as she recalled Gar's tumble into the open grave, with its dire portent for disaster.

"It's doubtful but I am bound to investigate all possibilities." He straightened, tightening his grip on her hand. "Perhaps you will be so good as to see me off."

When Rane straightened and made to follow, the baron turned him back with: "No need to exert yourself, your lordship. Do stay and enjoy the view a bit longer."

Rane simmered silently as Pinnow disappeared into the darkened tower with Charity. And as he stood watching the doorway, phantom flashes of Pinnow and Charity in the dark together . . . on the steps . . . in each other's arms, occurred in his mind. It took every ounce of rational thought and determination he possessed to keep from charging down the steps after them. He limped his way over to the stone crenels and forced his gaze out over the placid green countryside.

Minutes later, Charity and Sullivan Pinnow emerged from the dark keep into the reassuring light of the upstairs hallway. He showed every sign of slowing both their pace and his departure.

"I'm sorry, Baron, I have no time for a stroll along the sea-path this afternoon," she demurred, glancing at his sharp, unyielding features and wondering how she'd ever thought him elegant. She led him hastily out into the court and would have left him there, but he caught her hand and insisted she accompany him to his horse, which was tied near the stableyard fence, out of view of the front court. Once there, he took up his pursuit.

"I've spoken with your grandmother earlier." He

178

pulled her closer and she resisted, to little avail. He reeled her close enough to snatch her other hand. "She's given me permission to speak with you," he murmured thickly, sliding his gaze over her shoulders and down her chest. "You must already sense my boundless admiration for you. Your graces and beauty rob me of all eloquence to praise them, leaving me a poverty of expression. Nonetheless, I must boldly declare my mounting affection for you as best I might." She was so caught up in trying to think of some ladylike way to rebuff his verbal advances that she was utterly unprepared to avoid his physical ones.

He grabbed her shoulders and brought his mouth down on hers. Shock prevented an immediate reaction and he took inaction for acquiescence. His arms snaked around her, hauling her against his bony frame. His head wobbled back and forth, grinding his thin, hard lips into hers to impress upon her the strength of his passion. Belatedly she began to squirm and pull at the back of his coat, actions he chose to interpret as an overwhelmed response to his manly grip on her senses.

She whimpered distress; he heard it as a womanly purr. She pushed and wriggled against him; he took it for the wantonness he wished to find in her. She gasped revulsion and he shoved his wet tongue between her lips, congratulating himself on recognizing the latent carnality of his bride-to-be. She pushed away, with her cheeks red and her bosom heaving, and ran back into the house.

Sullivan Pinnow smoothed his dapper waistcoat and stared darkly at the doors where she'd disappeared. Then his gaze lifted to glide along the graystone walls and paraments of Standwell Hall itself. With a bit of redoing, it could be made quite presentable. And the lands that went with the hall were a fat plum that the foolish Upton Standing hadn't had the nerve to pick. He'd researched the prospects and weighed the assets

179

carefully; the place had real potential. And Charity Standing's delectable charms in his bed would be a delicious bonus . . . when he married her and claimed Standwell.

Then a gray-eyed cloud rose on his horizon and he scowled and rubbed his chin, scanning the outbuildings and nearby fields with a covetous eye. He wasn't overly worried that the Viscount Oxley might snatch his lucrative prize permanently; from what he'd been able to learn, the Viscount Oxley wasn't the sort to want the beehive . . . just the honey. But he had no desire to marry another man's leavings, even a full nobleman's. He'd have to begin protecting his interests here, calling on her frequently to make sure the viscount didn't get to the "honey" before him.

Above them, Rane was limping irritably around the battlements with his hands clasped behind his back, fuming silently at the tangled, bewildering mass of feeling inside him. He looked up to find Wolfram sitting by the steps, glaring at him. "Come near me and you're a dead dog," he growled.

He turned and went to the battlements, leaning on the stonework to stare at the placid waters of the bay and his gaze caught on something—someone—at the far corner of the house, by the stableyard fence. He startled and squinted and charged around the battlements, leaning furiously through the stonework.

It was them! Charity and the obnoxious baron—and they were—He blinked and squinted and craned his neck and viewed it from more than one angle. *Kissing!*

He wheeled from the sight to confront the glowering Wolfram. "What the hell are you doing just sitting there?! The bastard's kissing her! Everytime I kiss her you try to eat me alive! Why aren't you down there protecting her from him?!"

180

He saw her jerky movement backward, saw her widen the distance between them and stop. Then she turned abruptly and ran — *ran* — toward the front doors. Rane replayed that telling movement over and over in his head as he watched the baron pause, then step jauntily into his saddle.

"She never runs when I kiss her." A moment later his knees went weak with relief. "She didn't like it!" The next instant, a hot, confusing surge of indignation welled in him. "Well, of course she didn't like it! The insolent bastard . . . what the hell was he doing kissing her? How dare he?!! She's—"

It was an excruciatingly short step from "how dare he" to *"she's mine."* He fell back against the stone wall, hearing it in his mind, louder and more insistent with each repetition. *She's mine.* With each look exchanged, each touch, each of those soul-wrecking kisses, he'd been laying claim to her. He'd been coaxing and commanding and acquiring her, bit by delectable bit. He knew she was a rank innocent and, despite his self-conscious attempts at propriety, he'd been deliberately introducing her to pleasures . . . educating her to his tastes. The thought both horrified and fascinated him.

He wanted Charity Standing; he'd known it for days now. He wanted her luscious little body and her radiant sensuality and her openness and her irresistible logic and her quixotic charm. He wanted all of her, was half mad with wanting it. Or maybe he was entirely mad with it, just like his profligate father and grandfather before him. Their mad pursuit of unattainable women had driven them each into penury and informal exile from England's shores.

He closed his eyes and felt the spring sun on his face . . . and felt her rippling through his very blood. He relived the sweet taste of her mouth, like the nectar of island flowers. He conjured the burning softness of her breasts moving against his ribs, like the warm, island

181

waters. And he recalled her breathy whimper of delight as she discovered her own sensuality in his hands, like the whispers of a hot tropic breeze.

His entire body contracted as the thought struck. She wanted him, too; it was in every sweet shudder of her shoulders, in every questing stroke of her shyly curious hands, in every dart of her hot little tongue. She had braved his temper and his defenses and even his past, to get to know the man inside him. And just minutes ago, she'd declared in her seductively sensible way, that he didn't have to be an exhalted gentleman to claim her, he only had to be a man.

The hot blue flames in his eyes flared at the thought. His desire for Charity Standing wasn't mad or futile at all! She was his. All he had to do was claim her.

Below, Charity had fled to the privacy of her room. Her lips felt swollen and abused and her cheeks were aflame. Her chest was heaving and she was strangely unable to expell the breaths she gasped. She sank onto the bench by the window wiping her mouth frantically with the backs of her hands.

How dare the wretched baron kiss and paw her like that?! She'd been angry enough to scratch his eyes out! The mystery of why she'd always disliked the tall, palorous baron was instantly solved. Those oddly oppressive looks he'd given her, the possessive grasp of his hands, the physical hovering . . . he wanted her for *night work!* The very idea made her skin shrink.

She certainly never felt like this when Rane did such things to her! Rane's kisses were long, liquid caresses that coaxed and adored. His touch was like cool flames dancing over her skin. His body and his embraces were by turns hard and soft, but always gentle in their total command of her response. Rane Austen gave her things . . . intimacy, pleasure, joy. Sullivan Pinnow only took.

She reeled from the sudden insight. That was the difference between *night work* and *night magic,* she was sure of it . . . the "taking" and the "giving"!

Rane Austen made pleasure, gave pleasure. She smiled, understanding fully now and more determined than ever to have him. *Rane Austen had the night magic in his hands.*

For the next three days, Lady Margaret watched the telling looks Charity and Rane exchanged by day and watched the moon approaching fullness at night. The calamity she read in the convergence of the two phenomena was coming closer. Their mounting, volatile passions . . . under the full moon's tumultuous influence . . . it was a recipe for disaster that didn't bear thinking about! So she set her head to thinking of new ways to keep them apart, instead.

Charity watched her grandmother's maneuverings and sighed irritably. Lady Margaret conjured every spring-cleaning task known to humankind to occupy her time, and began to welcome the horrid baron's daily visits with suspicious enthusiasm. And to make matters worse, she became positively fanatical about her superstitions. She forbade knives at the dinner table, on the off chance that the butter might be cut on both ends, put quenched coals under whatever chair Rane chose in the parlor, insisted that Rane's and Stephenson's beds be moved so that their heads faced north and their feet south, and collected spiders from the stable to let loose on the house ceilings . . . to bring good luck. This last was particularly aimed at Rane, Charity realized, and she did her best to keep him from seeing them.

Clearly Gran'mere disapproved of her growing feelings for Rane and was doing her best to keep them apart. Charity didn't fully understand Gran'mere's objection, since Rane was an unmarried man and not promised to anyone else. She didn't know how to assure Gran'mere that Rane Austen was an honorable man and that she intended to marry him . . . when she had nothing more than her own feelings to base either assurance on.

When Charity announced one afternoon that Rane was well enough for a walk down the sea path to the old abbey ruins, she was hoping for a rare bit of privacy with him. But Lady Margaret hastily recruited expert interference. The baron eagerly answered her summons to Standwell and the old lady feigned surprise and invited him to accompany Rane and Charity, insisting that Charity take her "mangy beast" with her as well, to get him out of the way.

Thus Charity set off for her walk wedged between Rane and Sullivan Pinnow. Neither would give up his tacit claim to her and her hand, and they were forced to walk three abreast, more off the narrow path along the cliffs than on it. It made wonderful sport for Wolfram, who insisted on dodging and streaking without warning through the gaps between Charity and her two swains, jostling them violently. The baron rambled on about local doings and local gentry that Rane could know nothing about, and Rane retaliated with stories of London and ton doings that the baron couldn't possibly know.

Charity could almost feel the heat of the fiery looks being exchanged over her head and in desperation, suggested they stop for a "sit" on the stones that overlooked the ruins. She stepped carefully around the great stone slabs and blocks that had once formed the outer perimeter of the old abbey and the baron bolted after her, steering her to a seat on a stone just large enough for two.

Rane steamed silently and made his way to a stone behind them, his face as dark as his thoughts. The irksome near-peer removed his fashionable, high-crowned hat, to mop his brow with a handkerchief, and laid it on the rock behind him. Rane stared at that hat . . . wishing. . . .

A half moment later, Wolfram came lumbering up and stopped a cautious distance away. Rane stared at that hat, then at the great beast's lolling tongue and massive jaws. A slow, wicked smile spread over his bronzed features and he got to his feet and went to stand behind the stone where Charity and the baron were seated. Pinnow made a point of pressing closer to Charity and ignoring Rane, which made Rane's job all the easier.

He snatched the expensive hat behind his back and retreated. A devilish smile creased his face as he turned to Wolfram and waggled the headgear with a seductive flourish. Wolfram came to immediate attention, reeling in his tongue and fixing his eyes on that eminently chewable bit of silk-clad beaver. A bit more waggling and the dog was on his feet, eyes aflame, his tail slapping back and forth like a whip.

Rane uncoiled his arm and sent the hat sailing silently off on the gentle sea breeze, into the nearby field . . . with Wolfram in hot pursuit. He watched with a diabolical grin for a moment, until he was sure the dog would catch it in his massive, slobbery jaws, then covered his glee with a look of sober horror.

"Ye gods, Pinnow!" He pretended to turn with a start. "That cursed dog has your hat! Your expensive hat, man, he just darted in and grabbed it!" He straightened, seeming outraged for his rival. "Bring that back here, you mangy brute—it's worth at least two quid!"

"T-ten pounds s-seven!" Pinnow bellowed as though he'd been gored and lurched up. Wolfram shook the hat playfully, obviously pleased with the commotion he and his new plaything were causing. The baron groaned and bolted after him, shouting, "Come back here! Relinquish that hat—immediately!"

Wolfram watched the purple-faced baron coming toward him, probably to claim his new toy, and realized that this was a prime opportunity for a game of keepaway. His great brown eyes began to glow with excitement. Keep-away was his *favorite* game. He could play forever. . . .

The irate baron chased and snarled and cursed under his breath. Wolfram dodged and feinted and bounded off . . . staying just beyond the baron's fingertips.

Rane's shoulders were shaking with silent laughter as he turned and pulled Charity to her feet. He pressed a finger to her lips when she started to speak and led her down the sloping path to the ruins, as quickly as his stiff leg allowed.

"Shouldn't we—" She managed a breathless glance back over her shoulder at the hapless baron.

"Shhhh!" Rane slowed at the sight of her glowing eyes and flushed skin. "Unless you want him to come along. . . ." She raised a mischievous look to him and shook her head. His devilish grin broadened. "Come on then!"

Chapter Eleven

Hand in hand, they hurried through the littered stones and old grasses, on a zigzagging course toward the old stone chapel that rose above the rest of the ruins. The inside of the chapel was cool and dim, and so hushed that they could almost hear their heartbeats echoing in the vaulted stone chamber. She led him down a set of steps and down a roofless corridor of stone arches to another set of steps leading down to the old Brothers' House. It wasn't long before they heard the baron's voice, calling to them, echoing through the ruins.

Rane pulled Charity behind a stone pillar and cradled her against his hard body. His hand came up to press his grinning lips in a silent "shhhh," then came to rest on hers. They were hiding, the gesture said. And Pinnow would eventually have to give up and leave.

Twice he came close enough to threaten them with discovery; they could hear his puffing and stomping and muttering. They held their breaths and slipped from pillar to doorway to votary niche on silent feet, giggling like naughty children. After a while, the calling stopped and Charity led Rane to an upper window, where they glimpsed Sullivan Pinnow, still hatless, stalking along the sea path back toward Standwell. Around him, leaping and cavorting in broad, taunting circles, was a gray, four-legged form . . . with a piece of exceedingly expensive silk-clad felt in its mouth.

The laughter they'd been holding inside erupted, filling the cold, somber stonework with billows of warm, human sound. It seemed the most natural thing in the world for her to lean against his side, and for him to put an arm about her waist. She lifted her face to him and watched the glow of mirth in his eyes mute to a softer light. He bent and brushed his lips over the tip of her nose, her chin, and then her mouth. She became very still, intent on that subtle pleasure. Then to her surprise, he released her, taking her hand.

"Show me the ruins."

She nodded. The unexpected tenderness of those light brushes made them seem somehow more intimate than any kiss he'd given her before. And in the grip of a complex new feeling of pleasurable anticipation, she took him by the hand and began to lead him around the abbey, telling him the history of the place and her family connection to it.

They walked in sunlight and in shadow, talking of her family and Standwell. More than once his gaze drifted to the subtle sway of her skirts. Several times her eyes were drawn to his long, booted legs and the fit of snug wool over his muscular thighs. Each stole looks at their joined hands . . . his so dark and powerful, hers so fair and slender . . . gently entwined.

When they came to the lower levels of the Brothers' House, the storage areas and cellars, Rane stiffened, and his hand tightened on hers. When she turned to look, he was as stony as the great walls themselves and it took her a minute to realize he was glaring at something over her shoulder . . . and around them.

"Do you mind if we leave?" he said through clenched teeth.

Spider webs, lots of them, she realized. She pulled him toward the door. Once they were up the stairs and out in the sunshine, he relaxed somewhat, and she led him across a grassy clearing that had once been an open court in the midst of the abbey. They strolled, hand in hand and in deep silence for a few minutes, leaving the cold and damp behind for the sun and the terraced slope overlooking the bay.

They came to a sheltered spot among the great tumbled stones of the old round watchtower at the edge of the abbey. The grasses were lush and thick under their feet and a low, drumming cadence of distant waves pounding rocks invaded them, unnoticed. He paused beside her and she turned to him.

"I'm sorry." She searched the defensive set of his jaw. "I honestly didn't think. Why do you hate spiders so much?"

Rane turned a troubled look on her and she swallowed hard, obviously worried that he would be angry with her for asking. Her eyes were warm and clear, and her hair glowed in a soft spun-gold halo. Suddenly he had an urge to tell her what he'd never told another living soul, what caused him real discomfort to even recall. "I . . . was trapped in the hold of a ship once . . . with hundreds of them." She nodded, accepting it, but he could see she didn't understand. How could anyone from this climate understand?

"In the tropics there are spiders . . . as big as a man's hand. Tarantulas." He swallowed, feeling a little panicky just talking about it. "When I was a boy on Barbados, one of the few treats we had was bananas, most of which came by boat. I crept aboard a boat with some other boys to steal a few bananas once . . . and got trapped in the cargo hold with the bananas and . . . spiders, dozens and dozens of them. Tarantulas hide in the banana stalks as they're harvested and the workers don't know they're there. I was there for hours . . . with the cursed things crawling . . ."

His hand had tightened fiercely on hers, and when she returned the pressure, his eyes shifted and he rolled the nightmare from his broad shoulders. His voice came with a familiar, sardonic tone. "I suppose that must seem amusing . . . a man being so . . . so . . ."

"Afraid of spiders?" she supplied, reaching up to touch his cheek. She stopped halfway there, reddening, and would have withdrawn but he caught her hand in his and held it. "I don't think that's so strange."

Where their hands touched, a familiar warmth began spreading through him, loosening the cold knot in the pit of his belly.

"Everybody's afraid of something," she said softly. "I was afraid of the dark when I was small, and I've always been afraid of the water. Gran'mere's afraid of bad luck and Gar Davis is afraid of horses and lightning . . . and most people are afraid of dying. My father always said the important thing was not to let your fears keep you small. Not to let them keep you from doing things you have to do . . . or want to do." Her eyes misted unexpectedly as the mention of her father sent a wave of loss rolling quietly through her. "You still like bananas, don't you?"

Rane caressed her cheek, feeling a bit unnerved by her comforting logic and by the brief sadness he had experienced with her. Increasingly, whenever her father was mentioned, he could feel the pull of her hurt and longing as though it had originated inside him. It was more than just knowing what she felt . . . it was as though he somehow *shared* her feeling.

"He must have been a very wise man, your father, as well as a very lucky one. I wish I could have met him."

She smiled up at him through damp lashes, surprised by his tone of regret. "I wish you could have, too." The little smile she gave him had a sad, angelic quality to it that begged for more intimate comfort.

His hands slid to her shoulders and his head bent slowly to the softness of her mouth. She rose on her toes to meet him, needing him, wanting the sweet solace of his kiss. Gentle pressure, the soft, coaxing caresses of his lips beckoned her to respond, allowing her to set their pace. Gentle embraces, the light tantalizing massage of his hands on her back and waist slowly dismantled her inhibitions, allowing her desires to unfold in unhurried fashion.

He ended the kiss just as her knees were weakening, and Charity gazed up at his darkening eyes with her lips throbbing and her breasts tingling for the feel of him. Had she done something wrong? Had she seemed too eager? She flushed hotly and looked away. Why couldn't she ever manage to control her urges in his presence?!

His lips burned and his body groaned for more as he took her hand and began to walk along the top of one of the old terracing walls made of unmortared stones. For nearly two weeks he'd dreamt of having her alone like this, of feeling her against him . . . beneath him . . . And now that he had her to himself, he was beset by all manner of wild, conflicting impulses. He was determined to make love to her, to rouse and satisfy and enjoy her as no other man could. But now he also wanted to listen to her and tell her things, to watch her, and even protect her. The gentleman in him was scrambling to maintain his footing. What if he hurt her somehow? What if he lost control. . . ?

Suddenly the ground began to shift and give beneath his feet. Part of the eroded terrace wall collapsed under his weight, sending broken rock sliding and setting him flailing and scrambling with it.

"OhhhHHH-OWWWW!!!" His feet flew from under him and he went sliding and thumping down the crumbling wall on his injured buttock and leg, bashing his shoulders on the tumbled wall and landing sprawled on the grassy area below.

"Your lordship!" She scrambled down the wall and hurried to his side. "Are you alright?" He was momen-

191

tarily breathless and so stunned by his fall that he allowed her to take his arm and help him up.

"I-I'm n-not sure . . ." He winced as he gingerly flexed his bruised shoulders and felt his ribs and arms, taking stock of his condition. She watched anxiously as his hands moved down over his body. Then her eyes caught on the scrape marks up the sides of his boots and breeches. Without thinking, she sent her hand straight to the taut, much-abused mound of flesh he had fallen on yet again.

"Oh, no. Did you hurt your . . . your . . . again?" She found herself with her fingers questing knowledgeably over his left buttock and her eyes widened. She froze.

Her impulsive act unleashed a white hot bolt of excitement between them, setting both of them burning with expectation. She tried to pull her hand back and found it trapped beneath his, clamped over his buttock. For a long moment, she stared into the button holes in his elegant gray coat, unable to speak or to think how to excuse her brazen behavior. Then he lifted her chin on his hand to look into her crimson face.

"I'm sorry. I-I just meant. . . ."

"I know what you meant." He knew exactly the concern and openness and sense of intimacy that had prompted her to such familiarity with him. It was the same bewildering conglomeration of feelings and discovery and desires that he had just been feeling.

He reached for her with his other hand, curling it about the back of her neck, pulling her against him as his fingers molded hers over his aching rear, coaxing her caress. Then as her lips parted to receive him his fingers slid down the nape of her neck, pressing warm promises into the silky skin beneath the edge of her bodice. They came together, senses widening as rough velvet tongues plundered sleek oral hollows. Their bodies pressed closer, recalling that pleasurable fit of

192

contours they had managed so briefly in the darkened stone keep. Through her simple clothing, she could feel each line and curve of his body, the lean musculature of his ribs against her breasts, the hard plane of his stomach against her waist, and the swelling ridge of his male shaft against her belly. Each point of contact recalled to her mind's eye, the smooth, tanned skin and taut symmetry of his hard, male body. Where her mind wandered, her hands followed, seeking familiar treasures in a new way.

He felt her hands sliding beneath his coat, rising up his back, and groaned. Each stroke, each tentative caress, added to the pressure building in his loins. He slid his mouth down her chin and along her jaw, to her ear. Between breathy kisses and seductive nibbles that sent hot shivers down her neck and into her tingling nipples, he whispered her name over and over.

It wasn't "Miss Standing" or "Miss Charity" now, just *Charity*, richly woven with feeling and summoned from the depths of his very being. "Charity, I've wanted to hold you like this since the first minute I set eyes on you. To touch you . . . to feel you against me. . . ," he rasped, toying with her reddened lips. Then he paused and the flames in the backs of his eyes flared. "Well — not exactly like this. . . ."

His kiss was fierce, consuming, and when it ended, it left her dazed and swaying. When she managed to open her eyes, he had removed his elegant gray coat and spread it on the ground nearby. He lowered her to it and sank to the ground beside her, pressing her back against the body-warmed silk, into the softness of the moist earth and cradling grasses.

"This is more what I had in mind . . ." His wide chest rolled slowly over her breasts, molding that pliant flesh to his harder frame. His kisses trailed from the side of her mouth, down her cheek and neck, and his fingers wrapped over the front of her dark bodice so that his fingertips grazed the bare skin of her breast. "I want to love you, angel," he murmured into her throat. "But a gentleman never goes anywhere uninvited . . ."

"Touch me." It was the purest invitation he'd ever received.

He lifted her slightly and worked the ties at the back of her dress. He peeled back her black bodice to reveal the light boning that guarded her treasures. Those pale, perfect globes, nested in a whorl of black, were the incarnation of his deepest desires . . . light on dark, his blonde in black, his earthly angel. His tanned fingers slid over that fair, silken skin, dark claiming light, fulfilling the master scheme of his erotic desires. He rubbed his cheek over that living satin, then with trembling fingers, levered her nipples above their confinement and traced their tightly budded tips with his tongue.

She gasped as slow, swirling eddies of pleasure stirred through her breasts and narrowed to plunge and writhe in sinuous, hot streams through her body. Her shoulder flexed, arching to offer him more, seeking a deepening pleasure. And as his mouth fastened on one tight coral bud, suckling, she jolted physically, flung sharply onto a higher plane of sensation and erotic awareness. Her skin ached for his touch and her woman's flesh grew hot and sensitive with the memory of his hard body moving against it. His hands roamed and caressed her sides, her shoulders, her thighs, creating warm fluid surges in her blood wherever they went.

He shifted to press his swollen shaft against her hip as his knee nudged between hers. Her legs parted as he slid over her and his aching loins came to rest against her tender woman's cleft. Then he arched, sliding his swollen shaft over her responsive flesh, riding gently along its sensitive groove. Even through her clothes, the sensations were shattering. Each thrust pushed her excitement higher, and near the end of each she felt a crowning spasm of raw pleasure that radiated quickly through her woman's mound and was absorbed by the rest of her body as a delicious wave of warmth. Again and again it came, buoying her desires ever higher on a rising sea of liquid heat.

Her body now arched to meet his movement, rhythmically, in a sultry, driving synchrony of need. Her knees raised slightly to cradle his narrow hips against her, concentrating his force, focusing her pleasure as she undulated beneath him. One of his hands left her shoulders and hair to skim her half naked curves and seize her skirt. The fabric slipped slowly upward, a retreating tide of innocence that revealed the curvy hip and silky thigh he had once glimpsed in devastating silhouette. Now the shape, the texture, the erotic reality of them were his.

His hand roamed and caressed, gently at first, then more firmly as she gasped and pressed into his palm. Powerful hot currents of pleasure poured around and through her, flowing from his fingers across her bare hip and down the inside of her thigh. She felt him shift his body aside and started as the cool air and his hot fingers touched her in the same moment. The chill was instantly replaced by the steamy swirlings of his fingers against her flesh. Over and over he triggered breathtaking flashes of lightning through her senses that were accompanied by thunderous shudders of pleasure in her lower body. His hands . . . she managed to realize . . . he was making her pleasure with his hands. . . .

Magic. Her hands on his back stilled and her breath stopped. Her body tightened around an unseen hollow as she was propelled sharply upward on a towering rogue wave of sensation that released pleasure in a crashing white wall through her. Her senses erupted and her body arched and quivered. She felt suspended in brightness, expanded, given up to the elements that comprised her. It was a long minute before the white storm in her body subsided and she again felt the light kisses he rained over her face.

"It *is* magic," she managed to whisper into the molten disks of his eyes.

"Yes, it is," he smiled with tender hunger, not realizing fully what she meant or just how true it really was. "And there's more, my angel . . . much more."

When his mouth touched hers again, her body rippled under his. The pleasure that had seemed to be subsiding, resurged to fill her consciousness. But with it came a new hunger that made her want him against every inch of her body, a driving need to somehow join with him, to share his very body. The feel of his hot, bare shaft against her was strange, but the movements of his body as he rubbed it silkily over her moist heat were reassuringly familiar and stunningly pleasurable.

He cradled her head between his hands and his kisses became consuming as he relaxed the reins of his desires and let the pressure build in his loins. Breath by breath, the need focused in him, narrowing his senses, shutting out all but the soft, responsive being beneath him.

"Woof . . ."

He kissed her deeply and answered her throaty whimpers and helpless undulations with a subtle change of position that brought him against her unopened flesh.

"Woof!"

Something riffled through his constricted senses and he tightened against it, intent on claiming his seductive angel.

"Woof! Wrrrroof! RRRRROOF!"

He froze at the brink of paradise, listening to the nemesis of his desires fast approaching.

"RRROLF, RRROLF, RRRRROLF!"

"Noooo," he groaned. "Not that. Not your damned—"

But, the thought galvanized him, it could be more than just her damnable dog! Pinnow could be coming back, or even the old lady! He was suddenly up on all fours, braced above her stunned form, battening his breeches flap and covering her with her skirts.

Wolfram streaked across the terraced slope, bounding effortlessly over terrace walls in his mission to protect his mistress. He'd been distracted by his hat game with baron, but was all attention now. The sight of Miss Charity lying limp on the ground, beneath the lordship's possessive canine-male stance, sent a quiver of protective rage through him.

Rane didn't make it to his feet before Wolfram was on them, crouching and growling, showing his teeth at Rane and barking frantically at Charity. Rane braced, confronting the dog with fire crackling in his eyes. It was suddenly "bulldog" to wolfhound, male to male . . .

"You mangy, slavering . . . just come one step closer—just *one*," he beckoned furiously, "and I'll have your guts for garters!!"

"No! Please—he thinks he's protecting me." Charity recovered her senses enough to sit up partway, clutching at Rane's shirt to restrain him. "Wolfie, stop! I'm all right—really! *Wolfie!*"

The dog gradually eased and quieted to a growl, turning his big nose her direction for confirming sniffs. Then as Rane pushed to his feet, the dog darted in to stand over Charity, growling at Rane from the same position Rane had occupied seconds before. Rane stumbled back a step, unable to believe his eyes . . . or his thoughts. Jealous, the damned dog was jealous!

"Look bonehead," his voice was hoarse with frustration as he punched a finger at Wolfram. "You belong to her . . . she doesn't belong to you!" Wolfram growled accusingly and snarled nastily when Rane started toward her. "I am not going to hurt her—I just want to love her!" Frustration overwhelmed him and he

197

clenched his fists and shouted, "I'm crazy about her!"

The next moment, Charity scrambled to her feet, holding her drooping bodice against her breasts with crossed arms. Her hair was a glorious jumble, her lips were swollen from his hungry kisses, and her skin bore a revealing flush. But it was her caramel eyes, so irresistibly wide, that held him.

"You're crazy about me?" The girlish softness in her tone sent a wave of pure longing through him that had nothing to do with the thudding misery in his loins. He swallowed, feeling himself melting irretrievably into those clear honey pools again.

"Mad as a March hare."

A slow, bone-melting smile grew on her winsome face and he found himself smiling back. For some reason, he didn't seem to feel the burning confusion in his loins anymore.

Lady Margaret had seen Sullivan Pinnow storming up the sea path alone, then spotted Wolfram trotting and frolicking along behind him, and she knew without asking what had happened. Charity and the viscount were together . . . still at the ruins . . . alone . . .

"Worthless as cow thumbs!" She'd hurried to the kitchen door to snag the dog by his one scraggly ear and deliver him a blistering tirade that made "hell's backwater" sound a very refreshing place indeed, in comparison. "Now get your mangy carcass back out there and find them!"

Nearly an hour later, the old lady watched her granddaughter and the viscount walking up the sea path, from an upstairs window. She read in their glowing faces and joined hands that her fears were well founded. It was plain as a pikestaff that something drastic had happened between them!

She hurried downstairs to meet them and stopped

short on the steps, gaping at his lordship's grass-stained coat, ripped breeches, scarred boots . . . and the way he limped and the nasty red scrape in the palm of one of his hands. Whatever pleasure he had taken from her granddaughter, she inferred grimly, he'd certainly been made to pay for it. Then her gaze shifted to Charity and her heart folded and sank at the sight of Charity's tousled hair, rumpled dress, and love-flushed skin. Charity felt the disapproval in Lady Margaret's gaze and lowered her eyes as she hurried past her grandmother on the steps, heading for her room.

Rane watched the old lady's tight expression as she came down the stairs and obeyed her irritable hand motion ordering him into the "parlor." He could guess what she had on her mind.

"My granddaughter was an innocent." The old woman faced him with a fiery look that didn't quite conceal the pain it caused her to speak such words.

"She . . . still is," Rane answered her hot look with a steady gaze. "Though perhaps a bit less of one. I've not dishonored her." He did have the grace to redden, realizing that Charity's continued virtue was more to old Wolfram's credit than to his own. Lady Margaret searched his face for a long moment, then eased and turned away to stare out one of the long windows.

"It will leave her in pieces . . . when you leave." The old lady's voice was low and earnest, filled with the special pain a parent feels in letting go. "I can't protect her from you anymore. Nor you from her."

"I won't leave her in pieces," he declared. It hadn't occurred to him until this moment that his days at Standwell were numbered . . . and running out. He stalked closer, feeling an odd, hollow aching inside at the new thought of being parted from her. "Lady Margaret, I care about Charity. I don't intend to just leave—" He halted, a bit shocked by what he was about to say. If he didn't intend to just leave her . . .

199

what in heaven did he intend to do? Take her with him?

He stood in the middle of the parlor, realizing that was exactly what he intended. But *his* life, his future were supposed to be in London, with the lady-wife he'd sworn to keep! He'd worked eight long years to restore his family fortunes and recoup his family name. And the crowning of his success was to have been the acquisition of a proper lady-wife . . . a pale, perfect daughter of the almighty ton. He suddenly realized he hadn't even thought about his ambition in marriage in nearly two weeks!

He staggered and had to brace himself to stay upright. What had happened to his burning determination to make London society swallow its disapproval of him?

Massive, unquenchable desire for Charity Standing had happened. That and a dozen other disasters . . . being wrecked and bashed and shot and burned and cut and attacked by wild beasts. He'd been knocked in the head almost daily for the last fortnight; perhaps that accounted for the softening in his thinking! Or perhaps it was just her . . .

Charity Standing was bright and compassionate and giving, not to mention the most desirable young woman he'd seen in his entire life. And she had rather spectacular effects on him; instantaneous relief from pain and discomfort of all kinds, intense sexual arousal, and bewildering lapses of both anger and ambition, to name a few. She'd consumed his thoughts and rearranged his desires and wreaked havoc in his priorities. He'd come to want Charity Standing with every particle of his being.

Charity Standing wasn't ton. Neither was she a woman that a man could bed and leave, or keep secreted away in some neat little corner . . . or a country house in shambles. She was the kind of woman a man had to have in the middle of his life with him, not dangling about the edges, pulling him off center.

He thought of the pale, elegant debs he'd courted, the Carolines and Janes and Glorias . . . all so perfect, and so perfectly *interchangeable*. Eager and sensual, forthright and sensible, Charity Standing was utterly unique. She had been shaped and cast outside society's rigid, conformist mold, just as he had been. They were two of a kind, perfectly matched. She wasn't a "London lily," true. But who would dare judge an angel by such paltry measure?

He recalled glimpses of her reading to him, and bringing him kittens, and shaving him. He relived the deep pleasure of lying wedged against her soft heat, feeling her responses rising. Then he conjured the sight of her presiding over the tea tray and at the dinner table and savored the natural grace of her carriage and the effortless elegance of her movements.

She was his own personal angel, and he was going to make her his *wife!*

Lady Margaret had slipped out of the parlor, but not before she witnessed the telling play of longing and feeling on his aristocratic features. The Viscount Oxley had survived long enough to fall in love with her granddaughter. She could only pray he didn't take it into his head to do anything genuinely catastrophic . . . like marrying her!

The upper hallway had a cool, gray-silver glow from the light of the nearly full moon that streamed in the window at the far end of the corridor. But from beneath Rane Austen's door came a warm golden slice of light that drew Charity's eyes as she peered from her doorway into the hall. She chewed her lip watching that tantalizing golden slit, knowing it meant Rane was still awake, too.

She had spent the evening tending and occupying Stephenson, since Lady Margaret had suffered one of her infrequent attacks of lumbago and was unable to see to him. All evening she'd thought about Rane and what had happened between them at the ruins, and she was still thinking about it when she went to bed. Now she lay awake, feeling tantalizing echoes of pleasure whispering through her blood. As she squirmed and tossed, she felt his caress in the bind of her nightdress, felt his weight in the press of the comforter against her, felt his tongue in the rasp of fabric against her sensitive breasts.

She'd experienced the magic in his hands. It had been wonderful, breathtaking . . . like whole oceans colliding in her very body. It was a discovery so powerful that it eclipsed everything else.

Almost everything. Above the chaos of her desires and fears and longings, her mind fixed on the sight of Rane standing there with his body trembling and his gray eyes burning, declaring that he was "crazy about her." *He cared for her.* A powerful new ache of longing swept her from head to toe. She wanted, needed that caring even more than she wanted the night magic in his hands.

She took one step, then another across that moonlit hall, when out of nowhere came shuffling, thudding sounds. She looked up to find Wolfie materializing out of the darkness behind her. He threw himself against her, nuzzling her and demanding affection forcefully enough to bowl her over. She smiled and bent to give him a hug and to scratch his chin and his ear. His dark eyes raised, questioning her. "I want him, Wolfie," she explained softly. "And he wants me. I have to go."

She opened Rane's door and slipped inside.

Wolfram watched her go, watched the door close and heard the latch click. His ear drooped first, then his head. He huffed in a way that sounded remarkably like a sigh and spread himself across the threshold of Rane's door. His great head sank onto his paws and his dark eyes glistened in the dimness.

Chapter Twelve

Rane was standing by the window, dressed only in his shirt and breeches, half-prepared for bed. He turned with a start, broad shoulders coiled from defensive habit. Charity's heart skipped erratically as she watched his eyes lighten and his posture warm. She felt his gaze roaming her loose cotton nightdress and her unbound hair and hoped he didn't find her disappointing. She hadn't given any thought to what ladies wore on such occasions.

He took one step toward her, then another, and stopped. The gathered neck of her simple gown hung off center, baring most of one smooth shoulder, and her long silky hair clung to her like a possessive cloud. Her eyes were taffy-centered sweets in the dim candlelight and her generous lips were like bitten cherries. She was desire and innocence in such equal proportions that he didn't know which to address.

"I couldn't sleep," she confessed, running visual fingers through his silky black hair, then over the tempting slice of tanned skin that showed through the opening of his half-buttoned shirt. He was so big and bronzed and hard . . .

"Neither could I," he admitted, losing his eyes to the tantalizing cling of the nightdress over her breasts. The play of light from the single candle shaded two little bumps at the tips of her breasts that sent a galvanic tremor through his body. Hard, crinkled velvet points, just a snatch of cloth away . . .

"Well, as long as we're awake . . . perhaps we can not sleep, together," she proposed with a tantalizing blend of suggestiveness and sensibility. He laughed, bronzing.

"I believe it was just such thoughts of us 'not sleeping'

together that were keeping me awake." He stepped closer and his voice lowered to a deep, vibrating rumble. "Why is it that everything you say to me sounds so reasonable and proper . . . and right?"

"I have no idea," she confessed, wonderingly. "I don't seem to behave very properly, where you're concerned. It wasn't very ladylike of me to come here."

"And if I were any kind of a gentleman, I wouldn't let you stay. But, I don't always behave very properly where you're concerned, either. I was thinking of crossing the hall myself, angel."

She came a step closer and the whisper of her movement, with its hint of thigh brushing thigh, sent heat curling through his blood. She was within his arm's reach, glowing, asking to be touched. He ran his fingertips along her bare collarbone and she shivered, wanting to curl around his hand. But, she couldn't move, couldn't swallow, could scarcely breathe. He could see the tension in her shoulders and the flicker of uncertainty in her eyes and smiled, thinking of the innocence they betrayed . . . the innocence he would soon claim.

"Close your eyes," he commanded softly and she obeyed, trusting him. His hand slid down her arm and caught her wrist, pulling her across the room. He blew out the candle on the way to the window.

"Now look," he murmured drawing her against the windowsill with him.

She opened her eyes on a sweeping night view of the bay below Standwell. It was familiar and yet strange, seen by such strong moonlight. The slopes above the bay waters were dark velvet mounds edged by crumpled satin cliffs and rimmed by an ephemeral lace of foaming breakers below. A great, yellow medallion of a moon hung above the black waves, gliding the bolder crests as they rose against the nightwind. His arm slid around her, pulling her back against his front, gently wrapping her in his warmth beside the chilly glass.

205

"I was looking at it when you came. It's beautiful," he murmured.

"Yes, it is." She looked up to find him looking at her, not at the view. "I haven't looked at the moon in years."

"Nor have I. I suspect there are quite a few things I haven't really looked at in years."

"Gran'mere says moonlight is dangerous," Charity whispered, half forgetting to breathe, intent on the feel of his sheltering strength all around her. "Gazing at the full moon can make you go—"

"Mad? Too late. I'm already 'mad,' remember?" He turned her by the shoulders and pulled her against him, wrapping her waist with his arms. "Mad as a hatter. I can't sleep at night, I can't concentrate, and I can't seem to control my balance or my body temperature or my own wretched feet. Everytime I turn around, I'm bungling into some minor catastrophe or other . . . and the insane part is, it doesn't even seem to hurt anymore when I bang my head or smash a finger or go sprawling arse-over-elbows." He threaded his fingers into the silky flood of her hair and she felt her heart pounding harder as she absorbed the tenderness in his touch and the pained wonder in his voice.

"I find myself remembering things and feeling things and thinking things . . . Right now I don't care if I ever get back to London or if my business turns sour or if I'm never invited to another society bash. Everything in me and around me seems to be in turmoil. I don't feel like the same man anymore."

It was true, she realized, listening with her heart as well as her head. He didn't seem to be the same man! The impatience, the guarded air he'd worn like a cloak, the perpetual storm in his eyes, all were gone. The flame inside him still flared, but with desire, not anger. The startling intensity of his physical presence and his forceful character now seemed focused, channeled, more strength than threat.

"I'd swear it was one of those vile potions your grandmother made me drink, but I know better. You're to blame, Charity Standing," he charged softly, "or to credit." She roused, coming back to him, staring up into his night-luminous eyes.

"I am?" Her head began to spin dizzily, deliriously, as the full meaning of his words sank through the heat in her senses. He was saying that she had *helped* him! In their days together, in their talks and touches, the tender, thoughtful, sensual man inside the commanding aristocrat had slowly been released.

"All I have to do is look at you and every hurt, every ache in me begins to melt away. Having you near changes my perceptions and rearranges my thoughts and rouses my feelings. . . . I don't understand what happens between us every time I set eyes or hands to you—" Her fingertips on his lips stopped him.

"I think . . . it's a bit of magic." Her eyes sparkled in the dimness. "Gran'mere told me about it, the needing and the wanting between a man and a woman. And about the special pleasures that make your bones soften and your blood burn. . . ."

"Your grandmother told you about . . . pleasures?" He strangled on a laugh. "Lord, the old girl never ceases to surprise me."

"I don't think she meant to tell me quite so much." Her lashes lowered briefly. "I think she was trying to warn me about you."

"Ah, now that sounds more like her! Pleasures, eh? Tell me," his grin flashed with pure devilment. "Did she tell you about this?" He clasped her waist and skimmed up her sides to cup her breasts through her thin nightdress. Warm, hard fingers, lifting, caressing her gently . . .

"N-n-no . . . n-not exactly that." Her eyes widened and she shivered as he rolled the sensitive tips of her breasts back and forth between his fingers. Each twist and curl vibrated through connections in her that reached all the way into her tingling womanflesh.

"Ummm." He nodded thoughtfully and bent to nuzzle her hair back and tongue the whorl of her ear. Then he nibbled his way down the side of her throat, murmuring, "What about this? Did she mention this?" A hot, moist mouth kissing, tasting her skin . . .

"N-no-o-o, I d-don't . . . believe so." She felt her legs melting and leaned into his body for support, circling his waist with her arms. His arms tightened hard around her and he rubbed his body slowly down hers, flexing against her, caressing her with sinuous undulations of his muscular frame.

"Surely she included this. . . . ," he declared huskily, pulling her bottom half against his burning loins and thrusting slowly upward, against her womanly softness. She tightened, quivering, remembering the steamy pleasures that particular movement invoked. It was a moment before she could swallow her desire enough to speak.

"A-actually . . . I think it had more to do with h-hands," she murmured weakly.

"Hands?" His voice was a smoky rasp as he loomed over her, staring down into her dazed, desirous expression.

"Gran'mere lived with the gypsies when she was a girl and she learned gypsy ways." Everything in her body was becoming hot and liquid, trickling down into her loins, melting her bones. "She told me about the way a man's hands can turn 'night work' into 'night magic.' " She lifted his hand and he spread it for her as she ran her fingers over its hardened creases. "Though not every man has the night magic in his hands. Mostly just gypsies and Frenchmen."

"And you think I might have it, this 'night magic'?" He watched the glow in her eyes deepen as her mouth turned up in a very womanly, very alluring smile.

"I think you might." She rubbed her cheek against his palm and her eyes closed as she kissed and nuzzled it adoringly. He was a little surprised to realize she was recalling the pleasures he'd made for her that afternoon . . . with his hands. "I like your hands; they're so strong and tanned. I like all of you." She undulated against him. "You're so hard and so powerfully shaped. I never dreamt a body could be so beautiful."

Desire exploded up out of his loins and roared up the inner walls of his body, trembling his entire frame. He swooped to capture her lips, ravishing her senses as she circled him with her arms, giving herself up to him. Moments later, he pulled back, heaving, reaching for the ties of her nightdress with searing blue flames in the backs of his eyes. The garment slid and she caught it with trembling hands and searched the hunger in his face.

"I want to see you, angel," he demanded softly, invading her reluctance, coaxing her permission with quick, tender kisses along her temples and down the side of her neck. "I love to look at you, too. Your skin is so creamy and white, so different from mine." When his hands slid beneath her opened gown, prying it from her shoulders, she allowed it to slide. His hands followed it down her bare form, stroking and caressing and his eyes followed, watching his tanned fingers claim and charm the rounded, tightly-budded breasts he recalled so vividly.

He froze mid-kiss and spoke against her lips.

"Where's . . . your dog?"

"Outside, in the hallway." She rose to join their mouths and entreated a deeper pleasure by pressing her breasts harder against his palms. When he hesitated a moment longer, she began to understand and smiled. "He can't work doorlatches."

"I wouldn't be so sure," he growled huskily, unleashing his fingers to close around her taut nipples, making her gasp and wringing an involuntary wriggle from her. On the heels of those icy quivers, warmth billowed inside her, preparing her for the pleasure that was to come, for the love that was about to be fulfilled and sealed in their very flesh. His caresses lowered to the curve of her waist and flare of her hips, then he filled his hands with the softness of her buttocks. He lifted her against him, luxuriating in her warm responsiveness to his touch and in the shy, seeking movements of her body against his.

It was time, he realized, and he lifted her and carried her to the bed, laying her gently on the sheets. Lying half in moonlight, she glowed with a marble-like luster, cool perfection cloaking tumultuous heat. Her long hair tumbled across the pillows like an exotic waterfall. His hands fumbled with his clothes.

Her eyes drifted over the rippling fan of muscles that spread in his back as he bent to remove his breeches. Muscles worked visibly beneath the taut, bronzed skin of his shoulders. Her eyes slid down his narrow waist to the contrasting paleness of his pelvis and buttocks. There was a vivid red streak across one buttock, the wound she had once tended so carefully. When he came to stand by the bed, drinking her with his eyes, she whispered her heart's longing.

"Come . . . make magic with me."

He sank onto the bed and into her arms, pressing her back into the bedclothes, covering her cool breasts with a dark blanket of desire. He toyed with her lips, licking, nibbling, raking them with his teeth, then dipped into the yielding wet heat of her mouth. The faint sweetness of her breath, the silkiness of their joining, filled his head then seeped into his lungs, filing his chest with an aching fullness.

Kisses followed caresses, drifting over her shoulders, and floating downward to her breasts. The smooth, rhythmic friction of his fingers over one nipple was almost indistinguishable from the lush, liquid rasp of his tongue at her other breast. A broad spiral of pleasure turned through her, beginning at the top of her head and descending through her body to wind in a tightening coil around her deep woman's core. A creamy flood of anticipation spread through her womanflesh and she moved against his swollen heat, tightening around the emptiness in her, seeking once again.

His hands slid over her belly and down her legs, stroking, learning the shapes of her, discovering the odd little places at the edges of her breasts and on the insides of her knees that made her gasp and shiver when his fingers brushed them. Then languidly, in dreamy heat, her hands returned his curiosity . . . and his pleasure.

The night magic began. With touches and whispers of longing and needs unfurling, they came together, the elements of their beings arrayed like strands on loom, chosen with infinite care by a higher order, strength matched to weakness, trait to habit, custom to inclination, longing to fulfillment. The weaving was begun in a slow dance of pleasure, winding, wreathing those brightly colored strands of self with another's, each thread of self and experience and desire made richer by the surrounding other's. Bodies intertwining, senses merging, pleasures mounting, they followed destiny's unseen pattern, which was visible only to the celestial weaver.

She opened to him, welcoming his weight, making his power her own as he wedged against her trembling softness. He closed over and about her, absorbing her gentleness into his own response. They arched and flexed in instinctive rhythm, trading sensation and discovery, until somewhere in their movement the joining began. Slowly, sinuously his hardened flesh invaded her yielding heat, stretching, filling her, rising in her against the resistance of her untried body. A velvety whisper of a moan rose from her mouth into his . . . filling his head, his chest. It was surrender and pleasure and joy, captured in low, enveloping vibrations that resonated in his blood and in his heart.

He arched above her, lifting her with each thrust, and she tightened about him, wrapping him with her legs. Over and over she whispered his name as she absorbed his driving energy and began to soar on his desire. Higher, brighter she burned until her body and senses exploded and all was bright white and soundless . . . dazzling.

211

Through that blinding release of heat and pleasure, she felt him arch and contract, finding his own release in her, and she celebrated his presence with her in that boundless white plane of feeling.

Colors . . . she realized as her heart began to beat again . . . she was being drenched in beautiful liquid streams of colors. From the pervasive white came pale yellows that took on a fiery golden glow that reddened to orange and crimson and umber. As her breathing calmed, other reds began to blue, becoming winey crimsons, then deep azures and rich purples. It was just as Gran'mere said . . . the colors . . . and the loving pleasures.

"It is magic," she whispered, her sense widening to include him.

"So it is, angel." He withdrew gently and slid to the bed beside her, feeling oddly expanded, too big to be contained inside his own body just now. He pulled her against his chest, curling around her, relishing the sensation of her damp skin against his. "Though I think it involved a bit more than just hands."

When she turned to look at him, his eyes were dark glistening windows on his deeply roused feelings.

"Hearts, too?"

He smiled a haunting, winsome smile. "Hearts, too."

She smiled back, her earthly angel sort of a smile, and ran her fingers over the tender velvet of his wide, sensual lips. Rane Austen belonged to her now, as she belonged to him. He caught her hand and kissed it and fondled it, his eyes lidding with still echoing pleasure.

And together they sank into sweet, steamy sleep.

Much later, Charity wakened to the strange but pleasurable feel of Rane's body wrapped about hers. Tucking her chin, she stared at him in the silvery moonlight, marveling at the odd mixture of power and tenderness that held her so possessively.

212

Rane. He'd been just what she needed. His presence here had pulled her from a storm of grief and pain into the healing influence of caring and discovery. In helping him, she'd uncovered the woman hidden in herself and had grown and experienced new feelings. He'd broadened her world and let her see the value of her instinct for caring and helping. And now he'd introduced her to the power of the night magic . . . and of love.

She didn't understand all the wonderful things that had happened to her in that delicious storm of loving, though she sensed a great deal more had occurred than just the giving and receiving of pleasure. For a time she had miraculously shared his senses, his feelings, his very body. And she had shared hers with him, holding nothing back, opening, offering everything she had. She closed her eyes, savoring the feel of him against her body as she drifted back to sleep.

In that sharing, in the magic of love, in the weaving they had begun, Charity had indeed shared her body and her pleasures and her growing love for Rane. But in that joining she had shared one other thing . . . she had shared with him, her *luck*.

Charity slipped from Rane's lingering hands, casting a warm-honey look over his muscular chest and love-tousled hair as she lifted the doorlatch and stepped into the dim hall. Gray morning light filtered down the empty hallway, as she paused, listening. It was still very early, just past dawn, and her grandmother was probably still asleep. She should have left Rane's bed hours ago, but he'd roused when she tried to slip from the bed, and one thing had led to another. . . . He'd loved her again. She smiled, fingering her tender lips and recalling how exquisitely he'd adored her body, how beautiful he'd made her feel.

She hurried across the hall to her door and darted inside. Small, steamy aches whispered through her muscles and her tenderer flesh, reminders of the night's unaccustomed usage. She could wash quickly and with any luck she could manage . . . She stopped short, halfway to the postered bed.

There, in the dim morning light, sat Lady Margaret on the bench at the foot of Charity's bed. Her face was as gray as the dawn light and her dark eyes were ringed with sleeplessness. Her weathered hands were clasped over the ends of the shawl she wore over her nightdress. She roused and straightened, staring at Charity's rumpled nightdress, her tousled hair and love-stung lips. But it was the luminous topaz glow in her granddaughter's eyes that caused the old woman's heart to sink. It was a loving glow . . . a given-heart kind of glow.

"Did he. . . ," Lady Margaret's voice was oddly hoarse. "Did he make the night magic for you?"

Charity chewed her tender lip, watching the unhappiness in her grandmother's eyes. It was worse for her than any scolding or punishment. She nodded, searching for her voice. All she found was a whisper.

"He has it in his hands, Gran'mere, the *night magic*. It was all you said . . . and more."

Lady Margaret rose stiffly and came toward her. Her eyes glistened. "Was he good to you, child?"

Charity nodded. "Oh, please . . . don't be angry with me, Gran'mere."

The old lady's face filled with loving pain. A taste of love, a bit of sweetness amidst such trouble. How could she begrudge them that? A tear rolled down her weathered cheek and she wrapped Charity in her arms and held her for a moment. Then she left without a word.

Sun and sweet spring air came streaming in Rane's open window, filling his lungs and senses, expanding his already buoyant mood. He stretched broadly, luxuriating in the slow, steady pulse of his blood and the sensual ease in his

214

body. He hadn't felt so relaxed, so satisfied in . . . hell, he hadn't ever felt *this* good! And look what a morning it was—sun all golden and birds singing, all the world alive and humming.

He turned to the washstand and on the way past the rumpled bed, he paused, staring at the jumbled sheets and getting a glint in his eye. She was his now. His angel, his lover and, soon, his *wife*. All he had to do was . . . convince her old grandmother to let him do the proper thing by her.

He shaved and dressed carefully in his grass-stained coat, and even polished his scarred boots before descending the stairs to the dining room to breakfast. Melwin informed him that Miss Charity was out and about already, being an early riser, and served him tea and porridge, and scones with fresh butter. After breakfast, the old retainer directed him to the library where Lady Margaret was reputed to be laboring over the state's "books."

He entered the creaking door and stood quietly near the writing desk by the window, smoothing his waistcoat and waiting for the old lady to recognize him. When she finally looked up at him over her scratched tin-rimmed spectacles, the darkness in her eyes hinted that she knew what he'd come about . . . and didn't like it a bit.

"Lady Margaret, I wish to speak to you, Charity's guardian . . . formally. You must know that over the last fortnight, I've come to know your granddaughter well—"

"Too blamed well," she muttered. He reddened, braced, and continued.

"I have come to hold her in the highest regard and have reason to believe that she holds me in simi—"

"You took her to your bed," she stated bluntly, removing her spectacles and glaring at him. He stiffened, reddening further.

"Very well." He kicked his gentlemanly self aside to get straight down to the brass of it, since that seemed to be her preference. "I want to marry her. I am well-fixed financially and have no legal or moral entanglements that would impede a marriage with her. I can provide for her and see to her welfare," he flicked a meaningful gaze around him at the faded library, "far better than you can here."

Lady Margaret's eyes narrowed irritably and she fidgeted with her spectacles, then with the rabbit's foot amulet and silver crescent moon about her neck. "Unthinkable! No good would come of it. You—you don't *suit*."

Rane stared at her, stung in a very vulnerable place by her attitude, which paralleled uncannily that of London's elitist fathers. *He didn't suit?* Even here, even in tumbled down old country houses, he wasn't good enough?! His defenses rose. He stalked closer, and jutted across her littered writing tale on his fists, forcing her to sit back in her chair. At that moment, he was every inch "Bulldog" Austen.

"I'm a titled man of sound education and decent moral fiber, a man of some wealth and accomplishment in life . . . and I'm not particularly hard on the eyes! What the hell else could you hope to have for her in a husband . . . the bloody Prince of Wales?!"

Lady Margaret glared at him mutinously. "You're the unluckiest lump of human flesh I've ever seen!"

Rane startled. Luck? She was worried about his damnable *luck?!*

"What in hell has *that* got to do with anything?! If it hadn't been for my being shot in the bloody arse, I wouldn't have been carried here, and I wouldn't have met your granddaughter or wanted to marry her—so I can't be that damned unlucky!"

Lady Margaret huddled back in her chair with her chin raised, looking as if he'd just proved her point. "Something could happen to you . . . and it would break her heart."

"That's it? You're afraid I'll kick under and leave her? Well, if I did, I'd leave her rich—" He tripped mentally over an insight and stumbled to a halt. Charity's grief for her father was still fresh and, obviously, deep. Perhaps the old lady's concern wasn't so absurd, after all. He had been

216

wounded badly. He could see Charity's lovely face, glowing with the care she had for him. If something were to happen to him . . . Then every bit of bulldog determination he owned came surging in to rescue his mushy thinking.

"Nothing's going to happen to me, you old croaker." His features sharpened with legendary Austen stubbornness. "Your granddaughter thinks I *suit* perfectly. I'm going to marry her . . . and I'm going to bed her and have children with her and enjoy life with her . . . and I'm going to live to a ripe, disgusting old age. And I'll do it with or without your blessing." He punched a finger at her, then straightened. "But, for Charity's sake, I'll ask this once. . . ."

She watched the unholy stubbornness in his handsome jaw, the passion's fire in his striking gray eyes, and knew it was out of her hands. Her knotty little frame seemed to shrink and she heaved a hard sigh.

"If she accepts you, I'll not say you nay."

Rane strode from the library with a wickedly determined grin on his face. It had gone rather well, he decided. The old lady really did want what was best for Charity, beneath all her gloom and doomsaying. Now he had only to find Charity and propose. Then he'd see that irresistible glow enter the backs of her eyes and she'd go all womanly and responsive as he took her into his arms . . . Lord, he was hot as a griddle just thinking about it!

Melwin scratched his head a minute, thinking, then declared that he'd seen his young mistress out by the kitchen gardens not long before. But Charity wasn't to be seen around the neatly tilled kitchen gardens when he arrived. Austen scowled, raking the stone and timber outbuildings visually for a glimpse of her. Failing that, he decided to try the stable, where he would also check on how his horses had been faring since they'd been brought from the livery in town.

She wasn't in the stable. He spent a few minutes, checking his high-blooded blacks, then paused in the stable doorway to smooth his waistcoat and look for her again.

A quick movement on the periphery of his vision caught his eye and his head snapped around to follow it. Not black and blonde; not her. It was a man, a small, thinnish fellow in drab clothes and old boots, and something in his half-crouched posture and wary movements made it seem like he was lurking. The fellow paused by the corner of the cow byre and, suddenly, from around the corner, an arm could be seen waving, beckoning. The fellow lurched around the corner after it.

Rane took one step, then two, in his direction. Without quite knowing why, he followed the skinny fellow who was following a beckoning arm. Stealth crept into his own movements, and when he reached the corner where the fellow had disappeared and peered around it, he saw the two of them. They were hurrying away from Standwell, talking—arguing!—and the second one had a cloth sack slung over his shoulders. Rane started with recognition. Short and square, short and scrawny—he knew those two!

It was the two conniving little bastards who shot him! Here, now. Red flooded his neck and ears, and his fists clenched. A dozen times he'd vowed to find and personally thrash them within an inch of their worthless lives! And now to have them—What in hell were they doing *here*, at Standwell?

He hurried toward the spot where they were disappearing into the trees. He followed them into a rocky, stream-cut ravine that led down toward the cliffs above the bay. The path was treacherous, and his leg and buttock soon ached from the constant stress of unstable footing. But with his eyes fixed on the two that had shot him, he overcame the physical discomfort in his determination to find and confront them.

Unwittingly, they led their former victim down the rocky ravine to the edge of the cliffs and then through a crude hand-hewn passage, complete with steps, that was hidden

218

from view by boulders and scrubby growth of bushes. A narrow, rocky ledge led to the mouth of a limestone cave. Rane paused, catching his breath, watching for them to come out. Then he closed in on the rats he'd trapped, cold mayhem written in the hard bronze of his face.

Charity saw Rane in the stableyard from an upstairs window and called to him, but he didn't seem to hear. He was intent on something she couldn't see, something between the byre and stable, out of her sight. She'd hurried downstairs to see him with a spring in her step and a rosy flush in her cheeks. The love-warmed aura of the night they had passed still clung to her like a cloak, and she longed to see him, to revel in the special touch of his eyes and the charged sensuality of his presence.

But when she arrived in the stableyard, he wasn't there. She caught sight of him stalking across the grassy field that led to the rocky stream below Standwell. She frowned. Why was he going down to the stream? There was an odd wariness to his movements . . . then he began to pause behind first one tree, then another. She chewed the corner of her lip, deciding, then she followed him.

Chapter Thirteen

Flattened against the damp cave wall Rane crept closer, listening to their voices and looking out for something to use as a weapon. The cave was larger inside than the opening suggested, and stacked fortuitously near the entrance were numerous old crates and barrels, some of which were falling apart. He seized a stout looking old barrel stave and hefted it, smiling grimly.

They were pouring over the loot from their canvas bag on a table in the center of the cave. Their voices were low, but Rane could make out that one was unhappy about how the stuff was acquired. As he looked for a second exit, he noted the lived-in look of the place, the straw pallet and blankets on the floor, lanterns, table and stools, and cooking pans, and buckets. Not a weapon in sight. He took a deep breath, tightened his grip on the club in his hand and stepped out.

"You!" he growled like a great, angry cat. "You conniving bilge scum! I swore I'd find you!"

They started and whirled to find him filling the cave behind them, silhouetted chillingly against the light from the entrance.

Ominously he smacked his palms with the barrel stave and had the pleasure of watching their faces drain to ghastly white and their eyes bulge satisfyingly from their sockets. An encounter with the walking dead couldn't have stopped their blood quicker!

"It's him, Perc!" the skinny one strangled, grabbing his

accomplice by the coat and hanging on for dear life.

"Yes. It's me," Rane snarled. Permit me to introduce myself. Rane Austen, Viscount Oxley, at your service." He bowed with a sardonic flourish. "This must be your lucky day . . . meeting me . . . *meeting your Maker* — " He lunged, and they scrambled frantically out of the way, leaving him bashing the stave down into a loaf of bread on the table. He recoiled, shocked to find himself unopposed. He swung around and found them huddled together, shrinking toward the cave wall with stricken looks that jarred Rane's memory of that fateful night just two weeks ago.

"P-p-please, yer lordship," Percy Hall pleaded. "We didn' know ye wus a lordship."

"An' we didn' mean to shoot ye," Gar Davis whined. "It were jus' a bit o' bad luck we plugged ye. We jus' meant to give ye a little scare."

"Gar, here, ain't never hit nothin' before in his life! We jus' wanted to make ye take back yer money an' go — " Percy finished for him and rattled on. "We didn't have no more brandy . . . cain't get no more . . . don't even know where that other stuff come from. The squire alwus took care of the buyin' an' sellin'. We jus' did the haulin', in our boat!"

Watching them quivering and sniveling, Rane suffered the most infuriating pang of conscience. They had shot him — why should he have qualms about trouncing them within an inch of their blessed lives?! But wait — what was it that they had said about —

"The squire, he got kilt on our last run, bringin' the barrels ashore. Our luck's been running foul of late," Percy tried to explain.

"The squire?" Rane stalked a step closer, glowering as he put things together in his mind. "Squire Standing? *Upton Standing*, Charity's father? He was involved in your smuggling ring?"

"Him an' us *wus* th' smugglin' ring," Percy admitted

221

miserably. "Now it be jus' us. Except, we ain't got nothin' to smuggle no more. The squire, he needed money bad an' there didn't seem no harm in it, jus' a few tax fellers out a few quid."

"You're lying to save your own hides!" Rane tightened, glaring, searching them for some evidence of treachery, some sign of deception. But their guileless confessions were simply not the work of cunning; he had the foulest intuition they were telling the truth. Apparently, Squire Upton Standing, Charity's wise, loving and protective father, hadn't been so upstanding after all. The idea stunned him. Gar's voice came with a raspy quiver.

"I didn' mean to hit yer lordship—it were jus' Miz Charity's jinx agin." He swallowed hard and eased his grip on Percy's coatfront. "I went an' fell in th' squire's open grave, an' everybody knows a feller what falls in a grave dug fer another man is bound to die next. I ain't died yet, but I be jinxed fer sure. It's why I hit ye."

"It's alwus like that around Miz Charity," Percy took it up, glancing miserably at Gar and nodding agreement. "We known an' loved her since she wus a wee thing. She be like a daughter to us. But she be jinxed fer sure. It was writ in th' moon on the very night she were birthed! Acci-dents and troubles foller her around like a shadow . . . I had a broke arm and a split head, myself, in the last four years. An' Gar, here, he gets bashed an' bunged up regular—cain't get near no horses on her account."

"T-that's abs-surd!" Rane sputtered, coiling to defend her against such an unexpected and unbelievable charge.

"It be th' truth, we swear!" Gar stiffened, greening sickly. "She got an angel's tender heart an' wus alwus bringin' home stray animals. But none of 'em survived long, 'cept old Wolfie, an ye prob'ly seen what shape he's in. And her pa, the squire, even he had his share

222

of troubles. Broke somethin' near every year—an arm, a collarbone, a nose. Lost most o' his stock over the years and part o' his land and had to take to smugglin' to keep the house together.

"An' of late even the smugglin' were goin' bad. That night he were kilt, the guide lanterns blew out an' the weather were foul an' the ship wouldn' come into the bay. We had to go meet it in high seas . . . an wi'out the guide lanterns, we was on the rocks a'fore we knowed it. . . ."

Their eyes darkened and their faces tightened as the bitter memories of that tumultuous night were stirred and poured out of them in half coherent ramblings. Darkness and roaring all around . . . the spray cutting their faces . . . no sense of up or down . . . mountains of churning water falling on them . . . no light, no guide . . . no hope.

In the mouth of the cave, Charity stood frozen, hearing for the first time, the horrible details of her father's violent death, and hearing the blame for it laid at her feet by two men she loved as part of her family. *Jinx.* She reeled. Troubles and accidents . . . like a shadow always following her. All her life, troubles, so many troubles . . . Her grief-stricken heart was momentarily paralyzed, unable to beat. It was as though a great dark hole had been uncovered in the very ground of her being, and everything she'd built her life on, every assumption, every bit of surety and structure, was crumbling into it. As she reeled and grappled, trying to deal with it, the killing thrust was delivered. The lanterns . . . the guide lanterns had been snuffed on the night of her father's death . . . sending him onto the rocks . . . *killing him.*

"No-o-o," she whispered soundlessly, her eyes wide with anguished horror. Pain cut through her chest and

223

splintered in her leaden heart, scattering merciless shards all through her. She just managed to lift her skirts and stumble out of the cave.

Rane watched the hapless twosome experiencing the wreck anew, mourning the loss of their partner afresh, and felt his righteous ire sliding. They were half daft the pair of them, he realized. Whether from the trauma of the shipwreck and the death of their friend and partner, or from the taint of old Lady Margaret's fanatical superstitions, it was impossible to say.

Charity. He thought of her sensibleness, of her irresistible logic, and thanked God that Upton Standing had managed to get one thing right in life. In the midst of such overwhelming superstition, the beleaguered squire had managed to balance Charity's life with his earthy pragmatism and reason and blessed skepticism. It never occurred to him that Charity might not *know* what they believed about her.

"*Jinx?!* B'dammit, there's no such thing as a jinx—or *luck* for that matter!" He tossed the wooden stave away and stalked toward them, looking like he might be deciding to tear them apart with his bare hands instead. "Look, you pathetic poltroons, a man takes what he gets in life and makes what he can of it—and that's all there is to it! There's no damned thing such as luck. If anyone should know, I should!" He stomped closer, looming over them, crowding their breathing and their fears. His voice dropped to a menacing rumble that vibrated their very teeth.

"If I ever hear such vile, poisonous drivel coming from your mouths again, I'll thrash you within an inch of your worthless lives—*you hear me?!!*" They nodded, thunderstruck, and nearly collapsed when he pulled away. He raked them with molten silver eyes, setting their faces afire with the heat of his contempt. "From now on, you stay away from Standwell," he ordered, "and away from Charity."

They nodded, their faces puckering, their knees buckling, and he wheeled and charged out of the cave.

Charity ran across the sunlit fields, blinded by tears and struggling for breath. Some minutes later, she found herself well along the winding wood that curled through the valley near Standwell. Half thinking, half feeling, she tightened her hold on her black skirts and headed for the little stone chapel that stood on Standings' land. By the time she reached the door, her lungs were burning and her stomach and legs were cramping; she couldn't go another step. She threw herself on the doors and rattled the handles, finding herself locked out, barred from her last place of refuge by the parish committee's new padlock, which was meant to keep vagrants and other undesirables out of the little-used chapel.

Her fingernails raked the curled paint as she slid down the weathered door, heaving, crying. "P-please . . . please let me in . . ."

But her pleas died at the door, where she had collapsed on the worn step and in the dust beside it. Every breath was like a knife in her lungs. Every thought turned that same knife in her heart.

It came rolling over her like the suffocating black waves that had taken her father's life. *The lanterns.* It all came back to her, everything that happened that evening . . . the door she'd heard slapping with the wind in the little-used west wing . . . the two lanterns she'd found burning . . . and had extinguished, thinking Melwin had probably been working on the broken glazing in the window. She recalled thinking it odd, Melwin working so long past sunset, on such a task. And to leave the lanterns burning; it wasn't like him. Now she knew. She had extinguished her father's guide, perhaps his very life, with those lanterns.

A *jinx;* that's what Gar and Percy had called her. A jinx who brought trouble wherever she went, even to those who loved her most. And now as she lay in the grip of pain and guilt, as tossed and directionless as her father had been in that heaving sea, she seized their revelation as the explanation for things she had never been able to explain. The knowledge sank its cruel tendrils into her vulnerable heart and mind.

It had always been there, just at the edge of her consciousness, the most logical reason for the feeling of responsibility she carried for the misfortunes of those around her. She'd always felt just a bit guilty for having such wonderful luck, when others around her suffered so. Now the unthinkable had been said, and once said, it took root in her aching heart as the truth she'd sought, but feared to find. She'd spent her whole life trying to comfort the troubles around her, trying to help wherever misfortune had trod and left things crushed and broken beneath its heel. Could it possibly be that she had been the cause of the very misfortunes she'd always sought to relieve?

Her heart rebelled at the thought, but the logic her father had tried to instill in her was now pressed into superstition's dark service. Wave upon wave of bad fortune passed before her mind's eye: bad crops, and illnesses, and mishaps, broken bones and household accidents. Gar's horse problems, her father's broken bones and poor luck with his tenants, and the slow demise of Gran'mere's elegant china. . . . What else could account for the bees that refused to swarm to Standwell hives, the rugs that caught ablaze from popping cinders, the things that seemed to just topple from shelves when she passed? All the bumps and falls, even Gar's fall in the open grave, and the shooting of Rane Austen . . .

Rane. Charity's heart stopped dead. He'd been involved in a carriage wreck when she first saw him . . .

Suddenly the sight of black horses and a carriage thundering at her boiled up in her mind. The wreck! She'd been running and got caught in front of his carriage. *She'd caused his wreck!* She trembled violently, seeing it in her mind's eye again. And then Gar and Percy had shot him, after Gar fell in the grave, and Rane had been carried to Standwell where he'd suffered mishap after mishap. Falling and bashing and scalding and cutting and tripping—she'd watched him go about on the very brink of oblivion, never dreaming that she could be causing it! In fact, the only time he'd not been in peril of life and limb was when he was in her arms, surrounded by her abominably good luck. Or perhaps that was really the worst misfortune to befall him . . . kissing her, coming to want her.

In her mind the fatal connection was inescapably made. Her father and Rane . . . she loved them both, but had brought them both nothing but pain and peril. Her father was dead . . . and Rane was perpetually on the brink of destruction . . . because of her. In her grieving heart, present and future were now filtered through her grim new reality. It was only a matter of time, she understood, until one of those accidents or mischances took Rane from her, too. A fall, a wreck, a fatal blow to the head . . . And until then, misfortune would keep nibbling at him with small hurts and wounds and business set-backs and humiliations. And she would see it happening and know herself to blame.

If she really loved Rane Austen, she would do whatever was necessary to keep him safe, even if it meant losing him in the process. If she loved him, she must try to protect him from her calamitous influence, to send him as far away from her as possible, praying it wasn't already too late. Her heart twisted and ground painfully in her chest at the thought.

She lay in the dust at the foot of the locked chapel doors, drawing strength from the one thing in her being that hadn't been changed by her terrible discovery about herself . . . her capacity to love. In loving, she must find the strength to send Rane away from her . . . and to somehow go on without him.

Yet how could she go on with this terrible emptiness in her, the place where her heart had been?

Rane watched her come down the center stairs, just past noon, and his heart swelled with poignant desires to hold her and keep her safe. She was beautiful, her blonde hair a tawny, liquid honey color that glowed in the dusty light, her face a delicate ivory oval, enchanting in form and in expression. She was loving and generous, radiantly sensual and endearingly sensible. And she was *his*, his woman, his love.

He met her at the bottom of the stairs, capturing her hand, his face beaming. "I've looked for you everywhere this morning. Where were you?" But as she framed a careful lie, he turned, brushing aside his own question to pull her into the empty parlor with him. He led her across the great chamber to a settee near the long windows, and without bothering to cast a cautionary glance round them, he pulled her into his arms and kissed her, an achingly sweet adoration of a kiss. The ebullience of his mood blocked recognition of how little she'd returned his affection.

"Sit, Charity," he insisted, nodding at the settee behind her and taking her hands so that she had little choice but to obey. When she settled on the edge of the seat, he settled on one knee on the floor before her. He smiled into her honey-brown eyes, and only then noticed the telltale puffiness about them. "I looked for you all over, angel. I have good news, wonderful news." The way she lowered her eyes just then was a minor confusion, but it deterred him none. His news would soon brighten her mood.

"I spoke with your grandmother this morning . . . about us. Angel, she's given me permission to speak with you." His bronzed features were alight with excitement.

Charity's mouth dried, her eyes burned. She knew exactly what came next. Once it would have been a dream come true; now the expectation pierced her heart.

"Miss Standing, you must know that I hold you in the highest regard and in the warmest affection." He grinned; warm was a tepid description indeed for what he was feeling just now.

Charity lifted her eyes very briefly, but long enough for the warmth glowing in his face to begin melting her resolve. She panicked and turned her face away. "Really, your lordship, that's very nice of you. Would you mind letting me up? I've a bit of a cramp in my foot." She stood, setting him back on his heel in surprise. He frowned, bemused, as she drew a few steps away, making a show of soothing her foot. Then he pushed to his own feet, determined to make a better start.

"Charity, I've something to discuss with you, something important . . . something wonderful." He came to her and snagged her hands, lifting them to a soft kiss, then covering them with his own. "Your future . . . and mine."

Charity dared not meet his eyes; the image of them in her mind was quite bad enough. Her jaw clenched as she felt emotions rising in her throat. She had to reject him, had to refuse to marry him without telling him her real reasons for doing so. He didn't believe in luck and he wouldn't believe in her jinx, either. He'd insist she marry him anyway. And, knowing him, she knew he would persist until she was all puddles inside and gave in to him. She had to make him *believe* that she didn't want to marry him.

"I'm a wealthy man, Charity . . . or at least I was

229

when I arrived here a fortnight ago." He laughed ruefully, but his humor cut her to the core. If her determination had needed prompting, he had just provided it.
"And I've no attachments or liabilities to speak of. I'm
of an age and of a mind to marry. And I'm of a mind
to marry you, if you'll have me."

Charity pulled her hands from his as if he'd burned
them and stepped back, still refusing to meet his eyes.
"Really, your lordship . . . it is most ungracious of you
to make sport of such things."

"Sport?" He was stunned, totally unprepared for such
a reaction. "I assure you, Charity, I am utterly serious."
His hands dropped to his sides, feeling frighteningly
empty.

"Then you will be answered seriously, your lordship."
She straightened her spine, raising her eyes to his top
waistcoat button, no higher. "In place of your own good
sense, I must advise you that there is utterly no possibility of such a thing occurring."

"No poss—" He blinked, unmanned by her cool demeanor. "Charity?!" He stalked closer, and stopped
when she retreated by the same measure. "Charity, I'm
asking you to marry me . . . to go to London with me
. . . to be my wife—a viscountess." His face began to
redden, his skin began to heat with delayed dread. He
searched her posture, her averted gaze, and her stubborn chin for a sign contrary to her cool rebuff, finding
none. She appeared to be perfectly serious.

"I am flattered, your lordship, but you must know my
situation. I am undowered."

"Of course I know your situation," he declared, scowling. "And you must know that the only dowry I require
of you was rendered last night."

Charity's head snapped up. Her eyes were dark, littered with pained sparks. "How ungentlemanly of you to
remind me of it." She raised her chin challengingly.

"How unwomanly of you to forget it!" he snapped,

230

horrified by his rising irritation and by the drastic turn of what was to have been a joyful occasion. What had he said, done? Whatever it was, he was not about to let it continue! "Charity . . . angel . . . I apologize. Come, let me start again." He reached for her shoulders, meaning to pull her against him, meaning to conjure the warmth that always rose between them. But she succeeded in resisting being drawn to him.

"There is no need to start again, your lordship. I would save us both the discomfort of saying this again, but since you insist . . ." She pushed away forcefully, staggering as he let her go abruptly. "I will not, cannot marry you. Even in my girlish, ignorant mind the differences between us have always been clear, as have my expectations regarding you. You're a wealthy titled man, a gentleman of education and culture. I'm a penniless girl, a squire's daughter, a mannerless country mouse. I know my place, even if you seem to have forgotten it. Anything more between us would be . . . unsuitable, your lordship."

Unsuitable. That damned word again! Unsuitable. The sound of that dread judgement on Charity's lips shocked him speechless. After all the time they'd spent together, all the pleasure they'd shared . . . She'd always accepted him . . . wanted him. . . .

He took a step toward her, searching the guarded heat of her eyes, and quickly she stepped back, enlarging the distance between them. The violent flush of her face and the way her eyes fled his jolted him. Was she mourning the loss of her innocence, thinking herself ruined and undesirable?

"Charity, what happened at our bedding was nothing to be ashamed of." His voice became gentle, stroking, reassuring . . . cutting her to the quick. "It was natural and good. It was and is right for us to love each other—"

"I don't believe you quite understand, your lordship. I

231

don't want to marry you . . . or any man," she gritted out. A pure lie. It was the first she could remember telling in her life. It made her feel foul, sick inside.

"You expect me to believe that after what passed between us last night?" His face was now ruddy bronze, and his big frame coiled defensively as he searched her. The darkening of his beautiful gray eyes was physically painful to her. As her refusals slowly extinguished the light in them, it seemed the light in the center of her was going out, too.

"Last night was . . . unfortunate." She braced, watching him grapple with it, and could scarcely draw breath. Her heart seemed to be twisting in her chest.

"Unfortunate?" A slap in the face couldn't have stung as much. He lashed back. "That wasn't your opinion last night, angel. You came to my bed of your own free will, because you wanted loving . . . and you wanted it from *me!* You wanted to know what your *night magic* was about and you wanted *me* to teach you!" He stopped. In his mind and heart, his claims to her went much further . . . into her needs and feelings. But he dared not make such claims now; to hear her deny them would be too crushing.

"I cannot deny possessing a certain curiosity about the deed," she bit out every word, "and about your rather unique *attractions,* your lordship." A harsh, rasping tone entered her voice as each word was ripped from her very heart. "Is that what you insist on hearing?" She faced him with fists clenched at her sides, her nails biting into her palms. She could see the anger rising in him and almost welcomed it. "That should certainly come as no surprise to you. I would imagine most women find you . . . interesting . . . in that way."

"Dammit! Interesting?!" He quivered with angry frustration.

"But my 'curiosity' hardly changes the reality of the situation. Unsuitable is still . . . unsuitable, your lordship."

In the centers of his shimmering gray eyes, that little boy with the sunburned cheeks appeared, peering out at her with a look of betrayal and disbelief. Her eyes burned and she felt her throat close as if a hand had squeezed it. She was hurting him!

Unsuitable. From her lips it was killing. He grappled to make sense of it, struggling above the chaos inside him. Beneath it all, somewhere, was the implication that he wasn't good enough. He didn't deserve a wife . . . or tenderness or respect. He was a sensual curiosity, a pleasurable diversion—not a man, with needs and feelings. The acceptance and caring he had felt from her, the sweet awakening of her body and her feelings, the resurrection of his memories and his emotions . . . could it all have been a lie?

She watched him wavering, clinging to hope, and leveled one last, desperate thrust and sank it home.

"One night was . . . quite enough."

"Dammit—one night?!" One night *with him* was enough?!

Hunger and anger irrupted simultaneously in him and he lunged at her, dragging her against him, taking her prisoner in his arms. His mouth came down on hers fiercely, brooking no resistance, demanding all, taking what he wanted and needed. He plunged into her mouth, raking the honied sweetness, starving for her love and desperate enough to settle for her desire.

Charity was swept into the center of a raging firestorm. Hot blasts of desire and anger roared around and through her, oblivious to both her helpless responses and her efforts to escape. His hard body flamed against hers, his steel-thewed arms surrounded her with relentless heat, his mouth on hers was searing. It was too much for her burdened heart. The longings rose inside her, honed to cutting sharpness.

Her arms ceased pushing, her body stilled against his,

accepting, submitting to his power around her and in her. She was his . . . as he must never be hers.

In the center of that storm fury, in the deepest heart of her, rested the immutable core of her love for him, a bastion powerful enough to withstand his anger and desire and need, in his behalf. It was that love that filled her now and spilled out through her eyes. It was that love that caused his desire for her to become a dark, suffocating pain that coiled mercilessly through her.

He felt her resistance dying, and the fury in his blood eased. His mouth gentled over hers, commanding, then coaxing, then entreating her response. As his senses cleared, he searched them for traces of the passion he wanted, needed from her. But she just stood in his grip, trembling, breathing raggedly. And he became aware of a new taste in her mouth, salt. She tasted of . . . His breath stopped and he raised his head and opened his eyes. Tears.

Her eyes were shut and tears were flowing down her reddened cheeks . . . to her bruised lips. He felt like he'd been slammed in the chest and was unable to breathe. The sense of his deliberate violence, the anger that lay still coiled in his body horrified him. Dear God. What was he doing? What had he done?

He released her, gasping for breath against a vengeful hand squeezing at his throat. "Ch-Charity . . . I . . ."

She staggered back, her eyes dark and luminous with pain. He watched her struggling with feelings roused by his assault, watched her hand come up to touch her savaged lips. He'd unleashed all his bottled anger and passion on her, blaming her for his loving and wanting her, blaming her for not wanting him the same. He'd bruised her and hurt her.

"I *won't* marry you," she managed hoarsely, backing toward the door. "If you have any consideration for my grandmother . . . or for me," she swallowed hard and bit her lip, until she could continue, "you'll leave

234

Standwell today . . . now."

She watched him standing there, looking crushed and empty . . . alone. It was all she could do to turn and run to the door.

He stood for a long minute, unable to move, still seeing the hurt in her and feeling it growing inside himself, the way he had come to feel so many of her emotions. He blamed himself for it. He didn't understand her reasons for rejecting him, but he couldn't believe she hadn't wanted him or that she'd come to his bed from mere curiosity or even out of sensual need. Her loving had been too real, her caring too genuine. And yet today, she was an entirely different person, so cold, so detached and untouchable, every inch the "lady" she claimed not to be.

In a fit of raw frustration, he'd unleashed on her the bitterness of all his former failures. Whatever her reasons, they might have talked, he might have persuaded her, until he lost his temper and betrayed his own standards . . . and her trust. For years he'd worked to constrain the passion and intensity of his Austen soul, to acquire the character and bearing of a true gentleman. Now, in the one time it really mattered that he be a gentleman, his painstakingly assembled control had utterly failed him.

He'd lost her . . . without even understanding why.

The household was stirred to a flurry by the viscount's abrupt departure. Melwin sent one of his grandsons scurrying to Mortehoe for a hired rig, then packed up his lordship's smashed trunk and trundled it downstairs. The viscount begged an audience with Lady Margaret and gravely thanked the old lady for her kindness in taking him in. He gave her a sizeable draft on his personal account at the Bank of England, which she protested was too much and would never be used.

Together they bundled Stephenson down the stairs and into the carriage, since he refused to be left behind if his employer was leaving. And with a last, gray-faced pause and a suffering look at the empty stairs, Rane bade farewell to Lady Margaret, Melwin, and Bernadette . . . and even to Wolfram, who pranced about the carriage, utterly delighted by the commotion of his departure. As Rane stepped up into the small curricle-hung gig, he paused and turned a dark look on Lady Margaret, asking her to give his regards to Miss Charity. Lady Margaret scowled and nodded. Rane settled into the carriage, seized the reins, and slapped the horses into motion.

Far above, from the front-facing window of the room Rane had used when first carried to Standwell, Charity watched his departure through a haze of grief. It was the best thing, the loving thing to do, she tried to tell herself. But no amount of telling could dispel the tearing ache inside her as he carried her heart away with him. She watched until the gig was out of sight, then turned and wandered aimlessly about the room, pausing to stare at the bare ropes and planking of the bed.

Lady Margaret found her there, later, sitting on the barren bed, looking like the life had been punched out of her. The old lady came to stand by the bed, scowling, trying to discern what had happened.

"He asked permission to speak with you . . . I presumed he would," the old lady said with open puzzlement.

"He did." Charity scarcely glanced up from her knotted fingers in her lap.

"*And?*" There was exasperation in Gran'mere's voice.

"I refused him."

With that, and no more, Charity rose and left the room.

But that night, Lady Margaret learned all she needed to know when she found Charity in Upton's old room, standing by the window overlooking the bay in the powerful light of the full moon. When Charity turned to face her, she was wearing amulets, several very powerful ones.

"Tell me about the moon, Gran'mere," she said sadly. "You must know. Tell me about the moon . . . on the night I was born."

Lady Margaret tottered to a nearby chair and sat down with a thud. The calamity she had read in the approaching full moon had come to pass, but it wasn't the calamity she had expected. It was worse!

Charity knew about her jinx.

Chapter Fourteen

The London Road was rutted and difficult and the major coaching inns were noisy and crowded, but Rane scarcely noticed. His mind was filled with painful anger and confusion about his feelings for Charity and her inexplicable rejection of him, and with dread at the chaos he would probably face when he arrived in London. He made wretched company indeed for Stephenson, who could only seem to talk about Lady Margaret and Miss Charity and was trounced verbally every time he mentioned either. By the time they reached the outskirts of London's West End, both were sunk into grim forbearance.

Rane drove straight to his house on the fashionable St. George's Square and had the abominable luck of arriving just as the Countess of Swinford's, his neighbor's, morning callers were exiting next door. He reined the hack horses and the battered, muddied gig to a halt before the brick and ironwork fence surrounding the entrance to his Palladian-style residence.

The matronly countess and he had lived side by side for three years and, in all that time, the august dame had yet to call on him or to accept his personal call. Notwithstanding that, she managed to entertain the rest of London every morning in her fashionable parlor. And just now, they all seemed to be staring at Rane's paltry conveyance, his green-stained coat, his unkempt hair, and his dirty boots. And when he dismounted and pulled a cane from the gig to limp indoors, he was certain he could feel the vibrations from the tongues wagging.

He stalked through the understated elegance of the boxed shrubs and newly planted flowers of his entry garden, and mounted the graceful tier of steps to the columned half-portico surrounding the massive white doors. He paused, expecting the door to open, but apparently the footman and butler weren't at their usual posts. Thus he waited on his own doorstep under the ton's eyes, his face reddening, his buttock aching, his ire rising. Finally he seized the doorhandle himself and barged inside, ready to take someone — everyone — to task for making him appear to be an unwanted caller in his own home.

He swung the massive door shut with an irritable thud and turned to find himself facing a veritable mountain of baggage and wooden crates of every size and description. The spacious, domed entry hall, with its curved mahogany staircase, Florentine marble floor, and crystal chandelier, was practically filled with the stuff. He stopped just in time to keep from tripping over a small, leather satchel that appeared to have fallen from the pile. A half-second later, he heard raised voices approaching.

Into the entry stormed a stocky, formidable looking woman in dove gray silk . . . with a furious red-granite countenance. Nearly nose to nose with her was Eversby, the butler, shuddering under her blistering tirade, looking ashen and exasperated beyond bearing. Brockway, the footman, and Edward the underfootman looked on, owl-eyed, from the nearby doorway. Rane drew his chin back, his eyes widening on the volatile scene.

Lady Catherine Austen, the dowager Vicountess Oxley, turned on her grandson, gave him a searing look of appraisal, and issued him a bald order. "Tell this bufflehead of yours to carry my things upstairs! He's let them languish here in the hall for an entire day! Such treatment is unthinkable, inexcusable!"

"Your lordship!" Eversby hurried toward him, then stopped, seeing his disheveled state and his reliance on a cane. "Are you alright, your lordship? We got your message and didn't expect you for at least another week . . ."

"My convalescence went better than expected, Eversby. I chose to return early." Rane used the exchange to cloak his shock and digest the fact that his imperious grandmother had finally deigned to grace his household with a visit. His eyes slid to the mountain of baggage. Evidently it was to be a long visit. He lifted his eyes to her burning glare of disapproval at the way he'd spoken to his butler before her. He could see she was marking it down against him on some mental slate, and the thought mildly infuriated him.

"I decided to grant your request that I come for a visit, Oxley." She came forward, her stiff silks swishing and her eyes narrowing.

Never mind that the invitation had been issued five years earlier and that for the last two years all communication with him had been spurned . . . she was here now, with a vengeance. It left him wondering why the irascible old bird had chosen now, this particular bleak moment, to descend on him. She must have read his thoughts in his face.

"I thought it was time I had a look at my grandson," she divulged imperiously. "Perhaps reestablished family connections."

So, he thought, this was to be an inspection visit. Long overdue, was his next thought. Too damn long. After arriving in England, he had sought her recognition and she'd spurned him as if he were a pariah. Then, when he'd begun to make his fortune and had made overtures to her, wishing to establish his family ties and win access to her influential circle, she refused to recognize him, on one occasion actually snubbing him socially. Her shunning had led directly to his being excluded from her avenues of society. So, now she was ready to give him a chance. . . .

"I'm sorry, your lordship. Without orders from you I was reluctant to assume. . .," Eversby said nervously.

"I understand perfectly," Rane glanced at the loyal butler. "See that her things are carried up. And see Stephenson in from the carriage and to his room." He turned to his granite-jawed grandmother. "Welcome, Lady Catherine. Now if you'll excuse me, I've had a very tiring journey."

He ordered a hot bath and a plate of fruit and picked his way through the baggage toward the stairs. He was on the third step, when a fuzzy white streak, launched from somewhere atop the pile of baggage, hurtled past his shoulder and thudded onto the stairs before him. He recoiled, and would have lost his balance, but for the cane that Charity had given him. He found himself glaring at a fat, long-haired, white cat with sullen yellow eyes and a bold feline sneer. It arched at him and hissed furiously.

"There you are, you poor baby," Lady Catherine barreled past Rane on the step to scoop the furious beast up in her arms, cooing and stroking his raised fur. She looked up at Rane with full indignation. "That butler of yours refused to provide proper nourishment for my Caesar, and it's put him altogether out of sorts. He's got to have kippers from that little Italian fishmonger in Lupole Street, and small bread balls stuffed with chicken. I told the fellow exactly how they were to be made."

Caesar glared at Rane with dull yellow indignation, then decided not to be so easily pacified and clawed and wiggled his way out of Lady Catherine's startled arms. "See there?" Lady Catherine stiffened regally as the beast pounced down the stairs and began sulkily sharpening his claws on the lacquered mahogany of the newel

241

post at the bottom of the staircase railing. "He only does that when he's terribly upset."

Rane's jaw clenched and the cords in his neck tightened as he watched those claws raking streaks in his imported woodwork. He turned to red-faced Eversby at the bottom of the stairs and spoke through his teeth. "For God's sake, man—stuff the creature some bread balls. And be quick about it!"

Rane remained at his house just long enough to bathe and dress in his customary gentleman-of-fashion style. Then he called for his carriage to be brought around and went straight to his trading company offices. Whatever problems he might encounter there would seem small compared with the turmoil his grandmother and her damnable cat were brewing in his house. His leg and buttock were aching again; that accounted for part of his dark mood. The rest was the result of wishing Charity were there to stop the discomfort. Her warm eyes, her healing smile—the thought was just too painful. He straightened, clamped his Austen jaw and forbade himself to think of her again. He had to get hold of himself somehow!

His offices were located in a large warehouse in the burgeoning commercial district London. He found his head clerk, Addison, in the accounting room, embroiled in a heated argument with several disappointed victualers and hosteliers who had been expecting French brandy and were furious at having to go without. When Rane appeared, they transferred their ire to him wholesale, and he had a very long afternoon of it, explaining and promising and negotiating his way back into their good graces.

With his energy at low ebb, his buttock throbbing, and his head pounding, he finally permitted Addison to show in one last appointment, who had appeared late in the day, as word of Rane's return had spread. Rane slanted uncomfortably onto one side in his high-backed leather chair, behind his broad mahogany desk. He appraised the round-faced caller with the calm, pleasant demeanor, then perused the fellow's card. He was a solicitor with the firm of Markum, Baegley and Billforthing. Rane's hands tightened with expectation on the edge of his desk when the fellow eyed and complimented the mahogany paneled office, Aubusson carpet, and gilt-framed Turner landscape hanging on the far wall.

He'd come at the behest of a coalition of clothiers and mercantile establishments, none of whom rang a bell of recognition in Rane. He produced a monumental stack of bills that widened Rane's eyes and he very politely requested payment. Rane snatched up first one, then another, staring, glaring at them. Gloves? Statements from several mantua makers? Laces and wines and a ruby brooch from the king's own jeweler . . . at least two dozen pairs of ladies' shoes . . . an expensive oriental vase and ivory carvings. . . ? Across the bottom of each was written in clear feminine hand: "Apply for payment to the Viscount Oxley, St. George's Square, London."

He was stunned. Who would—Fanny? Spending his money all over town . . . advertising their "arrangement" by sending her bills to him? That wasn't like her . . . nor was it their agreement. Fanny maintained her own house and he provided a generous allowance and occasional special gifts, as warranted. His face bronzed as he came up straight in his chair, looking at another and another . . . milliners and lace merchants and silk drapers!

Then he saw it . . . the signature . . . and his jaw dropped with astonishment. "Lady Catherine Austen, Viscountess Oxley." His eyes widened on the mound of bills on his desk. The old crow had been about town charging things to his account?! He blinked, realizing that she must have planned her gracious "visit" for some time.

"There must be several hundred pounds worth!" he gestured to the pile.

Mr. Baegley winced sympathetically and lifted a card on which he had tallied the total. "Five hundred and seventy-three pounds, six and nine-pence, to be precise, your lordship."

"Good God." A wave of hot chagrin flowed over Rane. He should have realized there would be a price to the old woman's appearance in his life.

By the time he had arranged a transfer of funds and a bank draft, he'd managed to learn a bit about his free-spending grandmother from the accommodating Mr. Baegley. She had apparently decided to bestow the honor of her presence on his household only after out-spending her own means.

When Addison had sent the junior clerks home and doused the lights, Rane sat a while in his dim office, feeling like the weight of the world was on his shoulders and wishing with all his heart for a pair of soft, feminine arms wrapping around his shoulders, supporting him. Inescapably, Charity came to his mind, soft and accepting, her warm-honey eyes glowing, sliding sweetly into his. The ache that grew inside him took his breath momentarily. Dear God, how was he going to live without—He shook himself, pained by his violent response to the memory of her. He had to stop this nonsense, here and now! What could he do . . . ?

There was nothing he could do . . . except . . . What he needed was another woman, a simple, uncomplicated woman who didn't make him think too much or feel too much, and didn't invade his very soul with a single smile. He needed a hot, salty bout of lovemaking, a mindless immersion in pleasure, not another jump into a fathomless well of untapped emotion. Something hot, something simple. Fanny.

He seized his hat, called for his carriage, and strode

out into the warm London night with the grim determination of supplanting the feel of Charity Standing in his blood and under his skin . . . and the desperate fear that it might not be possible.

Red-haired Fanny Deering was the young widow of an aged Suffolkshire gentleman, who now resided in a suite of rooms in a quite respectable street in Chelsea. Rane Austen wasn't her one and only, but he certainly was her *primary*, as well as the main support of her comfortable, if not quite elegant, life. Rane knew abut her occasional *others* and made no complaint as long as they were men of worth — and as long as it didn't interfere with his own schedule.

Of late, however, his preoccupation with the ton and his marriage plans had taken precedence in his life. As he rode through the London streets toward Chelsea, he realized he hadn't paid her a visit since . . . Lord, more than two months ago! He hadn't even thought to have someone carry her word of his injury and the reason for his most recent absence. He winced. Perhaps he should have sent a message first, given her a day or so to prepare. Certainly, he should have bought her a gift, something suitably expensive, in case his prolonged absence had put her in a miff. But, he could probably make up for it by taking her shopping tomorrow.

He thought of Fanny's generous mouth and guileless gray-blue eyes, and her breasts that ran to the plump and pillowy. It was a mildly rousing picture, but it was soon overshadowed, then dispelled completely, by the memory of sweet, golden caramel eyes and firm, rounded breasts with long, velvety nipples. He felt his arousal soaring and smacked the roof of the carriage with his cane to signal the driver to go faster.

By the time he had reached Fanny's lodgings and sent his coach back home for the night, he had clamped a tight rein on his passions and was able to enter the house and climb the stairs to her suite of rooms with gentlemanly restraint. He applied his knuckles to the door and waited. He knocked again, scowling; then again, reddening. Where in hell was she? If she wasn't home, her maid always answered.

He stiffened and turned to go, finding himself facing the middle-aged landlady, who bustled up the stairs.

"Your lordship!" She arrived breathlessly on the landing with him, clutching a letter packet to her heaving bosom. "Didn't see your carriage, sir, else I'd 'ave caught you before you came up. Mrs. Deering is gone. She left this for you." She shoved the letter into his gloved hands and watched expectantly as he scowled, then cracked the waxed seal on it.

"Dearest Oxley," it began. "Please don't think too ill of me when you read this . . ." His eyes widened on her girlish script. ". . . Thought it over . . . to accept Mr. Trevor's kind proposal of marriage . . . to Southampton. . . ."

He was stunned. Fanny, *married?!* He burst through the door to her rooms and found them mostly empty; just a few furnishings that had belonged to the landlady remained. He stalked from darkened room to darkened room, frustration rising. The only thing that remained of her was the faint lingering scent of her powder in the bedchamber. She'd abandoned him for marriage to a plump, fiftyish linendraper!

Once out on the street, he began to walk, clutching her crumpled letter in his hand. He paused under a newly lit streetlamp to stare again at her explanation. ". . . If you can understand . . . you were gone so much . . . not complaining, really, you were more than generous. But a woman of my age . . . companionship. . . ." Lord. His red-haired mistress had deserted him, abandoned him. And for a paunchy bit of public commerce and some regular conversation!

He came to a major thoroughfare and just stood there, torn between bald fury and raging incredulity. Fanny had apparently wanted, needed, more in her life, the kind of "more" he hadn't known existed until he had begun to experience it with Charity Standing. Again, Charity's plaguing warmth rose up inside him, wrapping around his lungs, softening his anger and deepening his frustration. He battled back those physically painful remembrances of her. He didn't want to think about her, couldn't let himself dwell on those killingly sweet might-have-beens. But in his deepest heart the love still lingered and the question still echoed. *Why?*

"There must be some unwritten law in the universe," he groaned, "that says things are never so bad . . . that they can't get worse."

Within seven days, his new axiom was proven beyond the shadow of a doubt in his mind. There was a steady stream of strident creditors and unhappy customers to his South London offices, and several times he was forced to remove to his home, intending to gain some measure of peace. But what he gained there instead was just another gargantuan dose of frustration.

Lady Catherine was not the slightest bit timid about making "improving suggestions" for Rane himself and for his household, beginning with the evil effects of too much raw fruit in his diet, and going on to the proper storage of bed linen and the "uncongenial" arrangement of furnishings in the grand parlor. The imperial Caesar, who had developed an instant antipathy toward Rane, had a nasty habit of pouncing on the breakfast table without warning, to attack the kippers on Rane's plate and anything else he found edible, then always managing to look unjustly set-upon when his mistress appeared to defend him.

Rane sought refuge at his club in the afternoon, and

when he returned home, he growled at Eversby to do something about the way the place was beginning to smell like "a damned catbox." Lady Catherine heard him and explained huffily that cats disliked being relocated and simply had to "mark" their new territories in order to feel at home. It was, she sniffed, abominable of Rane not to be more considerate of the poor creature's distress!

A week after his return to London, Rane found himself sitting in his study, covered with cat hair and nursing an ugly scratch on the back of his hand that he'd gotten while defending his breakfast muffins. Further, he was realizing that his domineering old grandmother probably hadn't the slightest intention of publicly claiming him as family. She was here only because she'd exhausted her own resources, not out of any regard for their blood tie. In seven days she hadn't once mentioned inviting him or sponsoring him anywhere. And the worst part of the whole thing was: he didn't even care. He seemed to have left all his social and matrimonial ambitions . . . with his heart . . . somewhere in Devon.

As he sat in morose thought, he sniffed and screwed up his face at the acrid smell permeating even his private sanctum. How much worse could it get? His business was degenerating into chaos; he walked around like a shell of a man, his reason and feelings and reactions all ashambles. He couldn't have the woman he wanted and couldn't get rid of the woman he didn't want anywhere near him. He had to fight fang and claw for his breakfast every morning, and his house smelled like a blessed *piss box!* Where the hell would it all end?!

Maybe old Lady Margaret was right, he mused dismally. Maybe he really was just the unluckiest lump of human flesh on the face of the earth.

"You mustn't trouble about it, Baron, really." Charity

sat forward in her chair opposite the settee, staring at the last of Gran'mere's hand-painted china cups and saucers, lying in a dozen little pieces on the floor before her. She lifted her eyes to the red-faced baron who was struggling to lower his bandaged leg from its perch on the pillows beside him in order to pick up the pieces. "Here, I'll do it. You must remember your hurt knee!"

"I'm so dreadfully sorry, Miss Charity, Lady Margaret! I don't know what's come over me; I'm all butter-fingers of late."

Charity smiled stiffly and tried not to look too pleased or too guilty. Indeed, he was a butterfingers of late—and a slew-foot, and a twaddle-tongue. And an irksome, boorish lecher who scarcely waited until her grandmother had stepped from the room before assaulting her with his slippery hands. Though, she thought, the wrenched knee he'd gotten while evading one of Wolfie's jealous lunges had slowed him down a bit in that regard.

Beside her, Lady Margaret was watching the way the baron's acquisitive eyes came to rest on the smooth skin of Charity's breasts. Over the last week, she'd watched his ill-disguised and ill-managed maneuverings toward her granddaughter, taking vengeful pleasure in the way fate had retaliated with nasty little nips at his health and dignity. A wrenched knee, a ripped thumb incurred from a bit of broken harness, an elbow cracked in a tumble off a ladder while he attempted to retrieve a kitten out of a tree for Charity. He'd ruined a pair of fancy boots, a perfectly good saddle, a perfectly good saddle mount, who'd come up lame, and now, her last painted-china cup and saucer!

Unknown to both Charity and her grandmother, a much worse disaster was riding the sly, manipulative baron's thoughts, something so calamitous he'd kept word of it from everyone, even from his own clerks and bailiffs. He'd just received word of an inquiry by the

Crown into the administration of local districts. A letter had come announcing that the king's auditors would arrive with the fortnight to peruse his books and study the quality of his administration. He had covered his financial sleight of hands fairly well with regard to the issuance of stamps and permits and the ringing down of judgments in favor of grateful friends. But his blatant "borrowing" of tax monies and seized properties would be far more difficult to disguise. The time had come, he decided, to move from public life into private life.

And what better excuse for resigning from his post than a fortuitous marriage? Thus his pursuit of Miss Charity Standing had taken on a new urgency. She wasn't as wealthy or influential as he might have wished, but she was the most desirable little thing he'd ever set eyes upon. And now that the wretched viscount was out of the way, he was confident he could make her agree to a marriage soon.

To that end, he requested that Charity see him to his mount when he departed. Without giving her a chance to decline, he was up from the settee and towering expectantly over her. He helped her rise and led her out the front doors. But as was his habit, he changed his intent the moment they were outside and dragged her toward the weedy woodland garden, ostensibly for a stroll among the lilacs and blossoming trees.

As Charity felt the tightening of his hand over hers, her anger rose. She hated his smugness, hated the feel of his clammy hands on her skin, hated the sly lechery in the looks he gave her. But most of all, she hated the fact that she was coming to *enjoy* his misfortunes. It was a sign of a frightening change occurring in her . . . an abandonment of feeling, a locking away of her heart, a denial of her very nature.

Lost in her dismal musings, she suddenly felt herself being pulled from the path and reacted too late. The baron pulled her against a tree, trapping her there with his lanky form. His eyes were burning, and he was breathing heavily from between thin, wet lips.

"Really baron, how ungentlemanly!" She pushed against his chest with all her might only to find her wrists seized and pinned to the tree on each side of her head. "I must protest! This is un—" His hard mouth swooped toward hers, but landed well short of its goal when she jerked her face away. "Let me go!"

He laughed, clearly excited by her resistance. He pressed his body hard against hers as his knee blatantly probed her skirts. "You delicious little witch, playing tight and timid. I do enjoy these little games of yours."

Then his aim was perfected and his mouth crushed hers, oblivious to her muffled noises of outrage. His tongue probed, then stabbed its way into her mouth and she shuddered with revulsion. "Open up, lovely," he rasped as his knee pushed forcibly between hers and he ground his bony pelvis against her. "Open up, and we'll both enjoy it more." When she didn't respond to his carnal cozening, he kissed her again and coaxed cruelly, "I know you must have played a bit of tip and tickle with his lordship, lovely . . . so you can't pretend to be entirely shocked by the feel of a man's hands."

His taunting use of Rane's lovemaking had pierced her to the quick. Dark, suffocating waves of despair and remembrance rolled over her. Rane's quicksilver kisses, his tender giving of pleasure, his erotic caress of her body, were suddenly all there again, filling her mind and heart, fresh and painful. The contrast with the baron's crude pawing and repulsive kisses was so sharp that it cut her deeply. Rane had called her his angel. To the repulsive baron she was a witch. The pain left her unable to respond on any level.

She scarcely felt his fingers tugging at her bodice, fumbling, seeking her softness. But when he lowered his mouth to her, she strangled a cry of horror, and he laughed, certain he'd found the secret of her ardor.

251

Through a haze of inner pain and horror she felt him break off the assault and force her chin up, forcing her to meet his gaze.

"I've got you writhing and whimpering for it, you little witch. I knew beneath all that sweetness was a hot little hatch! Your lack of money needn't stand in our way; I'll accept Standwell with you as your dowry. I'll turn it into a rich estate and dress you in the finest." He forced another bruising kiss on her and, confident now of her agreement, insisted, "You will marry me, won't you, lovely?"

Charity stared up into his hawkish, greedy face and out of the deep well of despair in her came a roaring, hot surge of anger and disgust. Never, not in her whole life, could she remember wanting to deliberately hurt something or someone. But her loathing for the baron was now so deep, so implacable, that she stared him in the eye and whispered hoarsely, "Yes, I'll marry you."

His face creased with a despicable grin. Before he could seal their bargain with a kiss, she pushed him back with a condition.

"But it has to be soon; a week from now, no later."

She was thinking that the less time she had to dread it, the better. But her stipulation overjoyed him; he'd wed and bed her by week's end, and all would bemoan his romantic distraction and his inattention to his duties, while secretly envying him his sensual little bride. Who could blame him if things were in a bit of chaos in his offices, records incomplete or mislaid? It was perfect!

He was foul even in victory, giving her sensitive breasts a last tweak of promise and vowing wickedly to make her wait until after the vows for the fulfillment of it. Then he straightened her bodice and led her shocked form back to the house to announce the news to her grandmother.

Lady Margaret suffered through the pronouncement

with Charity, staring in disbelief at her sweet grand-daughter's bruised lips, rumpled bodice, and shame-stained cheeks. Charity would not, could not meet her eyes. And Lady Margaret could not, would not accept that this was what Charity truly wanted . . . *marriage* to that vain, rutting cock.

When the baron departed, Lady Margaret grabbed Charity's hand to keep her from fleeing the parlor and pulled her to a seat near the windows.

"What happened, child?" Her voice had absorbed some of its bleakness from Charity's lovely eyes. "Did he . . . hurt you?"

Charity avoided her grandmother's too-perceptive gaze and shook her head. Another lie. Each one seemed to come a bit easier.

"You wouldn't marry his lordship, but you will marry the baron. I don't understand." Lady Margaret wagged her head in dismay. "Surely you don't want to marry him."

"No." Charity's head came up and the pain in her luminous eyes was awful to behold.

"Then . . . *why?*"

Charity's desperate determination slipped enough to reveal the true depths of her loathing for her new be-trothed. "Because he's the wickedest man I know." Anguish crept into her terrible declaration. "And he deserves a wife like me."

Lady Margaret watched her flee the parlor and felt utterly powerless in the face of this new calamity. She was shocked to the bottom of her soul by Charity's grim pronouncement and by the anger and bitterness that had prompted it. Charity knew now that she was a jinx. And she was marrying the wretched baron *hoping* to bring calamity down upon him!

Over the last week she'd watched Charity struggling with the devastating recognition of her jinx. She had approached her time and again, to try and offer her some comfort, to talk with her. But Charity always shrank from such contact, looking at her with such pathos and self-loathing that it took the old lady's breath. Day after day, Charity wandered wretchedly about the house and down the sea path to the cliffs above the bay, her suffering clear and painful to all who loved her.

It was only now, faced with the pain of Charity's soul that Lady Margaret began to understand the full, devastating impact of Charity's jinx. The troubles that occurred around her were sometimes difficult, but the troubling inside her, in her tender, loving heart, made those external mishaps and misfortunes seem paltry by comparison.

Lady Margaret had lived all these years with the secret and had grown almost comfortable with it, becoming preoccupied with her charms and folk practices and absorbed in her pursuit of Standwell's "luck." Never once had she given thought to the impact it would have on Charity to discover that she was responsible for the misfortunes of others, even of those she loved best. Lady Margaret realized she'd been so occupied with the small, mundane disasters that she'd failed to prepare for the greatest one of all . . . the slow, painful destruction of a bright, loving spirit.

Tears rolled down the old lady's cheeks and she buried her face in her hands. Now Charity was compounding the calamity by throwing her life away . . . giving herself to a man she hated in order to blight his miserable life. A deep sense of guilt came over her. Perhaps she had been wrong to interfere between Charity and Rane Austen. At least with his lordship, she might have found some happiness to balance the pain.

It came to her: Charity had refused Rane Austen and sent him away to protect him from her jinx! It was the only explanation that made sense. Loving, helpful Charity—she'd broken his heart and her own, in order to spare him. And in so doing, she'd removed the light of

254

all hope and love from her life and her future. She'd consigned herself to a life without joy, without the one thing that might have comforted her . . . Rane Austen's love.

Lady Margaret straightened, her heart rebelling at the idea of Charity's giving nature slowly hardening with bitterness and betrayal. Something had to be done. She couldn't let Charity destroy herself, or even the wretched baron. Dare she tempt fate by interfering?

A still, small voice inside reminded her that she'd already interfered, thinking she knew what was best. What was one more little bit of interference if it meant sparing Charity . . . or saving her?

That night two solemn figures crept inside Standwell's kitchen door, reluctantly answering Lady Margaret's summons. The old lady hurried Gar and Percy over to the kitchen table and sat them down, trapping them in her most compelling stare.

"You have to go to London," she declared. "You have to find his lordship and tell him that Charity is marrying the baron on next Friday. And you have to tell him: I'm issuing him a special invitation."

Gar and Percy looked at each other, speechless with astonishment. They didn't know which was the more shocking: Miss Charity wedding the crimp-faced baron, or the thought of going all the way to London to carry their former victim the news! Gar found his tongue first.

"We cain't do that, m'lady—his lordship swore to thrash us proper when next he laid eyes on us! A-and we ain't never been outta Devon!" Her silence and her determined scowl sent him scuttling for another excuse. Percy came up with it.

"How'd we get there?"

"Horses," Lady Margaret said resolutely.

"Horses?" Percy stiffened back.

"We can borrow a gig of some sort and you can drive

255

his lordship's blacks; they look to be fast enough. He said he'd send for them." The old lady's eyes narrowed craftily. "We'll say you're just delivering them." Their horrified looks deterred her none. "You have to do this for Charity — we've got to do something, or she'll marry the baron and ruin her life, in spite of us all!"

"B-but . . . *horses* . . ." Gar turned a little green and looked at Percy. When he turned back to plead with the old lady, her eyes glittered with warning and her hand raised so that two fingers pointed threateningly from her eyes, a potent gypsy sign they knew all too well. Gar's shoulders rounded in surrender.

"Well, I'm gonna die anyway. . . ."

Chapter Fifteen

The next morning, travelers along the London Road were startled by the sight of a light trap bouncing and hurtling along behind a pair of powerful, rampaging blacks, with one startled bumpkin frozen at the reins and another hanging over the side retching for all he was worth. The hapless twosome careened past inn after inn, captives to wild-eyed horsepower, too stupefied with fear to wave or call out for help.

Eventually the blacks tired and slowed and turned themselves off onto the side of the road at a walk. When they stopped near a farmer's cottage, Gar and Percy were just able to peel themselves from the seats and wobble down from the small vehicle under the farmer's incredulous stare. After a bit of ale and food and a night's rest, Percy dragged Gar back into the vehicle the next morning. The blacks surged into motion and soon were galloping along at their customary blistering pace, Percy hanging onto the reins for dear life, and Gar pressed into the corner like green plaster.

They pulled into St. George Square mid-afternoon, two days later, drawing curious stares as they begged directions from the elegantly clad people strolling the grassy park and promenade in the middle of the square. The battered rig lurched to a stop in front of the Viscount Oxley's house and Percy managed to uncurl the reins from his fingers and pry Gar from the side of the vehicle. They stumbled onto the pavement, hanging onto one another, feeling weak-kneed and light-headed, and dreading the ordeal to come.

The great white door swung open and a nattily dressed fellow with gold braid on his shoulders looked down on them. They rambled and stuttered and gasped out their purpose to the footman, then had to repeat it all when the butler arrived to settle the noise. Then Lady Catherine appeared in all her pristine gray hauteur, impaling them with her icy stare such that their teeth chattered as they spoke. They needed to see his lordship the viscount, they maintained; something about his horses and a wedding . . .

Lady Catherine looked them over; superciliously peering at their plain, travel-stained clothing, their wind-whipped hair and sun-reddened faces, their dirty boots and frantic, owl-eyed looks. Then she ordered them removed from the premises, post haste.

But they hadn't come all the way to London, surviving numerous brushes with disaster, to be chucked out on their ears! They set up a howl and a scuffle that penetrated the depths of the house, all the way to Rane Austen's study. He came blasting out, ready to lay somebody—anybody—flat for disrupting what was left of his peace. He came to a flat-footed halt when he saw who was to blame.

"You?!" he bellowed, freezing the butler and head footman in mid-mayhem. He stalked closer, blinking, scarcely able to believe his eyes. *"You?!"* He took in their harried and disheveled state and their woeful expressions. "What the hell are you two doing here?"

"Some nonsense about horses," Lady Catherine stepped into the fray. "They're obviously beggars or miscreants. Well, don't just stand there," she turned on Eversby. "Get them out of here!"

"Yer lordship," Percy broke free of the footman's hold to stumble toward Rane. "We brung yer horses back to ye." His voice squeezed past the knot in his throat. "Lady Margr't, she made us."

258

"And she bade us tell ye—" Gar struggled out of Eversby's grip to join Percy in facing the hot-eyed nobleman. He swallowed hard and tried again. "She said fer us to invite ye . . . special . ." His courage failed as he recalled that same savage look on Rane's face the last time they had spoken of Miss Charity.

"Horses? You brought my blacks here?" Rane scowled, distracted momentarily by their pathetic condition and by the realization that they'd probably driven his high-strung blacks all the way from west Devon themselves. Then the bits and snippets came together in his mind and he stiffened.

"Invite me? To what?"

"To. . .," Percy swallowed miserably, ". . . Miz Charity's weddin'."

"Charity's what?" Rane stalked forward, swelling inside his gentlemanly coat.

"Her weddin'," Gar choked out. "She be marryin' up wi' Baron Pinnow, come this Frid'y. An' Lady Margr't's plum beside herself wi' grief. Cain't talk her out of it. So Lady Margr't sent us to in-vite ye to the weddin'."

Rane stared at them, trying desperately to make sense of it. "Charity? Marrying that mealworm Pinnow?!" His gut contracted violently at the thought. How could that be? Angry confusion boiled up in him, bronzing his skin, clenching his fists. And the old woman had the collossal gall to send for him to witness it?!

"B'dammit, *Pinnow?!* Why the hell would she marry Pinnow?!" he roared, biting off the part that said, *and not me?* Gar and Percy blanched and huddled closer.

"Lady Margr't says s-she . . . don't w-want to marry him," Percy stammered.

"Of course she doesn't—*she's in love with me!*"

Rane's furious declaration echoed in the marble dome of the entry hall: ". . . me . . . me . . . me . ." He stood in the shocked silence, hearing his own words whispering back at him, feeling like he'd just plunged,

259

heart-first, into reality's icy waters. For days he'd been blundering about in a daze, trying to flee her memory, trying to avoid the hurt that came whenever he recalled and tried to make sense of her rejection of him. Now one raw outburst of pained, raging truth had purged the haze in his thoughts and feelings.

Charity appeared in his mind with devastating clarity, smiling at him, touching, listening, helping. She wrapped through his senses and sinews, curling through that empty hollow she had carved inside him. She had come to his bed honestly, admitting her desire for him and giving him the joy of her awakening as a woman. And with each kiss, each caress, she'd given him another little bit of her sensible, giving, loving self.

She had given him her very heart, her love. She had nothing left to give another man! In the charged silence, icy hot waves of confusion and despair crashed over him, burning and freezing him in the same instant. She loved him, and yet she was marrying Pinnow?

Like bloody hell she was! He wasn't about to let Pinnow have her without a fight! It struck him like a blow; the old lady hadn't invited him to witness the wedding, she had invited him to *stop it!* His mind began to race, to plan. "Friday? But—Lord!—this is Wednesday!"

"Wull, them blacks near done Gar in, yer lordship," Percy winced. "We couldn't get here no faster."

Rane turned on Eversby, ordering, "Get me the fastest coach and four you can find. And give these fellows something to eat and drink." He turned on his heel and found himself face to face with Lady Catherine's tight glare of disapproval.

"What is this all about? Where are you going?" she demanded.

"To Devon, to stop a wedding."

"You—you wouldn't dare!"

"Oh, but I would!" He flashed a wicked Austen grin

260

of determination. "You see, I intend to marry the bride myself!"

Rain. Charity leaned her fair head on the leaded glass and stared out her bedroom window at the dismal, gray-streaked landscape. It always seemed to rain on the worst days of her life. It was probably an omen concerning her upcoming marriage . . . betokening the dank and dreary years ahead. She lifted her head and squared her shoulders. She smoothed her freshly pressed black bombazine and exited her room for the last time as Charity Standing.

Lady Margaret stood at the top of the stairs with her hands clasped and her face filled with the strain of sleepless nights and futile arguments. The shawl over her shoulders was wet from the fretful vigil she had kept, traipsing up and down the steps of the old tower, keeping watch for the viscount. She had been so sure he would come for her granddaughter, so sure that he wanted her. Now she had to wonder if she'd been wrong about him and his desire for Charity.

Charity slowed as she approached and she made her icy hands into fists that were hidden by her skirts. She avoided her grandmother's care-smudged eyes by fastening her gaze on the old lady's crescent moon amulet.

"Have you changed your mind?" Charity asked in a pained whisper. "Will you come?"

"No." Lady Margaret's voice was hoarse with strain. "I'll not come to watch you throw your life away." She summoned one plea. "Please, child, don't do this—"

"What better way to work some good with something so . . . terrible? I can still be of benefit. ." Charity's voice cracked, "i-if I keep away from good people . . . and let my jinx work on those who aren't."

"But, it's sheer folly—" Lady Margaret stretched open hands that went unfilled to her.

"Then tell me another way!" Charity raged in a desperate whisper that rose in volume and in pain. "Tell me how to undo my jinx! Give me a new charm or tell me another custom to observe, another ritual to practice, another of your beliefs to fulfill. Tell me there is hope for me in your moon signs, Gran'mere, and I'll not marry him!"

Lady Margaret felt suffocated by Charity's despair and lowered her head. Over the years she had tried everything; nothing had worked. She had nothing more to give Charity, no remedies or answers. Now, she had not even hope.

The front doors opened below and the sound of Melwin admitting the baron wafted up in the aching silence. Charity's eyes burned, her throat and chest ached, and her stomach was squeezing itself in two. The time had come and she had to go. She turned and was halfway down the steps when Lady Margaret roused and came racing down the steps after her.

"Wait, child! You can't wear that dress! A bride can't wear black at her wedding—it's the worst of luck!"

Charity pulled her hand away and leveled a look of pained, wordless rebuttal on her grandmother. Bad luck, that look said, was precisely what she intended.

Charity was met in the entry by Sullivan Pinnow, who was momentarily put off by her appearance in mourning clothing. "It is the finest gown I own," she explained, wincing at the harsh way his fingers tightened on her arm. "And all know I have been in mourning for my father. I shall change later, after the vows, if you want."

This seemed to pacify him. He stiffly ushered her out into the carriage he had borrowed for the occasion.

Lady Margaret labored down the hallway to her room, feeling crushed, old, helpless. From her window, she watched the departing carriage lurch along, taking the circuitous roads to Standwell's little chapel, where the rector and a few town dignitaries were assembling. It was a calamity in the making, a true tragedy of the heart.

She sat down on the bench by her window and her eyes filled with burning tears. She wasn't aware of how much time had passed . . . minutes . . . half an hour, perhaps. The appearance of a great black barouche thundering down the road toward Standwell brought her back to the present. Six horses, running full tilt, she realized distractedly. Reckless to the point of idiocy and a blamed lot of noise and—She shot up straight on her seat, searching the approaching vehicle. The great, dark husk of despair around her heart cracked. The viscount!

She snatched her heavy shawl and went barrelling for the stairs, reaching them just as Rane Austen blew through the front doors like a typhoon run aground, bellowing Charity's name. She raced down the steps to meet him, calling, "They've gone to the chapel!"

"She's really doing it?" he demanded, his face dusky, his eyes glittering. "She's marrying Pinnow?"

"She thinks . . ." Lady Margaret stopped before him, shaking her hands frantically, wondering how much to tell him. "She thinks she's doing the right thing. But she gave herself to you . . . and it's you she truly wants, your lordship." She felt Rane's gaze searching her, evaluating her assertions.

"Then why—"

"There's no time to explain! If we stand here jawboning, it'll be too late! They're at the chapel, even now!"

She grabbed his sleeve and dragged him out the door, sending the gawking Gar and Percy scrambling back out of the doorway they were just entering. "Forget the carriage!" she pulled him away when he veered toward it. "If we cut across the fields," Lady Margaret puffed, scurrying past the garden wall and into the nearby field, "we can make it quicker!"

They hurried through the soggy fields, getting wet to the bone from the puddles and wet grasses and the steady drizzle. Rane's jaw was set grimly as he thought about what he would find at the end of this mad journey. Would she belong to another man by the time he got there? He didn't see Wolfram bounding up behind and when the dog barked thunderously and leaped on him, he nearly collapsed of shock. He stumbled to a halt and beat the creature off with a panting snarl.

"Not now, you hell-spawned heap of fleas. Get off me!" But Wolfram only barked and jumped around delightedly as Rane struck off again. If he hadn't known better, he would have sworn the beast was glad to see him! But the dog continued to interfere in his path, and finally Rane roared, "Why don't you make yourself bloody useful? Go find Charity and gnaw on Pinnow until I get there!"

Lady Margaret heard his snarling and stopped, panting, clasping her heart. "Wolfram! Find Charity! At the chapel," she flung an authoritative finger ahead of them. "Find Charity!"

The great dog's lone ear came to attention and he seemed to register his mistress's name. He raced off in the direction Lady Margaret pointed and was soon out of sight.

"We. . ." the old lady staggered and wheezed dismally, "we won't make it . . . she's lost!"

No other words in Christendom could have had such a devastating effect on Rane. His bulldog determination erupted and he burst into a run, following the path Wolfram had blazed a moment before. His long muscular legs stretched out, his fists clenched, his arms braced the way they had on Barbados, when he ran from angry wild boars in the brush. Now running again meant survival . . . but of a very different kind.

* * *

264

Charity stood at the low altar railing, hearing without really listening as a homily was read and sonorous platitudes on matrimony were pronounced. Her heart was twisting and thudding in her chest; it felt like death throes to her . . . the death of her feelings, hopes and desires. She looked up at the icy blonde baron, standing beside her, and shrank inside. Soon she would be at his mercy . . . and he would be at hers. And for the rest of their lives, it would be so. She bit her lip and dug her nails into her palms. Her ears registered a muffled "woof" somewhere outside. The sound was distant, scarcely audible.

Moments passed, then something lunged at the weathered chapel door. It shuddered and rattled loudly. The handful of local dignitaries and ladies on hand to witness the rite turned in shock, muttering amongst themselves. The crashing noise came again and again, and the ashen rector finally paused and nodded one of the gentlemen to the door to dispense with the racket. But when the gentleman opened the door, he was charged and beat back by a massive beast of a dog that streaked up the aisle barking and pounced on Sullivan Pinnow.

There was mass confusion as the ladies squealed and hid and the gentlemen shouted and cowered and the rector dodged and sputtered and Pinnow flailed and bashed. In the end it was Charity who brought back some semblance of order. She hauled Wolfie away, seizing him by the scruff of his mangy-looking neck, and dragged him down the aisle and outside. Pinnow watched her through a haze of red fury and vowed the cursed beast would meet with a fatal accident before the night was out. He felt the guests' shocked eyes on him and stiffened with humiliation as Charity again joined him at the altar. His dark look promised retribution to the beast's mistress, as well.

The rector straightened his stole and smoothed his

surplice. He was so unnerved by the attack that he had lost his place in the service book and had to start back at the beginning. Shortly thereafter, the door banged open at the back of the chapel a second time. In the doorway, wet and muddy and panting for breath, stood Rane Austen.

"Rector!" His full bass voice filled the stone chapel and reverberated in Charity's empty heart. Her head came up, but she was too stunned to turn and face him. "Rector, I apologize for this intrusion. I am here on behalf of Miss Standing's grandmother, who will join us shortly. She has asked that I have an urgent word with you before you proceed further. Afterwards, we shall leave it to you as to whether these vows should be spoken or not."

"Oxley!" The baron had whirled to face him and now reddened furiously. "How dare you . . . This is an outrage!"

"My thoughts, exactly Pinnow," Rane declared, waving the rector out the door and waiting commandingly until the little man obeyed. They could be seen out in the muddy yard of the chapel talking, gesturing. Whatever it was that Rane said was obviously having quite an impact on the rector, who paled and looked confused and a bit horrified. Soon Lady Margaret appeared, clutching her throat, and puffing and gulping for air. With red-faced nods, she corroborated Rane's story. The crimson rector braced and then marched back into the chapel to pull the outraged Pinnow aside and relate the difficulty.

Pinnow went purple and his eyes caught fire as he glared at Charity and then at Rane, who now stood at the back of the chapel. Charity watched him come slowly toward her and shivered at the hatred burning in his eyes.

"You dirty little puzzle," he growled for her ears. "Had I known, I'd never have soiled my hands with

266

you! And now you've humiliated me publicly!" His face
was aflame as he strode past her and down the aisle to
the door. Trembling with rage, he glared feverishly at
Rane.

"You'll pay for this, Oxley! I swear to God, I'll make
you pay for this humiliation!" He whirled and stormed
out the door, leaving a breathless vacuum in the little
chapel.

Charity looked up, crimson-faced, horrified, and met
Rane's gaze. As he came up the aisle toward her, her
heart began to beat again, began to rise to meet him.
This was indeed a calamity. But as she searched his
bronzed features and the heated shimmer of his light
eyes, all she could feel was an aching pleasure at seeing
his beloved countenance again. When he stood beside
her, staring down at her with a lock of his wet hair
falling over his forehead, it was all she could do to keep
from reaching out to touch him.

"I have to talk with you." He grabbed her wrist and
dragged her from the chapel with him, tossing an order
over his shoulder for everyone to keep their seats.

The rough movement jarred her wits back to func-
tioning and the full impact of what he'd just done came
crashing down on her. He'd broken in on her wedding
and told the rector and then the baron something that
had shocked and horrified them both . . . something
that had made the rector refuse to read the rites and
made Pinnow sneer at her with disgust.

By the time he pulled her to a halt beneath the dripping chapel eaves, she was both furious at his arrogant
disruption of her life and frightened of the melting, the
longing that the mere sight of him had produced in her.

"How dare you come barging into my wedding!" She
stared up at him with a furious glare and wrenched her
wrist from his hand to cross her arms defensively over
her chest. "What did you say to them?"

He leaned over her, searching for what lay beneath

267

the anger in her pale face. The sleeplessness of her nights was evident in the hollows beneath her eyes, and her face seemed strained, a bit thinner. She'd been as miserable as he had, he realized. And the realization released a tide of relief through him.

"I told them . . . that it was very likely you're carrying my heir at this very moment."

"You told them—Ohhhhh!!" Shocked anger choked off her speech temporarily, and he seized the moment to inform her what else he had in mind.

"And since I've announced your perfidy—and mine—to the world, I suggest you allow me to do the decent thing by you . . . and our future offspring."

"H-h-how d-dare you?!" She gasped and would have fled. But his reflexes were faster than hers, and he had expected resistance. She tussled back in his grip and glared daggers at him, while avoiding his eyes. "I am not with child!"

"Are you quite sure?" His mouth curled suggestively.

"Of course, I'm sure! How dare you say such a thing? That's vile—"

"According to your grandmother, there's at least room for doubt. And since I've ruined your matrimonial future with my hypothetical offspring, I insist you wed me . . . now . . . here."

Wed him. Now. Here. Charity swallowed hard, bracing against the pull of his hands on her shoulders, feeling her whole body reacting to the thought of it. Her knees were melting, her heart was pounding as if she'd run, and her head was lightening, dizzy with the impact of his presence. No! She couldn't allow herself to even think about it!

"No!" she ground out, turning her face away, gritting her teeth. "I'll not marry you, no matter how you try to malign and humiliate me. If you think to force me to it, you don't know me very well. I'm not one of your frail London lilies who shrinks and wilts at the merest

268

hint of scandal. I'm not with child . . . and I don't have a reputation to save, and I don't need a husband to cover my disgrace!"

"Charity—listen to me—" he pleaded. He wanted to shake her, to make her listen to him. And he wanted to take her into his arms and hold her and kiss her until she began to melt . . .

"No!" she shouted, succeeding in wrenching away from his hands at last. "You listen to me! I dont *want* to marry you!"

Every word was ripped from her soul. She stood there, aching for him and aching with him, watching his expression change from determination, to confusion, and then to anger. There was no comfort for either of them. She couldn't give in. To surrender would be to destroy him. She turned to go but he snagged her arm and held her. Her heart stopped when she turned and glimpsed the angry glitter in his eyes.

"You were set to take Pinnow," he charged contemptuously. "Why?!"

She bit her lip and turned her face away, refusing to answer. A moment later, her knees weakened with relief. Apparently Gran'mere had been too busy babbling other things, to tell him about her jinx. Perhaps if she could make him angry enough . . . refuse him enough times. . . .

"It can't be money—he doesn't have any. You run from him when he kisses you . . . you can't possibly want him as a man!" Still, she said nothing. He watched the stubborn set of her jaw and his frustration burned a precariously short fuse leading to an explosion of Austen determination.

"Be stubborn, then. But you'll marry me . . . or . . . I'll go to the authorities with the truth about your father . . . and about Gar Davis and Percy Hall. They were in a smuggling operation together. And I know that Gar and Percy are the ones who shot me." He tightened,

269

playing his last, desperate card, pulling her closer and taking her shoulders in his hard grip. "If you refuse me, I'll go to the authorities and see them prosecuted . . . fully."

Charity stood in the gray, rain-washed shadows of the chapel, staring up into his dark, fierce countenance, feeling her determination to reject him, to save him from her, softening. He was so powerful and so stubborn and so tenacious. And she wanted him so much.

"You wouldn't . . . really tell . . ."

"I will if you refuse me." The swirling hurt his threat produced in her mingled hauntingly with his own private pain. The hard angles of his face softened and he brought one hand to her pale cheek. She felt the brush of his fingers across her open, vulnerable heart.

"I don't want to hurt you, Charity."

She raised her eyes to his and her breath stopped at the pain and hope and need swirling in the stormy depths of his gaze. Her heart swelled, crowding her breathing. His taut, bronzed jaw, his high cheekbones and straight, noble nose . . . he was so beautiful. And he was so unlucky . . . to be in love with a jinx like her. She could feel her strength ebbing. Her resistance was worn from days of constant strain and inner conflict. She felt her resolve giving way, surrendering, and was powerless to stop it.

"Please, please don't make me do this." Her whisper was filled with pained longing that shook him to his marrow. She was so tense and pale and so very unhappy. All he could think about was the contrasting sight of her, warm and flushed with loving, her, soft hair tumbled over the pillows, her eyes aglow. He wanted to see her like that again, wanted to love the spirit and the warmth back into her.

"Marry me, Charity." It was an entreaty, not an order.

It was the third time he'd proposed to her, she realized. *And the third time, as every good gypsy knows, is always a charm.*

His broad shoulders filled her vision, his musky sandalwood scent filled her head, and his determination filled her aching heart. She hid her crystal-rimmed eyes from him and nodded.

They reentered the chapel and approached the altar under the widened eyes of Mortehoe's elite. Rane spoke to the rector in quiet tones and Charity nodded with lowered eyes when they referred to her for something. The cleric mopped his brow, fumbled with his service book, then announced to the murmuring guests that Miss Standing would instead marry the Viscount Oxley. Lady Margaret and Gar and Percy, who sat in the Standings' family box, heaved sighs of relief . . . briefly.

No sooner had the rector begun the rites again, then Lady Margaret jumped to her feet and bustled forward. "No—wait! Stop! She's wearing black! She can't be married in black!"

Rane's jaw clenched as he turned on the old woman. "Enough nonsense!" He turned his back pointedly. "Do get on with it, Rector!"

"No, stop—" Lady Margaret fairly jiggled with anxiety. "Child," she hurried to Charity's side and engaged her eyes meaningfully, "you cannot wear that dress! It's terrible luck . . . and this marriage will need all the luck it can get. You must have something else! Something *borrowed.*"

Charity read her grandmother's thoughts. Every good gypsy knew that a bride had to wear something borrowed at her wedding, to insure luck. She nodded with a pained expression. The old lady wheeled and began searching frantically among the guests for a lady's cloak to borrow.

But the weather had been abominably balmy of late,

and there wasn't a decent cloak to be had in the lot. The old lady was frantic by the time she spotted the rector's white, hip-length surplice. The cleric reddened and stammered and protested, but the old lady soon wrestled his outer vestment from him and bustled Charity behind a stone arch at the back, to strip the unlucky black from her.

Thus the Viscount Oxley and Miss Charity Standing exchanged eternal vows; he, rumpled, muddied, and dripping wet, and she, garbed in a cleric's short white surplice and bare petticoats. He looked down into her sweet oval face, promised to love and to cherish and to cleave only to her . . . and meant every living word of it. She looked up into his handsome bronzed features and outwardly promised to love, honor and obey . . . while inwardly vowing to do whatever was required to protect him from his own hard-headed desire for her. If she refused to sleep with him, if she kept their lives as separate as possible . . . maybe she could forestall disaster, keep the inevitable at bay.

Then it was over and the rector proclaimed them man and wife with nervous relief. Not a breath was let in the chapel as he turned her by the shoulder and pulled her close. He wrapped his arms determinedly about her stiff form, surrounding her with his warmth, giving her shelter against his big, hard body. Then his head lowered to her trembling mouth.

The warmth and the liquid caress of his lips both comforted and tormented her. With her vow not minutes old, her resistance to him was tested to the limits. Another second, another breath, and her arms would wind about him, her mouth would open hungrily to his hot velvet probing, and she would seal his doom by linking his passions to her forever.

She pushed away and he staggered back one step, caught off guard by her resistance, his whole body contracting with unpleasant surprise. He stared at her with

272

a dark, piercing expression, trying to discern what lay beneath her unthinkable rebuff of his wedding kiss. Failing that, he grabbed her wrist tightly and dragged her to the parish register to sign the marriage documents, then turned to the guests with a new sharpness to his features and in his tone.

"I know you must have expected a proper celebration . . . but with the change of grooms, there has been a change of plans. I have obligations in London, and we will leave within the hour. . . ."

With that and with a glitter in his eyes, he scooped Charity up in his arms and strode down the aisle and out the door with her, headed straight for Standwell.

"Put me down, you—Wait! My dress!" Her voice wafted back to the guests as they sat, still immobilized by shock. They heard his ragged laugh and his shocking rejoinder.

"You won't need a dress tonight, angel . . . and tomorrow I'll buy you dozens of them!"

True to Rane's word, within the hour, they were stuffed inside the elegant barouche jouncing along the London Road. Charity's last glimpse of Standwell was of Melwin and Bernadette standing forlornly in the front door, and of Gar and Percy, in whose care Standwell had been placed, standing nearby and waving pitifully after them. In the elegant coach, however, across from Charity and Rane, sat two of Standwell's more catastrophic elements: Lady Margaret, who was bedecked with every bizarre and malodorous amulet she possessed, and Wolfram, whose great muddy paws were close to wrecking the elegant cordovan leather upholstery of the seat and who filled the coach with the overpowering air of wet dog.

Rane had relented to allow Charity time to don a real dress, and Lady Margaret had seized the chance to bustle into the house and snatch her store of amulets and her rarer herbals and notions. Then she had presented

273

herself at the carriage door, announcing that she intended to accompany them, to see her granddaughter settled safely and properly in London, with her own two eyes.

During the confrontation with the old lady, Rane glimpsed Charity's strained, bereft look as she peered out of the carriage and found himself blustering, reasoning, and finally agreeing to a short visit . . . only to help Charity's adjustment. Then as soon as he had helped the old lady in, he found himself knocked aside by a wet, bull-elephant of a dog bent on climbing into the coach, too. Rane grabbed Wolfram's patchy tail, then snagged one of his back legs and pulled with all his might.

Wolfram growled and clawed and whined, his great dark eyes pleading with Charity for help as he was dragged from the coach. But this "lordship" was a very tenacious animal indeed, and Wolfie eventually found himself on the ground again, flopping and twisting in the weedy, wet gravel. The lordship proved a very quick beast as well, for he scrambled into the coach himself and closed the door with a resounding bang, ordering the driver to, "Move!" Wolfram ran after them, barking and leaping at the horses, worrying the animals into balking and rearing.

Rane leaned out the window and shouted irritably at him. Wolfram stopped and trotted hopefully back to the door. The carriage lurched and moved down the road again, only to jerk and halt again as Wolfie harried the horses to another standstill.

Charity watched Rane's handsome features darken with frustration and saw the vein throbbing in his temple. It was all she could do to keep from reaching out to touch him, to soothe him. Poor Rane, he was so set-upon, so very unlucky. . . .

Rane ran his hands back through his damp hair and felt her eyes on him. He looked up to find her staring

274

at him with a longing, hurting look . . . that he took for a plea on Wolfie's behalf. He growled and slammed the door open.

"Alright, b'dammit! Get your arse in here!"

It was a long, jostling and miserable ride. Charity felt her nerves reacting to every shifting contour and angle, every restless movement of his big body in the dim carriage. She heated and tightened inside at the casual, unconscious flexing of his big, tanned hands. She kept remembering how those hard, square-tipped fingers that had teased her nipples to burning points of pleasure and had touched and explored her sleek, secret places with knowing tenderness . . . how they could work *night magic* in her. Her head jerked and her throat cleared irritably. But a while later her eyes drifted to the sprawl of his long, muscular legs and slid over the wool that hugged his thighs the way she wanted to . . . intimately, openly . . .

Her face flushed and she fidgeted crossly in her seat, smoothing her plain muslin dress over her knees and thinking of the battle that lay ahead. Rane had served bold notice of his expectations for their wedding night. And he was going to be furious with her when she told him he had to forego nuptial pleasures with her.

Rane watched her burrow back into the padded seat, as far from him as she could get, and ground his teeth together. She was obviously furious that he'd forced her to say vows with him in such an unorthodox manner. He determined to spend the first part of their wedding night uncovering and settling whatever was the cause of the misunderstanding between them. And then, one side of his mouth curled up in a carnally confident smile, he'd spend the second part of the night showing her all the reasons she should be pleased he had taken such drastic action upon her life.

He knew quite a little bit about her now. He stole a look at her, remembering the way she shivered when he tongued her ear. He knew how she reacted to the sight and the feel of his browned hands on her breasts. He knew the places on the sides of her neck and in the curve of her smooth waist that made her squirm when he nibbled them with his teeth. He knew the places she liked to be stroked lightly . . . and the places that hungered for a firmer touch. He was suddenly as hot as a tavern poker, just thinking about those warm, inviting places. He flushed and shifted in his seat, crossing his long legs to camouflage his untimely eagerness. There were ways of making her come around. . . .

Chapter Sixteen

The Kingery Inn was crowded and noisy. Rane had to trot out his rank and cross the innkeeper's palm with silver to acquire even his two meagerest rooms for the night. And when the innkeeper saw that Wolfram was to be an occupant in one of those rooms, a bit more "palm grease" was required. Then the fellow declared he had no time to ferry food and water upstairs, and they were forced to take nourishment in the noisy tavern of the inn, amongst ham-handed freightmen, local farmers, and gawking mail coach passengers.

It wasn't a particularly conducive atmosphere for a wedding night, Rane thought irritably.

It was a mercifully distracting and unromantic place to have their first confrontation, Charity realized with relief.

By the time they had secured a sooty oil lamp and mounted the worn stairs, both Charity and Rane were coiled like springs inside. Rane escorted Lady Margaret to her room, then steered Charity into their own. As soon as the door closed behind them, Charity braced and turned to him with her heart racing and her fists clenched in the folds of her skirts.

But she still was unprepared for the way Rane seemed to fill the small room around her. All she could see was his wide chest and his light eyes and the bold, sensual sweep of his lower lip. The warmth radiating from him invaded her skin and the smells of sandalwood and damp wool and wine filled her head.

"I . ." She stepped backward, trying desperately to recall her planned order of excuses and objections. "I should have asked Gran'mere for a sleeping powder to rid me of this terrible megrim," she launched forth, adding a judicious massage of her left temple and a suitably pained and accusing expression. "All that rough jouncing and jostling . . ."

"Megrim?" He took a step in the direction she had, staring at her. "You've a headache?"

"A terrible one." She averted her face and made to go around him, but he blocked her way again. "If you'll just . . ."

But he didn't move, and after a while she was forced to raise her chin and look at him. His gray eyes shimmered and his expression was a devilish half-smile that didn't seem to have a bit of outrage or indignation in it.

"I don't think we need bother your Gran'mere. I'll simply apply an old Austen remedy for a wedding night headache . . ." He came toward her, hands rising and reaching, and she jolted back a step, then another, glaring at him.

"I hardly think you're likely to prove the remedy, your lordship," she said irritably, "when you are the cause." Her eyes widened as he came for her, backing her past the stout bedposts and the lone chair. "A-actually, it's more than a headache." She smacked the wall with her shoulders and panicked briefly as he closed in. "It's worse, much worse . . ."

He massaged her temples in gentle, knowing circles. She couldn't protest properly for the tightness in her throat.

"Here," his voice was low and filled with smoke, "isn't this what you need?" Before she could answer his tantalizing fingers were working their way up into her hair, along her scalp, then down the back of her head to turn the muscles in her neck to butter.

"N-nnnooo." She stiffened, shaking off his touch. "Would you kindly remove your hands from m-me." He did lower his hands, but only to her shoulders, where they rested too warmly.

"Tell me," he coaxed pressing closer, "where else do you hurt?"

"I hurt . . . all o-over." She coiled and began mentally measuring the distance to the door, fearing her legs might not be functional. "Do you mind?" She shrugged off his hands, feeling more than a bit panicky, and then summoned the courage to give him a shove. "I have quite enough discomfort as it is, without your pawing me. My feet hurt, my legs ache, and my back is torturing me . . . and my head is pounding like a drum."

He stepped back, frowning, searching her, and she added a judicious wince while rubbing the side of her neck. A second later, he was pulling her to the ancient chair, pushing her down on it. He dropped to one knee before her and pushed her skirts up over her knees, taking one of her cold ankles in his warm hands.

"What are you doing?" She tugged and twisted, shrinking from him as she realized what he intended. He was going to . . .

"Rubbing your feet," he mused aloud, massaging her foot, "and your limbs." His hands drifted up her calf as he divulged his itinerary for the evening. "And your back and your head. No doubt, your bruised little bottom and your poor shoulders also." He lifted a challenging look to her. "I'm going to rub every single one of them until they forget all about hurting and concentrate on . . . more pleasant things."

She stilled, feeling her blood and body heat rushing to follow his fingers as they moved over her skin. Lush liquid rivulets of pleasure were defying gravity, trickling up her legs. It was only a matter of time before they reached the moist heat of her womanflesh and set her atingle there as well. Her eyes fixed helplessly on his

279

hands, watching them weave their special magic under her skin.

"No—no!" She flinched and wrested her ankle from his hands to stand up. Icy fingers of panic raced over her shoulders. All he had to do was touch her . . . anywhere . . . and she forgot all about vows and jinxes and troubles and protecting him. "You miss the point, your lordship. Thus I shall have to spell it out for you. You cannot, will not share my bed or my body this night, wedding night or not! Nor tomorrow, nor the next night—and you may as well accustom yourself to it!"

He watched the flash of her eyes as she skittered away, listened to her chilly declarations of denial, and was suddenly furious with her again. She could stand there with that rosy flush of anticipation his touch had produced in her and still deny him?

"I cannot . . . will not?!" He pushed to his feet and towered over her, coming after her again as she retreated. "What makes you think you can prevent me, angel? I'm your husband . . . and I've been your lover. I've just proven to you that you don't find my touch particularly repulsive." He backed her straight into the wall, trapping her there with only his hot silver gaze. She was desperate . . . frantic.

"It's my 'time,'" she whispered hoarsely, staring up into his angry face. "My woman's time. It's how I know I'm not with child. It started . . . this morning. . . ."

He blinked as it sank in, then he pulled his chin back, feeling as if she'd slapped him. Her woman's time? Of all the unexpected, absurd—Chagrin washed him from head to toe. All his male pride and manly force and sensual power . . . and he was reduced to carnal beggardom on his long-awaited wedding night by the mysteries of a woman's internal plumbing!

Or was he? He searched her clear, caramel gaze and found what appeared to be resentment and discomfort and even a tinge of righteous anger . . . but no deceit. Would she say such a thing just to escape his touch? Was she still so angry that he'd forced her to marry him?

"If you'd married Pinnow . . . would he have found you inaccessible tonight as well?!"

"Yes." She flared, angered by his suggestion. "It was his bad luck—and now you've made it yours! You've no one to blame but yourself."

He stared at her, unsure whether to believe her or not. There was no surety in the matter unless he braved and invaded her very person. And with his luck . . . she would be telling him the truth and he'd be a wretch and a cad and a royal fool for mistrusting her. Lord, this was Charity! His sweet, generous, sensible angel . . . his giving, sensual, eager lover. Just now, he had scarcely recognized her. Hell, just now he scarcely recognized himself—thinking about throwing her onto the bed, ravishing her to prove a point, to catch her in a possible lie.

He shuddered through a bout of self-loathing and backed grimly to the door. When he stood alone in the hall, he pounded one fist impotently into the other and headed for the liquid comfort of the tavern below.

No wonder women called it "the curse."

Later, when the noise from the tavern below had died, Rane finally climbed the stairs to his room. In the dimness, he could make out Charity's form on the bed. She lay on her side, bundled in the worn quilts, her light hair now brushed and braided loosely, lying across the pillow. He came to stand by her, gazing at her in the candlelight, savoring the sight of her and wishing he could savor the warmth of her as well.

Why wouldn't she marry him? Why was she so angry with him for doing what had to be done? Pride? He

281

honestly hadn't thought she had that sort of pride in her; she was too sensible, too pragmatic about things. Fear of being thrust into a position for which she felt unprepared and unacceptable? Numerous times she'd lamented her unladylike behavior . . . Fear of leaving her home? She'd never really been away from Standwell in her life. It was that realization that had caused him to bring Lady Margaret along . . . and her wretched mongrel. But none of those things, not even the sum of them, seemed a proper explanation of her rejection of him, or of her determination to avoid his loving.

Charity felt him staring at her and her face warmed, but she remained still, feigning sleep. The light disappeared and his boots thudded on the floor. Then the faint rustle of clothing reached her hungry ears. When he lifted the quilts and slid into bed behind her, she jumped, but he didn't notice it for his own movement. He curled his body around hers beneath the covers and laid his head on her thick braid. His strong arms wrapped gently over her, pulling her close, sharing their warmth with her. His every touch was tenderness distilled.

Charity lay in the cradle of his body, absorbing Rane into her parched being. She was desperate to touch him, to return his caring, to give him some of the love she had stored inside for him. But she kept seeing his face as it had been when they first brought him to Standwell: gray and cold, bloodless. It would be that way again, if she allowed him to share her body and her life; she was convinced. So she lay quietly in his arms, forcing her pained heart to calm and her breathing into a slow, shallow pattern counterfeiting sleep. Then she heard his quiet murmur as he settled to rest around her.

"Sleep well, angel."

Her misery finally escaped in silent tears in the darkness.

* * *

Their journey was delayed briefly the next morning as
Lady Margaret gave the carriage and horses a going-
over with green pusley and dried henbane. She brushed
and rubbed and muttered. After Rane had helped Charity and Lady Margaret inside, he stepped on the
mounting step himself, and the thing tore from the carriage under his weight. Charity watched with her heart
in her mouth as he scrambled and caught himself
against the side of the carriage.

"Rane! Are you alright?!" She sank to her knees on
the carriage floor, reaching panicky hands to him.

He straightened and took a deep breath, then
glimpsed the anxiety in her eyes and frowned. "Almost
went tumbling arse over teakettle. At these prices, the
blasted carriage should be in better repair." He watched
her stiffen and resume her seat, lifting her chin and
smoothing her skirt as if brushing off all concern for
him. He closed the door with a bang and went around
to the other step.

Charity met her grandmother's worried gaze. Small
troubles; they read each other's thoughts. This was the
way it would start.

It was a very wearing trip indeed. The carriage was
subject to numerous small and irritating breakdowns
that made Rane gruff with impatience and Charity stiff
with anxiety. When he climbed the stairs to their rented
room each night, he always found her still in her
clothes, even her woolen spencer, beneath the covers, as
if she feared removing any part of them with him
around. His sensual control and his temper both frayed
from the constant tension of wanting, and his speech
was increasingly peppered with Barbados French. He
grunted comments and questions that she answered in
monosyllables. Each growl and grumble fed her hope
that he was growing unhappy with his decision to marry

283

her. Each half-hidden flicker of pain in her eyes, each shiver of ill-suppressed longing fed his determination that when they reached London and gained some privacy, he was going to confront her anger and whatever it was that she held between them like a shield.

St. George Square was breathtaking in the bright spring afternoon. The granite facades and marble paraments of the houses gleamed with a polished luster, and the pristine glass of the long windows flashed in the sun as they passed by in the carriage. In the center of the square was a large green garden of hedges, spring flowers, fenced-in trees, and stone benches. A paved promenade bounded the park on all sides. The towering three- and four-story houses that formed the square were mostly of Georgian and Palladian design, set back from front walkways by small, tasteful, boxed gardens of topiary hedges, expensive Dutch tulips, and imported lilacs.

It was magnificent; grander than any of Charity's girlish dreams. She watched the well-dressed people strolling the promenade and tried not to be unladylike in her staring. But Lady Margaret craned her neck to see and Wolfram hung out the carriage window, panting with excitement. They rolled to a stop in front of a palatial house, and Rane, Lady Margaret, and Charity lunged in concert to keep Wolfram from jumping straight out of the carriage. Rane called to the driver to come and hold the beast and the fellow reluctantly obliged. Rane lifted Charity, then Lady Margaret, to the walkway and ushered them toward the doors.

As if by magic, the great portal opened wide to receive them and Charity had the oddest sensation of being swallowed up by a live thing as they stepped inside. But the doors had been operated by Brockway, the head footman, who took Rane's hat and welcomed him home with obvious surprise. Rane was in the process of introducing him to Charity when Eversby came running into the entry hall, coattails flying.

"My lord!" He jerked to a halt and smoothed his waistcoat, striving for greater dignity as he approached. "We did not expect to see you for some time, your lordship. Lady Catherine said—"

"This is Eversby the indispensable," Rane cut the butler off as he turned to Charity. "Come meet your new mistress, Eversby. The Viscountess Oxley. And her grandmother, Lady Margaret Villiers."

Eversby came forward through the domed entry hall, staring at the stunning, bonnetless blonde with the face of an angel and a rumpled muslin gown. He bowed deeply and expressed a sincere greeting and a welcome to Oxley House before turning to the master of the house again.

"I beg your indulgence, your lordship, but we've made no preparations. Lady Catherine said you wouldn't return for some time and . . . we've been so busy . . ."

"Busy?" Rane frowned deeply, then caught the uncomfortable squirm in his houseman's look. "Busy with what?" He tightened. "What has the old crow been up to now?"

"W-well . . . she's . . . we've been . . . entertaining."

"Entertaining? Here? In my house?" The old bat had waited until he left and immediately started trundling in her noble cronies to entertain . . . at his expense?!

"Callers . . . every day, m'lord." Eversby winced. "The Countess Swinford, from next door, is here even now, with a contingent of lady friends. In the drawing room, m'lord, having tea and cakes." He waved weakly toward a columned archway that led to an inner reception hall, which turned right to a stately dining room and left to the grand drawing room.

"I see. While the cat's away, the mice do play." Rane

285

grabbed Charity's arm and pulled her along with him, tossing an order over his shoulder for Eversby to see to the hired coachman and the baggage. He ignored Charity's resistance and dire whispers of protest over her unkempt condition, tightening his grip on her elbow.

"You look delicious," he growled without real heat. "You always look delicious."

Something in the grim way he said that tugged at her insides. Then she thought to ask, "Who is Lady Catherine?" He pulled back the great arched door to the great drawing room himself and pushed her through the doorway as he answered.

"My *grandmother.*"

Charity had no time to react to the news, no time to pat or straighten or even to dread. She found herself standing just inside the massive doors in a huge, airy chamber that dwarfed both her and her expectations. The column-studded walls were done in cream white and decorated with friezes, gilt-framed mirrors, and soft, elegant landscapes. There were two hearths, one on either side of the chamber, mantled in creamy Florentine marble and framed in elegant dark green serpentine. The window hangings and furnishings were a continuum of lush golds and vibrant greens nestled amidst polished mahogany and positioned over thick Persian carpets. Above them, twin chandeliers glittered in the golden afternoon light.

Rane pulled her with him to the center of the room, where the furnishings had been rearranged into an unbalanced little knot around a tea table. Perched upon those furnishings were several smartly attired ladies, most with high necklines and immaculate gloves and graying hair. They were staring at Rane's disheveled coat and Charity's rumpled blond beauty in evaluative surprise.

"Good day, ladies . . . Lady Catherine." There was a harsh edge to his tone that drew Charity from worries about her embarrassing appearance to look at his expression. She shivered at the angry glitter in his eyes and the very controlled set of his jaw and shoulders. She followed his eyes to the gray-clad woman at the center of the gathering, and his words and the old lady's appearance brought the woman's identity home to her. She had the same square, stubborn chin, the same light eyes, the same erect carriage and air of command. This was Rane's grandmother, Charity realized. And just now he seemed angry enough to bite her head off!

"So good of you to call, Countess," his attention turned to the violet-clad woman seated on his grandmother's right, "after all this time. A pity you had to wait until I was away." Rane's voice was filled with barely restrained mayhem. He pulled Charity forward and planted her hand on his sleeve in a more gentlemanly fashion. "However, you've come just in time to meet my bride. May I present, the new Viscountess Oxley, daughter of Squire Upton Standing, Lady Charity. Since I am unacquainted with some of your friends, Lady Catherine, perhaps you would do me the honor of introducing the rest of these ladies to my wife."

Lady Catherine had overcome her unpleasant shock to stare daggers at Rane for having had the audacity to arrive home unannounced and inflict himself upon her and her friends. But she was caught in a predicament and was forced by the bounds of decency to comply. She sat forward, shifting the great ball of white fur on her lap and wakening the indolent Caesar from a very comfortable nap.

"Lady Atherton . . . and the Countess of Ravenswood, Lady Agnes . . . and of course, the Countess of Swinford . . ." As she went around the circle of aging doyennes, Caesar became annoyed at all the fuss and began to sink irritable claws into his mistress's gray satin skirts, while watching Rane through slitted yellow eyes.

Charity noticed the cat, big and surly-eyed and obviously overfed. But she was so busy trying to recall proper manners that she shoved notice of him aside. Then suddenly Rane was leaving her to retrieve Gran'mere from the doorway and escort her into the group as well. Chins all but hit chests when he announced her as Lady Margaret Villiers, the new viscountess's grandmother. They stared unabashedly at her bold blue turban, her sun-weathered face, the hoops in her ears, and her gaudy green and red print gown.

Lady Margaret's mouth pursed and her spine straightened defensively. She could read their thoughts in their faces as they baldly inspected her garments and the odd conglomeration of objects about her neck. She looked like the veriest old gypsy they'd ever seen in their sheltered, pampered lives. Her hackles raised, her lips moved mutinously—then she suddenly squinted, staring at one of the ladies. She bent to shove her wizened face into that of the Countess of Ravenswood.

"Ellie Farquhar? Is that you?" Lady Margaret stared the old girl up and down, drawing outraged sputters from her subject as well as from the others in the tea party. "It is you!" she pronounced jerking upright with a wicked glint in her eye when the countess didn't deny it. "Rumnoggins—I hardly knew you. So you finally filled out proper." She gestured insolently to the countess's portly frame. "Well, you went a bit overboard on the filling part. And I see your teeth never did straighten out—"

"M-madam!" Lady Catherine sputtered, sliding Caesar unceremoniously onto the floor as she shoved to her feet. "I think you must be mistaken—"

"Not hardly!" Lady Margaret glared into the aging countess's melon-red countenance. "I'd know those teeth anywhere. She bit me once when I called her old 'piddle pockets' on account of the way she used to never make it to the—"

288

Charity watched her grandmother with wide eyes and felt oncoming disaster creeping up her spine like physical, icy fingers. Catastrophe approaching. Unstoppable . . . a relentless juggernaut of jinxed occurrence. She could only stand there in horror, watching it gather and come, knowing she was to blame. . . .

"Really! We've heard quite enough!" Lady Catherine clutched at her heart and staggered back against her chair, treading squarely on Caesar's fluffy tail.

"YEEEOOOWWWW!" He went howling and hurtling up into the ladies' laps and across the tea table and down again, to the nearest table leg, where he hunkered and hissed and began to sharpen his claws angrily on the already scratched mahogany.

"Oh my poor, poor baby." Lady Catherine blistered Rane with a look and started after her petulant pet just as that first, faint "woof" resounded faintly in the polished halls outside.

Over the whispers and gasps and Lady Catherine's cooing entreaties to the cat, Charity's mind fixed on that second "woof" and the third. "WOOF!" She could see him in her mind's eye, pausing to sniff between rounds of barks as he tracked them. Her heart sank, her stomach lurched upward, squeezing everything between them.

"WOOF . . . WOOF . . . *WOOF!*" The barks became thunderous and more frequent as they neared. Charity cast a panicky look at Rane and realized from the shocked comprehension in his face that he understood what was happening, too. Together they turned toward the door . . . just as Wolfie loped into the opening and paused.

He was a hundred and thirty pounds of quivering, wet nose and pure canine instinct. *"Food!"* was his first thought. Close on it came his second: *"Cat!"* He heard Charity calling his name, saw the "lordship" coming after him, saw the clutch of shrinking human females staring at him from the middle of the room. But one thought burst supreme on his brain. *"Oh, boy—CAT!"*

It seized his senses, it captured his brain, it pounded through his blood. *"Cat . . . cat . . . CAT!"*

Charity could almost read the fiery glint in his great dark eyes as she ran for him. He dodged her to charge the seated ladies, baying and woofing. Rane and Lady Margaret scrambled out of the way to keep from being bashed as he skittered across the smoothly-waxed floor and onto the rug. Wolfie quickly regained his footing and lowered his nose, bounding down the trail that led straight to Lady Catherine and Caesar. Lady Catherine squealed and tried to shield the table behind her skirts, but Wolfie dove straight at her feet and she scrambled out of the way, abandoning her pet, who was now frozen beneath the table. There was a moment's horrified pause as Wolfram and Caesar confronted and evaluated each other.

"REEOWWRRRR!" Caesar's back came up, his hair stood on end, and he hissed for all he was worth. A very impressive display, but nothing to seriously deter an old campaigner like Wolfram, who'd fought badgers to a standstill.

"RRRROLF—RROLF—*ROLF!*" Wolfram lunged.

"FFFFFFTTTTTT!!" Caesar swung a stiff paw with claws extended.

Wiry claws met sensitive nose and the whole room exploded with furry fury. Wolfram scrambled under the table after Caesar, overturning it as he darted out the far side after the great white cat. They raced over and under furniture and guests, barking, hissing, snarling and clawing in a wild melee of animal delinquency.

The ladies dodged and screeched and covered their elegant bonnets, forgetting that they held tea cups, which sloshed and jostled and spilled, ruining sateens and watered silks and several china cups as they tumbled and crashed on the floor.

It was pure mayhem, a disaster of the first order and all Charity could do was watch it unfold in ever-widening circles like ripples in a pool. Wolfram ignored her pleas and calls and dodged her attempts to grab him whenever he streaked past. Crimson-faced, she turned to Rane for help and found him scarlet-faced, too — but with *laughter!*

He was doubled over, laughing so hard that his eyes were filling with tears. He watched pudgy Caesar claw and scramble vainly, trying to climb the carved marble mantle to safety, and howled, holding his sides.

Twice Wolfram trapped the overfed cat and each time Caesar escaped, leaving him with only a mouthful of long white hairs. But the chase was, after all, the real fun and Wolfram threw himself into it again and again, joyfully. He hadn't had so much fun since playing the cane-game with the "lordship"!

Charity watched in a mild state of panic; she had to DO something! She backed toward the door, calling Wolfram repeatedly and eventually her summons bore fruit. But it was Caesar, who saw her near the door and seized the possibility of escape. He went streaking across the room and ducked out beneath her feet. Wolfram, intent on following, found himself crashing into his mistress, the captive in her arms, as she held on for dear life, to make him stop.

The wild spree ended abruptly as Rane hurried to help her, bellowing a call for Brockway and Eversby to come and retrieve the beast. There was tomb-like silence as the servants wrestled the dog from the room, panting, "What'll we do with him, your lordship?!"

Rane straightened and brushed his beleaguered coat and once-elegant trousers. He stared down at Wolfram, who was panting hard and looking supremely satisfied with himself. He met the brute's dark, laughing eyes briefly and decided to make the most of his cat-repelling potential.

"Put him in my study."

Charity straightened and brushed her printed muslin and her woolen spencer, suddenly very conscious of Rane's eyes on her every movement. She was humiliated to her very toes, aching with disbelief at the calamity she'd brought down on him. When she looked up there was only a warm amusement in his gaze . . . a private, speaking sort of look that seemed to put them in a rogue's league together. How could he make light of something so disastrous, so humiliating?!

He turned to the ladies, who were recovering quickly, gaining their feet to find themselves stained with tea. As broken china crunched underfoot, they stiffened and brushed and stammered stunned apologies for having been so clumsy while Lady Catherine babbled frantically about their ruined dresses and her "poor baby."

The ladies took leave just behind Rane and Charity, hurrying for the front doors, making overpolite excuses where none were required. When the last one had skittered out the door, Lady Catherine turned on her grandson with righteous fire in her eyes, declaring she had never been so humiliated in her life, and demanding how he dared bring such a brute into the house.

"Well, it's *his* house, isn't it?" Lady Margaret answered in his stead, drawing Lady Catherine's ire upon herself.

"And you—insulting my guest! How dare you! Have you no couth at all?!"

"I've enough couth not to bellow and rant at a man in his own house . . . in front of his new wife and family . . . whom you have yet to greet!"

It was suddenly grandmother to grandmother, nose to nose, one a perfectly groomed doyenne of London society, the other an eccentric old half-gypsy bedecked with bizarre dried animal bits around her neck. Charity stared at the ripening argument, horrified, then turned a pleading look on Rane to urge him to do something.

292

She found him watching them, fascinated, his lips curling upward at the corners. Lady Catherine purpled and gasped and finally ended the confrontation by turning on her heel to flee through the dining room, calling frantically for her precious Caesar.

Rane looked inordinately pleased as he took Charity's elbow and steered her toward the sweeping mahogany staircase in the vaulted entry. "Come, let me show you upstairs," he beamed baffling good humor. "I'm sure you'll welcome a bit of rest and a chance to refresh."

But at the top of the stairs they were met by Eversby with a bit of a logistical problem. It seemed Lady Catherine had earlier installed herself into what normally would have been the viscountess's apartments, across the hall from the viscount's. That left only the smaller guest rooms at the ends of the hall . . . or chambers on the next floor up, which would have to be freshened and cleaned and decorated properly.

"I shall be pleased to have one of the small guest chambers," Charity spoke up quickly, drawing Rane's darkest look.

"You're hardly a guest here, Charity. This is your home," he growled. Her expressed preference for "guest" accommodations stung him unexpectedly. Then like lightning, it struck him, the most desirable and natural of solutions. Charity would simply have to share his rooms and sleep with him every night! His grin broadened with wicked irony; he had his grandmother's grasping, assuming nature to thank for making so delectable an arrangement necessary. It almost warmed him toward the old girl. He straightened, smiling.

"No need to unsettle my dear grandmother. Just put the viscountess's things in my chambers, Eversby. She'll stay with me for the forseeable future."

Charity knew nothing about proper sleeping arrangements between noblemen and their wives. But from the implication of the butler's earlier comment and the fleeting dismay in his face now, she guessed that sharing sleeping accommodations was not routinely done. Before she could protest, she heard Eversby inquiring.

"And is the viscountess's baggage to follow?"

"That *is* the viscountess's baggage, Eversby." Rane nodded at the worn leather satchel sitting in the middle of the hall. The butler flicked an uncomfortable glance at Charity and she reddened and lowered her eyes. Rane caught the exchange. "Which reminds me . . . We'll need you to send for the best mantua maker in London . . . to arrive tomorrow morning to see to her ladyship's new wardrobe. Send also for a milliner and a shoemaker. Once we have the basics established, I shall take the viscountess shopping for the rest, myself." Eversby's brows raised in surprise and as he turned to go, Rane's voice called him back.

"And baths, Eversby. We shall all need a good hot soak and fresh clothes. And I don't suppose you've found any bananas?" Rane shook his head doubtfully, even as the butler confirmed it with a sympathetic wince and a shaken head. "Then oranges. Bring us several oranges."

Rane escorted Charity through the great mahogany doors to his chamber while Eversby showed Lady Margaret to one of the guest rooms. Rane's chambers were exquisitely done in pure masculine elegance, with heavy, wine-colored velvets at the long windows and around the bed, thick Aubusson carpets underfoot, and great winged chairs, upholstered in rich cordovan leather, near the massive soapstone hearth. The furnishings were graceful but solid mahogany pieces in the Adams style, and there were gilt-framed hunt scenes strategically placed about the walls. In the center of the chamber, on a dais, was a massive, carved poster bed, draped in damascene-lined velvets and trimmed in gold cording. Charity's eyes widened on the profusion of silk and velvet pillows at the head of the bed, and the rigidity of her body melted at the thought of plunging into that luxurious softness . . . with him.

A half-second later, she was appalled at her thoughts, bracing again as she turned to him. He was watching her reaction and had seen her telling softening as she gazed at the bed. She flushed with the knowledge, and feared he would use it against her.

"This will not do, your lordship. You've scandalized even your own butler. Pray, what will your grandmother think of me when she learned I share you rooms? I won't be humiliated in such a fashion. I've quite enough to live down already, thanks to Gran'mere and Wolfram!"

She turned on her heel and went striding back out into the hallway, looking first this way, then that. And before he could drag her back into his rooms, she was in motion, headed for the end of the hall and one of the guest rooms. He caught up with her just inside the doorway of the room and, out of pure exasperation, grabbed her shoulders with his hands.

"This will be quite adequate for my needs, thank you!"

"But not for *mine!*" he declared hotly, pulling her tighter and tighter against his hard body until she could scarcely wriggle. "You're my wife, Charity!" But his claim only seemed to fuel her opposition. In pure desperation he declared, to himself as well as to her, "Enough of this nonsense!" His mouth closed over hers, overpowering her resistance to hold her mouth captive.

She stilled slowly and he gentled, meeting her measure for reluctant measure. His mouth eased its fierce possession to massage her lips, coaxing them to respond. Then he added tantalizing tracings of his tongue over the borders of her mouth . . . and along the moist slit between her lips.

Her knees began to go weak as her blood withdrew from them to rush into the parts of her that were pressed inescapably against him. Her empty hands writhed hungrily at her sides, hot longings rose in her throat, her body ached with restraint against his hard male frame as he struggled to withhold her passions. Another minute . . . another twist of his head . . . another dart of his tongue . . . It was only skin touching skin, she moaned silently, only form and texture in varying pressures and in changing patterns of movement. And yet her hands came up to clutch his coat, her body thrust sinuously against his . . . just before she collected all her energy and shoved hard against him.

"No!" Her voice was hoarse and her eyes were hot with fiery sparks. "Have you no decency at all? I've told you why. And it's three more days. . . ."

Rane watched her with stunned disbelief. His whole body was afire; his blood, his nerves, his loins, and, suddenly, his temper. "Alright," he irrupted, "you'll have your damned three days! And then—" His jaw worked but somehow the things he meant to say to her didn't come out. Crimson with humiliation, he turned on his heel and fled to the comparative sanity of his own rooms.

Charity stood, frozen to the spot by his new icy anger. It was inevitable, the change in him. She had to make him dislike and distrust her so much that he would send her away, or at least allow her to go on her own. It was the only solution. Every warm, caring look he gave her, every brief touch of his hand, every soft caress of his lips undercut her ability to deny him the loving that they both wanted so desperately. Distance — miles and miles of it between them — seemed her only hope.

She looked unseeingly at the room she would occupy for a while. Roses and pinks and greens, polished bedposts and soft rugs. Finally, for the first time since their vows, she would sleep alone. She was startled from her reverie by Eversby and an upstairs maid, come to freshen the linen and unpack her meager wardrobe. She turned, removing her spencer for the first time in almost four days. She turned to Eversby with a request and saw his eyes widen at the clutch of bizarre-looking amulets hanging around her neck.

"Salt, Eversby. Could you please bring me half a pound of salt?"

Chapter Seventeen

No one slept well that night. Wolfram barked in Rane's study until Charity relented and crept downstairs to find him and lead him back to her room to sleep with her. Lady Catherine spent half the night consoling her poor Caesar, whose long, elegant coat had begun falling out in clumps following his unholy fright with Wolfram. Rane paced back and forth in his chambers, staring at his empty bed and consoling himself with French brandy that Upton Standing had smuggled into the country for him. And Lady Margaret spent half the night fashioning protective amulets from the materials Eversby had been able to secure for her.

Now, with the advent of morning, the turmoil only worsened. Lady Margaret was up at the crack of dawn, cornering servants and draping strung acorns, bags of garlic, horsehair, lucky pebbles, and bent nails around their necks while they scurried this way and that with morning duties. Then she went about the house rearranging mirrors and moving breakables from lower tables to higher shelves, snagging servants to help her proof the great house against untoward "accidents." They shook their heads in puzzlement and looked to Eversby, who nodded bewildered permission, and, fingering their amulets, they obeyed.

The dressmaker arrived at nine with a bustling entourage of seamstresses, porters, and baggage, then began to wardrobe the new viscountess as befit her taste and station. All morning, the upstairs was swarmed by dress-maker's assistants and silk-merchants and milliners, all requiring space and assistance. It seemed every single decision made as to color or style rippled through the entire group of clothiers, each spawning a dozen additional decisions to be made: trims, shoes, and spencers; bonnets, gloves, and shawls. Lady Catherine looked on all the mercantile furor with a jaundiced eye and withdrew to her rooms, announcing she would have nothing to do with it all.

Rane paced the upper hall, feeling like a spectator in his own life. He occasionally caught a tantalizing glimpse of Charity through the door as it opened and closed, and developed a burning desire to see her, to be with her. Was she pleased by his generosity? What would she look like, swathed in lush satins and sheer, seductive silks, Cluny laces and ermine trims? How would those exotic textures enhance the voluptuous feel of her against him? He was going mad imagining it! When he could bear it no longer, he summoned his worldliest air and invaded that enclave of femininity.

Charity stood in the middle of the room on a raised wooden step, clad only in her brief corset and a single petticoat. She felt conspicuous and embarrassed over the fuss she was causing and the expense she was generating, when she probably wouldn't even be staying long enough to wear such ladylike clothes. She stared down at the little French mantua maker with a hot spark in her eyes.

"I shall not remove them. They're my lucky pieces and I wear them all the time. You'll have to do your best to work around them."

"But, my lady, please," the little, dark-eyed woman pleaded, "they ruin the necklines . . ."

"Then they shall simply have to be ruined," Charity declared with a stubborn look. She was vastly relieved when the little dressmaker didn't pursue it further. She turned her eyes anxiously to the chaotic chamber and its contents. Silk pins, sharp scissors, and heavy trunks, flammable lint, littered scraps, and hot irons for "gophering up" the frills at daring necklines. . . . the place was a pure invitation to a disaster of some kind. She scowled and rubbed her hands together, worrying, feeling a bit peculiar. . . .

Her eyes came up toward the door and she saw him standing there, his light eyes silvery, his features sharp with hungry concentration. His whole being was focused on her in a way that made her heart stop, then race to make up beats.

She couldn't drag her eyes from his as he came forward and paused, planting his feet apart and his fists on his waist, ignoring the dressmaker's clucks of disapproval. His eyes slid down her face to her lips, then to her creamy throat, then to her lovely breasts, half hidden behind a wreath of amulets of sundry shapes and descriptions. He stared at her lush body, a bit annoyed by the obstacle of her wretched "lucky pieces." His face bronzed, his lips thickened and parted, and his eyes raised to hers.

"I . . . I don't need these clothes. They're a pure waste of coin," she managed, hoping half-heartedly to offend him. "I won't wear any of them." His eyes flamed with a private response that he soon shared with everyone.

"The prospect of you wearing no clothes doesn't trouble me in the least," he said huskily, oblivious to the dressmaker's gasp and the titters of her assistants. Their faces heated and their eyes met like flint and steel, striking sparks in the volatile atmosphere.

"Ohhhh—oh, no!" The charged silence was broken by one of the underhousemaids, who, while watching the master's and mistress's exchanges, had been neglecting the hot gophering irons she had been assigned to tend. A thin plume of smoke rose from a starched frill, and the dressmaker lunged to rip the scorched cloth from the girl's panicky hands. The dressmaker's lament over the layers of ruined, expensive ruffles rose, mingled with the housemaid's whine when she was given a sound swat. Charity hurried down from the wooden step to restore order and found herself embroiled in explanations and excuses. She felt his eyes on her and finally turned to him irritably.

"We'd get along much better without your 'help,' your lordship."

He stiffened, then his light eyes narrowed with irritation. "Very well. You have two days left, Charity. Two days . . ." And he pivoted and strode out.

He kept going, down the stairs, out the door, determined to take some air and to find some sanity and surcease, somewhere. Hatless and gloveless, he strode the fashionable streets until he found himself at an intersection of streets near his gentleman's club. He took a deep breath and braved the doorman's and the club steward's disapproval to enter that male domain without full gentlemanly attire. He deposited himself in a great leather chair in a corner, hoping to avoid human contact and to nurse his bruised pride along with a bit of brandy-laced coffee.

It wasn't long before his peace was interrupted by two smartly clad young gentlemen with full-length trousers, extravagantly pointed collars, and immaculate blue silk ties. "I say—Oxley—is that you?!" The intrepid young Earl of Meckton and the dashing Everly Harrison, son of the Earl of Brainerd, were two of Rane's more noteworthy sporting companions. They descended on him, ogling him with ill-suppressed curiosity.

"Good God, you're all we've heard about this morning. You're on every tongue!" Meckton crowed with uncommon glee.

"Married—you sly dog! Went and married some sweet country miss, did you? Must be quite a stunner—to lock her up so quick!" Harrison put in, smirking. "And I say, smart of you to get your nestling married off before bringing in a wife to roost. Saves bales of trouble . . . I

301

knew something was up when I heard your Fanny Deering had tied it up with some Southampton fellow."

Rane swallowed his coffee all in a gulp and stared at them. Smart of him to get Fanny married off? As if he'd had anything to do with it!

They sat down to pry the details of his courtship and marriage out of him, and afterward he wasn't sure exactly what he'd told them. He'd been too occupied by Harrison's comment about Fanny. He'd been so appalled to learn that she'd abandoned him at the time. And now it seemed to him an incredible bit of good fortune. Imagine coming back to London with Charity as his wife . . . and having to explain it all to Fanny and break it off with her. "Saves bales of trouble," Harrison had said. That was the understatement of the year. A disappointed mistress could make a man's life very difficult indeed. How strange that what had once seemed the wretchedest of luck had turned into a boon, given a bit of time and perspective.

It was the second time in as many days that he'd found himself rethinking a recent circumstance. His grandmother's wheedling, grasping presence in his house meant Charity couldn't have the mistress's rooms and would have to share his suite . . . in two more days. And now Fanny's leaving had solved a problem before it arose.

Both had seemed such disasters at first, and both were now proving to have unexpected benefits. Maybe it was all in the way you looked at things.

Dinner was a complete fiasco that afternoon. The cook toughened a very promising trout, and burnt the brais'd veal on account of a fire in the stack. The pudding had boiled over its sides, otherwise failing to rise, and the caramel flan came out watery and unappealing. Cook was in tears, Eversby was frantic, and Rane was grim-faced. Lady Margaret, reading in the demise of dinner a portent of things to come, bustled about the table tying acorns and dried purslane to every chair, then offered to sweep out the kitchen with a new straw broom to change the cook's luck. Lady Catherine arrived late, carrying a very patchy and very irritable looking Caesar in her arms. She took umbrage at Lady Margaret's remark that cats were bad luck at a table.

Rane insisted on waiting for Charity and sent word to her to that effect. But by the time she finished her last fitting and hurried downstairs, everything was cold, everyone had had too much wine, and nobody felt like eating the cream soup, cold meats, and hastily warmed rolls that Eversby supplied with profuse apologies.

Charity, seated at the foot of the table in the hostess's chair, felt Rane's glare on her and her old muslin dress and woolen spencer throughout the meal. When Lady Catherine, by way of advising Rane on the running of his household, related all the difficulties in the kitchen, Charity's cheeks reddened, her hands trembled noticeably, and she couldn't swallow another single bite of food. More troubles. She hadn't been in the house five minutes and they had started . . . and they would continue as long as she was here. She had some difficulty answering Rane's pointed inquiries about her fittings, and declined his offer to show her the house and introduce the rest of the household staff to her after dinner.

To escape Rane's deepening glare, Charity's gaze wandered the table, and when they fell on Caesar, he narrowed his yellow eyes at her and pounced down from his mistress's lap to waddle over to the great hearth in the dining room. Using a nearby chair, he climbed onto the mantel for his customary after-dinner stroll along the marble ledge. Only this time, the mantelpiece was filled with candlesticks and crystal vases that had been collected from more vulnerable places in the room during Lady Margaret's purge of breakables. And as pudgy Caesar

squeezed past, these began to topple and fall . . . one
. . . by one . . . by one.

Everyone at the table started and turned as the first,
then second candlestick smacked the floor, and all witnessed the leaded crystal vase that went next, shattering.
Caesar, startled by the commotion, bolted and skidded
across the slippery marble and tumbled off the end of the
mantelpiece, having emptied it completely of valuables in
the process. Then, before their disbelieving eyes, he
flipped as he fell, and landed square on his *back!* Lady
Catherine was on her feet in a heartbeat, strangling a cry
and rushing to her stunned pet.

"What the hell were all those things doing on the mantel in the first place?!" Rane roared as he pushed to his
feet. They all watched Lady Catherine struggling down
onto her knees to gather the fallen Caesar into her arms.

"I-I . . . had the servants put them there," Lady Margaret admitted. "So they wouldn't get . . . broken."

"B'dammit!" Rane roared, clenching impotent fists at
his sides. "This is not Standwell! And I'll not have you
skulking about rearranging things to satisfy some idiot
superstition! I'm bloody sick and tired of your 'luck' nonsense. Look at the damage it's caused! You'll put everything back as it was . . . and you'll get your ridiculous
amulets off my servants' necks!" He threw his napkin
down on his chair and stalked out, heading straight for
the comparative sanity of his study.

Charity looked at her grandmother. Rane was wrong.
It wasn't Gran'mere who'd caused the damage, or even
Caesar, the cat; it was her. Her jinx. What else could
make a cat land on its *back?!* And it could only be a
matter of time before her jinx again began to wreak
havoc on Rane himself. When Lady Catherine huffed out
of the room with her cat in her arms, Charity turned to
her grandmother, her face and her heart brimming with
fresh anxiety.

"Gran'mere, I have to do something! But what? Tell

me what I can do, Gran'mere."

"Maybe you could tell him about your jinx. Maybe he could—"

"He doesn't even believe in luck; he'd never understand my jinx. He'd be furious with me and he'd insist on . . . I can't tell him."

Lady Margaret's face drew into a deeply troubled frown as she fingered her crescent-moon amulet. It had been the dark of the moon, and she'd had no way to search for answers. But tonight the first sliver of the new moon should be visible. Perhaps if she tried again . . .

Charity watched Gran'mere's uneasy silence and suddenly felt angered by it. All Charity's life Gran'mere had insisted she had the answers to life's difficulties, a remedy or a practice or a charm or preventative for everything. She had made Charity believe that in her time with the gypsies, she had acquired access to life's and nature's innermost secrets. And now, when it really mattered—perhaps to the point of life and death—the fount of Gran'mere's "secret gypsy knowledge" was suddenly dry.

"Well, I can't—I won't just stand by and watch something terrible happen to him because of me." Charity's eyes burned with determined new fire. "I'll do whatever I have to do to change his luck, to protect him from my jinx!"

Two hours later, just at dusk, Charity finished tying mistletoe to each of the bedposts in Rane's rooms, tucking dried sprigs of angelica into the clothing in his chests, and rearranging the shoes and boots in his valet closet so that the toes all pointed north. She had stuffed acorns and dried bits of love vine and appleseeds into the pockets of his coats, and had sprinkled salt in a trail along the two window sills and across the hearth to keep mischief from entering. Now she pushed the pan of quenched coals a bit further under his bed and checked the pair of scissors she'd put beneath his mattress to cut his bad luck. He didn't seem to own any old shoes, so she took the scuffed pair from her own feet and placed one strategically under his bed and one behind the drapes on the window ledge.

She paused in the middle of his room, chewing her lip and wishing she had a few spare horseshoes and some splinters from a lightning-struck tree to complete her precautions. Her eyes roamed to the great bed with its silk pillows, soft sheets, and elegant satin comforters. It beckoned to her in the dimness, and she succumbed.

She leaned her head, then her side, against one of the great carved posts, running her hand lovingly up and down the smooth, polished mahogany. This was where he slept. For a brief instant she allowed herself to imagine lying with him beneath that luxurious tent of silk damascene and velvet, cradled against his firm flesh, tasting the faint saltiness of his kisses. . . . A powerful wave of pure longing welled in her and crashed, washing the strength from her knees and bringing her body taut against the bedpost, sending a churning spray of desire through her that set her nipples contracting and tingling.

The next instant she was blushing in the lowering light, recoiling from the bed and all its temptations. She hurried to the door and paused, peering into the corridor. There was only a houseman, lighting the candles in the mirrored sconces and she judged it safe. She slipped out the door and closed it behind her. She delved into the pockets inside her skirts for the brown paper packet of salt and began drizzling a trail of it along the sill of the large double doors. She was so intent on her task and on mentally repeating the little chant Gran'mere always used, that she ignored the sound in the hall behind her.

Rane stood near the end of the hall, watching her stoop and wave her hand past the foot of his bedroom doors. He squinted and leaned to make out what she was doing, but her body blocked his line of sight. He frowned, and decided to just let his eyes feast on her curvy little body until she had finished and straightened. Then he strode down the hall, surprising her as she turned toward her own room.

"Oh!" She flushed and fumbled, stuffing something into her skirts to keep him from seeing it.

"What were you doing there?" He waved a hand toward the doorsill and she glanced that direction a bit too quickly. The color in her cheeks deepened and her lashes lowered; clear signs of a guilty conscience.

"I . . . um . . . dropped a silk pin and was . . . looking for it," she said breathily. She felt his light eyes roaming her and her whole body responded. Her skin flushed, her lips thickened, her bones began to soften . . .

"Charity, we have to talk." He came closer, crowding her senses. "I was on my way to your room—"

"No!" Her head came up and her heart convulsed with the impact of his handsome face and sensual heat . . . so close. A few minutes alone with him and she knew she wouldn't be just talking. "Not now—please!" She darted around him and made it to her door first, closing it firmly in his face. She threw the key in the lock and leaned back against the heavy wooden panels, listening to his growls over the pounding of her heart.

He groaned and his fists came up to pound on the door, but halted short of smacking the wood. His frustration was multiplying by the minute. But unleashing his Barbados-hot temper, shouting and pounding, would only complicate things between them . . . just as it had before. He sent his hands back through his hair instead, and then let them flop at his sides. Lord, she really was going to drive him mad as a March hare!

Two more days, he told himself, then he would confront her fully and demand to know what was troubling her. Two long, long days . . . and him already randy as a stag in rut. He turned and walked down the hall, intending to change his clothes and leave the house, perhaps visit his club for a few hours. He found himself standing by his doors, staring at the floor, then bending down. . . . There was a fine, grainy white trail across the dark polished boards of the floor, all the way along the door opening. He squatted on his heels and touched the stuff, bringing some of it up on his finger. He sniffed, scowled, then with an idea in mind, touched it to the tip of his tongue.

Salt. She'd been putting salt over his doorstep. He frowned, surprised. Then he froze. Salt? Salt was one of Lady Margaret's charms against mischief and . . . bad luck. His heart beat faster. He pushed up, rubbing the salt together between his fingers as if he could squeeze some insight from it. By the time he stood in his dimly lit bedchamber, staring at the sprigs of mistletoe tied on the posts of his bed, his blood was coursing faster in his veins. Mistletoe for luck? Had she done this, too? But she didn't follow the old woman's crazy superstit—

Suddenly the sight of her in the hallway just now came back to him. She wasn't wearing her everpresent spencer . . . but she was wearing a handful of amulets! But she didn't wear lucky pieces; she said she didn't need them. His eyes widened. She'd had them on this morning, when the dressmaker came, and she'd refused to remove them; he'd heard her. She now wore lucky pieces . . . and followed her old grandmother's crazy superstitions? What the hell had happened to her?

He charged out into the hall, and was halfway to Charity's door when Lady Margaret arrived at the top of the main stairs, her arms filled with a basket of bizarre herbals and luck paraphernalia. He stopped. She stopped, her eyes widening at the deepening glare on his face. His gaze lowered to the basket and caught fire. An instant later, he caught her by the arm and dragged her down the hall to her room.

"I want to know what happened to Charity just before

I left Standwell," he demanded, towering above her knotty little form. "Something damn well happened to set her against marrying me, and I have a right to know what it was!"

Lady Margaret huddled back and her glare deepened as she searched him. He must love Charity a great deal to have come flying all the way to Devon to stop her from marrying Pinnow, and to put his reputation at risk by marrying her himself. But would his love be strong enough to withstand all their troubles?

"I guess you do have the right." Lady Margaret labored to a chair by the hearth and sank into it, looking and feeling old all of a sudden. "You won't like it." His eyes narrowed threateningly as he came to stand over her and she sighed.

"Charity's a jinx." She saw him coiling, saw his eyes silvering with irritation and held her hand up to stay his protest. "I know you think I'm a crazy old woman, but I love her more than life. I would never say it if it weren't true."

Rane watched the shimmer of pain in her age-faded eyes and realized she truly believed it. "Of all the asinine, idiotic—"

"Ever since she was a wee thing, troubles have followed her like a shadow. They never seem to involve her directly . . . they just always happen wherever she is. Sometimes it's little things, breaking china or popping buttons. Sometimes it's great disasters, like carriage wrecks and broken bones . . . and strangers gettin' shot in the . . . in the . . ."

"Arse," he supplied with a judicious sneer.

"Yes. Well." Her voice and shoulders lowered with the weight of her revelation. "You see, Upton never wanted to believe it, either, even though he couldn't explain the things that happened around her otherwise. So he insisted we keep it from her, and we did. We accident-proofed the house and kept to ourselves to reduce the damage she might do . . . and to see that she never blamed herself for the troubles around her. She's always had such a tender heart, we feared what would happen if she learned she caused the troubles that grieved her so."

"Charity doesn't believe in such nonsen—" He stopped. She *hadn't* believed in it. But now she wore amulets and left salt trails. "What happened to her?" The implications of the old woman's revelations had begun to crystallize in his mind.

"She found out. She heard you and Gar and Percy down in the cave that afternoon. And it nearly crushed her."

"Dammit—I don't believe any of this! You're saying she wouldn't marry me because she heard those two piddlewits call her a jinx?! She's no more a jinx than I am. There isn't any such thing!" His fists clenched and his shoulders swelled as he recalled that wretched encounter. The anger he'd felt then returned to him twofold. They actually *believed* that Charity was somehow responsible for the tragedy and trouble in the world around her—Charity, whose very presence was a potent antidote for pain!

"But there *is* such a thing and she is one. I read it in the moon on the night she was born. You haven't been with her all her life . . . you haven't seen all the accidents and mishaps and troubles. But as soon as she heard it, she knew. She understood. It explained so much that had happened in her life. It even explained how you came to be hurt and how you came to our house . . . and all the mishaps you suffered while you were with us." The pain in her expression deepened. "She was afraid that if she married you, something terrible would happen to you."

"She thought. . . ?"

"She was protecting you." Lady Margaret watched his anger and shook her head at his stubborn disbelief, so much like Upton's. "I tried to keep you apart. I didn't

310

want her to love you . . . or you her. She had just lost her father and she grieved so over losing him . . ."

Of all the old lady's ramblings, that one statement struck a chord of reason in him. Charity had just lost her father. Grief sometimes did strange things to people. It could make a person believe in things . . . or quit believing in things.

"But Pinnow!" He shifted and clenched his fists, grappling with his own anger and trying to make sense of a situation that made no sense at all. "What the hell was she doing marrying him?!"

"She was marrying him *because* she despised him." The old lady winced. "She said . . . he deserved a jinx for a wife."

Rane stiffened, sobered instantly by the ramifications of that. He didn't believe a word of what he was hearing . . . but Charity did. She obviously believed in her "jinx" enough to reject a life with the man she loved, and enough to agree to something as drastic as marrying a man she loathed. Her belief in her jinx gave it substance and made it a force to be reckoned with in their lives.

He knew about the power of destructive belief; he'd seen it in operation before, on Barbados, when he was a youth. He'd watched the native superstitions of his tropical home combine with illness and the destructive forces of nature, hurricanes, to whittle away at various native families and plantation owners . . . including his father. And if it hadn't been for his own innate skepticism and stubbornness, he might have succumbed to it as well.

A white-hot spurt of protective anger surged in his blood. He had to DO something! The thought of his loving and compassionate Charity, blaming herself and cutting herself off from those she loved in order to protect them, cut him to the quick. She deserved to be loved and cherished, to have a life and joy and pleasure. He was determined to give them to her, all of them. And he was determined to have the joy and the pleasure he'd

311

waited so long to experience.

If it meant he had to do battle with her belief in her jinx and her fears, so be it! It was a love and a challenge made for a man like "Bulldog" Austen. He knew exactly where to start.

Charity stood in her stocking feet as she prepared for bed, staring at the mounds of paper boxes, bolts of fabrics, and stacks of string-wrapped packages that were the evidence of Rane's generosity to her. Her gaze drifted to a wooden valet rack of partly stitched dresses and spencers in polished sateens, soft moirés, and luscious shot-silk brocades. The sight of such luxuries only added to the burden in her heart, for she could give him nothing in return, nothing, that is, but misfortune and heartache.

She slid her worn muslin dress from her shoulders, perhaps for the last time, and untied the waist of her old petticoat, stepping out of it. Her fingers moved to the lacings at the top of her brief corset, then she froze.

"Charity!" Her name and Rane's fist assaulted the door in the same instant, startling her. "Charity, open the door!"

She stared at the door with wide eyes. There was no mistaking the sensual timbre in his deep command, and she knew beyond a shadow of a doubt that his patience with her denials and rebuffs was at an end. Her heart convulsed in her chest and began to beat frantically as he pounded again, demanding that she come out . . . or he was coming in. She couldn't respond; her voice seemed frozen in her throat. She could only back away, staring at the door, clutching her petticoat to her. The time she had dreaded had come.

The banging stopped, but the silence only heightened her dread. And as it continued, it stretched her nerves taut and shortened her breath. At any moment she expected the massive door to splinter from its hinges.

Then, in the deafening silence, came a quiet rasp of metal and a click. The key in the lock on the inside of the door fell to the floor with a clack and a bounce, and the door swung open.

Rane was leaning a broad shoulder against the doorframe, filling the opening with his powerful presence. In his hand he held up one key out of many on a great metal ring. "The doors in this house are very thick," he observed with a casual flick of his eyes toward the inches-thick mahogany panels he'd just conquered with the civilized flick of a wrist. He let the key drop and let the heavy key ring slide to the end of his finger, dangling it before her delectably wide eyes. "And I don't like to be kept from anything that's mine." His voice dropped to a rumble of sensual menace. "I have the keys to everything, angel."

Charity felt his shadowed eyes on her like a possessive touch, sliding down her shoulders, over her breasts, down her waist and hips. The message he intended to send was clear: he had the keys to her as well. He knew exactly how to unlock her passions, how to free her imprisoned responses, one by one.

In one sleek movement he slid the keys into his coatpocket and pushed off with his shoulder, coming for her.

"N-no," she managed through the cottony feeling in her mouth. "You can't—"

"Oh, but I can, angel. And I am." He pulled the petticoat from her panicky hands and scooped her surprised form up into his arms. He was through the doorway before she began to struggle in earnest.

"Put me down! You can't do this! I told you two more days—" She wriggled frantically, trying to free her knees as she pushed at his hard shoulders. But his hand wrapped tighter about her knees to prevent her escape and his muscular arms clamped her body tighter against him as he strode for his rooms.

"I don't want to wait two days to talk to you," he declared hotly, glancing down at her curves straining against him. "And I don't intend to wait any longer to have you in my bed."

Gran'mere had run into the hallway and Lady Catherine stood in the open door to her rooms, across the hall. Both stared, openmouthed, at his bold claims and the spectacle he was making of her. Charity's ire shriveled under the raw humiliation of it — being dragged from her rooms, half naked, to furnish his bed and serve his husbandly desires! She covered her face with her hands and wriggled anew, wishing she could die on the spot.

Rane slowed enough to flick a commanding look at Lady Margaret as he entered his rooms. "If you would be so good as to close the doors after me . . . I seem to have my hands full."

Lady Margaret watched him carry Charity into his lair and started at his insolence. Then, a heartbeat later, a wry look came over her face and she scurried forward to do exactly as he had requested. When the doors were securely shut on them, she turned and found Lady Catherine coming out of deep shock.

"Well, I never!" Lady Catherine gasped indignantly.

Lady Margaret looked her squarely up and down and ventured the opinion, "No, I guess you didn't. It would probably have done you a world of good."

Chapter Eighteen

The great chamber flickered with the dim golden light from a single candlestand. Rane carried her straight to the bed and as he lowered her onto the velvet comforter, he covered her with his body, to keep her from fleeing. She gasped and struggled, demanding release.

"How dare you do this to me . . . and in front of my grandmother and yours?! You're acting like a brute—a raging barbarian," she growled, arching her back and straining to try to topple him from her.

He laughed raggedly, feeling his body responding massively to her writhing beneath him. "No, I'm acting like a love-starved husband on his wedding night. Because that's what I am, Charity . . . your husband. And that's what this is going to be . . . our wedding night." The seductive softening of his voice sent her into a panic and she strained to turn her face as far from him as possible.

"Carrying me through the halls naked—" She wormed her arms up between them and planted the heels of her palms on his chest, pushing hard. But he released more of his weight from his own arms to counter her force and all she gained was more of his heat sinking deep into her muscles, collecting in her sensitive places.

"But I had to." His voice became silky, blatantly caressing. She could hear that he was smiling and she knew exactly what his roguish, desirous expression would be. She didn't need to look.

"The groom always carries the bride over the threshold on the wedding night . . . for good luck."

His use of the word "luck" lodged somewhere in the mass of anger and fear and stubborn excitement which roiled in the middle of her. She stilled and, in spite of all the warnings her better sense was screaming, she turned her face to his. He *was* smiling . . . and oh, Lord . . . it was even worse than she feared.

His taut skin glowed like warm bronze in the candle-light, his eyes were heavy-lidded pools of silver heat, and his broad, sensual mouth was drawn up on one side so that a rogue slash of a dimple appeared in the plane of one cheek. Over his forehead, that same contrary lock of hair drooped, just begging to be tamed by her fingers. A smothering wave of dry heat swept her from head to toes, sending her into a raw panic. She jerked her face away and pushed harder, tightening furiously beneath him.

"Then you might as well have let me walk, for all the 'luck' it will bring you," she gritted out, clinging stubbornly to her prime defense. "You still have two days to wait, before you can inflict yourself on me . . . in that way." He laughed—*laughed* at that. Then his weight shifted so that his belly pressed squarely against hers and the hard swelling of his desire rested against the sensitive base of her woman's mound.

"I have it on good authority," his softly spoken words dropped like lead weights through her, making her stomach sink, "that you've never required a full seven days in your life. And I hardly think it's fair that I have to wait a full seven, if you don't."

"Who told you—" She flamed and turned to stare at him in horror.

"Your Gran'mere and I had a bit of a talk . . ."

"Y-you spoke to Gran'mere a-ab-bout. . . ? OHHHHH!" She began to struggle in earnest, her pride at full boil now. How dare he go behind her back—and how dare Gran'mere divulge such information, knowing he would only use it against her?! She wriggled and strained and fought . . . and he let her.

But it was warfare limited to a few very sensual inches. She succeeded only in escalating the heat between them and in deepening the sensitivity of her body to the heaviness and roused state of his. Her eyes closed as the sensations swirled higher and hotter, inside her and around her. She was being pulled into an overwhelming vortex of pleasure and her reason began to run in maddening circles . . .

She had to resist for his sake; she had to yield for his sake. She wanted desperately to protect him; she wanted desperately to please him. She loved him too much to let him . . . She loved him too much to stop him. . . .

"Angel," his voice intervened in those painful, confusing circles, taking charge, diverting her frantic thoughts. "Look at me." His hand turned her face back to his with gentle force. "Open your eyes, Charity."

The quiet urgency of his voice captured her will. She obeyed. He was staring down into her face with a look so fierce and so tender that she forgot to breathe.

"I want to make the night magic for you . . . and with you." His head lowered slowly so that he spoke against her lips. "Let me."

His mouth touched hers softly, as though it were their first kiss, tentative and exploratory. Then he drew back and dragged his lips over hers, feeling every part of her mouth with every part of his, over and over, in sinuous circles. It was delicious torture, wondering when he would end this toying and give her the full taste of his mouth that she craved. It was too slow in coming and she arched her neck, seeking that fulfillment. But for every degree she rose, he withdrew one, maintaining a steady, mesmerizing brush of satin lips on oral silk.

Her lips parted in aching invitation and still he hesitated, watching her, reading her opening responses.

"Say it," he coaxed against the dark fragrant opening

317

of her mouth.

She knew what he wanted.

"Make the night magic with me," she whispered. "Love me."

He joined their mouths fully and she moaned as heat billowed through her. Her hands slid from his chest, around his sides, to his back, to pull him tight against her breasts. His arms sank beneath her shoulders and his hands slid up to cradle her head. He toyed and tantalized her with his tongue, then raked and plundered the yielding inner sleekness of her mouth. From breath to breath his kisses changed, beguiling her relentlessly and yet setting her free.

When her body began to wriggle beneath him, seeking him, he lifted his head to watch her kittenish eagerness. Then he smiled, a sultry, silver-eyed smile filled with hot sensual promises. He slid from her body to the bed beside her and held her eyes captive in his as he untied the lacings of her corset. He dragged the soft chemise from her tingling breasts to expose her budded velvet nipples.

Her eyes still captive in his, he lowered his head to trace those sensitive peaks with lush, swirling laps of his tongue. The sight of his mouth at her breast, licking, toying with her softness, sent a volt of desire through her body that set her womanflesh burning. Then his mouth closed on the tip and he sucked, gently at first, pulling strings of sensation all through her, making her muscles contract. She arched into his mouth, demanding more, seeking deeper possession, that made her moan softly as he complied. Then he nuzzled the valley between her breasts, migrating to lavish the same hot attentions on the other peak.

Her whole body caught fire, consuming reason and caution, relacing them with driving sensual need. She writhed and whimpered as he began to rake his teeth over her soft flesh, teasing, nipping, so that hot, erotic

318

flashes of pleasure plunged along some unseen connection to the tingling, engorged center of pleasure between her legs. Her thighs clamped tightly together to relieve the ache, her hips rocked, intensifying the delicious burning in her tenderest flesh.

Rane read the total commitment of her arousal and made himself withdraw, dropping a light kiss on her lips as he sat up, bracing on one arm above her. Her eyes flew open as cool air replaced his heated body against hers, intensifying the ache of need in her.

"W-what—" She swallowed hard and raised onto her elbows, looking like a delectably naughty angel, with her lips kiss-swollen and her breasts exposed and her damp nipples contracted tightly with desire. "What's wrong?"

"It's bad luck for a groom to undo his own buttons on his wedding night, angel." His voice was a dark rasp of pure need. I'm a prisoner in my own clothes . . . unless you set me free." He reached for her hand and pulled it to the buttons of his waistcoat, pressing her palm against his chest. "You'll have to help me, angel."

A moment later, she was sitting opposite him on the bed, her bare breasts jutting eagerly from the neck of her chemise and her hair tumbling over one shoulder. Her trembling fingers fumbled with the small pearl buttons of his waistcoat and he laughed softly, lifting one of her hands to his lips and kissing her fingertips.

"There's no hurry, sweetheart." His eyes glowed with hunger that was tightly reined. It was the urgency of her desires that drove their loving now, and both knew it. She was beyond blushing. She took a deep breath and set much steadier and more determined fingers to work.

He ripped his gentlemanly coat from his shoulders, while she worked, and he tossed it from the bed. Then he nudged his shoes from his feet and they fell to the floor with thuds. She opened his waistcoat and her shoulders slumped when she spied the row of buttons on his shirt. He watched her attack the fastening and savored the nudges and brushes of her busy fingers descending against his chest and belly. His eyes fastened on the jiggles and sway of her breasts as she worked and he sucked a breath and peeled his waistcoat and shirt from his shoulders to bare himself to her.

Her eyes lit as her cool white fingers slid over the taut bronzed mounds of his chest to cup his hard male breast. His hand closed over hers, pressing her palm against him, rubbing it back and forth as his eyes closed and he groaned softly. Then he dragged her hand down his stomach to the buttons of his trousers.

"These, too."

She swallowed hard and released the buttons, one by one, peeling back the flap of his gentlemanly trousers coming even closer to the massive ridge that rose from the base of his groin. He watched her delicate fingers work to release him and just managed to control the powerful thrusting urges of his body. When the buttons were all undone, the flap of his breeches still covered him and he caught her hovering, uncertain fingers and pressed them against his swollen shaft, shuddering as they closed around him. He thrust against her hand and moaned, a deep, tolling sound of pleasure.

He shed his trousers and reached for the bottom of her chemise. She yielded it to him and lay back on the covers, feeling his hungry eyes on her body. She opened her arms to him in aching anticipation of his heat and weight engulfing her. But the expectation went unfilled a moment longer. He moved to one bedpost and searched among the drapes for something. Then he came to lie beside her, spreading himself against her side, and bracing on one elbow to savor the sight of his dark skin joined to her pale beauty. He raised his hand and in it was a sprig of mistletoe that she had tied earlier to the bedpost. He held it before her darkened eyes.

"If it's good luck to kiss a wench under mistletoe, then imagine what it must be to make love under the stuff . . ." While she was fumbling mentally with his remark, he lowered to kiss her lightly under the mistletoe. Then he rose, with eyes hot and hungry, and dragged the dried sprig of lucky herb gently down the side of her face, then down the side of her neck. He slid it across her chest and rubbed it tantalizingly across her tingling nipple, bringing it to aching attention.

"Rane . . ." When her hand fluttered up to hover over his, he brushed it aside and continued the slow, sensual rasp of mistletoe over her body.

"This is very good luck, angel, trust me. Can't you feel how good it is?" he murmured.

Luck. Oh, yes, it was good, so very good. Over each breast it trailed, in torturously lazy spirals, then it brushed the valley between and wound across her ribs to her waist. It tickled and she squirmed. He laughed, holding her in place with the weight of his chest and a muscular thigh clamped across hers. Trickles of pleasure rippled down the side of her hip and thigh . . . then down her calf and up the sole of her foot. He shifted back and traced the same erotic path down her other side, heat to toes, and began to rise up the inside of her arch, then her ankle and calf.

She moved slowly, like a molten tide, parting her legs, opening to him as he coaxed and charmed her sensitive inner thighs. Icy hot fingers of pleasure curled through her skin and seized her nerves, focusing that lush, penetrating sensation into a single burning point of pleasure in the center of her hot womanflesh. Somewhere in that slow, gentle ravishment of senses, her eyes had closed. And now she felt a slow sensual rustle in the curls at the base of her groin. She shifted, opening more, baring her creamy coral heat to him. Over and over, in ceaseless changing combinations he stroked her just enough to move the curls, just enough to send whispers of pleasure into the moist, tender flesh beneath.

She began to quiver, tightening as the pressure mounted, burning for release. Her muscles contracted, her body arched and made tiny thrusting motions, seeking the pressure that would end this glorious torture.

"Please, Rane . . . please . . . now. . .," she murmured, tugging at his shoulders, frantic for the joining that her body craved. She moaned softly as he spread over and around her, wedging his silky rod against her receptive opening. She welcomed him, folding herself around him in return, luxuriating in the strength of him, in the hard, focused force that now penetrated her flesh and filled her with its power.

The magic began again as their bodies moved and their kisses deepened. The weaving once begun was now continued, as though there had been only a heartbeat's delay. The bounds of self and other were dissolving between them and the tightly wrapped strands of each's being relaxed to permit the other's to intertwine with them in perfect synchrony. Over and over, they traded and yielded place, loving and giving freely.

They came together, spiraling and soaring, engorged with pleasures too many to contain. He rocked her body with his thrusts, focusing, plunging into the honeyed warmth that permeated her from the depthless golden pools of her eyes all the way to the sweet, steamy heat of her woman's cleft. She absorbed all of him, his length, his intensity, his passion. She accepted his hardness, his bronzed heat, his fierce possession, and met his need with her own, claiming him . . . becoming one with him.

Their expanding senses erupted in a blinding white brilliance that released the coiled hot potential of their bodies and the deeply welled passions of their hearts. There was no more sight or sound, only pure tactile sensations of expanding endlessly . . . to the edges of existence. And in that white endless sea of sensation, dream-bright color rose and flowed into the current of perception.

It was wonderful! She clung to him, rubbing her dewy face over his hard shoulder, luxuriating in the complete languor of her body. The tension and striving of only moments before were swept away and in their place was a warmth that imbued her very bones. It wasn't exhaustion; it was completion . . . a fullness of being that was utterly new to her. She looked up into the sated, softened angles of Rane's face and found him looking at her with the same sense of wonder she was feeling. As she poured her love into her eyes for him to see, she felt herself soaring . . . wafting higher on bright drafts of freed feeling.

"I feel like I could fly," she whispered.

Her words stirred the silver streams in his eyes visibly. He kissed the tip of her nose, then her bruised-cherry lips. "I feel the same . . . like I could move mountains or empty oceans. . . ." He turned her with him as he slid to the bed beside her and tucked one of her knees between his. He'd never felt so alive as he did watching her now. It was his loving that put such a dreamy heat in her face and made her body glow with such sensual allure. Those gorgeous honey-pot eyes of hers were pulling strings in him still, stirring parts of him he had never associated with physical loving.

"Lord, I've just had your body, angel, and for some reason I'm still ravenous for you. I still want to fill my senses with you, want to touch and kiss you still, over and over."

She nodded wordlessly but her eyes spoke volumes. He pulled her close and buried his face in her tousled hair, just at the base of her neck. She tasted sweet, with a hint of saltiness. His mind began to work again.

"Did you know . . . it's very lucky for a man to kiss

323

his bride here . . . on their wedding night? Well, it is."
His mouth lowered to the sensitive side of her breast
and he kissed and tongued her softly. "And here . . ."
His mouth slid to the tender peak of her breast and he
laved it gently. "And this spot . . . goes without saying."

One kiss, one flick of the tongue led to another and
soon she was being consumed by voracious kisses and
nibbles and was laughing at his outrageous litany of
lucky places to adore on a bride's body. "Elbows . . .
Lord, yes, elbows!" He tantalized that tender flesh, then
slid to her waist where he found a very lucrative spot
on her side that caused rapturous wriggles.

"And sides . . . most beneficial . . . and belly buttons
. . . and scrumptious earlobes . . . and the backs of
knees . . . ummmm, you have marvelous knees. So sensitive. Hold still, Charity. And toes . . . very lucky
things, toes . . ." Devilishly, he nibbled the fleshy pads
of her toes.

"Oh, please, Rane—stop! It tickles!"

He grinned wickedly at her and pushed her back
down, to begin working his way up her arch to the
sensitive run of nerves up the insides of her calf.

"And just think . . . these are only the lucky places
on your *front*. Ummm, the insides of your knees,
too. . .," he moved still higher, kissing, consuming her.
"If a fellow gets this far, he's probably going to be very
lucky indeed . . ."

"Rane—oh, lord—" she wriggled in earnest, seeing
where he was heading in his quest for bountiful luck.
"Rane, you wouldn't—"

He raised his head and waggled his eyebrows teasingly. "Watch me," he challenged huskily. When she
gasped and blushed crimson, he laughed. "Or better
yet, don't watch, angel. Just close your eyes and feel."
She seemed so shocked that he abandoned his original
purpose, though not his determination to please her.

"Trust me, angel." His grin softened to a loving glow.

"I won't do anything to shame you. Close your eyes and let me love you."

Doubt flickered in her face, but she lay back on the pillow and closed her eyes. He could feel her tension in her legs and smiled, applying his lips to her inner thighs as he rubbed the outsides of them reassuringly. He worked his way slowly upward, skirting the downy skin at the tops of her legs and pausing to kiss and caress her sweet belly. He felt her relax suddenly and smiled. She had trusted him . . . and he had honored it. And when he rose to spread himself over her again, she welcomed him with a beaming smile that made him feel rich and full inside.

He joined their bodies with slow, intensifying thrusts that shattered what was left of her sensual ease. Her responses sprang to life all at once, fully roused, primed by his playful seduction. The flexing muscles of his wide shoulders, the powerful contractions of his buttocks as he thrust, carried twice the energy of before. He was focused, as she was, in a way that brought their awareness to a new plane of intensity. The wet velvet heat of his mouth and the smooth rhythmic slide of him against her swollen flesh etched deeply, lastingly, into her vulnerable senses.

Before she had welcomed him; now she demanded him. Her deep, hungry kisses and hands, greedy for the feel of him, challenged his deepest control. Her legs wrapped his, forcing him tighter against her and she arched against him in bold, provocative rounds. The bounds of his gentlemanly restraint weakened and he tightened fiercely around her, plunging them both into a boiling sea of uncharted desires.

They came together powerfully, of singular mind and sense, paring away all sensation but the endless and deepening pleasure of their joined bodies. They moved as one. Their hearts shared a single driving rhythm. Their senses merged and bodies blended. Sinew and sensation and desire compressed in passion's raging heat to shape a single entity, an alloy of spirit and flesh, of past and promise. When their senses could hold no more, when their bodies ached and trembled, unable to contain expanding pleasures, they erupted together in a volcanic release of heat and pleasure. Wave after wave of molten feeling engulfed them, propelling them higher, buoying them up through a blinding maelstrom of passion.

The storm in her subsided, leaving sweet steam that was slowly cleared by a gentle, cooling rain of satisfaction. In the lulling patter of that gentle shower and in the protective cradle of Rane's body, she drifted into delicious dark exhaustion and slept.

She awakened some time later to his lazy smile and love-weighted eyes. He lay on his side facing her, watching her with a wealth of feeling in his expression. She smiled and raised a hand to trace his love-bruised lips.

"I told you knees are very lucky. Do you believe me now?" He grinned, coaxing her response with a hand skimming up her belly and across her breast. The caress was a shameless bribe and she shamelessly succumbed to it.

"Ummmm. Lucky knees. Lucky elbows . . . lucky toes. And mistletoe . . . and lots of buttons for me to undo. . . ." She put her hand over his on her breast and luxuriated in the pure tactile pleasure of his touch. She wetted her lips, looking at his. "I'd never heard about a bridegroom's buttons before."

"It's never been your wedding night before," he parried smoothly.

She tipped her head to watch the knowing twinkle in his eye and the wry curl at the corner of his sensual mouth. "It's never been your wedding night before either. How did you learn about the buttons?"

"We husbands . . . have our sources." It was clear he wasn't going to tell her. Her eyes narrowed suspiciously.

"I didn't think you believed in 'luck,' " she charged.

"I don't."

Something in his blunt denial raised a first pulse of anxiety in her. She searched his bold, black-rimmed eyes and found their charming ease turning to quiet determination. Something began to crowd the edges of her consciousness, something she had abandoned in the fierce idyll of their loving. She struggled with it now, wishing she could resist, knowing it would come.

"But if you don't believe in luck then why. . . ?"

"I know you do." His eyes lidded with meaning as he studied her reaction. His hand moved to her waist and tightened and his leg came up slowly over hers, preparing for what came next. "You wear amulets now."

Her skin began to contract. That something at the edge of her consciousness had begun to murmur like softly inrushing wind. It gathered intensity as it bore down on the center of her awareness. Suddenly it had a forlorn, familiar sound, like a sigh of anxiety. Like the breath of approaching disaster.

"You put mistletoe on my bedposts." He caught her eyes in his and his body tightened subtly around hers. "And you put salt across my doorsill and old shoes on my hearth. You never used to do such things."

Her mouth dried and her heart began to pound.

"You were set to give yourself to Pinnow, when you can't bear his touch and you run from his kisses. What happened to change you so, Charity? What do you know now that you didn't know then?"

She stared at him, chilling in his warm embrace.

He knew.

Her heart convulsed in her chest as icy tendrils of horror crept through her. He knew about her, all about her . . . and her jinx. But how—Gran'mere! The realization slapped her like frigid water, leaving her gasping. She erupted with wild resistance, pushing, wriggling, frantic to escape his knowing eyes and posses-

327

sive touch.

"Charity! Angel! Listen to me—"

He had expected something like this, even prepared for it. But he was still surprised by the frantic force she summoned as she grappled and thrashed, trying to escape him. "Charity!" He subdued her shoulders and trapped her arms with his. Then in desperation, he lowered his body onto hers, pinioning her with his full weight.

"Let me go!"

"Charity, look at me!" he ordered raggedly, shaking her shoulders. Her face was turned as far away as possible and her eyes were clamped shut, but she had to surrender to his superior weight and strength. Her struggles died beneath him, but her resistance only retreated inward. He watched her bite her lip and saw the horror and self-loathing in her face as it strained away from him. Pain slithered through the middle of his chest.

"Charity," he risked releasing her wrist to force her face back to his. "Angel, look at me. You're not a jinx. There's no such thing as a jinx."

His quiet words, so full of certainty and determination, fell like hammer blows on her heart. Her shame-darkened eyes opened into his. This was the moment she'd prayed would never come.

"I am a jinx!" she whispered desperately into his handsome face. "Are you blind? Disaster follows me like a shadow . . . everywhere. And heaven help whoever my shadow falls on . . . Gar and Percy, the baron, Wolfie, my father . . . you!" Anguish squeezed her throat, cracking her voice. "No one is sa-afe from me."

His hand gently on her face, he stroked her trembling chin. For a few moments they'd managed to seal out the world and again she'd been his loving, sensual Charity. Now the warmth in her eyes had been replaced by the chill of fear.

"Angel, I don't believe that—"

"I'm *not* your angel!" She closed her eyes to banish the tears that were formed. "Injuries and accidents and troubles . . ." When her eyes opened again, they were dark wells of despair. "Can't you see what happens every time I walk into a house or a room? Things fall from shelves and people tumble down stairs or choke on food or trip over their feet. Chair legs break and horses panic and things spill or catch fire . . . it's happened all around you! It's happened *to you!*"

"To me? Look, sweetheart, the only disaster to befall me is your pigheaded belief in this nonsense—and your attempts to keep me from the woman I love! Charity, I lov—"

"No!" She looked horrified, and as he gripped her wrist, her hand moved in a frantic repeating pattern that he realized was probably a luck sign. "Don't say that! Don't you ever say that to me!" she choked. Her eyes filled with tears, in spite of her blinking, and her heart twisted in her chest. She hungered for those words, ached to hear them yet she couldn't let him say them, knowing they would bring a tidal wave of disaster down on him. "You, of all people, should know what a jinx I am. I caused your carriage wreck—"

"Don't be absurd, Charity! I was driving hell-bent-for-brimstone on impossible roads—"

"And I ran out in front of you and startled your horses," she ground out.

"You?!" he scowled, pushing up a bit above her. "My wheel broke in a damned rut, the horses panicked, and I lost the reins—"

"From that minute on," her voice dropped to an agonized whisper, "you had nothing but trouble. You got shot in the . . . rear. . . ."

"It was those two piddlewits, Gar Davis and Percy Hall!"

"They were trying to *miss* you, Rane," she moaned.

329

"They've never hit anything with a gun before in their lives! Then you were carried to Standwell—"

"Straight into your loving arms," he growled.

"Rane—" He wouldn't listen, didn't want to see. It was a measure of his care for her, but she had to make him stop it! "Then you fell out of bed and you got scalded—and you cut your foot that night—"

"Thanks to your cursed fleabag of a dog! Every time I turned around he was attacking me. If anybody's a damned jinx in this house, it's *him!* He's disaster on the prowl."

"You kept bashing your head and tripping over your feet!" she charged.

"I was butt-shot!" he bellowed, burning with frustration. "My leg and hip were stiff, and I was unsteady on my feet. Furthermore, I was so hot for your curvy little body I couldn't see straight. It wasn't your *jinx*, Charity, it was my own blessed *lust!*"

"Well, your lust didn't make a shambles of your grandmother's tea party on the day we arrived!" she shouted.

"No, old Wolfram did!" he shouted back, wishing he could just shake some sense into her. "Disaster, like beauty, must be in the eye of the beholder, angel! I thought the entire thing was a damned howler!"

His words lay burning on the air as he stared at her and pulled back to slide from her soft form. His whole body was strung taut with frustration as his mind raced, searching. The silence charged as each plumbed the overwhelming gulf between them.

In the eye of the beholder—it echoed in his head. Suddenly his thoughts after his conversation with Meckton and Harrison, at his club, came back to him. Events that seemed difficult, even ruinous, at the time they occurred, could actually be benefits in disguise. Having a greedy grandmother and losing a mistress . . . getting shot in the arse . . . lying helpless in a run-down coun-

330

try house while the social season ticked away . . . all the small mishaps and humiliations that had cast him into her hands, *into her arms,* over and over . . . Lord, it was so true, it was painful. It really was all in the way a person looked at things!

"Listen to me, Charity." He sat up beside her, on the edge of the bed, and pulled her up with him. His voice and face filled with urgent persuasion. *"Luck,* good or bad, is just a way of looking at things. And it's only one way of seeing things. There are other ways to explain the things that happen around you . . . reasonable, rational ways. Accidents and mishaps happen because people are careless, or unprepared, or because they do foolish things—like putting all the breakables in the place on one mantelpiece, or like keeping a dog that's big enough to pull a plow yet hasn't got a drop of common sense in him." He could see the shimmer of disbelief in her eyes and ground his teeth.

"You don't understand. Over and over, all my life . . ." Her throat clogged with tears she wouldn't allow to fall on the outside. She couldn't recount every senseless disaster and accident that had occurred in her life. And even if she did, he'd find an explanation for them all . . . because that was what *he* wanted to see. And he would ignore the compelling sum of them that convicted her utterly.

She watched the dark frustration in his face, and in his coiled shoulders and clenched fists. She wanted to touch him. Her whole body was aching with the desire to comfort him . . . to love him. Her pained heart crept into her eyes.

"Please, Rane. Let me go home, to Standwell," she whispered.

"No!" He went rigid and slid off the edge of the bed, towering over her as she dragged the sheet over her body. The very thought of her isolated in that ramshackle house, buried alive by her grandmother's crazy

331

superstitions, positively enraged him.

"Rane . . ." She came toward the edge of the bed on her knees. Tears filled her eyes and clung to her lashes in haunting prisms. She poured all her anguish into her eyes for one last desperate plea. "Please, I don't want to hurt you. If I stay, something terrible will happen to you."

He felt as though he'd been impaled. She loved him and she was terrified of loving him. He glimpsed the agonizing depths of her conflict for the first time. She really believed her presence, her admission of love for him would put him in danger. He wavered for a moment, wondering if he really should take her home. But how could he give her up to long, futile days of blame and remorse, with no one to counter her destructive illusions?

She knew his decision the moment he reached for her. His arms closed tightly around her, pulling her hard against his bare strength, claiming her. She couldn't stop her arms from circling him, couldn't hold back the tears . . . or the desperate hope that surged inside her. She clung to him, her face buried in the salty warmth of his chest. The want, the need, filled her with a slow burn of pained pleasure. She gave herself to it, holding onto him desperately.

Above her head, the grimness of his expression was easing. The feel of her arms around him answered his deepest fear, his only hesitation. She did want him, even through her fears. She did love him. His tenacious heart began to reclaim lost ground.

"I won't let you go, Charity. I can't. You're my wife, my love."

"Please don't say —"

"I love you, Charity." He drew back enough to force her tear-streaked face up. "Saying it, or not, doesn't change it. It's not an incantation, it has no magic in it. It's only another way to express how I care for you and

332

need you."

She could scarcely breathe. He needed her. It was the hardest thing she'd ever done, looking into that need, while holding back the words of loving that would surely seal his doom.

"Say it, Charity." There was such hunger in his voice; it was terrible to hear. She closed her eyes to keep from seeing the hurt in his face, then shook her head.

Rane's throat tightened and his fists clenched as a wave of pure longing crashed through him. He wanted, needed to hear her say it, as much for her sake as for his. As long as she couldn't declare her love for him openly and freely, both she and their life together would be prisoners to her fear.

But how did he fight an illusion . . . a wrong belief? With the truth. With a belief in something real.

What else did she believe in? His mind raced as his eyes flew over her bare shoulders and love-warmed skin, over the love-tousled bedclothes. And it came to him. There was one thing she believed in, one thing that was powerful enough to make her forget her jinx and her fears—at least for a while. It would have to be enough.

The power of love. *The night magic.*

"I'm going to fight your damned jinx, angel, every step of the way."

When she looked up, there was an odd light in his eyes. "You're my wife, Charity, the Viscountess Oxley." He stroked her shoulders in small, intense circles. "Do you have any idea how long I've waited to say those words, how long I've waited to bring home a wife? I bought this house nearly three years ago, intending to bring my bride here. Only there was no bride . . . and no love and no joy in this house, either." His hands came up to wipe the tears from her cheeks and stayed to cradle her face lovingly.

"Do you have any idea what it means to me to have you here? To look up at dinner and see your big honey-brown eyes looking down the table at me, to watch them dress your sweet body in the silks and velvets and laces I can provide? Do you know what it means to me to know that at day's end, your arms will open to me in the sweet darkness of my bed?"

Every word sank straight into her roused, aching core. No dogged assault of logic, no bombardment with reason and debate, could have breached the protective walls around her will like those poignant admissions. He had been alone in his title and his grand house and in his life. He hadn't belonged to anybody. And he had wanted a wife, so desperately, to share those things with him.

"I love you, Charity, and want you in my home and in my life." He lowered his face toward hers and the flames in the backs of his eyes flared. Jinx or no jinx, you're the mistress of this house and the lover I want and need. I'll fight for you every step of the way. But I have to know that it's what you want, too. Tell me, Charity. What do you want?"

She bit her lip and searched his earnest gray eyes, struggling with his demands. It was all she'd dreamed about in her naive, girlish dreams of marriage . . . and more. A fine home, beautiful clothes, servants . . . and life with a special man, a man she adored. It was a lifetime of living with Rane, loving him, sharing the good and the bad of life with him. The conflict of fear and longing in her winsome features was painful to behold. He wouldn't let her go and he wouldn't let her protect him anymore. He was demanding that she share his life and his loving, no matter where it led. She watched the challenge in his big frame, the determination in his face. And she had no defense against his demands. She wanted those things, too.

"But, if something should happen to you . . ." Her hands came up to press protectively over his heart.

"Charity, I can't guarantee our lives or our love. They

334

will become what we make them. Whatever time I have with you, I want to make it count. I want to love you a lifetime in each minute. I want to weave your 'night magic' through our days as well." His fingers played gently over her lips, caressing, coaxing. "What do you want, Charity?"

She looked up at him with her eyes shining, jewel bright with tears.

"I want . . . that sky-blue silk dress with the embroidered velvet spencer. And I want to get Wolfie a strong leather collar and a stout chain. And I want . . . the special magic you make, Rane Austen . . . every day and every night, for the rest of my life!"

Chapter Nineteen

Down the hall, Lady Margaret paced her room by candlelight, waiting for the moon to rise. It was the new moon, the moon of portent, and she was determined to be there when it first crested the horizon . . . or whatever there was left of a horizon in west London.

When it was time, she took a candle and made her way up the stairs at the end of the hallway to the third floor, then past the housemaids' room in the attic. She pushed through a little-used door and stepped out onto an old widow's walk that ran along the flattened top gable of the roof. She clutched the low wooden railing and inched along, scanning the horizon for sign of that auguring moon. It took a while, but she finally located it and concentrated all her powers of observation on it.

But try as she might to focus her eyes, the crescent remained an indistinct arc of light, dim at the edges and difficult to see. She rubbed her eyes and squinted and cocked her head at seven different angles. Was that a shadow or a shimmer? Did it have a greenish cast tonight or was that silver? The familiar smudges, knobs, and bumps . . . where in blazes were they? Despite her gyrations, the new moon remained a luminous up-ended grin that kept its mysterious secrets.

The old lady wrung her knotty hands and rubbed her forehead with anxiety. Her eyesight wasn't as good as it had been, she knew. But she'd not guessed that it had deteriorated so far that she couldn't see a new moon properly! Lord, what was she going to do? She had to have answers, had to find some way to help Charity and her hard-headed husband.

She dragged her shawl tightly about her and knew the time had come. She'd have to find help . . . someone who knew as much or more about the moon than she did. . . .

The next morning the sun was shining brightly and the room and the bed were warm around Charity when she wakened. Warm like the sun of Rane's smile. Warm like the touch of his generous hands. She lay on the great plane of his bed, swathed in down-filled comforters and luxuriating in the traces of his magical loving that lingered in her body. She stretched and wiggled her toes, letting her eyes roam over the tented silk canopy overhead, and over the dark, lustrous mahogany of the bed and other furnishings. It was all *too* grand, *too* wonderful . . . She strangled that gloomy thought and slid from the bed. She had promised Rane she would try to be his wife in every way, and she meant it.

An efficient serving woman of middling years appeared with a tray on which sat coffee and chocolate and buttery scones. She also brought the news that the dressmaker had been waiting for more than two hours for Charity to waken . . . as per Rane's instructions. Charity winced at that and would have hurried down the hall to her old room. But the maid stared at the comforter she gripped around her, and tactfully suggested that she might wish to avail herself of the bath the viscount had ordered for her and then to dress before meeting with the dressmaker.

Charity blushed, realizing that there was quite a bit for her to learn as a viscountess . . . starting with the idea that one didn't meet with dressmakers unless one was already amply clothed. She took a deep breath and allowed herself to be led into an adjoining room that was covered in white and blue moorish tiles, both floor and walls. A huge copper tub of hot water sat waiting amidst fresh linen and marvelously perfumed steam. It was a bathing chamber, the maid explained, reaching for the comforter and averting her eyes as Charity slid into the tub of rose-scented water. "Comin' all the rage amongst th' uppers an' betters."

The maid reappeared later, to help her from the bath and promptly slipped on the cake of soap that had fallen from the side of the tub. She landed with a plop on her ample rear and sat blinking, more surprised than hurt. When she heaved to her feet, she suffered an even greater shock as Charity paled and apologized profusely to her . . . for not keeping the soap under better control.

By the time Charity had dried and dressed in the new French chemise, embroidered petticoat, and dressing gown that the servant had brought from her old room, anxiety was creeping up her spine again. She faced the dressmaker with waning enthusiasm, and this was dealt a lethal blow when it was discovered that two lengths of very expensive Italian shot-silk had been cut wrong. The dressmaker went into an artistic temper and smacked one of her assistants, who backed into a stack of hatboxes, sending them toppling onto a seamstress, who scrambled out of the way and elbowed the errand boy, who yelled and jumped back, smack into the middle of a velvet scoop bonnet that had spilled from the top hatbox when it fell!

It was a perfectly *explainable* chain of disaster. But somehow, when the horrified milliner lifted her ruined creation and started to sniffle, *how* it had happened wasn't nearly so important as *why*. It was her jinx, Charity thought. What else could it be? She recalled her promise to Rane and lifted her chin, trying to counter the heaviness in the middle of her. She had promised to live with him and be his wife, but that didn't mean she wouldn't worry about his safety . . . and that of his household.

Rane had risen early that morning and gone to his offices long enough to set a few matters on course, before returning home. Learning that Charity was still occupied by her fittings, he retreated to his study and called Eversby to remove Wolfram to the nearest livery and have him fitted with a collar or harness of some sort, to make him more manageable. The butler looked at Wolfram's massive frame and jaws and his perpetual half-snarl, and paled. He called for the footman and the under footman to bring their ropes, and soon the reluctant footmen were being dragged out the front doors of Oxley House by Charity's exuberant horse of a dog.

Rane watched them through the entry hall, grinning. It was a prudent first step in regularizing their unusual household and unsettled lives. He strolled back into his study and sent Eversby to ask Lady Margaret to join him there . . . to take the second step.

"You will not refer to Charity's *jinx* in any way, while under this roof," he declared in a firm tone. "You will place every breakable object you've moved back into its original position, and you will cease stuffing strange animal and vegetable matter into every nook and cranny of my house. And if you expect to continue living with us, you will put on decent clothes and get rid of those wretched, malodorous animal parts around your neck." The old lady blanched and huddled mutinously in her chair. For a long moment, they engaged in a visual clash of wills.

"I will not get rid of this one!" She finally held up the silver crescent moon hanging around her neck. "It's been with me for years and it doesn't stink. Nor does this pebble, nor this lucky penny." Her weathered chin trembled and her age-faded eyes took on a haunting, vulnerable look so much like Charity's that he felt his irritation crumbling.

"All right, b'dammit." He relented and she melted with relief. "Keep the ones that don't stink. But from now on, you'll wear them beneath the neck of your new dresses."

"New dresses?" Her gratitude slid into a scowl and she crossed her arms protectively over her favorite purple smock. "I don't have any new dresses."

He came round his desk to tower over her with his most compelling look.

"You will, *Gran'mere*. You will."

He sent for Lady Catherine next and she arrived in a rustle of gray silk, looking rather put out at having been summoned just as she was about to depart on her morning calls. Rane invited her to be seated and came straight to the point.

"There has been a great deal of tumult in this house of late," he began. Lady Catherine's eyes narrowed and she humphed agreement. "I understand there is already talk of my unusually 'quick' marriage and some confusion and curiosity about my bride."

"Your irrational behavior positively invites censure; you've brought it all on yourself." She lifted her chin to stare down her imperial nose at Rane. "It has naught to do with me."

Rane's genial look frosted. "It was everything to do with you; you are my grandmother, the dowager Viscountess Oxley, and a part of my household now." He strolled around his desk and perched insolently on the side of it, returning her heated glare.

"I think it best to meet all speculation head on. I would like you to sponsor Charity, socially. She needs to stay busy and she needs to learn about London life and social matters in order to make a proper adjustment to her new life. And it would help quiet gossip if we were seen together in public, perhaps at a dinner or party

. . . or even the Duke of Sutherland's ball. You could secure us an invitation."

"Sponsor her? Secure *you* an invitation? Out of the question!" Lady Catherine pushed to her feet. "You went charging off to Devon, against all advice, interfering in the girl's proper and rightful marriage. And you've created a howling scandal by impulsively marrying your little milkmaid—or whatever she is—yourself! I'll have nothing to do with it, or with her, do you hear. She's out of her depth and above her station and she knows it . . . even if you do not. You've made your bed, now lie in it." She turned on her heel and was halfway to the door before she turned back to deliver one last burning thrust.

"You're just like your grandfather, a heedless, libidinous beast. I was right about you all along. You don't deserve to be in decent society."

Rane felt anger licking up his spine, and when it burst into flame in his eyes, it was hot enough to scorch his thorny grandmother half a room away.

"Perhaps I'm not enough like my grandfather. He certainly had no difficulty in getting rid of you."

Lady Catherine gasped and recoiled as if struck. She turned and fled the study, then the house itself, in high dudgeon. Blinded by righteous indignation, she had failed to see Charity standing, partially hidden, beside the open door of the study.

Charity had come downstairs seeking Rane's warmth and certainty, escaping the chaos of fashion and the tension caused by the morning's mishaps. She had planned to show him her first completed dress and thank him. Instead, she caught him in the midst of an argument with his irascible grandmother, an argument over her.

Until now, she had only worried about the troubles her jinx might bring down on him. She hadn't realized that the very fact of their marriage might have a calamitous effect on him as well. A wave of weakness went through her knees at the thought. More trouble. He wanted, needed, an introduction to society to put an end to the gossip about his marriage to a country miss with no money or connections. And Lady Catherine wouldn't sponsor him in society for precisely that reason: she felt he'd married, both rashly and ruinously, a penniless, mannerless girl who was beneath him.

She hurried toward the stairs.

"Charity?" Rane caught sight of her as she slipped past his study door and hurried out after her. "Charity, what are you doing here? I thought you would be occupied with fittings the entire morning." With a broad smile, he pulled her into his mahogany-paneled study and closed the door behind them. She stood a moment, her hands in his, looking about the large, comfortably furnished study, with its filled bookcases and sturdy leather furnishings and polished desk. It was so like him, so masculine, so substantial.

"I thought you might like to see how your money is being spent." She pulled her sprigged muslin skirt out at the side and pirouetted slowly under his hand to let him see. "I hope you approve. I'm afraid it's rather expensive."

His eyes glowed as they roamed her curvy form, then narrowed at the unsettled air in her girlish manner. "Has something happened, Charity?"

"Happened? No." She answered too quickly and flushed, lowering her eyes. "I mean, it's just tiring and confusing. So many decisions to make."

Rane watched the veil of her lashes hiding something from him. Anxiety? Fear? Was she finding the weight of her new role constricting and disagreeable? Did she need to talk, or perhaps the reassurance of his "magic" touch? He smiled knowingly.

"Let me see. Lovely soft fabric . . ." He brushed an evaluative hand over one short, poufed sleeve, and grazed the tambour-work frills inserted in her rounded neckline, then pressed his hand fully against the side of her breasts and slid it down to her waist. "Lovely soft skin . . ." She shivered and he smiled roguishly.

. "I see you're adopting wicked London ways, angel." To her widened eyes, he explained, "You're not wearing a corset."

"Mrs. Carstens, the dressmaker, says corsets haven't been 'the thing' for several years now."

"She would certainly know. Although, I confess, as a married man, I am beginning to see the wisdom in them. It will be a powerful distraction—and something of a worry—knowing your sweet breasts and silky hips are so . . . accessible." His fingers closed over her breast, kneading gently, turning her body molten with their seductive motion.

Her eyes closed and her breath rattled to a stop in her throat. His fingers rippled and swirled over her, seeking the tightening nipples of her breasts through the soft layers of fabric. She leaned into him, raising her mouth, inviting him into its warmth. His lips came down on hers, searching coaxing, pleasuring. And soon she was wrapped in his arms and wriggling closer, molding her body tighter against him, rising onto her toes to meet his hungry kiss.

Panting, quaking from the eruption of need in his veins, he murmured, "I want to love you, angel. . . ." And he pulled her out the door and up the main stairs with him to their rooms.

"Rane!" She protested the sensual set of his face and the glint in his eye with a hoarse whisper. "Rane, it's the middle of the day!"

He laughed at her ladylike shock and paused in the upper hallway to pull her against his hardening body. "Everything works the same in daylight, angel. Have you forgotten?" he murmured, absorbing her protest between his parted lips. When her knees weakened and she melted against him again, he pulled her into the

343

master suite and threw the key in the lock behind them.

He took her into his arms and kissed her with long, plundering strokes of his tongue and erotic nibbles of her lips. His hands flowed over her possessively, claiming the lush new textures and contours of her. She flicked a desirous gaze at the big comfortable bed, but he only smiled into her hot caramel eyes and slid his hands over her hips.

"Do you want to know what else is fashionable with London's bolder ladies?" Before she could swallow and speak, his fingers were raising and bunching the soft muslin of her skirt, pulling it up to her waist. His fingers worked the tie of her petticoat and it tumbled into a pool around her feet. Her skirt slid back down her legs and his hands followed. "They wear no petticoats, so their dresses drape more revealingly around their legs." He sent his hands down her hips and buttocks, caressing, exploring the feel of her through her clothes.

"But it's so . . . I feel so . . ."

"Naked," he murmured, kissing the base of her throat, sending hot vibrations in all directions beneath her skin. "Ummm." He clearly approved of all he was feeling. "I believe that's the idea; to feel and look as naked as possible, while still clothed. Want to know more, angel?"

She nodded, hypnotized by the feel of his hands on her bottom and his throaty murmurings. She allowed him to back her toward the bathing room and found herself against the washstand by the door, captive, his arm tight around her waist. He raised the pitcher of water and, before she realized what he intended, had arched back and poured it in a slow stream over her breasts and down her waist and belly. She jolted at the feel of the cool water on her warm skin, gasping and squirming.

"Rane! What are you doing?! You'll ruin my—ohhhh!"

"Muslin doesn't ruin in water," he answered hotly,

pulling her tightly against his chest, heedless of his own gentlemanly clothes. "Trust me, angel . . . Let me show you." Her wriggles died under the sultry pull of his gaze and his voluptuous kiss. Caught against the wall of his hard body, she stilled, borrowing his heat. He moved back and turned her, holding her by the waist with one arm. That erotic stream now focused on and tantalized her nipples and slid down her belly to intensify against her woman's mound. The water seeped through, running like cool, erotic fingers along her woman's cleft and running in warming rivulets down the insides of her heated thighs.

"London's shameless ladies dampen their gowns." He set the pitcher down and released her waist to take her hands in his. "The dresses cling to their hips and legs as they walk and dance, caressing them like a lover." His eyes drifted hotly down her body, savoring the sight of her protruding nipples and the boldly outlined curve of her breasts, and luxuriating in the erotic molding of the fabric to her belly and the entrancing little V at the top of her legs.

Her initial shock passed as Rane's hands and mouth followed his eyes down over her wet front, tracing her shape, fastening hotly on the wet mounds of her breasts, warming her. Hot flashes of arousal streaked along her nerves, as he drew her across the floor, whispering, "Walk for me, angel. Move for me."

He was right, she realized. The wet fabric was like a caressing hand over her body, sliding, clinging, molding against her most sensitive skin in an utterly decadent display. She felt exposed, naked in a way she'd never imagined. And her body began to respond with lush, swaying, movements, then, as he watched, with indecent wriggles and arches, motions she had only made in the throes of loving. Rippling, seeking movements displayed her hunger, revealed her most private shapes and her desires. The dress hugged her legs and rode snugly over

345

her belly as she moved and undulated for him . . . closer, coming closer to his body, pulling him toward her lush, wet heat. She felt him watching the movement of her legs and the provocative roundings of her hips and the shameless thrusts of her woman's body and felt a new power in the desire she was building in him.

She paused before him, looking up at him with hot promise swirling in her eyes and in her woman's body. And she swayed against his front, brushing him slowly, touching and caressing him with her breasts, her waist, her belly and woman's mound. She found the inflamed ridge of his manhood and undulated slowly against it . . . from base to tip . . . up that steely satin length.

His arms clamped around her and his mouth came down on hers with a primal growl of pure need. He consumed her with ravenous kisses as he peeled the wet fabric from her shoulders and breasts to feast on the skin beneath.

Somehow they made it to the bed, clothes dropping, shoes flinging, seams straining. Clad only in stockings and lacy garters, she slid back onto the soft pillows and pulled his body over hers. He sank into the wet, receptive heat of her desire, and began to weave his special magic again in her body, her senses, her heart.

Her cool skin absorbed his warmth as they arched and came together, over and over. Their senses fused, their sense of self and separateness expanded into a world of feeling enlarged by the limitless heart. Together they soared, exploring new regions of sense and sensuality, until they approached that final barrier and went crashing through into stunning bright pleasure.

Satisfaction seeped through her like steam, bathing her roused feelings. She lay nestled in his arms, feeling utterly at peace, and wished they could just remain here, in each other's arms, sealing out the rest of the world. He kissed her forehead and she shifted to offer him the side of her face, then arched to make sure he could reach her neck and the hollow of her throat.

"Ummmm." He hummed into her skin, setting her nerves atingle. "I knew roses would be your scent."

"And how is it you know so much about wicked London ladies, who wear nothing beneath their dampened gowns?" She turned a look of sultry demand on him.

"I've . . . I've heard all about them." He nuzzled her ear and rubbed his face in her hair.

"Beast." She laughed, punching his shoulder ineffectually. "You've more than heard about them."

He raised his head and his eyes contained a worldly glint. "Beasts . . . do get around." A wry grin appeared on his love-swollen mouth.

"I'll bet you do . . . *did.*" Her eyes narrowed and she wriggled against him meaningfully. He laughed at her emphatic use of the past tense and hugged her.

"*Did,*" he agreed.

As she lay in his arms, the word came back to her . . . "Beast." It was what his grandmother had called his grandfather, and him. Somehow it had found its way to her tongue, as though to remind her of it. A lecherous beast, or words to that effect. She thought back to the rest of that exchange and puzzled over it.

"Why does your grandmother dislike you so?" she finally asked. His laugh was a short, sardonic huff of surprise that let her know she'd struck a sensitive nerve. She raised onto her elbow beside him and poured all the care and acceptance she had for him into her expression. "Please, tell me."

He rolled onto his back and drew a tight breath. She could see he was searching, sorting things mentally, deciding whether and what to tell her. She squeezed his hand to reassure him.

"She doesn't know me well enough to hate me," he began defensively, "but it doesn't seem to stop her. The one she really hates is her husband, my grandfather. He's long dead, but her loathing for him certainly isn't.

347

And every time she looks at me, she sees him. I look something like him." He turned to her with a firm set to his chin.

"He left her for other women. Not just one woman . . . lots of women. He was a randy old hound and a spendthrift to boot. There was scandal after scandal, until the king politely asked him to absent himself from England. That's where Barbados came in. My father followed in his footsteps, except his yen was for only one other woman, who was already a duchess and filthy rich . . . and married. Barbados again. My mother died when I was six years old and he sent for me. I grew up in my father's informal exile with the taint of Austen disgrace. And with the intense Barbados heat in my manner, in my skin." He drifted away from her, across time and distance.

"Then I came back to London after my father died. Barbados was harsh, at times. But London's almighty ton is harsher, by far."

Her heart paused, aching for him, then proceeded to beat cautiously. His Barbados background and exotic looks . . . his grandfather and father exiled for their wayward lusts . . . wives betrayed and bitter . . . Apparently his family troubles hadn't begun with her jinx; they were of long standing.

"Then it isn't me?" she whispered, scarcely able to believe it. "She doesn't hate you because of me?" He came up onto his elbow, facing her, searching the surprise in her expression.

"Is that what you thought, angel? You believed you were to blame for my grandmother's anger toward me?" His hand came up to caress her cheek. "How could you possibly . . ." Then he realized: her belief in her jinx, and the guilt it caused were so strong that she took responsibility for all the troubles around her.

"I was unacceptable to my grandmother and her cronies long before I married you, long before I ever came

348

to Devon, Charity." His laugh had a bitter edge. "Probably even before I was born."

Relief poured through her in a surprising flood. She might have aggravated the situation, but she certainly hadn't *caused* his grandmother's acrimony toward him. With that flood came a cold sobering draft; she had been set to blame herself for family problems that had likely begun with Rane's grandfather, long before she was ever born! It struck her like a lightning bolt, even as he said it.

"Charity," he groaned, turning her chin up to delve into her eyes, "you can't possibly be responsible for *all* the troubles around you; it just isn't reasonable. Your father knew it wasn't. That's why he refused to let your grandmother say anything about your supposed 'jinx.'"

It was true. Logically, she couldn't be responsible for every bit of trouble around her. And yet, somehow, she'd made herself *feel* responsible for all of them. For the first time in weeks, she actually felt a glimmer of hope. She didn't cause all the troubles around her, only some of them. It brought back Rane's assertion that there were reasons and explanations for everything.

"It's true. I'm not responsible for all the troubles," she admitted, melting with relief against him, reveling in the possessive way his strong arms wrapped and held her. It didn't change the fact that cats landed on their backs when she was around or the way horses shied. It didn't change the fact that if there was a weak seam or button anywhere near her, it was sure to pop. But it was such a relief to know that Rane's grandmother didn't hate him because of her.

Lady Catherine's scornful tone and disparaging words suddenly came back to her, but this time without the added weight of her own self-blame. Her face and pride heated furiously. She was most certainly not a milk-maid. She was a squire's daughter, from an old and honorable lineage, and her grandmother was a duke's

349

daughter . . . and a duke's sister!

She looked up into Rane's handsome features and thought of his tenderness, his generosity to her and her grandmother and even to her exasperating horse of a dog. He deserved better. He deserved the best. And she vowed to somehow get him the introduction, the invitation that he wanted and needed into the almighty *ton's* midst. She was going to help him!

When he met her eyes, they were glowing with joyful determination at the prospect of helping again . . . helping *him!*

"Charity?" Her smile was such a contrast to her earlier mood, it unnerved him. "What is it?"

"I was just wondering," she murmured suggestively, pressing against his lean, rising heat. "Are you going to pour water over me like this when we go out?"

His face reddened and he met her eyes with a flame in his. "I have to confess, I overdid it a bit with the water. The naughty ladies *dampen* their dresses, they don't *drown* them. Once I got started, I just couldn't seem to stop."

"That's something I've always liked about you, your lordship," she purred, undulating slowly against him.

"What's that?" he growled, rolling her onto her back to give her what she seemed to be asking for.

"You don't stop."

Charity appeared in Lady Margaret's room after dinner that afternoon with a spark in her eye and a mission in her heart.

"Gran'mere, do you know anyone in London?" she settled on the footstool beside the chair where the old lady sat darning her stockings. Lady Margaret looked at her, looked thoughtful, and frowned.

"No, not really. Oh, well, that hog-toothed Ellie Farquhar, but I don't know what happened to the others. Oh!" She brightened, recalling one other. "Of course, there's Teddy. Lord, I haven't seen him in years!"

"Teddy?" Charity frowned now.

"Your Uncle Teddy, my younger brother."

"I didn't know I had an Uncle Teddy." Charity looked puzzled. "Why didn't you ever talk about him?"

"Oh, but I did, from time to time. He's the Duke of Clarendon."

Charity's eyes widened with pleasure. "Uncle Teddy. Oh, Gran'mere, it would be unforgivable of you not to call on him now that you're in London! And while you're there—Gran'mere, does he owe you any old favors?"

Two days later, the Duke of Clarendon's butler arrived in the grand drawing room of the duke's house in Grovenor Square, just steps ahead of a very persistent and self-possessed guest. "Your Graces, Lady Margaret Villiers."

The silver-haired Duke of Clarendon looked up from his paper to his duchess and then to the door where Lady Margaret stood in a new dress and matching turban, complete with elegant ostrich feather. But it was the great gold hoops in her ears that raised a flash of recognition in him.

"Good Lord." He thrust *The Times* aside and rose, staring at the weathered little knot of a woman in the doorway.

"Teddy?" Lady Margaret squinted and stared from her brother to her sister-in-law and back, seeing them decades older than she'd remembered and feeling poignantly just how much time and life had been lost in the distance that had lain between them. "Lord, I would hardly have known you if it weren't for that beak of yours."

351

The duke sputtered and hitched about to stare at his wife, then looked back at the old woman near the doorway. Nobody had called him "Teddy" in decades . . . or referred to his "beak." In fact, nobody had ever done so except . . .

"Y-your G-grace," the duchess stammered. "W-who is this woman?"

"I think it's . . . my older sister. Margaret?"

"It's me, Teddy." She came forward and paused in the middle of the elegant drawing room, feeling waves of longing and remembrance rolling over her. A moment later, the duke's thick shoulders sagged and his eyes misted as he smiled and held out his hands.

"Maggie."

Chapter Twenty

That next afternoon, as they sat down to dinner, Lady Margaret withdrew a packet of snowy vellum from the pocket of her new smock and handed it to Rane with a flourish, under Lady Catherine's narrowed eyes. He scowled, staring at it, then lifted a puzzled look to Charity, who sat in the hostess's chair down the table, beaming at him. The glowing pleasure in her face arrested him so that he paused and had to be reminded by Lady Margaret.

"Well, don't just sit there. Open it up."

He came back to the task at hand, and broke the seal on the packet and opened it. His eyebrows raised at the elegant ducal crest at the top of what had the measured, metered appearance of an invitation. His eyes widened as they flowed down the engraved script, catching on the name of the sender, the Duke of Sutherland, and on the words, "ball to celebrate the end of the season." His jaw dropped and he sat forward in his chair, staring disbelievingly at the coveted invitation.

"What could possibly be so important as to delay dinner?" Lady Catherine's cheeks pinked as she clasped her hands in her lap and strove to hold her curiosity within ladylike bounds.

"How did you . . . where. . . ?" Rane looked up at Lady Margaret, then checked the name on the outside of the letter packet to be sure there was no mistake. *The Viscount Oxley, the Viscountess Oxley, and Lady Margaret Villiers*. His face filled with unabashed pleasure and he lowered the invitation to meet Charity's gaze. "You know about this?" He could read her answer in the twinkle of her eyes.

"It was Gran'mere, really. And Uncle Teddy." Charity's smile blossomed to pure joy at the light in his handsome features. She'd managed to please him, to help give him something he couldn't have acquired or attained alone.

"How unthinkably rude. Will someone please have the manners to inform me what is going on?" Lady Catherine demanded.

"It's an invitation." Lady Margaret faced Rane's grandmother across the table, drawing herself up straight and raising her chin. "To the Duke of Sutherland's ball at week's end. You're in society, or at least you claim to be. Don't tell me you haven't heard of the Duke of Sutherland and his bash . . ."

"The Duke of Suth—I don't believe it. How—where would *you* get such an invitation?!"

"Yes, how did you come by it?" Rane echoed, pulled back from Charity's absorbing glow to stare with open fascination at the ripening conflict between the two old ladies.

"From my brother, Teddy," Lady Margaret crossed her arms over her chest, mirroring Lady Catherine's indignation, tit for tat.

"Your brother?!" Lady Catherine pushed to her feet, heedlessly upending the ratty looking Caesar from her lap as she turned on Rane. "Ye gods—she's stolen it—she or one of her gypsy cohorts!"

"*Stolen—?!* Teddy is not a gypsy, nor is he a thief, you tongue-sore old drouse!" Margaret twitched with rising fury. "He's a full duke of the realm, the Duke of Clarendon. It was he that secured his lordship and Charity the invitation, upon my request."

"Your brother . . . a duke?!" Lady Catherine made an expiring sound of pure derision. "That's absurd!"

"Clarendon is your brother?!" Rane choked, equally astonished. Then he saw Charity's earnest nodding and recalled something she had once said about Lady

Margaret's family connections. "Good Lord, why would the duke wish to sponsor me? I've never met the fellow in my life."

"I paid him a call yesterday, to renew old ties." Margaret spoke to Rane but her pointed explanation was aimed at Lady Catherine's swelling ire. "He'd heard about your marriage and when he learned his grandniece Charity was your bride, he kindly offered to take you out into society, since you had no family of your own to sponsor you."

"He h-has family of his own!" Lady Catherine erupted, abandoning all decorum to lean angrily across the table at Lady Margaret.

"Well, it was me who got him the invitation that his *family* wouldn't . . . or *couldn't!*" Margaret met her across the table. They were nearly nose to nose again, faces red and furious.

"I could have gotten him that invitation!"

"But you didn't! Nor did you get him an invitation to call on the Duke of Clarendon tomorrow morning, where he and Charity will meet a few of the duke's and duchess's intimates! And there's no telling where I'll get them invited after that!"

Catherine snapped upright, as if slapped. Her gray eyes crackled at the challenge. She wasn't about to let a bizarre old half-gypsy with delusions of nobility outdo her in her own social set!

"Well, they shall have to be back early to receive calls from the Countess Swinford . . . and the Countess Ravenswood . . ." Her eyes flicked back and forth as her mind raced, thinking of others she could count on to appear at short notice.

"Humph! Ellie Farquhar? You expect them to hurry home from the Duke of Clarendon's to wait on 'old piddlepockets'?"

Rane saw Charity's horrified look, urging him to do something. But his eyes were bulging and his shoulders were shaking; it was all he could do just to keep his incredulous laughter inside. The old girls were at it fang and claw, an exceedingly well-dressed old gypsy and a bred-in-the-bone doyenne of the almighty ton, locked in mortal combat over the chance to sponsor him and his bride socially! It was almost more than he could contain. When Lady Catherine turned on him with a strident attempt at grandmotherly regard, he had to grip the table edge and chew his lips to keep from bursting into gales of laughter.

"Oxley, I cannot imagine you could want your entry into society managed by. . .," she gestured to Lady Margaret, pulling herself back from the table and from the brink of an unladylike explosion, "a dilettante. There are pitfalls everywhere, in society. I suggest you put yourself in better hands!"

"Like yours?" Lady Margaret snorted, drawing back into a huddled, arms-crossed posture. "You had your chance; now step aside for your betters, bitter-bones."

It was either resort to mayhem or retreat graciously, and for a long, charged moment, it seemed even odds on bloodletting and civilized withdrawal. Finally, breeding and habit prevailed. Crimson-faced Lady Catherine drew herself up with great dignity, giving Lady Margaret a look that was hot enough to scald her for peeling.

"At least I can recognize my betters when I meet them, you smelly old hob. Oxley, I seem to have lost my appetite."

She lifted her chin and sailed out of the room with Caesar padding regally at her heels. When the door banged resoundingly behind her, it was the beleaguered Caesar that felt her emphasis most.

"REOWWRRRR!!" His long fluffy tail had not quite cleared the doorframe. The door rattled and parted slightly and from the far side, Lady Catherine's voice was heard cooing, "Poor, poor baby. Wait—where are you going—?! Come back!"

Rane exploded in spasms of laughter, holding his sides and his head, rolling back in his chair and stiffening his legs. Then he sighted Lady Margaret's prune-like scowl as she hauled a contraband amulet from beneath her bodice to sniff it . . . and went off on another thigh-pounding round of helpless amusement. Lady Margaret snatched her sulfur and garlic concoction out of view and glowered at his unholy mirth, realizing that part of it was aimed at her. Her shrunken chin came up and she took leave in similar indignation, muttering about "ingrates" and "invitations."

When only Charity was left in the dining room, he sobered and wiped his eyes. "Oh, God. I haven't had so much fun . . . since Wolfram nearly ate Caesar!" It was another minute before he could quell his convulsive outbursts and manage to look even halfway contrite.

"I'm sorry, Charity," he took a deep, shuddering breath and tightened his stomach against a third wave of laughter. "I didn't mean to offend your Gran'mere, but — lord! — she was a hoot! The two of them, at it dig and gouge —" She was chewing the corner of her mouth and frowning at him. He strangled yet another chuckle and was on his feet in a flash, striding down the table to take her hands and pull her to her feet.

He wrapped his arms around her stiff form and worked to produce his most sincere and loving smile. "You had a hand in this, I believe. I can't imagine your Gran'mere with a deep desire to enhance our social standing. Admit it, now. You put her up to it."

She sighed and melted shamefully, seeing the deep pleasure in his eyes and getting caught up in his buoyant mood. "I *helped*. I suggested she visit the duke . . . and that she mention the ball."

He laughed, a soft, endearing laugh that invaded and encompassed her, resonating in the deepest regions of her heart. As he searched the clear, untroubled depths of her eyes, the significance of her "helping" dawned on him. It was a sign that she was coming back to her old self, back to the irresistible combination of spirit and sensibility that was the core of her. The earnest heart he'd fallen in love with was slowly mending. For the first time in weeks, his smile contained no reserve of worry.

"Thank you, angel." He bent to press adoring kisses on her temples, on her eyelids, the tip of her nose, and finally her mouth. She responded, opening to his kiss, leaning into his hard body, beguiled by his touch into forgetting place and circumstance.

A discreet bit of throat-clearing brought them abruptly back to the present. Eversby was standing down the table with his eyes averted and a rather uncomfortable expression. "Dinner, my lord?"

"By all means, do serve, Eversby." Rane looked up, refusing to relinquish his hold on his curvy little wife, even when she seemed to be insisting on it. He scooped her up into his arms and strode down the table with her to his great chair, settling in it with her on his lap. He was grinning like a devil, ignoring both Eversby's shock and Charity's silent, crimson-faced horror.

"It seems Lady Catherine and Lady Margaret won't be joining us. You can take them trays, later," Rane addressed the rattled butler. "I'm positively famished." He ignored Charity's covert tugs and whispers to engage Eversby's eye. "Just lay the food out and be sure the doors are closed behind you."

Eversby nodded, flushing even redder, and signaled the servants at the door to hurry in with the tureens, dishes, and trays. The doors finally closed, and it was a minute before Charity could open her eyes and glare at him.

"Rane! What must they think?! Poor Eversby, he's the epitome of courtesy and decorum. . . ."

"He'll get over it," Rane laughed, a wicked twinkle in his eyes. "This may be our last opportunity for such privacy in our own dining room, angel, and I think we'd better take advantage of it. We may soon be too fashionable to behave in such an indecent manner."

His hands propped her arms around his neck and he caressed her waist, her sides and hips, coaxing her agreement. Then his fingers moved to a dish of pickled olives and he slipped one into her surprised mouth. When she stared at him, he laughed and kissed her, sharing the taste of her olive.

They took their dinner in just such fashion, Charity ensconced on Rane's lap, the most delectable dish present, and the only one to raise his hungers as well as satisfy them. He nibbled the food and nibbled her, between ever-more-private caresses and long, twining kisses. They fed each other . . . dollops and mounds and drips and bites . . . combining sensual and physical hungers like greedy children, until the honey on the bread became inseparable from the honey of their mouths and they abandoned the rest of dinner to satisfy that more urgent hunger.

He slid her from his lap, then carried her up the stairs to their rooms in scandalously broad daylight. And once there, he pulled her stunning new gown from her and clothed her, instead, in a weaving of his own special magic . . . in the ardent, sensual devotion of his body and the lavish, healing warmth of his love.

Life at Oxley House had gradually taken on a more predictable flow, thanks to Rane's dogged determination to regularize their lives. He had quietly ordered the servants to be especially careful to avoid household accidents, and to report any such mishaps to Eversby only. He ordered Wolfram quartered in his study for the forseeable future, and established a strict schedule of freedom for him and for Caesar, to insure that their paths didn't cross. Wolfram seemed quite amenable to the arrangement; he was inordinately proud of his new, studded collar and relished his daily turns about the park with the two footmen that were required to handle him. Caesar, however, was put out of sorts by the restrictions placed on his accustomed territory, and vented his indignation on every upholstered piece of furniture in Lady Catherine's suite of rooms.

Things on the two-legged front had also seemed to settle into a routine. Each day Rane had risen early and spent the morning at his offices and the docks, while Charity endured fittings upon fittings and began to learn about the workings of Rane's house and the nuances of her position and London life. Increasingly, Lady Catherine had absented herself from the house, having thrown herself into paying social calls.

Now, though, that placid pattern had been disrupted by the advent of the duke's invitation and the resulting competition between Lady Catherine and Lady Margaret for social invitations. The head footman was kept quite busy answering the door the next morning. He ferried bits of vellum to Eversby, who ferried them to Charity, who dropped them into a pile on Rane's desk as though they burned her fingers—then rubbed her hands nervously to soothe them, afterward.

For a day and a half, the pile of invitations grew, spurred by Lady Catherine's determination and by their visit to the Duke and Duchess of Clarendon.

It was this visit that gave Charity her first uneasy glimpse of what it really meant to be in society. Rane was his most gentlemanly self, dressed in impeccable dove gray and possessed of a natural air of command. Charity looked exquisitely fair and beautiful, and yet somehow approachable, in her beloved sky-blue silk with the fine tambour-work frills inserted into its square neckline, and her embroidered velvet spencer. They arrived at mid-morning, and the silver-haired duke welcomed them broadly, while the gray-templed duchess could not have been more gracious. The duke drew them about the gold and crimson splendor of his massive drawing room, introducing them to a small horde of intimates, and insisting they stay more than the customary quarter of an hour to take some refreshments.

It was a small miracle, Charity believed, that she managed to remember all her very best manners and even smiled on occasion. Inside her, a screw of tension was turning ever tighter. Out of habit, her eyes kept returning to the mantel, with its Venetian porcelain figurines, and to the teatray, with its fragile china. She found herself eyeing the sturdiness of chair legs and wondering how well the gilt-framed portraits and landscapes were hung. The sight of all those pristine white gloves and all that vulnerable broadcloth and silk set her nerves on edge, and her anxiety soared when she noticed Gran'mere moving about the edges of conversations, covertly pushing figurines and miniatures back from the edge of the mantel and secretively ferrying vases of flowers and crystal candle globes to a table in a far corner.

Then the Earl of Albermarle set his teacup and sweetcakes down on the settee while he demonstrated something having to do with his hounds, and Lady Priscilla Granville sat down, smack in the middle of them. The cup and saucer broke, of course, and tea and gooey sweets were ground indelibly into both portly Lady Priscilla's silk dress and the settee. Gran'mere scowled and muttered that the old girl was just lucky that nothing got *punctured* in the process.

Charity's face drained, her shoulders went rigid, and she shrank from the commotion. Rane turned to find her withdrawing and glimpsed the cloaked horror in her lovely face. He read her thoughts in that look and glanced back at Lady Priscilla's exiting form and the murmur of commotion in the other guests. He realized Charity was blaming herself, her jinx, for Lady Priscilla's humiliating accident. He snagged her hands and made her look into his heated eyes.

361

"Charity—" His voice came in a low, emphatic whisper. "It had nothing to do with you. It was Albermarle's damnable carelessness!"

She swallowed hard and looked away, aching with confusion and feeling stained and guilty. As the others returned to their conversations with reddened faces and a sparkle of gossip in their eyes, Rane drew her along with him to the duke's side. He expressed their gratitude and extended an invitation to call at Oxley House any time. Charity somehow managed gracious comments to the duchess, agreeing to come again, for a more private chat, before the duke left London for his summer residence. Then Rane, Charity, and Lady Margaret departed for Oxley House . . . to numerous spoken assurances that they would see their new acquaintances again at the Duke of Sutherland's ball on Saturday.

All the way home, Charity was silent, and when they arrived, she avoided Rane by announcing she'd contracted a terrible megrim and going straight to their rooms. She felt his gaze on her, and prayed he wouldn't follow. She couldn't bear to see the disappointment, or the anger, she knew would be in his eyes.

Rane watched her go, feeling frustrated and impotent against her tenacious belief in her jinx. He considered storming their room, seducing her reason and her senses with another hot bout of lovemaking. It always seemed to help, always made her forget all about her wretched jinx. But only for a while. Something always happened to remind her. How long would it be? How much loving would it take to free her? Or would she ever be really free from it? Lord, he was starting to think in the same hopeless circles she did!

He heeled and blew through the front doors, onto the street. He had to get some air and exercise to clear his thoughts!

Charity rested on their bed for a while but was unable to sleep. She kept recalling the desperation in Rane's expression earlier and wished with all her heart she could just absorb his certainty and his skepticism, make it her own. If she could only just accept his rational explanations . . . and let the rest go. He'd said that everything had an explanation; it was probably true. Things got broken because servants—or belted earls of the realm—were clumsy or careless. People ruined expensive dresses and settees because they didn't look where they were sitting. Still, all the logic and causation in the world couldn't explain why such things always occurred in her presence. The slackened pace of calamity during these blessed days in Rane's house had lulled her awareness of it, but all she had to do was venture outside to be reminded of it.

She rose and drifted restlessly about the master suite, touching his things, wanting to give him the life he wanted with her. When the ache and confusion became too much, she fled their rooms and soon found herself at the door of Rane's study, being trammeled and licked thoroughly by Wolfram as she battled her way inside. She hugged the great beast like a dear old friend and admired his fancy new collar . . . and his elegant new accommodations. Then when she could avoid it no longer, she turned to Rane's desk and the forbidding pile of vellum on it.

She circled the desk warily, feeling anxiety creeping up her spine. When she had thought of helping Rane get the invitation and the entrance into society that he wanted so badly, she hadn't thought about the fact that she'd be expected to accompany him. Every one of those linen-textured packets was probably a disaster just waiting to happen. But it was what Rane wanted. It was the acceptance he needed.

Her heart began to thud and her mouth dried. She made herself reach for one and break the seal on it. The

363

Marquess of Weymouth wanted them for dinner in two days. Her fingers trembled as she opened another. The Earl of Brainerd summoned them to an intimate "soiree" . . . whatever that was. By the time she broke the wax seal on the third, her knees were weakening and she could actually feel the blood draining from her head. She put it down, unread, and started for the door, her head reeling. She opened it and smacked right into Rane, who was just returning from a long walk and a visit to his club.

"Charity?!" He caught her as she fell back. As she mumbled an excuse and fumbled to pull away, he glimpsed her pale face and dark, unsettled eyes. He tightened his grip on her arms and pulled her closer.

"Charity, what's the matter, what's happened?"

"It's nothing, really." She flashed a pitifully unconvincing smile to distract him. "I just came down to answer some of your invitations . . . but I must have risen too quickly after my nap. I feel light-headed. . . ."

"Charity," he gave her a shake, "look at me." It was a long moment before she surrendered to his hard grip and raised her eyes to his. The dark uncertainty, the fear in those clear, honey-golden eyes made Rane feel like he'd been gut-punched. He tore his eyes away to look at the pile of invitations and realized that they had something to do with her fear. "Tell me. What's wrong?" But even as he said it, he knew.

"Rane . . . I can't go. I . . . things will happen, terrible things. I'll embarrass you, or you'll get hurt somehow. . . ."

He stood, staring at the love imprisoned in her eyes, and knew he had to set it free. He had to break down those defenses, to rouse and touch her. And he knew of only one way. He swept her up in his arms and strode down the hall and up the stairs with her. Each labored breath, each wriggle of protest, fired his determination a bit more. Damnable superstition! He was going to have to love it out of her, every damned bit of it!

"Rane, please . . ."

But he was past listening, past talking. He kicked the door to their rooms open and ordered the startled chambermaid out. He plopped her on the bed and stood over her with his fists on his hips, looking dark and fierce . . . and hungry. A thrill of new fear ran up her spine, mingling shockingly with sensual excitement. Was this what the London ladies felt when they looked at him?

"Take off your clothes, angel," he ordered, his voice a menacing rasp. A wickedly carnal smile creased his features as he watched her eyes widen and her jaw droop. "I want to see your pale English skin under my hands. I want to feel your soft, cool body under my Barbados heat."

When she hesitated, he dragged her to the edge of the bed and began to peel her light spencer from her shoulders and grope for the ties at the back of her soft silk gown. Her panicky hands flew to rescue her blue silk and soon he was pulling her from the bed and dragging her soft dress and thin French chemise from her quivering shoulders. When she stood in nothing but stockings before him, he captured her hands and pressed them against his chest, rubbing them down his row of buttons to the flap of his trousers.

"Now mine," he demanded softly.

She chilled from both excitement and anxiety. Her nervous fingers moved to his top button and worked their way down. When they reached the buttons of his trousers, he watched, breathing hard as she released him. He caught her hand against his silky shaft and tilted his hips, thrusting against it.

Suddenly she was engulfed, surrounded by his heat and invaded by his desire. He poured around her and into her kiss, claiming her, driving everything but the rightness of that possession from her mind. Her legs weakened and her body blossomed in that exotic warmth, opening to him like a rare tropic flower, yielding him the sweetness of her response.

He pulled his clothes from his body without relinquishing her lips, then he lifted her against him and strode for the cheval mirror across the room.

"Rane! What are you—"

"Look at us," he commanded, turning her and banding her with his arms to hold her before the mirror. She clamped her eyes shut in shock.

"I can't—it's terrible luck, two looking in a mirror at once!"

"It's just silvered glass that reflects whatever is set before it. Have you ever seen your naked body, angel? Do you know how beautiful you are?" He lowered his mouth to her ear and murmured, "Look at us, Charity . . . look at the contrast of our skin. Look at your lovely breasts, your body . . . and mine. Look."

His hot whisper slid down the side of her neck and flowed caressingly over her bare breast. Her eyes opened helplessly on the sight of her own nakedness, framed and bounded by his bigger, darker form. There were her breasts, rounded and dark tipped with desire. Her eyes slid involuntarily down the curve of her waist and traced the flare of her hip and lingered in shock on the dusky curls that hugged her woman's mound.

As her wriggles stilled, the corded bands of his arms loosed across her and his hands splayed over her waist and slid down the pale curves of her hips. His touch was like liquid fire and the sight of his sun-darkened caresses claiming her body burned into her mind. Her heart was pounding, her nerves were tingling, preparing, as his palms raked her belly and rose to lift and cup her breasts. Her breath caught in her throat, watching and feeling his tanned fingers teasing, tantalizing her burning nipples.

Her hands came up to close over his, deepening his possession. Her slender white fingers coaxed and caressed

366

his, urging, directing them. A ragged sigh poured from her lips and she leaned back against his hot body, wriggling, luxuriating in the power that held her and in the shocking visual display of his dominion over her desires.

He turned her in his arms and turned them both so that their bodies appeared in profile, pressed intimately together. The curves of their backs and the erotic rounding of their buttocks . . . the seam where light skin was joined to dark . . . the soft bulge of her breast pressed against his hard ribs . . . the sinewy strength of his thigh pressed against her belly and smoothly tapered leg. It was breathtakingly erotic . . . shameless . . . sexual.

"Look at the way we fit, how we complement each other," he whispered hoarsely, tightening around her and pulling her fiercely against his aching hardness. He cupped her buttocks and raised her against him, bracing with his powerful legs and sliding between her parting legs. "Oh, angel," he groaned, "open to me . . . love me. You are meant to love me."

"Rane . . . I want you. I want *us*." Instinctively she tilted her pelvis and he found the center of her hot, creamy flesh. The reflection of their joining bodies in the mirror seared into her mind as he filled her, lifted her against him. Dark and light, hard angles and soft curves.

His muscles coiled and straining, he could wait no longer. He carried her to the bed and sank above her and deep inside her.

Their bodies moved in fevered synchrony, flesh lapping flesh in gentle abrasion, soft absorbing hard, bronze fused to marble in a tribute to passion's power. There was no fear, no hesitation in their hands and hearts and bodies. They moved and thrust, rising on drafts of pleasure, introducing passion's burning palette into the magic being woven, continued, between them. Their senses erupted with blue-white heat that exploded through their straining bodies. Clinging to each other, they abandoned all sense of space and separateness, expanding, merging in other planes of being . . . lost in each other . . . lost in love.

It was some time before Rane turned her onto her side and stroked her passion-bright cheeks to bring her back to him. The dreamy heat, the opened, unguarded look of love in her eyes meant she was his again, for a while. For how long?

"I love you, Charity." He pulled her fingers from his lips when she tried to stop him, and kissed them. "I intend to spend my life with you and to spend all my love on you. But I have to have you with me in the whole of my life. I won't settle for less. Invitations and entertaining and travel and work, whatever life brings us, I need you there with me."

Her eyes glistened at his certainty. "What if I make a fool of myself? What if disaster follows every place we go? What if—" She halted, summoning her courage. Her voice was hoarse with fear. "What if something terrible happens to you because of me, like it did to my father?" He heard her grief for her father so strongly that he missed the nuance of guilt in her question.

"Charity, I can't promise to live forever, any more than your father could. But I can promise you that you couldn't possibly do anything absurd in public that I haven't already done myself. I won't be ashamed of you, angel, ever." He took a deep breath. "The only thing that could possibly drive us apart is in your control." He felt her stiffen and tightened his hand on her waist reassuringly. "Your fears, Charity."

She tried to move away but he held her fast.

"Your jinx exists only in your mind and heart, but your fear gives it power over you . . . over us. It very nearly made you marry the wrong man, and it keeps you from doing things you want and need to do. It's keeping you from loving me fully and from making a new life with me, here, now." Tears flooded her eyes and he caressed her cheek to encourage them to fall.

"What was it your father said? Fear keeps you small. You told me that once, when I needed to hear it. And dear God, how right he was. Fear is like a cold hand in your gut that crumples you in inside . . . makes you feel dirty and useless."

It was true. She could hear her father's words, his voice, across the boundaries of life itself. Fear would rob you of life if you let it; it was the devil's tool, he had sometimes said. Fear would keep you small and alone. And fear itself was always worse than the thing that was feared. Only now did she realize why he had felt so strongly about it, why he had shielded her from her jinx . . . and from the fear it would introduce in her life.

Tears of grief and regret flowed down her cheeks and he pulled her against his broad chest and wrapped her in his arms.

"I've been afraid, too, Charity. Of spiders. Of not being good enough. Of being alone the rest of my life." He held her, feeling her slender shoulders quake, praying that some of what he said sank in, praying that the love that he felt for her and the loving they'd made would make a difference somehow. When she quieted and drew a shuddering breath, he lifted her reddened eyes to his.

"Believe in me and my love for you. Or believe in yourself and your own caring, generous heart. Or just believe in the magic we make together. Love is strong magic, angel, strong enough to counter your jinx."

"I do believe in you." She looked up at him through prisms of liquid crystal. "I believe in your strength and your goodness and your love. And I believe you love me." She bit her lip and her aching heart rose into her eyes. "I want to share your life and your magic. Rane, I'll try, I really will. I'll go to your ball and your dinners and entertain the duke . . . whatever it takes. And I won't be afraid . . . if you're with me."

He waited, hoping, then heaved a breath of relief and hugged her. She couldn't say it yet but it was there. She

369

did love him. And each time he loved her, he conquered a bit more of her "jinx" and claimed a bit more of her heart.

Someday, he vowed, he'd have it all.

That same night, Lady Margaret paid a second call. Well past dark, just before the moon was to rise, she hurried to a seedy little district at the edge of London's great sprawl, a place where cramped city and nature's open space met in a semi-permanent gypsy encampment. In the middle of a field, just off the road, sat a circle of faded gypsy caravans. And in the center of that circle was a communal fire that cast dark, dancing shadows on the trees and caravans around. Familiar smells of grease and greenwood smoke and garlic filled the air, stirring Lady Margaret's distant memories.

She had searched out the location of the renowned gypsy sage and seer, Princess Janov, reputedly an unparalleled authority on moon signs and lunar phenomena. One of the gypsy children, for a coin, led her to a caravan separated a bit from the others. She was met by a young gypsy girl, the old princess's great-granddaughter, and she explained her mission. After settling on a suitable gift in return for the princess's help, Lady Margaret was shown into the dimly lit caravan and found herself re-entering a long-ago world of childhood and wonder and awe.

In the dim, cluttered caravan, the old princess sat on a bed of feather cushions, looking quite aged and very wise. Around her, the walls of the caravan were painted with luck signs and symbols, and Lady Margaret was a bit unnerved to recognize so few of them. Princess Janov leveled a dark-eyed stare on Lady Margaret, listening to her story and to her problem. The old gypsy nodded soberly throughout and when "jinx" was mentioned, made several hand signs that Lady Margaret scarcely understood. For a long time after Lady Margaret finished, the princess sat in thought, the furrows in her aged brow deepening, her faded eyes lidding with assessment of the one seeking help. When at last she spoke, there was little comfort in her words.

"A true jinx is a rare and terrible thing," she said in a voice filled with the smoke of a lifetime of gypsy campfires. "There is only one born in a hundred years or more. And always the moon speaks of it." Her eyes narrowed and she sent the young girl out of the caravan to fetch a light for her pipe.

Lady Margaret found herself fidgeting like a child on a log around a campfire. "Well, I-I'm sure my granddaughter is one. I've told you about the black horses; they're scared witless of her. And the accidents and troubles since she was a wee thing . . . I've tried everything I know." Desperation crept into her voice. "Isn't there anything that can be done to break a true jinx?"

The old princess looked grave indeed. When she leaned forward, the great gold hoops in her ears rolled forward, as though to catch and enclose her secrets. "There is but one way . . . for a true jinx."

The hushed horror in her voice made the hair tingle on the back of Lady Margaret's neck. Her throat tightened so that she could scarcely breathe.

"A life for a life." The rasping words fell like hammer blows on Lady Margaret's heart. "A life given in love. A sacrifice of the heart. It is nature's way of restoring the balance of luck."

Lady Margaret stumbled from the caravan, horrified, wishing for all her life that she'd never come here . . . wishing she had never tried to read the moon. A life for a life. It would have been far better not to have known! She pulled her shawl tightly about her icy shoulders and somehow made her way back to the road where the hackney waited.

The old princess labored to the doorway of the caravan

371

and watched Lady Margaret fade into the darkness outside the circle of campfire light. "Amateurs . . . dabblers," she snorted. "They come and they stay with us for a little while . . . and they go off thinking they can read the moon. It takes a lifetime to know that sly old man . . . and still he keeps things back from you." She made a luck sign on the air with her hand and spat on the ground. "By the Light, I hate dabblers!"

The girl handed her great-grandmother the pipe and lit it for her, watching the old woman's dark mood with a respectful eye. "Do you think the girl is really a true jinx, great-grandmother?"

The ancient gypsy heaved a tumultuous sigh and lowered herself to a seat on the door sill. "Who can say? But that old dabbler has declared her one. That alone is enough to start strange things happening." The old lady stared at the girl's puzzled face and waved her to a seat on the steps by her feet.

"Once a person or a thing is declared to be a certain way, folks start to see it that way, whether it's true or not. And after a while, folks' beliefs and doin's begin to *make* it true. You'll learn, child, when you begin to read the palms and the cards . . . people see what they expect to see . . . and hear what they expect to hear." She turned her ancient head to look in the direction Lady Margaret had disappeared.

"That old dabbler believed she read a jinx in the moon. Now, she's probably got one."

Chapter Twenty-one

The next few days at Oxley House were blessedly un-eventful. Rane suggested, and Charity gratefully agreed, that they decline other invitations until after Suther-land's ball, to give them a bit more time to prepare. And Lady Catherine, with surprising generosity, offered to assume responsibility for all callers to Oxley House, entertaining them briefly, then sending them on their way. Lady Margaret kept to herself and her room a great deal, citing her lumbago and other minor com-plaints. Charity had worried about her grim look and chronic air of pain at first, but was reassured when the old lady finally bestirred herself and began to meddle in Lady Catherine's elegant entertainments. Charity and Rane were thus free to spend a few hours together each afternoon.

He took her for a carriage ride about London, point-ing out those places he had described to her from his sickbed at Standwell, and promising her a closer look at each in the near future. Then he drove her through the rowdy, bustling waterfront to show her his offices, and took her to two fine millineries to complete her ward-robe. Also together, and against Rane's better judge-ment, they took Wolfram for a walk each day in the park in the square. The great dog always perked up his lone ear and picked up his step to a jaunty prance. He was scrupulous about obeying Rane's commands, and by the time they reached home, Rane couldn't resist those laughing brown eyes and that mischievous lopsided grin; he found himself affectionately scratching the brute's good ear.

The sheer normalcy of it, the placid pace of things began to stretch Charity's nerves. Did it mean Rane was right—that the power of their love and their loving could somehow counter her jinx? Or was it only a lull in the inescapable course of disaster?

Contained within a fenced park of its own in the midst of London's fashionable west side, the Duke of Sutherland's London home was nothing short of a Georgian mansion. But for one magical night each spring, it also served as the portal to social renown and acceptance in the London ton. Everyone who was *someone* was invited to that glittering gathering that celebrated the triumphs and commemorated the notable social transactions of the passing season. And this year, the presence of Rane Austen, Viscount Oxley, was not only requested, but positively mandated by the curiosity generated about his abrupt marriage.

Stories abounded in whispers and sighs, both envious and indignant. It was a great love match; it was a grave moral scandal. His wife was a stunning blonde beauty he'd abandoned all to possess; his prize was a fortune-hunting temptress who'd taken advantage of his hereditary weakness of the flesh. She'd nursed him tenderly back to health; she'd beguiled him with love-philters. He'd stormed into her wedding and snatched her from beneath her rightful husband's nose; he'd gallantly rescued her from a forced marriage to a monstrous wretch.

However it was recounted or embroidered, it was a fascination to the staid and rigid ton, who suffered no breaches of their strict rules and conventions . . . except that rare violation so grandly romantic and so breathtakingly flagrant, that it must be forgiven. The dark, passionate viscount appeared to have met the ton's criteria for forgiveness on every count.

* * *

374

The air was thick and sultry for May, weighing on plumes and starched ruffles . . . and nerves. By the time the great, glassed carriage had inched up the line of vehicles outside the gates and entered the carriage turn at the entrance to the duke's house, all conversation had been plunged into expectant silence. Lady Margaret was humped and mumbling wordlessly and Catherine was stiff and vengefully silent. Rane had finally settled their vying over the right to accompany and introduce him and his wife by declaring his preference for the companionship of the Duke and Duchess of Clarendon. Neither grandmother could argue sensibly against such splendid company . . . and both sank into sulky silence.

Once or twice, Rane thought he caught a sniff of something unpleasant, but when he sniffed again, and again, it seemed to vanish. He looked up to witness Lady Margaret fussing with the multi-layered lace dickey over her bodice. When their eyes met, the old lady seemed to flush, and jerked her head away to stare out the window. He gave a suspicious sniff in her direction, but the trace of unpleasantness was gone, swallowed up in the sweet essence of roses which wafted from the woman sitting by his side.

Charity descended from the carriage into Rane's arms, radiant in an ivory silk gown with green and thread-of-gold cutwork embroidery on the squared bodice and short poufed sleeves. Her slippers were trimmed with stylish silk bows that, as she mounted the grand marble steps, peeped in and out of the matching embroidery that bordered the hem of her skirt. Draped casually around her shoulders and over her arms was a stunning, moss-green shawl, shot with tiny golden threads that shimmered in the golden glow of the dazzlingly lit entry hall. Her glorious blonde hair was caught up in a delectable mass of curls that flowed from

375

the crown of her head and swayed intriguingly as they mounted the grand, curving staircase to the ballroom on the second floor.

But for all her elegant appearance and seeming poise, her hands were icy inside her elegant long gloves. She looked up at Rane as they waited to be announced at the entrance of the ballroom, and was reassured by his warm, solid presence and his big hand covering hers on his sleeve. He wore a black double-breasted coat, cut away at the sides, and form-fitting ankle length trousers. His waistcoat was re-embroidered white brocade and there was a profusion of tasteful linen ruffles on his shirt. His pristine collar was banded by a pearl gray tie that matched his striking eyes. He stood in the doorway, a head above most of the men around him, looking dark and elegant and dangerously virile. Charity's heart skipped a few beats, and the wave of possessive warmth that coursed through her set her anxiety back on its heels. This was Rane's night.

Every head turned, every eye sought the doorway when they were announced. When the Duke and Duchess of Clarendon came forward to greet them, all present recognized the gesture as the endorsement it was, and soon Charity and Rane were engulfed in a slow, perpetual wave of powdered faces and perfumed presence.

Charity felt as though every part of her were being examined with an eye for fault; her hair, her use of fan and shawl, every nuance of her posture, the timbre of her voice, even the very shape of her body! It was little consolation that they scrutinized Rane with the same judgmental eye. That realization pulled her from her self-consciousness to study the curious and critical faces around Rane. It seemed that the paunchiest and pastiest fellows were most displeased with him, and it didn't take a gypsy sage to discern the envy in their sidelong glances and duplicitous greetings.

Jealous, she realized. Rane Austen was unique in a society that demanded conformity above all else. They counted him a threat to their bland and stiffling standards of manhood. He was too big, too dark, too intense . . . and too interesting. So they had excluded him. She lifted her chin at the thought and determined to make him as proud of her as she was of him.

At the edge of the group, Lady Catherine maneuvered with tenacious patience, waiting for the chance to introduce her grandson and his wife to her personal acquaintances before someone else did. But Lady Margaret, true to form, was not content with polite distance; she insisted on being at Charity's side, and constantly and shamelessly used her status as the duke's sister to manage it. Rane watched the old ladies at their maneuverings and sighed quietly. When the Oxleys and Clarendons began to stroll, the old grandmothers jostled each other for position none-too-discreetly, drawing dubious looks.

In pure desperation, Rane made mention of the fact that Lady Margaret undoubtedly knew how to read secrets in a person's palm. The old lady stared at him, slack-jawed. Shortly thereafter, she was besieged and swamped by lovesick young girls, fashionable matrons, and fortune-hungry younger sons. She watched, anxiously as Rane bore Charity away. Her plan had been to plant herself beside them for the evening . . . to extend them whatever protection she could from the very powerful amulets she had secreted in her clothes.

Lady Catherine appropriated them for a time, basking in the reflection of the attention focused on her recently claimed grandson. The young couple was eventually rescued by the young Earl of Meckton and Everly Harrison, who crashed the circle surrounding Rane and Charity and spirited them off toward the serving tables. Charity found herself the recipient of yet another sort of scrutiny, equally as thorough and equally as disturbing. Harrison captured her free hand and kissed her fingers a bit too passionately and Meckton followed him, gazing raptly into her flushed face and unusual honey-brown eyes.

"Ye gods, Oxley," Meckton moaned, as though in pain. "You said she was lovely; you didn't say she was absolute perfection." His eyes absorbed her with shameful eagerness. "She's beautiful . . . she's . . . positively divine . . . she's —"

"My wife, Meckton," Rane supplied meaningfully, removing the speechless Charity from his grasp and settling a possessive hand on her waist. The gesture and the silvery spark in Rane's eyes chastened Meckton. He suddenly recalled his manners and flushed, giving his blocky face a boyish appearance. Harrison stepped in with a twinkle in his eye.

"Has he told you about us, his reckless, Corinthian friends?" At the demure shake of her head, he smiled broadly. "Tsk, Oxley, are you ashamed of us? Or is it rather that you'd not have her ears sullied with the details of your prior life."

"I've been . . . busy, Harrison," Rane said casually, but with a less than casual eye on Charity's delectable little person. "Married life is much fuller than I had imagined." He left it to them to imagine exactly what filled his days and especially his nights. "And of late, I've taken up the study of magic . . ."

She started and looked at him, blushing furiously. But his devilish twinkle and Meckton's and Harrison's blank looks undercut the scandal of his statement. The suggestiveness was for her ears only, she realized, and was surprised by a small trill of excitement at the thought.

Meckton and Harrison watched the intimate acknowledgment Rane and Charity exchanged and were positively tantalized by it. For the next hour they were Charity's rapt attendants and Rane's good-natured annoyance.

378

Lady Catherine caught up with them as they swept from room to glittering room, and both she and Charity were occasionally pulled from Rane's side by a bevy of curious ladies. In one such covey, Charity found herself face to face with a slender, blonde young woman who might have been called pretty, but for the drawn quality of her face and the pinched air of hauteur about her mouth.

"Is it true, then, what is said? The viscount was wounded by ruffians and recuperated at your home?"

"The viscount was wounded and brought to our house by the local magistrate . . . to recover," Charity answered evenly, unsettled by the young woman's covert hostility. The screw of anxiety in her made another half turn and she glanced warily at Lady Catherine. The dowager viscountess had a perfectly inscrutable expression on her face as she watched Charity and the young woman.

"How perfectly ghastly. And how like him," the young woman said with obvious distaste. "He always did have a penchant for *reckless associations.*" Her dripping honey tone and lidded look carried the suggestion that Charity was to be included among those unwise liaisons. "Could it be — his intemperate ways have caught up with him at last?"

"Oxley seems to have a genius for narrow escapes, Miss Sutterfield," Lady Catherine declared with a meaningful look at the young lady, who stiffened. The old lady took Charity's arm and steered with regal poise toward the door. When they reached the hallway, Charity pulled her to a halt. For the moment, her righteous indignation eclipsed her social anxieties and even the fact that Lady Catherine disliked her.

"How dare that Miss Sutterfield say such things about Rane?!" she declared, twice angry for not having had the presence of mind to put the witch in her place. "She called him 'ghastly' . . . and named me the comeup-

379

pance of his 'reckless' ways!" To her surprise, Lady Catherine's face creased in a cool little smile. "Do you know that wretched girl?"

"I'm afraid I do." Lady Catherine's eyes narrowed evaluatively on Charity's anger. "Oxley made a public bid to marry her not long ago."

"He—he did?"

"She refused him, I heard. She or her father . . . it's one and the same, I suppose." Lady Catherine watched Charity's reaction to the news closely.

"Refused him?!" She was totally indignant. "So . . . he wasn't acceptable or fashionable enough for the limpet-faced Miss Sutterfield?! How perfectly stupid of her. He is the handsomest, kindest, most generous man I've ever known. He's a gentleman through and through, no matter what kind of language he uses. He's strong and honorable . . . even if he does have a stubborn streak a mile wide. He is sometimes high-handed, I'll grant you that. But you'll never meet anybody more thoughtful or considerate of those he cares for. Anyone with two good eyes can see what a perfectly wonderful man he is!"

Charity suddenly recalled to whom she was lecturing on Rane's strengths and virtues . . . Rane's prickly grandmother, who didn't have an especially high opinion of him either. She reddened violently and lowered her eyes, but she wouldn't take back a word of it or apologize for it. It was all the truth—and maybe the old lady ought to hear it, for once.

Lady Catherine stood feeling strangely convicted by Charity's bold and balanced defense of her husband. She'd watched Charity in the last few days. The girl was no moon-struck ninny, beguiled by a title and a few fancy gowns. She showed surprising sense and sensibility. For all her inexperience in social matters and managing a great house, she did catch on quickly. Now, when she described her husband, it was with surprising clarity as well as with affection. She knew his faults full well, and she loved him and defended him fiercely anyway.

The old lady's throat tightened. She didn't want to be wrong about Rane Austen. But over the last week she'd gradually come to see him in a new light. He had managed to amass a decent fortune and he'd had the brass—or the uncommon sense—to marry the woman he truly wanted, instead of marrying just for advantage or position as his handsome father and grandfather had. Perhaps it was time she got out her "two good eyes" and looked at him, really looked at him.

"Remarkable, how things that seem disastrous often work out to be blessings in disguise," Lady Catherine observed after a productive silence. "If Miss Sutterfield hadn't refused him, he wouldn't have been free to marry you, my dear. Do bear that in mind."

Charity's ire and defensiveness melted strangely. Those words could have come from Rane himself. She recognized the deeper level, the broader scope, of their meaning and was utterly unable to resist or refute it. The evidence was inescapable; good often did come from bad, benefit from disaster. Then she realized with genuine surprise that it was her marriage to Rane that prickly Lady Catherine was offering as the "good" to come from a difficulty.

"I shall, my lady," she answered with a soft twinkle in her eye.

"I say, Oxley—isn't that Miss Sutterfield with your wife?" Harrison had craned his neck to look past Rane's shoulder. Rane had turned in time to catch the reddening of Charity's cheeks at something Gloria Sutterfield had said. Then he watched his grandmother turn Charity away from Gloria's company and steer her out the door. He had to stay another minute or so, to not make too obvious an exit. But he excused himself as soon as possible to look for them. He found them in the hall, staring silently at each other with odd, almost pleased, expressions on their faces. And when they turned to him, both smiled.

He ushered them into the Duchess of Clarendon's company for a short while and was drawn into a conversation on the economic hardship caused by the protracted difficulties with France. But his eyes and thoughts strayed to Charity's lovely blonde form, then to Gloria Sutterfield, who was visible across the room. He couldn't help noting and savoring the contrast between them. Gloria was pale and thin-shouldered and her expressions and movements seemed lifeless beside Charity's vibrant coloring, sweetly voluptuous figure, and gracious, genuine manner. It baffled him that he had once coveted Gloria Sutterfield to the point of distraction.

He had wanted a lady-wife, not a woman, he realized. He'd wanted a trophy, something pale and perfect and uninvolving, something to be acquired and set on a shelf to be appreciated for the status it bestowed. But he had *needed* a woman. Someone, not something. A warm feminine presence in his life, a challenge to his defensive pride and a balm for his troubled heart, a partner for his passion and a focus for the feelings he'd long denied; he had needed a love. And Charity was that love, a caring heart that had disrupted his narrowing, hardening world and resurrected the heart and soul of him.

He looked around him at the forced smiles and guarded eyes of proper society. Each word amongst them was fraught with levels of meaning, each action or comment was meant to display and impress, every human transaction was governed by ponderous rules of place and decorum, and was valued only where it produced "advantage." How could he have wanted this posturing and pretense so badly?

Some while later Rane and Charity found themselves face to face with the unpleasant Miss Sutterfield and her betrothed husband, the frog-faced Viscount Harrowford. It seemed every eye in the ballroom was on them as Harrowford kept Charity's hand a trifle longer than propriety allowed and gazed a bit too openly at her evident sweetness and sensuality. Miss Sutterfield was goaded to rashness and turned to Rane with a burning look.

"You'll have to forgive his lordship's inattention. He's just come up from a time in the country. But I'm sure you already know how bad country air can be for one's manners . . . as well as for one's skin."

Charity bristled, on the verge of a hot retort, but Rane coolly insisted that they were being summoned by her host and escorted her off. When they were safely out the door, he pulled her down a dimly lit hallway and watched her fume and sputter.

"She's marrying him? That poor, scrawny little Harrowford fellow?" Her eyes narrowed vengefully. "Somebody ought to remind her that if you play with toads, you get warts."

"Lady Charity, I do believe you'll hold your own quite well in society." Rane laughed and, without even looking to see if they were alone, pulled her into his arms and into an achingly sweet conspiracy of a kiss.

Through the light super at midnight, Charity felt the dark looks and not-so-secretive whispers that Gloria Sutterfield aimed across the rows of banquet tables. Her ire began to smolder. Rane and Lady Catherine made a point of ignoring Gloria's snide behavior, and Lady Margaret was too busy watching over the luck of the dining procedures to notice much else. But Charity had never encountered such blatant malice in her life, and reacted to the injustice of it with every fibre of her being. This was the envy and prejudice that Rane had

had to live with for years, she realized. Her blood heated a bit more in her veins with each sly, disparaging glance, each haughty comment Gloria made to her wine-warmed companions.

Rane saw the flush of Charity's cheeks and the stiffness of her spine and slid his hand reassuringly over hers beneath the tablecloths. She smiled gratefully at him and lifted her chin, trying valiantly to ignore Miss Sutterfield's spite. But when Gloria made an exceptionally loud and unladylike comment about "milkmaids and ridiculous old gypsies," then alluded to the "thickness of Devon's clotted cream," it was just too much.

Charity's eyes narrowed, her hands coiled into fists in her lap, and she turned a slow-burning look on Gloria Sutterfield, that was enough to heat the whole south end of the banquet hall. Her heart was pounding, and her muscles contracted with a massive urge to shake the crimp-faced twit until her head rattled. For the second time in her life, she actually wished someone bodily harm!

Gloria shot back an icy little smile, having gotten the reaction she wanted, and declared she was bored with "all this stuffing and swilling." She pushed to her feet and gave Harrowford a thump on the arm with her fan, insisting a bit too loudly that she simply had to have a breath of air.

Harrowford dutifully rose to remove her chair, swaying noticeably from his numbing indulgence in champagne. He bumped into Gloria when she paused for one last comment, startling her, and she tossed him a scathing look over her shoulder. When she jerked huffily away, there was a loud ripping sound, and she halted and whirled to find he'd caught the wispy silk of her dress underfoot. A third of her fragile voile overskirt had been pulled from its stitching and now hung limply down her back.

Sputtering hotly at the beet-red Harrowford, Gloria

recoiled irritably from both him and his assistance . . . straight into a tray of fruit compotes held by a servant who had paused in the middle of serving to gawk at her torn dress. Stemmed glassware and fruit went crashing, and Gloria stared around her in horror as necks craned and eyebrows rose and a few gentlemen pushed to their feet at the sound of the commotion. Embarrassed now, she snatched up her drooping voile, raised her chin to a proper English angle, and started for the door . . . only to have her heel hit a loose strawberry and go flying from beneath her. She squealed and flailed . . . and soon found herself sprawled on the marble floor amidst bits of squashed fruit and shattered glass and the collective stare of the almighty ton.

Charity watched, stunned, as the crimson-faced Gloria was helped to her feet and fled the banquet hall in full humiliation, her ineffectual viscount trotting along at her heels. Charity's face flushed hot with satisfaction and her eyes sparkled with unseemly glee as she fought to keep the corners of her mouth from curling up. When she looked at Rane he was chewing the inside of his lip and scowling, his shoulders twitching. Their eyes met, laughing, speaking the same thought before they were forced to look away. There was nothing quite like a well-timed dose of disaster. . . .

Disaster. Charity's smile faded slowly as that word caught and echoed in her head. She swallowed hard. Only an instant before, she'd been wishing all sorts of ruination on the insufferable Miss Sutterfield. And within the space of a few heartbeats, the object of her ire was being humiliated before the entire assembly!

A small embarrassment, a voice inside her insisted. But her heart lurched and began to thump desperately as though something were pursuing it.

A minor mishap . . . a mere tumble, her better sense pleaded against the gathering alarm in her middle.

Coincidence, reason declared desperately. *Perfectly explain-*

able.

She looked up and found Lady Margaret staring at her with a look that was clearly worried. Her stomach pulled into a tight knot and her heart began to beat erratically. Her mouth was dry and her hands were icy in her lap.

As they quitted the banquet room, she watched the wine-warmed faces of the people around her as they talked and gestured and postured, searching them anxiously and fighting the cold, creeping dread that was claiming her bit by bit. She tried telling herself what Rane would probably tell her: *What happened to Gloria Sutterfield had nothing to do with you.* But it didn't quite have his conviction or his reassuring warmth.

As they strolled through the ballroom, it began again in earnest . . . *the trouble.* The Countess of Ravenswood dropped her fan and the very portly Comte de Brionesse, who had consumed massively at supper, bent gallantly to retrieve it . . . and popped the straining rear seam of his breeches. The sound of fabric parting company was audible several feet away, and the poor comte made an inglorious tactical retreat, backing straight into a lit candlestand and knocking it over so that it bounced and rolled under the brocades at one of the long windows. One of the few still-burning candles nipped the edge of the fringe of the drapery and the dry, dyed fringe pouffed into quiet flame that licked merrily up the border of the drape, crossed the volatile fringe along the elegant cornice, and plunged down the fringe of the drape on the other side of the window.

By the time the poor comte was ushered from the room, there was an eerie ring of light around the entire window and flames were biting into the drapes themselves. A strangled cry of "Fire!" rang out, and several gentlemen charged the flaming draperies, ripped them from the window, and stomped and beat out the flames in the bare nick of time. Even with the danger past, several ladies took the vapors and had to be assisted from the room. The Duke of Sutherland hurried in to assess the damage, ordering the musicians to play on while the servants cleared away the mess.

Charity stood along the wall, staring woodenly at the commotion and coming to her senses only when she focused on Rane coming toward her with Everly Harrison. She hadn't even realized he wasn't beside her. Both were breathing hard and wiping their sooty hands and faces with handkerchiefs. They'd been among that quick-thinking group that saved the ballroom from going up in flames.

"Is it . . . safe?" Her face paled and her knees weakened as she grabbed his sleeve. The smell of smoke that clung to his clothes enveloped her, invaded her, increasing her anxiety to a visible level.

"The flame is completely out; nothing to worry about." He looked down into her darkened, luminous eyes and the grin on his roguish features tightened, then began to fade.

"Rane, you might have been hurt," she whispered hoarsely.

"But I wasn't." He watched her fingers curl tightly on his sleeve as the hauntingly familiar worry crept into her eyes. He groaned mentally, taking her hands boldly in his. "Old drapes . . . and recently dyed . . ." He gave a judgmental sniff that parodied uncannily the disparaging gesture Charity had been seeing all evening. "One would think a duke could afford better."

"I trow Sutherland insisted on all those additional candlestands. He prides himself on setting an atmosphere," Harrison took it up with a conspiratorial sniff . . . that led to another sniff of his smoky clothes and a wince. "It must have started from those candles old Brionesse toppled. . .," his voice lowered to a wicked whisper, "after he split his breeches. Lord, the old boy's a walking disaster this evening."

Disaster. The word went through Charity like an icy blast and she stiffened. Breeches and candlestands and fires . . . a growing wave of misfortune that had very nearly set the duke's house ablaze! She fled Rane's cajoling look, trying desperately to hold onto reason. For the last several days, in the safe haven of their home and bed, it had been so easy to submit to Rane's tenacious reason, to adopt his certainty. But now, on her first venture into his world with him, all her borrowed convictions were slipping from under her feet, deserting her!

Rane watched her struggling with what had just happened and felt some of her anxiety affect him. He looked at her braced, rigid shoulders and the strain evident in her lovely face, and his free hand curled into a fist at his side, itching to fight for her. But there was no one, nothing to use it on. His rival for Charity's love was not vulnerable to physical resistance or economic force or any other mortal agency . . . it was her own fear and her belief in the destructiveness of her presence in his life.

Over Charity's shoulder, he saw Lady Margaret hurrying toward them and read the old lady's fears in her face. He knew he couldn't allow Charity to see them. Thus, declaring they both needed a breath of decent air, he turned her quickly and ushered her out the door.

On the main stairs, in the great marble entry hall, they passed two inebriated young gallants who were so busy ogling the bevy of young ladies preceding them up the stairs that they forgot their own feet. One stumbled on the stair runner and fell, clutching at the other, who was caught off-stride and fell into the wall with a great thud . . . that rattled a portrait of one of the duke's illustrious ancestors and sent it sliding down the wall. The fallen portrait cartwheeled corner-over-corner down the long curving staircase, where it bashed into a houseman who was just untying the ropes that held one of the two great crystal chandeliers, preparing to lower it to trim the candles while there were few guests in the hall.

Rane had hurried Charity down the stairs to avoid the confusion and now pulled her a few steps away . . . just as the servant was struck and lost control of the rope . . . which released the great chandelier. There was only a tinkling "whosh" from above and a strangled cry from the servant. Rane's head came up, and in half a heartbeat he was lunging out of the way, sweeping Charity before him and sheltering her with his body.

The shrill crash of brass and crystal penetrated nearly every room in the great house. The sound brought guests and servants running from all directions, crowding and shoving to see what had happened. When Charity and Rane finally turned to look, one of the great chandeliers lay on the marble floor in a sea of shattered prisms. And all around, crowding into the entry hall, were faces filled with surprise and dismay . . . turning on them.

Charity clung to Rane, her heart pounding, her senses reeling. When he loosened one arm about her to tilt her face up and ask if she was alright, she could only nod. He led her quickly through the crowd and chaos and through the empty halls until he found a nook at the far end of the long, window-lined gallery and pulled her trembling form into his arms.

"Rane!" She suddenly came to life against him, pushing back, covering his shoulders, his chest, his head, frantically with her hands. "You're alright?" By the bright flashes of jagged silver lightning visible through the window in the night sky, she searched his face for reassurance.

"I'm fine, angel." He caught her hands and brought them to his lips, sharing her relief. But as soon as that first sight of release was spent, he watched her expression change to one of pure horror and felt as though something had stomped on his lungs. Oh, Lord—disaster again.

"Rane, you were almost—" her throat squeezed so that she could barely say it, *"killed!"* The word beat in her mind, like a muffled drum heralding terrors yet to come. Her knees weakened and everything in her middle seemed to be melting and sliding toward her knees.

"Charity, I wasn't even hurt! It was an accident, a stupid mistake . . ." He halted, mastering his sudden flare of anger. "I'm whole and hale—"

"But not for long! Don't you see? Gloria and the fire and now the chandelier—I should never have come here!" She pulled away sharply, her body rigid with fear and self-blame. "We have to leave . . . now . . . this minute! Please, Rane—"

He caught her by the arm as she turned, and hauled her back to face him. "Charity, you're not responsible for what happened. Those clumsy fools knocked the picture down and it rolled—"

"Do you know what that means?!" Her voice was hoarse with fresh anxiety. "It means a death. When a portrait falls, it means a death soon—and you were nearly killed a moment after it fell!"

"Another damnable superstition!" He wanted to shake her and he wanted to hold her. He was aching for her and he was furious with her. Anger and compassion warred in his blood as he searched the tense, volatile silence between them.

"If you don't take me home, I swear—I'll walk," she choked, biting her lips as anxiety overwhelmed her. "I'll walk—all the way to Standwell!"

There it was. Her ultimatum. The one he'd dreaded.

Logic and restraint both exploded in him. He was past reasoning and arguing and persuading, and even past seducing. It was damn well time for an ultimatum of his own! His eyes narrowed and began to shimmer. His shoulders swelled as he straightened above her and his fingers tightened on her shoulders. His chin jutted, and he was suddenly "Bulldog Austen" with a vengeance.

"I am gut-flinging sick of your damnable jinx, Charity Austen." His voice came in a furious growl, rattling her down to her very toes. "There is no such thing as a jinx, woman! And I'm going to prove it to you!"

He released her so abruptly she staggered and, under her bewildered eyes, he ripped his elegant coat from his shoulders and turned it inside out. Then, with his eyes glaring white-hot defiance, he jammed his arms into it again and smiled furiously at her, his coat on inside out.

"R-Rane?" She swallowed the surprise in her voice and scowled frantically at him. "Just what do you think you're doing?"

"I'm proving to you that there's no such thing as luck . . . or jinxes." He reached down and pulled off one of his shoes, flinging it aside with a defiant flair. Then he seized her arm and dragged her down the gallery with him, striding with one shoe off, one shoe on.

"Rane—have you lost your senses? Put your other shoe back on!" She struggled to pull her arm free to go back for it. "It's terrible luck to walk with only one shoe on—" He pulled her to him and smiled rather nastily. "I know."

Horror bloomed in her as he dragged her bodily through the hallways, nodding with effusive gallantry to the people they met. He obviously intended to make an exhibition of themselves. "Rane! Stop this!"

She tried digging her heels in to slow them to a more dignified pace, but he pulled her into the drawing room, striding half-shod and with his coat inside out, under the quizzical eye of the ton's elite. She managed to keep up with his driven pace and to lift her burning face and square her shoulders as he stood making their excuses to the disaster-dazed duke and duchess. Her stomach sank as Sutherland's eyes widened.

"You are aware, Oxley, that you have your coat on inside out?" the duke mentioned hesitantly.

"Quite, Your Grace." Rane smiled his most devastatingly charming smile, kissed the duchess's hand, and ushered Charity briskly out the door. He doggedly ignored Lady Margaret's call from the far side of the entry hall.

Lady Margaret had seen the fire and seen Rane whisk Charity from the unlucky room. She had hurried out after them and begun to search . . . then she heard the terrifying crash and shatter and came running to find a ruined portrait and a shattered chandelier. They couldn't be far away, she reasoned, and she began to search in a dead panic. The troubles were escalating at a dangerous pace!

Then she saw them rushing for the door and anxiety overwhelmed her for a moment at the sight of Charity's panicky face and Austen's inverted coat and missing shoe. Something terrible was about to happen, she knew it! But by the time she pushed and shoved her way through the guests gawking at the ruined chandelier, they were out the door, gone. She looked up, shaking her hands frantically, and found Lady Catherine bearing down on her.

"What the devil has gotten into them?" Catherine demanded through clenched teeth and a plaster-tight smile that fooled nobody. "Oxley came charging into the drawing room with his clothing in disarray, spoke to the duke and whiffed out—"

"They're in trouble . . ." Margaret tried desperately to think.

"They certainly are! One can only hope people are in their cups enough not to recall his behavior—"

"I have to get home before something happens. A carriage—I've got to have a carriage!" Margaret hitched around, searching the crowd distractedly. Then it came to her. "Teddy!"

Catherine was appalled by the way Margaret wheedled and bullied the duke. But within minutes his carriage, placed at their disposal, was being brought around. She contained herself until they were stowed in the duke's luxurious landau, then vented her anxiety in outraged indignation at Rane's behavior. "Things were going so well until he started acting like a madman."

"He's not mad. He's probably just doing what any man would . . . married to a jinx."

"A what?" Catherine stared at Margaret. By the light of lightning flashes she saw genuine fear in her whitened face.

"My Charity's a jinx," Lady Margaret said hoarsely. "A bringer of bad luck. It was because of her the chandelier came down."

"That lovely child, a *jinx?*" Catherine made an unladylike snort of disbelief. "That's absurd. You've sniffed one too many of your smelly old chicken gizzards—"

"Livers!" Margaret snapped.

"Whatever!"

Chapter Twenty-two

The storm that had been brewing all evening had begun to break with a fury . . . both in the night sky and in Charity Austen's soul. The wind whipped fiercely and flashes of lightning ripped through the roiling clouds, coming closer. The sky growled and snarled like a live thing, setting the carriage horses on edge. They shied and reared as Rane pulled Charity amongst them, searching for their carriage, and Charity pulled him to a halt.

"Do you see—I always make horses jittery!"

"And I suppose a sky full of lightning and thunder have nothing whatsoever to do with it!" Rane growled with frustration and the veins of his neck were visible as his eyes rolled skyward, borrowing strength from the tumult overhead.

He stuffed her, bodily, into the closed carriage and ordered his driver, "Move!" She huddled back in her seat, torn between fear for his safety and anger at his high-handed flaunting of the most common luck-sense. Explosive flashes of blue-white light coming through the carriage windows burned the image of his determined face in her mind. They careened through the streets, and with each violent pitch and sway of the vehicle, her anxiety rose another notch. He was furious with her . . . there was no telling what he might do once they were home.

The first, huge raindrops pelted them as he pulled her from the carriage and up the front steps. He charged straight through entry hall and into the dining room, where he made straight for the salt cellars on the sideboard. Before her disbelieving eyes, he opened one and poured it out onto the floor with a vengeful flourish.

"You can't do that!" She bent to collect a pinch to throw over her shoulder, but he prevented her, bracing over the spilled salt.

"What damage could a bit of spilled salt possibly do? Charity, think, for God's sake. The worst that could happen is that somebody could slip on it." The dread in her face spurred him hard. "That whole superstition is nothing more than a simple prohibition against wasting a necessary commodity!"

"There's more to it than that. Rane, you can't just fly in the face of luck!"

"Oh, but I *can*." The gleam in his eyes promised retribution of all the irrational forces that had constrained and distorted his life with her. "What I *can't* do is live the rest of my life with half a wife . . . half a heart . . . half a love! I won't go through life looking for bogards behind every bush and doom in every salt cellar. I can't live like that, Charity, and I don't believe you have to either. You can choose not to. You can choose reason and freedom . . ." He paused. His voice lowered and need welled in his eyes. "And love. You can choose life, angel. You can choose me."

He took one step toward her, then another. Pained confusion and longing boiled up inside her, swirling like a vaporous, smothering cloud. Could it possibly be as simple as just *choosing?* How could she just walk away from the guilt and blame of a hundred small catastrophes, call it coincidence or pretend it didn't exist? She stumbled back, trembling visibly. The turmoil in her delicate face and dark topaz eyes was painful to watch.

"Say it, Charity," he whispered, letting his need reach out to hers. His roused senses absorbed every nuance of fear and hope generated by the battle he could see raging in her eyes. When she tore her eyes from his, frustration poured through his veins like hot coals. So close . . .

they'd been so close!

"Then I'll just have to face down your damnable *luck.*"

He snagged Charity's arm and pulled her along to his study, where he took the ladder from the bookshelves and lofted it over his head. With pure insolence, he struck off for the main stairs—*walking under the ladder.*

"Please Rane, put it down . . . you don't know what might happen!" She bolted after him, catching him on the stairs, then shrinking back against the wall to avoid the long, narrow ladder. She was caught somewhere between outrage and anxiety. "Please—we'll talk—"

"We've already talked."

He climbed the stairs and ducked through the doorway of their rooms with the ladder. Then he paused, looking around, deciding. He propped it against the canopy of their bed and stood under it for a long, mutinous minute. Then with a flash of remembrance, he strode to the hearth and extracted the old shoes she'd hidden there and carried them to the window . . . and threw them out into the storm. The shoes tucked behind the drapes went next, and then the pan of coals from under the bed and the mistletoe torn from the bedposts. As the wind blew rain in the open window, he wiped the salt from the sill and went to the hearth to do the same. Everything . . . he was going to purge every bit of superstition, no matter how small or seemingly harmless, from their lives!

Charity watched him disposing of her protective charms one by one and felt as though he were stripping them from her very soul. The sights and smells and sounds of her early life and the myriad little rituals that had been a part of every day, of every life event at Standwell, billowed in her mind and senses. She was suddenly smothering in dark, icy waves of memory.

The "lucky silver thimbles" of girlhood stitchery came back to her, and the admonition, to "Never stitch a garment still on a person, lest you stitch sorrow to his back." Bits of the stories that had made simple wooden spoons

396

and brooms and eggs seem magical recurred in her thoughts and dissolved into the little chants and rhymes that explained and predicted things. "Red sails at night, sailor's delight . . ." ". . . Friday's child is loving and giving, Saturday's child must work for its living . . ." "One crow, sorrow; two crows, mirth; three crows, a wedding; four crows, a birth." Her head filled with the remembered smell of leaves and potent herbals drying in the corners and around the doors.

But from the dark corners of her mind came darker memories of the nights she had lain in her big, cold bed, terrified of the goblins that the everpresent superstition had placed in the dark around her. No matter how long the night is, her father had reassured her many times, the morning always comes. She recalled her feverish, childlike prayers, begging for God to let the morning come and save her. And in her mind she was suddenly lost in that darkness again . . . alone and frightened . . . praying desperately for the light.

The room was lit eerily by the almost continuous flashes of lightning. Tension mounted around them like floodwaters as rain lashed the windows and the chamber vibrated with the low, powerful rolls of thunder. The fierce turbulence in the elements outside seemed to stir the conflict raging in her soul.

Was it really just salt, just old shoes, just dried leaves? Her father's voice rose inside her head, speaking her thoughts. What power could old shoes or coriander seeds or garlic in chicken livers or dead rabbits' feet, possibly have over a human life? How could they protect someone against heartbreak of illness . . . or death? They certainly hadn't protected him . . .

Rane watched her pale to a deathly white and saw the horror deepening in her lovely features. He felt her slipping further into her fears and, in sheer desperation, he removed his shoe and strode to the long, cheval mirror they had used so memorably on a sultry afternoon. Too late, she cried out as his arm whipped forward. With one stroke, the mirror shattered into a hundred pieces.

"Noooo," she groaned, rushing forward to grab his sleeves and pull him away from the ominous, glittering fragments. Her fingers dug into his arms. "That's seven years! Now something terrible will happen to—"

"Nothing is going to happen to me!" He grabbed her by the shoulders. "Dammit, Charity, there's no magic stored in mirrors or horseshoes or manmade charms! There's no mystical power, good or bad, in words or in luck rituals or avoidances . . . or in the damned moon. You've brought nothing but good things into my life, Charity. You've filled my house and my bed and my heart in ways I never expected, in ways I never knew existed. I love you—"

"So did my father . . . and he's dead! Oh, God, Rane—don't you see—I'm responsible!" The confession was ripped from the very bottom of her soul and her voice was tattered from the violence of it. "He'd lost everything but Standwell and had to turn to smuggling. It was my jinx that sent him out in that vicious storm, and it was me—*me*—who doused the guide lanterns that would have brought him safely home that night." The awful truth reverberated in her head and in her heart. *Me . . . it was me.* Dry sobs mingled with her half-strangled confession. "Don't you see . . . I killed him."

Her words and the torment in her face and quaking frame stunned him for a moment. He'd finally found the key. And a moment later he was reeling mentally from the impact of it. She honestly believed she was responsible for her father's death—worse!—that she'd actually killed him! He stared, breathless, at the pain visible in her eyes and understood, for the first time, the fierce guilt and grief that had driven her to accept the unacceptable . . . to believe in something beyond reason. Her grief had demanded an explanation for something as final and terrifying as death . . . and superstition had supplied

398

it. Then together, grief and guilt had manufactured her a role in the misfortune that had taken her father's life.

"Charity, you're not responsible for your father's death." His voice was low and fierce with conviction. "It was the damned rocks and the wind and the sea—"

"No!" She shook her head frantically and tried to wriggle from his hands, but he held her tight. "That night I found two lanterns burning in the window of the room Stephenson used and I put them out. They were the lanterns that were meant to guide the boat in. I thought Melwin had left them burning, and I put them out. So you see, I caused the wreck, I—and my jinx."

A terrifying crack of lightning and thunder exploded in the room and she convulsed with terror in his grip. The storm—it was just like the storm that had taken her father from her! Lightning and wind and tempest . . . and danger. Rane had already been in peril twice tonight . . . Her eyes widened in fresh horror. It was happening all over again! If she didn't get away from him, something terrible was going to happen to him! She began to struggle violently against his hold, and the panic in her heart gave her strength enough to wrench free.

"Let go—you have to get away from me!" she rasped, staggering back, staring at him, sliding beyond the reach of reason. "The storm . . . lightning could . . ."

In that searing moment, that next breath, that next pulse of blood, the decision was made. He lunged at her and dragged her to the door, overpowering her panicky protests. He pulled her up the darkened stairs at the end of the hall . . . one flight, and then a second, very narrow, set of steps that wound in a slow, creaking arc through terrifying blackness. He pulled her higher in the house, feeling his way toward the storm. The walls shuddered around them and the steps resonated beneath their feet with each fresh assault of thunder.

"What are you doing?!! Turn back, please!" she begged. But he pulled her through the doorway at the top of the steps, into a large and lightning-lit attic. Dark shapes loomed, draped and indistinct, ominous in the erratic light. She froze and he half-carried her across the attic to a door, where he set her on her feet and turned her to face him. His features were dim in the dying flashes of a lightning streak, but his eyes burned like coals as he spoke.

"I love you, Charity. And when I come back inside, I don't ever want to hear the word jinx on your lips again." He stripped the coat from his shoulders and stepped out the door onto the wooden widow's walk . . . straight into the hungry jaws of the storm.

"When you come—Dear God, no!" Her whisper was absorbed by the crackle and explosive pop of yet another bolt of lightning striking nearby. The white-heat of that cataclysm melted her fear-frozen response. "Rane! Stop this—come back inside! Please! I'll do whatever you say—"

His white shirt made a ghostly silhouette against the blackened sky as he spread his muscular legs and straightened his broad shoulders, bracing against the elemental fury. The rain lashed him in visible waves and the wind buffeted his big body bruisingly. He managed to turn so that he faced the doorway and in the surreal, blue-white flashes of light, his face was defiant.

Her heart beat in straining, painful spasms as she stood in the rain-whipped doorway, calling him above the roar of the storm, pleading. Each time she said his name, it seemed the thunder crashed and rolled . . . as if tolling for him. She watched him standing there, defying luck and nature and even death itself . . . his love for her burning in his eyes.

For one moment she was lost . . . sinking . . . drowning in fear as she clung to the doorway. Lightning would strike him . . . he would die . . . without ever hearing her tell him that she loved him. Down that treacherous wooden walk, he waited, loving her, wanting her freedom

400

more than he wanted his own life.

If he died, she didn't want to live without him. And it didn't make sense that she wouldn't live with him, love him . . . if he lived. Either way, she had to be with him now, had to share his peril and his hope and his fate.

She dashed out onto the widow's walk, grabbing for the railing, working her way toward him. The rain stung her face and tore viciously at her thin gown, but she felt none of it. She ran the last few steps, throwing herself into his arms and wrapping tightly about him, molding her quaking frame against his. She blinked against stinging rain and burning tears as she looked up into his face.

"I love you!"

A wave of pained pleasure surged through his body, releasing the tension. "Louder!"

"I love you!" she yelled again. And again and again, each time stronger, surer. "I've always loved you."

His arms tightened possessively around her and he pulled her head against his chest, sheltering her against nature's rage with his big body. They stood together, the wind and rain lashing them, braving luck and nature and even death itself . . . together.

It might have been minutes; it might have been hours that they stood there, above the London rooftops, in the very eye of nature's fury, joined in embrace and, finally, in love.

The winds slowed as the brunt of the storm passed. Soon the sound of the rain emerged from the trailing rumbles of thunder. It drummed, then pattered on the rooftops around them, plinked on metal flashings and gutters, and splashed on the wood of the railing around them.

"Charity?" Rane's voice sounded as drenched as the rest of him.

"What?"

"We're still alive."

"Are you sure? This feels heavenly to me." She spoke into his wet shirt, nuzzling the hard warmth beneath it. He had to strain to hear her.

"Oh, yes, angel. I'm sure," he laughed, tilting her chin up to cover her lips with his. "We're going to live to be a hundred!" It was a warm, splendid treasure of a kiss amongst the cool rivulets of rain trickling down their faces. And when it ended, Rane lifted her into his arms and carried her carefully back along the rain-slicked walkway and inside.

He had to let her descend the dark curving stairs by herself, but every few steps, in the dark, he paused to take her into his arms and kiss her breathless. And as soon as they reached the third floor, he lifted her again and carried her down the final flight and into the hallway leading to their rooms.

"They're here! Up here!" Lady Margaret saw them coming from the far end of the hall, near the steps and called to someone over the railing. She scurried down the hallway to meet them, slowing and halting as she came close enough to recognize that they were both dripping wet . . . and coming from the stairs leading to the roof. They were soaked through. They'd been out in the storm . . . on the roof! "Merciful Lord," she choked.

Lady Catherine arrived a moment later, puffing and panting. "Where in thunder have you two been?" She scowled fiercely at their drenched clothes and dripping hair. "You had us worried sick about you!"

"Really?" Rane's wet grin curled wryly on one end. "That was awfully decent of you, Lady Catherine. Worrying about us."

"The old gypsy here," she flung a contemptuous hand at Margaret, "kept babbling on about jinxes and danger . . . had me quite beside myself!" She glared hotly at Lady Margaret, who was busy searching Charity's glowing face. "Not that I believed a word of it, of course. But with the storm . . . Ye gods, how did you get so wet?"

"Are you alright?" Lady Margaret's eyes flowed anxiously over Charity and over Rane's possessive grip on her, obviously worried by the fact that he carried her. She started to make a gypsy hand sign and Charity reached out to grab her hand and prevent it.

"We don't do that anymore in this house, Gran'mere." She squeezed the old lady's hand lovingly and met her eyes, then looked at Rane. "We don't need it. We'll make our own luck from now on."

Lady Margaret saw the love glowing in their faces and knew they'd finally settled it between them. Charity had chosen his way of reason and logic and rational fact, and there wasn't a thing she could do about it. They had reached the limits of "luck" and she had no idea where they would proceed from here.

She squeezed Charity's hand, fighting the rising tears in her aging eyes, then released it. "You don't want to come down lung-sick. You'd better get out of those clothes," she muttered gruffly, stepping aside.

Rane laughed wickedly, staring at Lady Margaret's reddening face. "My thoughts exactly."

He carried Charity into their rooms and Lady Catherine roused to thoughtfully close the door behind them. When she turned, she found tears rolling down Lady Margaret's weathered cheeks.

"What's to become of them, bitter-bones?"

Catherine came to take Margaret's hands. "They'll be fine, old hob. Come, I'll make Eversby find us some brandy."

Rane plopped Charity in the middle of their big, dimly lit bed and spread his long, heated body over hers in one exuberant lunge.

"Rane!" She pushed him back, laughing.

403

"Ummm?" His smile had a devilish tilt as he ignored her resistance, holding her tightly against him, rubbing her with his whole body.

"What are you doing?!"

"Isn't it obvious? Then I must be doing something wrong. . . ." He lowered his mouth to the cool, wet skin of her shoulder and nibbled his way along her collarbone to the base of her throat.

"But we're wet."

"Umhummm. I like you wet, remember?"

She sucked a sharp breath at the heat of his hands as they closed possessively over the tightly molded silk of her dress and the chilled curves beneath.

"We'll get the bed wet . . . we'll . . . ruin the covers," she protested just as his lips captured hers, massaging, grazing, plundering hers in continually changing combinations. Fearing she might already be too late, she gave it one last try.

"You heard . . . what Gran'mere said," she managed between lush, consuming kisses. "You have to take my clothes off!"

That brought his head up. He stared into the seductive lights of her eyes and grinned his lascivious best.

"Lord, yes. How could I be so thoughtless? Your lungs . . ."

He lowered his weight to the bed and lifted her to untie the laces at the back of her wet silk, and soon he was peeling it from her cool, damp breasts. He paused, staring at that bare, rose-tipped bounty, then covered it firmly with his big, warm hands. "I do love your . . . lungs . . . angel."

Heat billowed through her like a delicious cloud of steam. "More . . . take them off . . . everything."

But he pulled her wet garments from her at a maddeningly slow pace, showering kisses and nibbles and hot caresses on every inch of gooseflesh he uncovered. She squirmed and laughed and held her breath, finally begging him to hurry. But he was determined to torture her with her own longings, and when he rolled the last stocking from her leg, he began a slow, thorough passage up through all the "lucky" places on her body. The arch of her foot, the insides of her knees, her hipbones, the sides of her breast . . .

When she could stand it no more, she pushed up to sit naked before him, and attacked his buttons and breeches with a ferocity that took his breath. Soon he was as bare as she and, in one last blast of reason, he slid from the bed and pulled the wet counterpane from beneath her, flinging it onto the floor somewhere.

"Is it alright if I still call this 'magic'?" she whispered, running her fingers over the smoothly mounded muscles of his chest. He shivered.

She was suddenly on her back, engulfed, trapped between down-filled satin comforter and lust-filled male body.

"What else could you call it?"

She felt his hardness pressed against her thighs and wriggled them apart, then quickly back together, trapping his hardened shaft in the silky grip of her thighs. He groaned and arched and thrust, over and over . . . sliding upward through the soft resistance of the sheath she'd created. As he reached the summit, she relaxed her legs, giving him the access he'd earned. And with a perfectly aimed thrust, he joined their burning bodies.

They began to move, lifting, arching in supple synchrony. Their senses welled, filled with pleasures too many to contain, even as their forms contracted, binding and compressing each other's passion so that the flame between them flared dangerously. Tongues of fire licked up the walls of their bodies and seared paths along their nerves, until their very bones seemed to glow white-hot. Once, twice more . . . and they exploded together, flung through searing suns and burning stars . . . consumed, transformed by the fire . . . leaving the dross of fear and pain behind.

Together they floated free, joined inextricably in the bright tapestry woven of their destinies and their very beings. Between them, there was no reserve, no fear, no hesitation. Between them was an enduring bond of commitment, woven by love's fingers on the loom of experience.

They lay on their sides, facing each other, their bodies touching only at toes and knees and noses . . . and hands. They listened to the dying storm in their blood and to the dying storm outside. Rain drummed softly against the great windows, a steady, reassuring murmur, like a lullaby.

"Do you know how I came to be called Rane?" he said softly, staring into her honey-gold eyes. She shook her head.

"Tell me."

"My mother always like the sound of the rain. And on the night I was born, she lay listening to it . . . and decided to name me for it."

Her hand came up to stroke the side of his face and trace the bold sweep of his lower lip. When she spoke, there were tears in her eyes.

"I hope it 'Ranes' every day of my life, for as long as I live."

Hours later, they wakened, touching and holding, smiling secret smiles, and sharing the evening's tumultuous events. They laughed again over the look on Gloria's face, and Charity actually managed a chuckle over the fat comte's split breeches. She still couldn't find any humor in their narrow escape from the chandelier, but had to smile at the memory of him stalking through the duke's house with one shoe off.

"Heaven, Rane, what will they think of us? You with your coat inside out and wearing only one shoe, dragging me through the halls bodily, rushing off—"

"They probably think I'm a madman holding you captive . . ." He ran his palm over one of her nipples in lush, repeating circles. "Inflicting my base animal desires on you . . . ravishing your enticing, delectable blonde beauty over and over and ov—"

"Be serious." She stopped his words with her fingers and her face reddened slowly as his hand continued those erotic volutions over her tightening budded-rose tip.

"I am serious." His mouth curled in a rueful grin as he lifted his eyes from his sensual play.

"Well . . . does that mean we won't be in society anymore?"

He laughed. "It's not exactly likely to enhance our acceptability." He kissed the slight crease in her brow, then trailed kisses down to her love-swollen lips.

"I'm sorry, Rane. I know how much being included in society meant to you. And now because of me and my—" His hand stopped her words and his eyes narrowed. When he took his hand away, she finished, "Stubbornness. I was going to say 'stubbornness.' Now you're probably back to being a pariah socially. Could we apologize somehow? Perhaps if Gran'mere talked with Uncle Teddy again . . ." His eyes were closed and his hands were making distracting circles over her buttocks and the backs of her thighs. She shivered. "Rane—"

"Let's just ignore it all."

"What? But you . . ." She paused, mid-wriggle.

"Let's do other things, like travel. I know you'd like that. And I've always had a yen to buy some land . . ."

"But you already have land."

"I do?" His eyes came open.

"Standwell. You acquired it when you acquired me." She watched his face grow pensive and thought he was probably connecting her home to some painful memories. But in truth he was realizing that he hadn't even considered that. Where she was concerned, his hard-driving business sense had failed him completely. "The land is very good." She smiled at his frown. "And we can take

407

down all the horseshoes."

He grinned, allowing the glow of her reassurance to warm him. But even through one of her lush, intensely rousing kisses, something lodged in his mind, something important, about Standwell. He raised his head to look at her and recalled the things she'd said before they went on the roof, the sense of guilt that had driven her to accept her jinx as truth.

"If the land is so good . . . then why was your father so penniless?" He watched her eyes darken and felt her stiffening, bracing against him. "I think I can tell you why. Because it wasn't well managed. The decline of Standwell's fortunes had nothing to do with you or any 'jinx.' Your father was a good man Charity, even a wonderful man. But he didn't manage the place well. And it was *his decision* to take up smuggling and *his decision* to go out in the boat that night in the midst of a raging storm. You can't go on blaming yourself for the decisions other people make, or for their carelessness, or their inability or weakness or foolishness. . . ."

She bit her lip, opened and listening. She was ready to hear it now, to face it. Her eyes misted as waves of childhood memory came rolling over her. She watched them through adult eyes now: the many times her father left his ledgers to go hunting or fishing with Gar and Percy, the times his tenants had come to see him and found him gone. She recalled the numerous times he'd told Gran'mere the rents were short again and shrugged, saying they'd have to let another servant go. She thought of their contrast to Rane's daily trips to his offices and his "hard work" on the docks. It was a night for truth, for confronting and putting away girlhood fears and illusions. Her beloved father, Upton Standing, was indeed a good man. But he wasn't a good manager. And Rane was right about the rest, too. It had been her father's decision to take up smuggling and to go out in that storm.

"But I did extinguish the lanterns that night, Rane."

Tears trickled down her cheeks and he wiped them with his thumbs. He could feel the letting go, the acceptance of it, in the subtle relaxation of her body against him. He felt a great slide of relief in his chest. Now to that last thorny point, that sin of commission. . . .

"Lanterns. You mean regular tallow lanterns?" When she nodded, he pushed up on his elbow and drew her up with him as he scoured his memory. "Charity, they couldn't have been using those lanterns to guide their boat in. It was a howling storm, and Gar and Percy said they had to go further out than usual, outside the bay. A regular tallow lantern wouldn't be visible beyond fifty or a hundred feet in a storm like that . . . much less all the way to the mouth of the bay." She shook her head and sat up, rubbing her temple with a trembling hand, confused and trying desperately to make sense of it.

"But there were two of them. They were the guide lanterns, why else would they have been burning?!"

"I don't know. Maybe those lanterns were meant to guide them to the house, after they got to shore." He could see her testing his explanation in her mind. "Charity—we were out in a storm tonight, a storm just like the one your father died in—you said so yourself." He sat up and took her shoulders in his hands, making her look at him. "Think. Did you see any lights around us tonight? There are houses all around, and there must have been a few lights somewhere. Did you see any?" His hands tightened on her, forcing her to face it as he lifted her anguished gaze into his.

"Did you?"

"No," she whispered.

The reality of it, the logic of it engulfed her and the hope that had been swelling in her now burst into fear-melting certainty. Through a blur of tears, she saw his smile begin and spread, a sign of his triumph in logic and in love. She embraced both him and the truth he

409

had brought her in the same delirious hug. It was true; she wasn't responsible for her father's death! A suffocating dark cloak of guilt had just slid from her shoulders and she felt buoyed, freed.

She showered him with big noisy kisses between tears and laughter and *"I-love-you's."* She wrapped herself around him, soaring, sharing her joy and relief with him. Within a kiss and a heartbeat, he was joining their bodies, coaxing her astride him, adoring every inch of her lovely body and every impulse of her freed and loving heart.

He made love to her like a starving man, voraciously, urgently, consuming her. And she gave him the full range of her passions . . . arching, purring, demanding, submitting . . . an erotic feast of response.

They sprawled and snuggled in sated exhaustion and finally relinquished each other to the healing arms of sleep.

Late the next morning, they awakened to Eversby's discreet cough. Rane sat up with a start and pulled the cover up snugly about Charity, who was pushing up beside him, blinking and rubbing her eyes. Both were puzzled by Eversby's presence in their rooms and by his cheery greeting.

"Your ladyship." He nodded at Rane but addressed Charity with a triumphant grin. "That commodity you ordered me to search the docks for each morning . . . we found it! Several pounds of it!" He turned and clapped his hands and one of the housemen wheeled in a linen-draped cart, set with a large silver tray bearing . . . a pile of yellow and black tube-like things arranged in clusters.

"Bananas!" Rane shouted, scrambling madly to pull a bit of cover around him as he bounded from the bed. "It's really bananas!"

Charity and Eversby exchanged wondering grins, then watched raptly as he reached out like a little boy to touch

410

and then take one. He fidgeted with anticipation, glancing up at them as he handled it.

"It's plenty ripe . . ." He tore at the stem, peeled it, and stuffed half of the white, fleshy inner fruit into his mouth at once, shuddering with ecstasy. He finished the rest in one huge bite and tore into another, then another.

On his fourth, he looked up to find Charity smiling at him from the edge of the bed, on her knees. He reddened furiously at being caught behaving like a gluttonous boy. "You? You ordered them to search me out some bananas?"

She nodded and he beamed pleasure, insisting that she taste one and declaring she was going to love it. The bland, sticky-sweet mush of a slightly overripe banana filled her mouth and she tried to smile as she made herself swallow it. She declared it "interesting" and insisted he enjoy the rest himself . . . which he did.

He pulled up a chair beside the cart and peeled another, stuffing his cheeks with it. The little boy with the sunburned cheeks that lived inside him appeared in his twinkling eyes, beaming gratitude at her.

"Angels and bananas," he said with a satiated grin. "I must be in heaven."

Chapter Twenty-three

Charity floated down the grand stairs in the entry hall, dressed in her new marigold-yellow sprigged muslin. She paused halfway down to survey the graceful sweep of the warm mahogany bannister and the pleasing contrast it made with the white marble tile and pilasters and the gilded cornices of the domed entry hall. It was warm, livably elegant, and it reminded her so strongly of Rane that she smiled.

It had been five glorious days since the ball and her decision on the rooftop. They had loved and romped and laughed and flaunted their affections shamelessly. Lady Catherine was scandalized by their behavior, Lady Margaret was grieved by it, and the household staff was alternately charmed and embarrassed by it. The only one who seemed genuinely delighted was Wolfram; their dalliance meant two long walks in the park each day, one with them, and one with the footmen. And once there, it meant that Rane and Charity were so absorbed in each other, they forgot about him, and he was able to slip his lead to chase pigeons and chew up flowers and nose around after that matched pair of sleek afghan hounds that the Countess of Swinford kept next door.

But on the fourth day, Rane rose early and departed for his offices and the docks, and things began to return to a more normal pace. Then the Countess of Swinford came to call. It was a regulation quarter-of-an-hour visit, marked by nothing more monumental than the exchange of pleasantries and milliner's names, and an itinerary of summer plans, now that the season was officially over. But the sheer ordinariness of it was an implicit declaration that the Viscount and Viscountess Oxley were not going to be shunned because of a bit of irregular behavior at Sutherland's ball. Apparently, those who had been sober enough to recall the incident were inclined to put it down to romantic excess and wink at it.

Now, as Charity stood on the stairs, Brockway came into view, struggling to pull something on a rope through the side archway into the entry hall and muttering hotly under his breath. She came down a few steps to look and, as she expected, saw Wolfram crouched on his haunches, feet splayed, resisting being dragged into the entry hall with everything in him. She hurried down the steps to assist and Wolfram gave her a guilty, petulant look when she appeared.

"I won't have this, Wolfie. If you don't cooperate, you won't get your extra walk at all." He huddled back, looking unrepentant and even insulted by her ultimatum. "Very well." She took the rope from Brockway's hands and trundled him back through the doorway and across the narrow hallway, into Rane's study. She stooped beside him to untie the rope on his collar, giving him a good scolding. "Shame on you! It's a good thing Rane isn't home. . . ."

The sounds of someone arriving at Oxley House drifted through the archway and as Charity worked fruitlessly at that stubborn knot, Wolfie lifted his ear and his nose, alerted by something. He listened and sniffed, training his senses on the low rumble of human voices. Suddenly he streaked for the door, knocking her back on her bottom. She scrambled up and gave chase, calling furiously, but came to a dead stop in the entry hall, staring at Wolfie, who was braced stiff and glaring . . . at Sullivan Pinnow.

"Baron." Charity's face pinked and she drew herself up straight to meet his scrutiny.

"Viscountess," Pinnow said with a slight hiss, bowing extravagantly. He took a step toward Charity, and Wolfie lurched between them and sank to a preparatory crouch, growling and snarling.

Pinnow staggered back a step and Brockway made a lunge for Wolfie's still-attached lead rope. A moment later, Eversby appeared at a run with an under houseman, and together the three managed to subdue Wolfram. Charity pressed a hand over her heart and apologized, ordering Brockway and Jordan to take Wolfie out for a good run. When they had dragged the great dog out the front doors, she turned a tense little smile on the baron and asked Eversby to have Lady Catherine and Lady Margaret join them . . . and to bring them some tea.

"So sorry, my lady," Eversby winced. "I forgot to tell you; Lady Margaret called on the duke this morning and Lady Catherine . . . insisted on going along."

Charity's heart sank at the news. She would have to suffer the insufferable baron's visit by herself. She led him into the drawing room and he paused, just inside the door, to survey the place. His icy blue eyes trailed from the ceiling friezes to the carpets on the floor, then coolly tallied the value of the sumptuous furnishings and paintings. And as he took stock of Charity's world, she covertly examined him.

His manner was oddly harried and his usually immaculate dress was slightly off. His gloves bore stains, his starched collar had been crumpled and restraightened on one side, and his blue broadcloth coat had a creased, lived-in look. There were deepened lines about his eyes and mouth, etched by frequent tension and strong emotion. When he turned his cold blue eyes on her person, she looked quickly away and felt a slight chill.

"What brings you to London, Baron?" She invited him to a seat and took one herself. But instead of sitting, he came to stand near her, staring at her in a way that was alarmingly personal.

"A business opportunity," he said, with a knowing tilt to his mouth. "I've left district administration and public life . . ." *Just one step ahead of arrest and imprisonment,* he snarled

414

privately.

He had fled Devon five days ago, even as the Crown's auditors were uncovering and collapsing his fragile network of financial shams and paper-shuffling contrivances. He was in dire legal straits, probably being hunted this very moment, and the money he'd managed to grab on his way out of Devon was too insignificant to count. Desperate circumstances required desperate measures, he realized. And once in London, he had begun to plan a bit of opportunity and a bit of revenge.

"You've got quite the little nest here, your ladyship." Pinnow smoothed his vest, smiling his cool smile as he cast eyes about him. "Oxley must have been better fixed than you realized." There was a flash of raw heat in the glance he turned on her. "Or perhaps you did realize. Quite astute of you. And not very perceptive of me . . . to miss the shrewd little opportunist beneath all that sweetness and simplicity."

Shock prevented Charity from responding, and Eversby appeared a moment later with the butler's cart laden with tea and sweet cakes. She turned to him and waved it off with a trembling hand.

"It won't be necessary, Eversby. The baron won't be staying." When the puzzled butler withdrew, taking the cart with him, she rose to face Pinnow with a cold sense of dread creeping up her spine and down her legs. They were alone in the house . . . except for a few far-flung servants and Eversby, whom she'd just dismissed. She realized now that this was anything but a social call. What did he want with her?

Pinnow turned with an unpleasant light in his eyes and read the discomfort in hers with vengeful pleasure. "You know, *Lady* Charity, in my capacity as Magistrate of the Mortehoe district it was my duty to have a thorough knowledge of the doings in the area. I became privy to numerous . . . secrets, things that the good people of Mortehoe would rather not have exposed to public scrutiny." A chilling smile appeared on his thin mouth and Charity braced visibly.

415

"Recently I came across evidence of your father's involvement in a bit of illegal commerce. Smuggling, your ladyship. Your father was a *smuggler*. And I have the testimony of Gar Davis and Percy Hall to substantiate it. I caught them in a bit of poaching . . . and they sang like birds to save their hides."

Charity blanched. The icy baron knew; it made her knees go weak. "Gar and Percy . . . would never say such things about my father," she raised her chin to combat the sinking inside her. "I don't believe a word of it."

"I don't care what you believe, chit." Pinnow stalked closer, irritated by her cool rebuttal. "The authorities will believe it . . . as will your precious husband, the ambitious Viscount Oxley. Think what would happen if he were to learn his toothsome little bride was no more than the spawn of a common criminal."

Her shoulders twitched and her hands balled into fists at her sides. Her cheeks caught fire. The wretch! How dare he come here!

"I could arrange to take that damaging knowledge with me, out of the country . . . for the proper price."

She jolted back, seeing the full scheme of it now. He wanted money in exchange for silence. Well he had chosen the *wrong secret* and the *wrong victim* to make his dirty fortune from!

"His lordship knows about my father's old activities. He learned just before we were married and is fully reconciled to it. I've kept nothing about me or my family from him," she declared hotly. She was pleased by the anger her announcement struck in him . . . briefly.

"Then, if you don't find my proposition interesting, the authorities will. I'm sure they will be delighted to launch a full investigation. Your husband's name will be dragged through the papers and perhaps even through the courts, when they attach Standwell for reparations."

She whirled away, wringing her icy hands, thinking furiously. He'd do it. He'd go to the papers or the authorities

416

. . . and whatever respectability they'd begun to acquire would be shattered. For one brief moment, she considered paying him to keep his wretched silence. Then Rane rose in her mind's eye, shrugging at their new social acceptance, suggesting that they travel and refurbish Standwell instead. Her head snapped up and she stared at Pinnow's pallorous face and sharp, conniving features. What if she called his bluff, told him to go to the officials and to the papers with his stories?

"Then by all means, Baron." Her voice was surprisingly steady. "Do your civic duty. Go to the authorities with your nasty little accusations. And we shall see who they believe." Her eyes slid pointedly over the shabby edges of the Baron's form. "The Viscount Oxley . . . or a *former* magistrate."

Her refusal and her queenly poise in the face of his threats sent a bolt of fury up his spine. His face reddened to a dusky orange color and his fists clenched impotently.

"You little witch. You don't think I'll do it, do you?"

"I don't care whether you do or you don't, Baron. Now if you'll be so good as to leave . . . before I call the servants to remove you."

She read defeat in the jolted look in his face, unaware that it heralded the snap of the last civilized restraint in him. She was totally unprepared for his lunge. He grabbed her by the shoulders, and snarled down into her shocked face.

"You conceited little bitch! You ruined my future before and you'll not do it again!" He met her struggles with rabid force, shaking her and growling. "I swore I'd make you pay for your treachery—and I will . . . in cash . . . and in flesh. You're coming with me!"

His eyes burned with unnatural light and his thin lips were foam-flecked as he spat his threats. She'd been right; he had no intention of going to the authorities. But her refusal had only raised the stakes in a more desperate and terrifyingly personal game.

"Let me go! You can't—" As she opened her mouth to

scream, he whipped a sharp stiletto blade from the inside pocket of his coat and waved it menacingly before her face.

"Shut up, witch." The yellowed gleam in his eyes said clearly that he would enjoy using it on her, and her cry strangled in her throat. "You're coming with me," he declared, his fingers biting into her upper arm as he dragged the tip of that sharp blue steel over her chin and down her throat.

"If you and your precious viscount make it worth my while, I may let you come back . . . when I'm through with you. How much are you worth in his bed, I wonder?" His ugly laugh stopped her blood. "A thousand pounds?"

"You'll never get away with this," she rasped, her eyes dark with shock and confusion. But the steely tip of his blade continued down the smooth skin of her chest and traced the visible mounds of her breasts with terrifying menace.

"He raced all the way to Devon to stop our wedding. Five thousand? More?" He straightened, savoring the traces of fear in her eyes. "We're going for a sociable little walk, your ladyship."

"You'll never get away with this! They'll find you!"

"But they may not find *you*." The tip of his blade nudged sharply through the muslin over her ribs as he wrapped her arm with his and held her tightly against his side. "Move!"

Another sharp nudge convinced her he meant it, and she began to walk, searching frantically for a glimpse of Eversby, or Brockway and Wolfie, or even a housemaid. But they made it to the front door unseen, and stepped out into the street. There were no carriages, no couples strolling the promenade, no passerby to note their departure. It fired her panic and she balked. She felt the earnest bite of his blade against her ribs and jolted.

"I said, move!" he whispered furiously. "Or I'll cut you right here!"

She swallowed her heart back into place and bit her lip, doing his bidding. She had to almost run to keep up with his long legs, but the physical strain of his frantic pace was an unexpected mercy. It gave her no time to dread what would happen . . . when they stopped.

To the casual glance, they looked like any fashionable couple hurrying along the street. But to Brockway, who, from the park across the street saw them emerge from the house and hurry down the street, something seemed odd. He was just about to remark on it to the under footman when Wolfram caught sight of his mistress and the unpleasant baron and came to immediate attention. A split second later he was at the end of his rope, lunging furiously, barking in great, angry "rolfs."

Brockway and his assistant struggled against the dog's frantic force, pulling and heaving together to reel him back. But as he came almost within reach, the knot at his collar that Charity had worked at loosening finally released. He went bounding off down the street, in the direction of the corner Charity and the baron had turned, barking furiously. Brockway gave chase for a block or two, led by the great dog's barking, but then the barks stopped and neither the mistress nor her horse of a dog were in sight. He staggered to a stop, puffing and wheezing, then turned back toward Oxley House, wondering how he was going to explain this to Mr. Eversby . . . and his lordship.

Wolfram stopped on a street corner, his sides heaving, as he raised his great head to search for them. Being a "sight hound," he couldn't rely on his nose at much of a distance. He needed visual cues as well. A movement just around the edge of a nearby corner enticed him and loped off in that direction, finding an empty alleyway when he arrived. He put his big nose to the ground and ran back and forth, sniffing earnestly.

Humans, he thought, sorting scents, *too many humans!* The narrow alley smelled like *chamberpot* . . . and *tomcat* and *old damp* and *no food.* He raised his head briefly and sniffed. He froze then, concentrating on a tickle of roselike scent . . . *Miz Charity!* He wagged his head, determining which direction the scent was strongest and took off at a lope with his head up and his eyes peeled.

Most of the time he smelled just *old fish* and *rotting* and *horse plop*. But twice more he got an encouraging noseful of roses and they led him toward the docks. He dodged kicks and swerved out of the way of trundling wagons and sotted sailors, looking and sniffing. *Grease;* he passed an open tavern door. *Food!* He paused before a bakery, inhaling deeply, salivating. That was a mistake; it took precious minutes to get the cling of yeasty wheat and cinnamon out of his nose. By that time, the trail was cold and he found himself near the docks, assaulted by a whole new set of salty and confusing smells.

His head sagged. His tail drooped. But in his canine mind rose a remembered scent, sandalwood, and a strong impression of stern, powerful hands. *The lordship!*

Now all he had to do was get home.

Pinnow forced Charity along the most deserted streets and alleys, sometimes dragging, sometimes shoving, but always with that cold steel scratching against her ribs, daring her to draw too deep a breath or to call out in any way. The buildings around them became tenements and taverns, then the shabby old depots and great looming warehouses which indicated they were nearing the docks.

He finally pushed her through a wooden door in the side of an old brick warehouse and forced her through a maze of stacked crates and barrels toward a lighted clearing. Three seedy-looking men looked up at them from a barrel on which they were playing cards, and their grizzled faces lit with interest on his knife and his prisoner.

"You!" Pinnow fixed the closest fellow with a stare and jerked a nod toward the door. "Go tell your captain I've got a new proposition for him. Now!"

A minute later Charity found herself dragged down a set of rickety steps. She was forced through a doorway into a crowded storage room containing piles of old cargo nets, canvas tarpaulins, and cable. Pinnow released her with a shove and stood blocking the doorway, brandishing his blade as though enjoying the feel of it in his spidery hand. She whirled, feeling a bit off balance, and rubbed her bruised arm to revive the circulation in it.

"You'll never get away with this." She lifted her chin to combat the cold clutch of panic in her chest. Shock and threat had immobilized her resistance earlier, but now that her head was clearing, she was physically trapped.

"I already have, sweetest. I've got you here . . . in my hands. And all that remains is to let your precious viscount know my conditions for giving you back to him. You humiliated me by spreading yourself for him, you dirty little trull, and I intend to see you pay for it in kind."

He stalked toward her, his eyes glowing dully, his face twisting into a sneer. She dodged and scrambled to escape, climbing over piles of cable and around small kegs and barrels. His third lunge was full on target and she found herself pinned against the far wall with Sullivan Pinnow forcing himself against her, his knife at her throat.

"I remember your lips, witch . . . and how I could make that hot little body of yours squirm with pleasure . . ." His pelvis ground against her and his hand came up to squeeze her breast.

"Your touch makes my skin crawl," she gritted out, bashing his hand away with her fist, then pushing him with all her might. He staggered back, surprised. His face flamed and in a blind fury he drew back a fist.

Her head snapped viciously to one side and fireworks exploded in her head . . . just before everything went black nd she crumpled down the dingy brick wall.

Lady Margaret and Lady Catherine arrived home late in the afternoon in a mutual snit.

"You had to drag out those stinky old amulets of yours!" Lady Catherine huffed, jerking the ribbons of her bonnet loose and removing it with an irritable flourish. "I thought

Lady Melbourne was certain to head over in a dead swoon!"

"Lumpy old newt . . . acted like she'd never seen ferret feet before!" Lady Margaret growled petulantly, thrusting her shawl into the housemaid's hands.

"I shan't be able to hold my head up!" Lady Catherine pressed her temples and closed her eyes, looking as ashen as her customary gray sateen. "In one short week you've reduced my acquaintance by half!"

Eversby hurried into the entry just then, and at the sight of the old ladies, his face fell. "I heard voices and thought perhaps Wolfram had come home."

"Wolfram? Gone?" Lady Margaret turned to him.

"It seems he got away from Brockway and Jordan earlier, and hasn't been seen for several hours."

"Good riddance, I say." Lady Catherine sniffed with an arch look at Lady Margaret.

"He ran off after Lady Charity and that gentleman . . ." Eversby glanced at Brockway and seemed a bit uncomfortable. "I don't wish to seem alarmist and perhaps it's not my place, but . . . she hasn't returned either."

"Gentleman?" Lady Margaret scowled. "What gentleman?"

Eversby straightened the tie at his throat and motioned Brockway forward to substantiate his story. "Her ladyship had a caller this afternoon; she seemed to know him. She ordered tea, but when I brought it she said they wouldn't need any . . . that he was leaving. Then Brockway saw her leave with him from across the street and he marked it as a bit odd . . ." He motioned to Brockway, who stepped forward.

"Couldn't put my finger on it at first, but somethin' seemed off. Old Wolfram, he commenced to barkin' and lungin' at his tether and it snapped and he run off after 'em. Later I figured out what was strange about it; her ladyship didn't have no bonnet nor gloves. And she was walkin' real close to the feller . . . and real fast."

422

"Hell's backwater!" Lady Margaret turned on Eversby. "Who was he, this 'gentleman'? What did he look like?"

"Tall and light . . . I believe her ladyship called him Baron. . . ." Eversby reddened and looked to Brockway for help.

"Baron Minnow . . . or Penny?" The trusty footman shrugged.

"*Pinnow?*" Lady Margaret half strangled. "Baron Pinnow?"

"That was it!" they chorused.

"Merciful Lord." Lady Margaret paled and clutched at the amulets tucked beneath her dress. "He's come to London."

"Who?" Lady Catherine demanded, her concern piqued by Lady Margaret's fright.

"Pinnow. He's the man Charity was marrying when his lordship stopped the wedding. He left the chapel swearing . . ." She twitched as if pinched and turned to Eversby. "You've got to send somebody for his lordship. Charity's in trouble!"

Brockway ran nearly all the way to Rane's offices, only to find him gone. He tried Rane's club and had no luck there either; he was off making a business call somewhere, they said. Brockway left urgent messages both places, then returned home with the grave news that Rane might not return for a while.

It was more than three hours later, and well past dark, when Rane arrived home to find Charity missing and Lady Margaret and Lady Catherine and Eversby all pacing the drawing room, beside themselves with worry. It only took one frantic word from Lady Margaret to raise his own anxiety. "*Pinnow.*"

He listened with one ear to their story and with the other to the memory of Sullivan Pinnow vowing revenge for his humiliation. He couldn't imagine that Pinnow's temper would have improved drastically in the month since his interrupted wedding. Neither could he imagine that a District

423

Magistrate would be so foolhardy as to abduct a young noblewoman from her own house in broad daylight.

He rose, deciding grimly that he would conduct his own search before alerting the local constabulary, when there was noise of confusion from the entry hall. He bolted for the door with Lady Margaret and Lady Catherine elbowing each other in his wake.

There, in Brockway's steely grip, hung Gar Davis and Percy Hall . . . looking even more crumpled and pathetic than usual. "Yer lordship," Percy called, "there be trouble!" At the wave of Rane's hand Brockway released them and they stumbled forward, hats in hands, their faces long and grave.

"What in bloody hell are you two doing here?"

"Oh, yer lordship—" Gar panted. "We come to warn ye! The baron—he knows about the squire an' the smugglin'."

" 'E caught us poachin' a few birds an' wrung our tails good an' tight." Percy took it up. "An' Gar here . . . he ain't much good wi' pain." Gar winced and hung his head and Percy continued. "The baron kept askin' 'bout you, yer lordship, real angry like."

"Had us in town . . . in the local clink, till three days past, didn' he, Perc?" Gar hauled on Percy's arm for confirmation and got a nod. "Then some other fellers come an' let us out . . . said there wus a new magis'rate . . ."

"So we come straight here," Percy took it up, "to warn ye."

"On horses," Gar shuddered.

"Pinnow's not magistrate anymore?" Rane demanded, grabbing Percy by the coat. And when Percy shook his head, Rane felt his stomach fold and slide toward his knees. Pinnow no longer had a position to maintain . . . He was in London . . . looking for revenge . . . and he had Charity. He released Percy and found himself staring into Lady Margaret's suffering gaze. "If the bastard harms a hair on her head, he's a dead man."

Everyone began talking at once, explaining, making orders and countermanding orders, until Rane shouted above the din to call a halt. He took charge, sending Brockway for the constables; the more pairs of eyes they had searching the streets for her, the better. But the rangy head footman had no sooner opened the door, than he was being bowled back by a great heaving ball of fur and muscle.

It was Wolfram! He came lunging and barking hoarsely, frantically at Rane. Rane braced and caught the panting dog and wrestled him to the floor.

"Charity!" Lady Margaret bustled forward. "He ran after them, maybe he knows something about where they are— at least which direction they went! Charity?" she asked the dog, waving her hand toward the open door. He barked and made a whirling jump at the sound of his mistress's name. "Go find Charity! Go on!"

Wolfram ran toward the door then came back for Rane, barking insistently. "Go for the constable," Rane ordered Brockway. Then he grabbed Gar and Percy by the sleeves and pulled them toward the door. "You come with me."

Lady Margaret made a protective gypsy hand sign over them as they hurried out the door and she turned to Lady Catherine with a desperate whisper. "I knew something terrible was going to happen . . . but I never figured it would happen to Charity. All the troubles . . . they've always happened to other people." She suddenly thought of Princess Janov and heard that terrible pronouncement again: *A life for a life. The sacrifice of a loving heart.* "Her jinx . . . something's gone wrong . . ."

Lady Catherine opened her mouth for a hot reply, but saw the tears gathering in Lady Margaret's eyes and didn't quite have the heart for it. She lifted her chin and looked down her regal nose.

"My grandson will find her, old hob. They don't call him 'Bulldog' Austen for nothing."

Wolfram led them through the darkened streets, first one

way, then another, retracing his own meandering course. But eventually they found themselves on a narrow, unlit street near the docks, standing by while Wolfram ran this way and that with his nose to the cobblestones. He had lost the trail.

"Well, at least we know they've come toward the docks. But is he running for a ship . . . or just a place to hide?" Rane's eyes glinted like molten silver in the wispy light. "No matter. He couldn't have chosen a worse place to come; I know these docks and ships like the back of my hand." He paused, his eyes darting over some mental scene, then he came to life. "A lot of people around here owe me a favor. Somebody has to have seen them somewhere!"

They split up to search the streets in a more systematic way, stopping and asking everyone they saw. Gar and Percy went one way; Rane and Wolfram, the other. At each tavern Rane paused, finding familiar faces, recruiting help. Soon a score of longshoremen prowled the streets, passing the word from tavern to tavern, crib to gaming hell. Bulldog Austen's woman had been taken. *And he wanted her back!*

Chapter Twenty-four

Charity lay in black, dreamless sleep on a bed of fusty old canvas . . . mere blocks from where Wolfram had led her rescuers to the end of the trail. Pinnow's blow had struck her on the temple, giving her a mild concussion. He had dragged her limp body onto a pile of canvas, cursing his own temper, and then left in an ugly mood for a meeting with the shabby captain of the vessel on which he had purchased hasty, anonymous passage to India. He had realized that he would have to help with his venture, if it were to be completed before he sailed, and decided the grizzled captain seemed a likely and resourceful partner.

For a long time all was merciful blackness in Charity's mind. Then, as she rose toward full consciousness, her head began to pound and she recoiled from the relentless onslaught of reality. But it would not be forestalled and, suddenly, she was awake, her head banging and her body throbbing. She was lying on her back in darkness, surrounded by fetid smells.

Suddenly there was light above her in the blackness. She shrank and tightened her still closed eyes, finding herself incapable of movement. A male laugh, ugly and suggestive, rolled over her, and the words righted themselves in her head.

"A rum-rumpin' piece of muslin there, Pinnow. Blonde as a buttercup . . . and wi' skin like pearl. Make's a man's mouth water, all right." The coarse, gravelly voice was coming from above and it was all Charity could do to keep her eyes closed. "You say her husband's a nobleman with a fat purse?"

"Got plenty of blunt . . . and friends in high places," Pinnow's voice came to her ears, oddly slurred. "I want to see him pay . . . plenty."

"Ransoming's a tricky business . . . lots to go wrong." That grizzled voice grated along her aching nerves. "He'll want her back, bad, a fine piece o' fluff like that. But if ye really want her husband to pay, then why give 'er back to him at all? If I swear on as yer partner, I say we jus' take the chit wi' us. She'll fetch a small fortune from a fat old pasha I know with a taste fer blondes."

"Well, I . . . I never thought of . . ." Pinnow stammered at the suggestion, then stopped, mulling it over. The graveled voice came again, tempting, tantalizing him with unexpected possibilities.

"It be a long way to India, Pinnow. She'll make the voyage plenty enjoyable for you and me. . . ."

There was a long pause before Pinnow's wicked hiss was heard.

"Yesss. We'll take her with usss."

"Then the sooner we be gone, the better." There was a terrifying smile in the sound of the tempter's voice. "I can be ready t' set sail first thing in the mornin'."

Charity heard the door creak and the sound of footfalls. When darkness and the sound of the door assured her she was alone, Charity wilted against the pallet, quaking and trembling. Slowly, she pulled herself up to sit huddled in the dankness, her arms wrapped about her shoulders. The thudding in her head pounded the frightening reality of her situation into her mind. They weren't going to ransom her at all! They were going to keep her . . . then sell her to some old . . .

She shoved to her feet, frantic to find some means of escape. She groped toward the dim streak of light coming from a crack around the door, only to find the sturdy door locked securely. There were no other doors, no windows. She was trapped! Stumbling back in the faint light, she sank to her knees on the canvas.

For the first time in her life, *troubles were happening to her!* She'd been threatened and abducted and struck . . . The future was filled with a string of terrifying calamities awaiting her, each more drastic than the last. Had fate stored up misfortunes over the years to set them all loose on her now? She'd be carried away from Rane, from England . . . they'd abuse her . . . then they'd sell her to some fat pasha who would—

The suffocating darkness of her prison seeped into her lungs, into her thoughts, into her very soul. Her aching mind fixed desperately on the one island of sanity in an engulfing sea of despair. Rane. His light eyes came to her, glowing silvery with determination. His jaw appeared, taut with his stubborn belief in their love. The rest of his features rose to complete his image in her mind . . . beautifully sculptured bronze, now sharp with resolve. His lips began to move, his relentless logic prying her from the shell of her fears.

She wasn't a jinx . . . "Fear crumples you up inside" . . . He'd fight for their love with everything in him . . . their love was strong enough to counter their troubles. . . . He had massaged those words into her heart and mind with his beautiful loving, and now they coalesced into a warm core of strength for her. That stubborn warmth slowly uncurled in her middle and began to spread along her icy limbs and up her spine, straightening it, fortifying it.

He had been willing to fight for their love, even to die for it. Now she had to be willing, too. New heart rose inside her. She'd fight Pinnow every step of the way! She'd kick and claw, do whatever it took, but she'd find some way to get free!

* * *

Rane and Gar and Percy haunted the docks through the deepest hours of the night with no luck. As dawn approached, dozens of longshoremen who had worked or still worked for "Bulldog Austen," scoured the gritty waterfront district for some sign or word of her. Gradually they were joined by a few seamen and even a few ships' officers. Finally Rane submitted to the good sense of a captain-friend who argued that if he continued his frantic movement, it would be impossible to locate him when they did find her. He confined himself to the centrally located Gray Gull Tavern and sent word to Oxley House where he could be found.

He paced and agonized, remembering Pinnow's fury and imagining it turned, full force, on Charity's vulnerable form. And he prayed that the docks' fleet network of information would do its work well . . . and soon.

In the wee hours of the morning, in the gray mist of a doomed dawn, they came for Charity. Relentlessly, she had honed her thoughts, paring away the fear that made her doubt every possibility. After they took her from the warehouse, once they were on the street, she would have a chance, *one chance,* to surprise them with resistance and screams for help. She'd have one chance to wrestle and bash free.

She positioned herself to make Pinnow think she was just as he'd left her, lying on the canvas, still unconscious. Pinnow growled and shook her and even smacked her face lightly, but she fixed her mind on the image of Rane's face and clung tenaciously to her pretense. The guttural male laughs and foul comments of the men accompanying him seemed to add to Pinnow's anger. They wouldn't need their ropes, he growled, she'd give them no trouble.

She was limp and difficult to carry, but he stubbornly refused to let those rough low-lifes handle his curvy prize. When they were through the warehouse and out on the street, she peered from beneath her lashes to get her bearings, summoning all her courage. Her muscles began tightening in spite of her, and her heart was pounding madly in her chest. Were there other people on the street? She waited a moment longer, praying. . . .

She erupted in Pinnow's arms, flailing and screaming at the top of her lungs. He half dropped her, and she scrambled and somehow found her feet. A moment later she was free of his shocked hands and lunging away, calling for help, starting to run. But one of the two seasoned tars with Pinnow was around in a flash, lunging, catching her skirt and snatching her back. She fought and bit as they tried to cover her mouth with their hands, and she was able to get out another bloodcurdling scream before one of them stuffed a dirty old kerchief into her mouth and they managed to get a rope around her arms to bind them to her sides.

In a few harrowing minutes, they carried her writhing, groaning form along the docks and out along the quay to their ship. She wriggled with muted horror as she saw the masts above and the water below the gangway. Her mind kept screaming that it couldn't be . . . it had to have worked! But they trundled her down a narrow passageway and into a bare, dingy cabin, where they dumped her onto a bunk.

Only the appearance of the furious captain saved her from feeling Pinnow's full wrath again. Pinnow and the captain argued and shouted at each other over the attention her screams might have drawn and the stupidity of not having tied her properly in the first place. Finally, the captain dragged Pinnow topside with him. Charity managed to wriggle from the loosely bound ropes and pull the cloth from her mouth, but she found herself locked securely in a dim box of a cabin with a small window . . . that might be large enough for her to shinny through. She stood on the bunk and threw it open, looking out the shoulder-wide opening. She sagged. The bare stone quay was only eight feet away, but it might as well have been miles. Below, between her and the dock, was only water . . . cold, black water. She swallowed a sob of frustration. She was deathly afraid of water.

A carriage rumbled up before the modest Gray Gull just after dawn. Lady Margaret and Lady Catherine descended and charged in to join the tense vigil being kept inside, declaring that they couldn't sit at home any longer, knowing Charity was in danger. Rane was at wit's end and the old ladies' appearance, factoring yet more confusion into the situation, pushed him to the brink of a massive eruption. Suddenly a scrawny fellow, a longshoreman from one of Rane's warehouses, came pushing through the group.

He had heard a woman's screams, he panted out, on the far east end of the docks . . . and he had seen a woman's form being trundled onto a ship preparing for a hasty departure. Rane grabbed the poor fellow and rattled him a bit until the name of the ship popped free. The *Lucky Lady*.

Rane went charging out of the tavern, running through the dockside streets with Gar, Percy, a motley crew of longshoremen, and a few constables. He snagged the few sailors he saw on the east docks, demanding, "The *Lucky Lady*—where is she?!"

Most shrugged, but finally one pointed . . . down a stone quay to a ship that was hoisting topgallants to catch a steering breeze.

Rane's heart was convulsing, his lungs were raw, but white-hot anger poured furious energy into his blood and he ran on, reaching the gangway of the *Lucky Lady* just as the sailors currying around on deck spotted the trail of people running down the quay. He was met by two sailors at the end of the gangway, but lowered his shoulder and plowed through them in a rage, knocking them back. He spotted Sullivan Pinnow on the quarterdeck and jolted toward him, bashing another sailor who came at him out of the way. Behind him there were sounds of running and shouts and conflict as Gar and Percy and the others tried to shove and bash their way on board.

Chaos broke out as the captain of the ship ordered his men to rip loose the gangway. The ship creaked and groaned as the topsails caught a bit of breeze and nudged out. Gar and Percy and the others on the gangway went scrambling off, narrowly escaping being dumped into the black water along with the gangway planking. Gar and Percy watched helplessly as Rane caught the shrinking Pinnow on the ship's quarterdeck and bashed him in the face and belly several times with his bare fists. When Pinnow staggered back and pulled a knife, Rane turned it on him, and soon held Pinnow by the neck with the blade against his throat.

"Where is she? Where's Charity?!" he shouted, at the captain, who glared murderously at him. "I want my wife—take me to her or I'll slit his mangy throat."

The captain waved his men back when they made to rush Rane. "She's below."

"Lead the way," Rane snarled. The captain complied, leading Rane, with the baron at knife-point, below decks. Rane kept his back to the wall as they moved down the short passage to Charity's door. "Open it!"

The captain shot a narrow look at the men blocking the end of the passage, then produced a key and turned it in the lock. The door swung open and Rane glimpsed Charity standing in the dim cabin, her face filling with shocked relief at the sight of him.

"Are you alright?" he growled, fighting the urge to use that knife on the wretched cur in his hands. She nodded wordlessly and ran toward the door. But the moment's concentration he'd spent on the sight of her allowed the captain to nod unseen at his men and they suddenly charged, while the captain dove from the other side. Rane was caught between them in the passage, and a glancing blow from a belaying pin sent him sliding down the wall.

Charity cried out and would have rushed to him, but burly arms pushed her back into the cabin and the door locked against her frantic cries. The captain ordered Rane thrown overboard, then stood over Pinnow, whose face was swelling and bleeding. "Mebee I should'ave let him stick you. . . ."

Charity banged on the door, pleading for Rane's life, but her cries fell on deaf ears. She ran to the small window above the bunk and threw it open. There was now thirty feet between the ship and the dock, and that breach was growing wider by the instant. Suddenly, into that great chasm, a body hurtled. Rane's body!

He was knocked in the head—unconscious—he'd drown!

The splash sent a cold, suffocating wave of terror through her, and for one brief moment she was paralyzed. If he died because of her, she wouldn't want to go on living. If he died . . . *if!* She looked down at the brackish oil-slicked water and could scarcely breathe. Her heart stopped. Rane . . . she had to help Rane! She couldn't let fear keep her—

Her heart seemed to explode in her chest and she shoved her head and shoulders through the window. She pushed and scrambled and clawed at the outer planking of the ship, wriggling through and dangling . . . then plunging, headfirst into that cold murky water. It closed over her, dragging her under . . . pulling her down . . . into cold, terrifying nothingness.

Above, Lady Margaret and Lady Catherine came running down the quay from where their carriage had been forced to stop . . . just as the crew of the *Lucky Lady* dragged Rane above decks and dropped him over the side. Everyone was shouting, pointing, trying to see where he'd surface—if he surfaced—and Wolfram was barking so furiously they barely heard the second splash.

"Dear God—it's his lordship!" Lady Margaret gasped, clutching Percy and Gar furiously. "Do something! He'll drown!"

"I cain't," Percy groaned, "I cain't swim! But Gar can— Gar—"

Gar paled and went stiff with panic as they turned on him. "No—I-I cain't, I—"

Lady Catherine broke in shouting, "It's Charity—there in the water!"

They turned and saw a speck of yellow and white . . . Charity, struggling to stay afloat, floundering and calling for help. She sank below the water's surface and Lady Margaret cried out for someone to help her. Gar watched, trembling as she failed to surface. Their little Charity . . . their loving little jinx. . . . He sucked in a shuddering, terrified breath and leaped off the side of the dock into the water.

When Charity went under a second time, her feet brushed something, and she flailed madly opening her eyes in the foul water, trying to make it out. She glimpsed a dim log-like shape and reached toward it. Fabric—a coat—*Rane!* She tugged and pulled desperately for the surface as her mouth filled with water and she choked.

When she broke the surface, she gagged and nearly sank again, but the thought of Rane, in her hands, depending on her, gave her the spurt of energy she needed to kick her feet and stay afloat. She managed to get his head above the water just as she recognized that someone was thrashing through the water toward them. Somehow she managed to realize that it was Gar Davis.

"Help him—take him—H-he's—h-hurt—" She tried to shove Rane between them.

"No—you come, too—Hold onto 'im—" Gar grabbed

435

Rane's head and began pulling for the stone steps, fifty yards away, that led from the top of the quay down to the water. Lady Margaret and Lady Catherine ran for the steps along with Percy and three other fellows who rushed down to the water's edge, calling to him. Stroke after stroke, Gar dragged them in agonizingly small increments, his small body struggling valiantly to buoy their collective weight in the cold water. Then, as they came within fifteen feet of the edge of the dock, Gar gasped. His hold on them loosened and he went under.

Charity began to kick her feet madly against the binding of her dress, shoving Rane before her toward the outstretched hands at the landing They grabbed him and dragged him out, then reached for her, and in seconds she was being pulled onto the landing and into Percy's and Lady Margaret's arms. Some of the longshoremen had carried Rane up onto the quay and Charity was frantic to break free of her grandmother's arms.

"Is he alright?! Please God—don't let him be—" She tugged at her wet skirts and struggled up the steps.

"He's breathing! He's alive!" someone called as she reached the top. She pushed past the dockworkers and fell onto her knees beside him, gathering him in her arms.

"Rane—you're alright!" Tears and water streamed together down her face. He felt chilled and looked so pale beneath his tan that her heart skipped beats. "Look at me, can you see me?" She shook him gently. "Rane!"

He suddenly doubled up, coughing violently to clear the last residue of brackish water from his lungs. Then he managed to open his eyes. He smiled at her woozily. "Charity?" he rasped, raising a hand to touch her face and the tears flowing down her cheeks. Then he struggled to sit up and grabbed her into his arms, holding her so tightly she could barely breathe.

They were both alive. *Alive and together.*

Charity's heart soared as she wrapped her arms about his shoulders and buried her face in his sopping coat.

They'd survived . . . they'd been in deadly peril . . . and they'd come through!

Lady Margaret and Lady Catherine embraced, laughing and crying all at once, sturdy longshoremen clapped each other on the shoulders, and Wolfram pranced and leaped excitedly, nosing through the group to lick Rane and Charity and bark with deafening joy.

"Gar?" Percy craned his neck above and around, looking for his friend with a broad grin of congratulations. "Where's Gar?" He slowly froze and a bolt of recollection went through him. "Gar! He never come out of the water!" He went tearing down the steps to the water's edge, calling Gar's name. Lady Margaret and Lady Catherine stopped and stared at each other, then hurried after him. They stood on the landing searching for a sign of him in the murky channel, calling frantically.

Wolfram pushed through the men clamoring down to the water's edge and nearly knocked Lady Margaret into the water. He stared at the people pointing and calling across the water, and connected concepts together in his canine mind. *Human . . . water.*

He plunged into the water, paddling and diving over and over as the humans on shore yelled and pointed frantically. Then, not too far out, he bumped into a human form and fastened his jaws on it, scrambling for the surface.

"There! There he is!" Lady Margaret shouted, pointing at Wolfram's nose and eyes barely bobbing above the surface. They could see he was dragging something—someone—and called encouragement, beckoning him toward shore. They pulled Gar and Wolfram out of the water and hurried the drowned Gar up onto the quay, laying him out on his stomach, pushing the water out of his lungs, then rolling him over. One of the fellows leaned down to listen for Gar's heart, then looked up with a sorrowful face and shook his head.

Rane and Charity, who had gotten to their feet, stood holding each other, looking down in horror at the pale, cold form of their little rescuer. Percy knelt by Gar's side, calling to him, frantically, patting his hands, rubbing his cold cheeks.

"Come on Gar, wake up . . . Ye gotta wake up!"

Charity stumbled forward and knelt on the other side of Gar. When she touched his hand, it was exactly as she knew it would be. Woody and cold . . . like her father's. "Oh, Gar . . . you, too?" She pressed his hand to her cheek and her chin trembled as tears welled in her eyes and burned down her face. She looked up into the desolation of Percy's blocky face and knew exactly the bleakness, the pain he was feeling. It was as though some vital part of him had been ripped out and only mangled feeling and crushing hurt remained.

"He died . . . saving us," she whispered. The ache in her voice was painful to hear.

"He loved ye, Miss Charity, like ye wus his own . . ."

The violent clash of fates and fortunes was past and, in their tumultuous wake, all was suddenly, eerily still. Overhead, the gulls ceased their crying to swoop and circle silently. And on the quay, there was only the muffled sound of hearts breaking. Lady Margaret heard Percy's quiet words through her tears and her head came up to look at Gar Davis. The perpetual worry that knotted his brow was gone; his face was smooth, at peace.

A life for a life, she heard the old gypsy's words ringing in her head. It had come to pass. The sacrifice of a loving heart. Charity's jinx was dead . . . gone with Gar Davis's life.

Wolfram pushed through to sniff at the human's feet and recognized his scent. *Gar!* He watched Gar's silent form with his ear perked and an intense look. He began to growl, nosing at Gar, nudging him with his head, then he began pawing at Gar's leg and barking. Some of the

438

longshoremen grabbed Wolfram's collar and tried to pull him back from the dead man, but he surprised them with a lunge and broke free . . . landing smack in the middle of Gar's chest with a great, horrifying thump.

Charity squealed and everyone shouted and lunged at Wolfram to pry him away from the body. Rane dragged Charity up and away from the chaos, and a moment later they were staring in fresh horror at the twitching, gurgling, choking form of the drowned Gar Davis.

Rane fell to his knees and quickly rolled Gar onto his side to give his back several good thumps. Suddenly Gar was coughing in earnest, gagging and retching and spitting up more water. . . . Charity had never seen such a wonderful sight in her life!

"Gar!" She and Percy crowded in on him, lifting him into their arms, hugging him joyfully. A cheer arose, and Percy sprang up and danced around for joy, hugging Lady Margaret and Lady Catherine . . . who hugged each other and together hugged Charity. Everybody hugged or patted Wolfram, who beamed and pranced proudly around, and in the frenzy of release and relief, Lady Catherine even threw her arms around her own grandson and gave him a crushing, grandmotherly hug. It was a veritable contagion of affection . . . longshoremen even hugged constables!

In the midst of it all, Percy knelt by Gar again.

"Ye had us near scared stiff, Gar Davis, fergetting to breathe, like that," Percy growled, swiping tears from his eyes. Gar's eyes opened wide, and a bewildered look came over him as he registered the faces staring down at him in concern. His lungs felt raw and soggy, his head was pounding, and he felt like he'd swallowed half the English Channel. He began to recall more, and his eyes widened further. He grabbed Percy's coatfront in both hands.

"I died, Perc—I swear!" he croaked. "I wus dead—"

"You didn't die," Percy blustered, frowning and glaring at Gar. "I couldn't be talkin' to ye if'n ye died, numskull!"

"But I did, Perc! I saw light . . . and an angel wi' blonde hair!"

"It were Miz Charity, ye saw wi' the fair hair, lunkhead." Percy waved at Charity and Gar turned his head to her. She was all wet and beaming teary-eyed joy. And Gar had to credit that she did look a great deal like the angel he'd just seen. But then, they had always known, he decided, smiling, that her looks and her sweet nature had been stolen from the angels.

Within minutes they were delivering the drowned hero into the Oxley carriage and loading the rest of their party inside. The second hero of the afternoon, Wolfram, plunged straight into the midst of the carriage after them and proceeded to shake off his shaggy wet coat. And this time nobody, not even Lady Catherine, had the heart to object.

By the time they reached Oxley House, Lady Margaret could restrain her happiness no longer and announced to all, including Eversby and the servants that hurried from all over the house to greet them, that Gar Davis's "death" had broken Charity's jinx.

"It did?" Gar's face lit with excitement as Percy helped him along. "Did ye hear that, Perc? I fell in that grave an'—by thunder—I went an' died and broke Miz Charity's jinx!"

"You didn't die, Gar Davis," he glared, turning that same look on Lady Margaret. "He didn't *die!*"

"Of course, he didn't," Lady Catherine stepped in to take Percy's side and go him one better. "And he couldn't have broken her jinx because there never was a 'jinx' to begin with." She leveled an acrid look on Lady Margaret. "Except in your knobby old head. And look what chaos you caused! Take a lesson, Margaret Villiers, and give up these absurd, pagan superstitions of yours! There are no such things as 'secret gypsy charms' and 'spells.'" She ended, shaking a finger at Lady Margaret, who stiffened and bristled with outrage.

Rane's face reddened, and he was about to enter the fray when Charity pulled him back by the arm and pressed his lips with her fingers. "Let them argue if they want," she whispered. "We've already settled it between us."

With a seductive, wifely smile, she tilted her head toward the stairs. "We have more important things to do. We have to get out of these wet clothes. Our lungs . . . remember?"

As they mounted the stairs, hand in hand, smiling and warming to the possibilities of loving, Lady Margaret's face was drawn up like a purple prune in the hall below. She was raising her index and little fingers to point them from her eyes, wriggling them furiously at Lady Catherine.

"Oh, Lord, m'lady!" Gar gaped at Lady Catherine in dismay. "Yer in trouble now. That be Lady Marg'rt's hexin' eye."

Catherine stared Gar in the eye with open disgust, then returned Lady Margaret's glare and her "absurd finger wiggles," tit for tat. After this display, she drew herself up tightly.

"There's no such thing as a 'hexing eye,'" she sniffed, turning and ordering Eversby to bring some tea and cold meats, and to lay on a fine dinner. When she turned, with a righteous nod at Lady Margaret, and started for the drawing room, she saw Caesar strolling through the hallway arch.

"Caesar! There you are, my po-o-or baby!"

The imperial Caesar took one look at his mistress and every hair that was left on his patchy body stood straight out on end. His eyes flew wide and he hissed in terror—then shot through the still open front doors as fast as his pudgy little legs would carry him.

* * *

Charity rose out of the great copper tub in the bathing chamber, straight into Rane's glowing, possessive gaze. He stood, damp from his own tub in the bedroom and wrapped in sheet-like toweling, leaning his shoulder against the doorframe. He'd watched the last minutes of her bathing and had seen her face grow flushed and dreamy as the heat invaded and relaxed her body. Now the sight of her, rising from the water, her rose-tipped breasts glistening, her hips and thighs rosy with warmth, set fire to his blood. When she reached for a towel, he pushed off from the door and pulled it out of her hands.

"I'll get cold." She wrapped her arms around her waist and over her chest, but too loosely and too carelessly to stem from either true modesty or true chill. It was a co-quette's pose, her tight, rosy nipples more framed than hidden, her knee bending and body curving to accentuate the bold line of her hip. Her eyes glowed like sunlit honey . . . sweet, beckoning.

"You won't get cold, angel." He tossed the unused towel aside and opened the cotton toweling wrapped around him, baring his tanned body to her eyes as he came to her. He lifted her out of the tub and against his bare body, wrapping his arms and the towel about her in the same delicious embrace. Then his hand slid over the tow-eling, down her back and waist and over the seductive rounding of her bottom, drying her back as she wriggled wetly, seductively against his front.

A moment later, he turned her in his arms and pulled her back against his belly, giving his hands free rein over her front. His strong fingers cupped and rubbed her soft breasts and hard nipples, stroked her curvy waist, and slid down over her belly to cup the damp heat of her woman's cleft . . . then to rub it slowly. She was caught between the caressing undulations of his hard body against her back and the marauding pleasurings of his hands over her front. And all she could do was respond . . . with every-

442

thing in her.

She arched and rubbed her shoulders back against his chest, and wriggled her bottom against his hardened shaft, moaning softly, luxuriating in the feeling of being surrounded by his big body, by his loving magic. And when she could bear his sweet tortures no longer, she turned in his arms and molded her breasts, her body, against his, opening to seek his kiss.

Fire billowed out of control between them as they locked in fierce embrace, their mouths joining hungrily, their hands clasping possessively. He pulled her up into his arms and carried her to the bed, sinking over her, then into her creamy enveloping heat. His hands adored her, stimulated every part of her, while her lips whispered soft erotic praises and her fingers massaged them into his tanned skin. Over and over, they came together, arching in frantic force, then easing to join with playful luxury. They rolled and writhed, entwined and exultant, until the flames of arousal crowned and burst out of control, rushing, consuming them like wildfire.

He felt the tremors of her body beginning and braced, giving her more as she demanded it, and more and more . . . until his own senses exploded and he joined her in that steamy plunge into fathomless loving pleasures.

"I love you, Rane Austen," she murmured into his ear as they lay snuggled together. He smiled a recklessly triumphant smile.

"I know."

"And do you also know that you owe me a mirror?"

He laughed, a deep resonant laugh that vibrated her body as it lay against his. "So you like 'two in a mirror,' do you?" He shifted back and tucked his chin to look at her alluring honey-blonde glow. "No more bad luck?"

She laughed and a mischievous twinkle came into her eyes. "No more bad luck. Didn't you hear Gran'mere? I'm not a jinx anymore." That brought him up onto his elbow above her . . . with a very determined look in his eye.

"You never were a jinx, angel. All the mishaps and troubles . . . it was all in the way you looked at things—" Her fingers on his lips stopped him and she smiled.

"I don't know if I was ever a jinx or not; maybe I'll never know. But I do know, I'm not afraid anymore. I'll face the harshest gossip, I'll brave the biggest lightning bolts, I'll fight the wickedest kidnappers, I'll jump into the deepest, darkest water . . . to be by your side, Rane Austen."

He watched the fiery, loving glow in her eyes and felt a sweet ache pounding through the middle of his chest. It was true. She'd done all those things and more . . . for love of him. His hand came up to stroke her face and she caught it and kissed it. His voice was thick with feeling and wonder.

"You're really not afraid anymore, angel?"

Her eyes glistened and she broke into a radiant smile.

"You loved it out of me, Rane Austen. You and your *night magic.*"

Afterword

There is an old saying amongst the sons and daughters of Romany: "With one behind, you cannot sit on two horses." It is a recognition that each person born must someday choose between logic and luck. Most of the world chooses logic . . . and builds machines and laws and bridges and cities. But gypsies choose luck . . . and spin stories and sayings, poems and dreams.

True wisdom comes in knowing that both paths, when fully traveled, lead to the same end. For both logic and luck will someday come to their limits . . . and to go beyond those limits, takes love.

Author's Note

I hope you enjoyed Charity and Rane and their irascible grandmothers. Their story was, paradoxically, one of the most enjoyable, yet one of the most difficult I have ever written. The research for this book led me into the very shadows of people's beliefs, into superstitions and fear and the feelings of power*ful*ness and power*less*ness that lie at the core of the way people look at their lives. It was an enlightening and fascinating experience for me, both as a writer and as a person.

You may have recognized quite a number of Lady Margaret's superstitions; spilled salt, lucky horseshoes, mistletoe, walking under ladders, and brides wearing something borrowed. Rest assured, the other luck practices—ash over doorframes, not stitching clothes on a person's back, salt trails, putting quenched coals under furniture, not walking in only one shoe, and portraits falling—are all genuine English superstitions, authentic to the period. Wolf shoulder blades and amulets made from bent nails, animal paws, lucky pennies and the occasional dried chicken liver, were all used to attract good luck and ward off the bad. Some superstitions took the form of ideas: Fridays were bad luck days; the moon had powerful influence over a person's mental state; numbers had inherent good and bad luck in them; and animals (especially black horses and dogs) could see things humans could not.

Some of the superstitions in the story stayed in the background; for example, the scratch on the back of Rane's hand (from his fight with Caesar over breakfast muffins) would have been a clear sign to any good gypsy that he would soon go on a journey. But only one superstition in the entire book was "made up": Rane's declaration that it was bad luck for a groom to undo his own buttons on his wedding night. (The scamp. There was absolutely no basis for it in my research, but he declared that if there wasn't such a superstition, there ought to be. I agreed.)

In fact, one of the real difficulties in writing this book seemed to be deciding which of the fascinating and often humorous superstitions to *exclude!* If you would like to research the origins of superstitions you encounter, I recommend to you Opie and Tatum's very readable *Dictionary of Superstition* (Oxford University Press, 1989), which includes historical citations from as far back as the 1500's.

Also, I wish to publicly credit my expert consultant in the area of dog-thought and canine behavior. It was Wolfram Krahn, an erudite, twenty-six-pound, salt-and-pepper schnauzer, who provided the insight into dog-vocabulary, dog-values, and dog-fun that became the character of Charity's "Wolfie." It was the real Wolfram's alarmed reactions to human kissing that provided the inspiration for "Wolfie's" dim view of Rane's displays of affection toward Charity.

And lastly, lest we twentieth century people, with our scientific outlook and superior knowledge, get too smug, ask yourself, when was the last time you tossed a pinch of salt over your shoulder, or picked up a pin or a penny saying, ". . . then all day you'll have good luck," or admonished someone not to thank you for the gift of a green plant, lest it quit growing? I have come to believe that each of us has a little gypsy tucked away in us somewhere . . . a stubborn little desire for things that seem mysterious, or out of reach, or unrealistic. And I believe it is that tenacious little bit of spirit in us that makes us long for, and believe in, the true magic that can be worked by love in our lives.

SUMMER LOVE WITH SYLVIE SOMMERFIELD